## "STRONGLY RECOMMENDED . . . EXCITING . . .

A legal thriller à la Grisham, this one is special in that the narrator, Malone, tells his story so eloquently and with such raw emotion."
—*Library Journal*

"Levy . . . has injected new life in a familiar genre with a massive dose of authenticity and a winning, wisecracking hero."
—*Newsday*

"[An] exciting debut novel . . . The best elements of a classic medical thriller and courtroom drama are combined by an author who keeps the reader in suspense."
—*Bookman Book Review*

"*Chain of Custody* is a good blending of a police procedural with a medical thriller that uses DNA tampering as the underlying premise. . . . The story line moves rapidly forward."
—*I Love a Mystery*

"Fast-paced . . . Levy has done a nice job with his first novel, blending in bits of medical and legal jargon without overwhelming the reader."
—*News-Leader* (Springfield, MO)

"Generates real tension and boasts a fascinating premise."
—*Booklist*

# CHAIN OF CUSTODY

## Harry Levy

FAWCETT CREST • NEW YORK

A Fawcett Crest Book
Published by The Ballantine Publishing Group
Copyright © 1998 by Harry Levy

Fawcett is a registered trademark and Fawcett Crest and the Fawcett colophon are trademarks of Random House, Inc.

www.randomhouse.com/BB/

Library of Congress Catalog Card Number: 99-90138

ISBN 0-449-00449-X

This edition published by arrangement with Random House, Inc.

Manufactured in the United States of America

First Fawcett Crest Edition: June 1999

10   9   8   7   6   5   4   3   2

FOR LESLIE

# ACKNOWLEDGMENTS

THE loneliness of writing was greatly relieved by the help and encouragement I received from Susanna Lesan, Murray Eskenazi, Professor Stephen Newman, Phil Rosenberg, Jill Smith, Dr. Ted Witek, Jr., Pat Doskocil, Martin Gardlin, George Cohen, Madelin De La Rosa, Don Deye, M.D., Jack Miller, and the staff of the Food and Drug Administration. I am especially grateful to Amy Pierpont for being such an enthusiastic fan. My book owes its existence to the skills of my professional family—Mike Rudell, my attorney, who went out of his way to take a chance on an unpublished author; David Gernert, my agent, who gently fine-tuned the manuscript and helped me keep my eye on the ball; Deb Futter, my editor at Random House, who raised the bar higher and higher; Amy Williams, Matt Williams, and Lee Boudreaux, who made things easier; and the unconditional love of my family—my wife, Leslie Carr, whose editorial and story suggestions proved prescient and shaped the book; my mother, Ethel Levy; Marilyn Miller, who made subtle edits; Jane Heffner, Frederick Levy, Esq., and Gary Chafetz; and my sons Zachary, James, and Sam, each with his own very definite opinions.

# PROLOGUE

*A dark cloud touched the horizon, blocking the early morning sun, and in the greenish light the white object rising and falling on the harbor waves appeared radiant.*

*Lieutenant Figlio motioned to the two rookie officers to snag it. No one moved or offered the rookies any help as they struggled like deep sea fishermen everywhere to rope a slippery catch. After many attempts, they finally pulled the floater aboard. Except for one dangling red earring, the woman was totally naked.*

*The waterlogged skin had the appearance of meat frozen and defrosted too many times. Everyone stood back, irrationally afraid of contamination, as water leaked out onto the deck. The bloating and decomposition had obliterated most of her features. Whether she was old or young, White or Hispanic, small-boned or large was impossible to determine. About all that could be reported with certainty was the absence of any man-made fatal wounds. A straightforward death by drowning.*

# CHAPTER 1

THE air whistled between the dock planks, sounding asthmatic. If Figlio didn't come soon I was going back to bed, to recover from my unfortunate habit of saying yes too quickly to friends.

It was nearly nine. The silence of a Sunday morning on Wall Street was disturbed only by the seagulls as they noisily traded garbage futures in midair. Figlio's excuse would be reasonable—there'd be nothing for me to get angry about. *Not his fault, Your Honor, I take full responsibility. The Defendant can't help himself.* NYPD's only water-based detective had an unruly work life—we all knew that. Whereas mine, in some fundamental way, is very predictable.

My name is Dr. Michael Malone. I used to be Assistant Chief of Cardiovascular Medicine and Interventional Cardiology at Mount Zion Hospital and an honorary police surgeon as well (I have kept the cardboard parking permit on my dashboard to ward off parking tickets). Ten years ago, I successfully treated Detective Figlio's arrhythmia. We've been friends ever since. Although Figlio would deny it, if asked.

Now I practice law rather than medicine. A change of heart, a change of venue is the way I view it, though some former medical colleagues still act, all these years later, as if a cult is holding me against my will and I'm the one who needs an intervention. Barney Glass believes my switch proves that evil will inherit the earth, but he's a urologist and they tend to exaggerate.

My reasons were less cosmic: it bothered me that too few patients stopped smoking, really dieted, or exercised or took the medicine I'd so carefully chosen for them, and just went ahead and died earlier than they should have. On top of which I felt on-call for everyone except myself, without any time to do anything other than coronary artery rotorootering.

Of course such memories can be self-serving. Sally, my soon-to-be ex-wife, who's a Deputy D.A., said I was a "competitive shit" who just wanted to "stick it to her." An ironic choice of words because in the preceding months, before I declared my law school plans, she'd initiated a unilateral withdrawal from the sexual playing field. My mom was more disturbed about the career change ("I let him watch too much TV as a kid and TV makes people restless") than she's been about the divorce, which should give you a good clue as to how I get my priorities screwed up. But it was my choice, she shouldn't blame herself. As for television, only last week I was regaling another litigator with the helpful pointers you can pick up watching late-night Perry Mason reruns.

In an attempt to save our marriage I'd agreed to see a therapist to examine Sally's notion that I was really a mean-spirited creep. The elderly gray-haired woman, with a German-accented lisp that suggested that she was in personal communication with Freud, declared that I had an "unconscious desire to exhibit myself in courtrooms to compensate for a lonely childhood." I didn't buy her logic then and don't now—in my experience courthouse groupies are the same people you see staring blankly on the subways. If you're really looking for a good crowd for display purposes, you'd do better at Yankee Stadium.

The unexpected horn blast from the approaching police boat resonated across the harbor, scattering the seagulls and sending a jolt of adrenaline into my food-starved arteries. Behind me two vehicles, a windowless black-paneled van and a late-model domestic sedan, rumbled across the crumbling pier. Something was up. Show time in the wasteland. Hopefully, soon Figlio and I would sit down at Odeon with the fancy people for brunch or squeeze into the tiny booths at Bodega, its new sibling, where they still serve breakfast, and I'd get the chill out of my bones.

A scraggly civilian crew member with an unkempt ponytail tossed a mooring line to shore just as the launch bumped hard against the pier tires, and the transmitted force knocked him to the deck. Unhurt, he quickly bounced to his feet and jumped ashore to secure the rope.

Two uniformed attendants hopped from the van, opened the rear doors, slid out a gurney, and gingerly carried it onboard, as if they were setting up for a picnic. Figlio came out of the cabin and met them on the aft-deck, looking tough in his navy blue windbreaker, the yellow NYPD letters stitched across the back.

Like explorers declaring possession of a newly discovered land mass, the three of them stood on opposite sides of the tarpaulin-covered mound, exchanging papers. When the dialogue ended, the two attendants nudged the body onto the gurney, hurriedly disembarked, and drove off, tires screeching, as if time still mattered. You didn't need an M.D. degree to know their human package was definitely dead on delivery.

I caught Figlio's eye. He acknowledged me with a slight wave of his hand, which could have meant, *I'm sorry I'm late,* or *You'll have to wait a little longer,* and then launched himself into an animated conversation. Figlio came from a long line of talkers and the man and the woman he was speaking to, both of whom had the intensity of detectives, never had a chance to say much. After a few minutes they too departed, probably feeling useless.

Finally Figlio turned to me and called out, "Still hungry, doc?" I nodded vigorously, the last effort before slipping into hypoglycemic shock. "Gimme a second," Figlio shouted, and ducked inside the cabin before I could protest.

When he emerged I could see he was going to apologize for all the delays. I saved him the trouble. "Looks like you had a successful outing."

"Yeah, we caught one *that* big," he said, stretching his arms as far apart as skeletally possible, the way my father began his fish tales. When I was small my father had taken me out into the Manhattan waterways with his friends. My first reel-in was a used condom. "That's a Hudson River whitefish, son," my father told me. When I'd asked where's the head, they'd all laughed so hard the boat almost capsized, and I'd never fished again. "Let's boogie. I'm starving. Where's your car?" Figlio asked, his appetite undiminished by his human catch.

"At the garage. Someone broke the window and lock on the driver's side last night. Cut my hand."

"Shit. Let's grab a cab," he said, uninterested, as cops are, in the ordinary crime all around us.


Bodega was doing a brisk business by the time we sat down to breakfast—it was crowded with a mix of truck drivers, hookers, and rainbow hair-colored, multipierced young artists dressed in various shades of black—but our orders came quickly, as if we'd phoned ahead.

I forked a melon ball from my fruit salad while Figlio submerged his pancakes in globs of maple syrup.

"We've been looking for that floater the whole fucking night," Figlio declared. He paused to saw off a piece of breakfast sausage. "You lucked out. I could still be out there. Those Christmas jumpers are tough. Third one this month."

Christmas jumpers sounded festive, but I was sure it wasn't. "Christmas jumpers?" I asked, letting my eye drift pointedly toward the puddle of butter coagulating on his plate.

"If you jump in the summer, you're up the next day. But when it's colder, especially if you land in deep water, you'll get trapped under the ice, and we won't find you till spring, when the waters start to warm up." I rolled my eyes. "It makes the gases form inside and float you up. Holidays get a lot of people down, Christmas more than any of them."

"Uh huh," I nodded. These past eight months, since Sally filed the divorce papers, I'd lived alone in a sublet. I understood. My Christmas morning celebration had consisted of a quart of fresh-squeezed orange juice and an awkward call to my son, Jess, at his mother's.

"This one looked like some prehistoric sea creature. Total body bloat." Dead bodies seemed to excite him, which surprised me, but I guess the alternative would've been worse.

I waved a hand over our food. "Must we?"

"Come on, Dr. Malone, you should be used to this." It'd been so hot and awful during my first week of gross anatomy that I'd passed out from the formaldehyde fumes.

"I'm trying to eat . . ."

"So. We're talking food chain," he laughed. Why weren't we talking about the inside stuff on the Lopez case? That's what I'd thought, or hoped, was the reason he'd invited me to have breakfast.

"I see why some of you cops go over the edge. You're one sick puppy, Figlio. You oughtta get yourself some professional help." Figlio smiled. "I'm not kidding," I added in a serious tone.

"You don't get it, Malone. I admire these women. Guys blow their brains out. That's messy. These gals are neat. Most of them leave everything behind—clothes, ID's, even their pocketbooks. They're like those old Eskimos who jump on an ice floe and go off to the happy fishing grounds."

"You're the one getting carried away, Figlio."

"No I'm not," he insisted. "We're talking natural, the way things were meant to happen."

"This is New York, you know. No self-respecting Eskimo would want to be caught dead covered in a lot of plastic garbage."

"Hey, everyone does the best they can."

I let it go, no point arguing with a true believer, and tried for the last word. "All I can say is I'd never take my clothes off in the middle of the winter and jump in a half-frozen river."

Figlio laughed, spraying some coffee. "It's not as if she was worried about catching a cold. Plus they figure no one will ever see them, that they'll never come up. That's the final pisser, you know. They all do. Once we fished out a guy who was chained to a newspaper box." I visualized bodies tattooed with newsprint littering the beaches, while Figlio finished off his griddle cakes. "Been a big year for recoveries. Fourteenth already."

"Why so many?" I asked.

"Hey, it's not as bad as the early Reagan years. We had a shitload back then."

I bit into my cream cheese and bagel. "Political protest or the economy?"

"Some people are just fucked, don't you think? Ain't no miracle cure for unhappiness, doc, or you'd still be pushing pills."

"I was a cardiologist, not a shrink."

"It's all the same. Which reminds me. A lotta guys on the Force are bad-mouthing you big-time."

"Really?" I said, feigning surprise.

"Why're you wasting time on that Lopez kid? From everything I hear he was a real dirtbag. He wouldda died someday soon anyway. Why bust the chops of those two detectives?"

"We're all going to die. That's your famous natural order. It's just that sometimes it happens a little too soon. They killed him, you know. I'm gonna nail them. Since when are you buddying with rotten apples?"

"Ain't. But you'd better watch your overeducated butt, doc. With all this," he made half a papal arm wave, "you don't have too many friends in blue besides me. Okay?" Despite his gregariousness, Figlio prided himself on being independent, on being a loner living on a houseboat who didn't need "nuthin' from nobody." If he's saying he's my "friend," the higher-ups must really want my balls. "Which reminds me," he continued, "how's your divorce going?"

"So we're still on death and decomposition?" I shot back.

"It's just that you look like shit."

"Screw you." Figlio didn't look too great either—his curly hair barely covering his scalp was heavily speckled with gray and his face was thin, almost pinched, as if everything had been squeezed out of it like a toothpaste tube on its last legs. But I said nothing—today's cops get enough simpleminded psychology training—I didn't want to give him the opportunity to say I was being defensive.

"Someone's gotta tell you. You're carrying some extra flab in the gut. And your eyes are bloodshot, kinda druggy."

"That's not true. Someone mistook me for Kevin Kline once," I protested, but I knew I was closer to Mr. Fat than Mr. Fit. And even Visine by the gallon wouldn't do a damned thing. In the midst of a wrongful death trial against the Police Department and a divorce action that revealed the two-faced nature of many of our social friends, plus bombardment from life's little irritations like my car break-in, a recent burglary at the apartment, crank calls after midnight from someone looking for Ramona, my eyes were doing the best they could.

The waitress ambled over. "More coffee, guys?"

I looked at my watch. "No thank you. Can we have the check, please?"

"Sure," she said, and stood there, rocking slightly to and fro as she totaled the bill.

Figlio seemed taken aback by the abrupt end to our breakfast. "You can stay. I've got trial prep for tomorrow," I said by way of an apology.

"No, I'm going to go home and get some sleep. I'm dead on my feet."

The waitress was having trouble with her arithmetic. After several erasures, she decided she had the addition right and handed the tab to me, but Figlio grabbed the check in midair. I protested to no avail. "Next time you pay."

"Okay," I said.

"Great. There's a French restaurant up near you that got three stars the other day. Le Mirage. How's Thursday evening?" he smiled. Figlio loved to eat out. Given his mid-forties salary and the constant probes into police corruption, it was truly amazing he'd never come up on anyone's radar screen.

"Looks like your loyalties are going to be divided," I told him.

"Why's that?" he asked.

"If you want to go there, you'd better root for me to win the case. Otherwise we send out for Big Macs."

"Hey, I never said those guys didn't have shit for brains. I just said to watch your butt."

When I hailed a cab uptown I fully intended to go to the office to review the files—tomorrow promised to be a big day in court. But the thought of breathing Friday's stale air, Figlio's warning, and the floater's message that life was fleeting turned my nose away from the grindstone and instead pointed it home to my small, modest, but in no way depressing, railroad flat near Gracie Mansion, which I sublet from the actress daughter of a friend. Recharging my batteries, I told myself, would help my client more.

# CHAPTER 2

NEW YORK'S court system mirrors the City: overcrowded, noisy, and in need of repair. This morning the rear benches in Justice Sherman's courtroom were dusted in white from a weekend of falling plaster and cordoned off with yellow police tape. Polyglot conversations bounced off the hard surfaces and the whole place smelled of papaya and mango, producing an atmosphere that seemed in its sweetness even more unpredictable. If they ever market a plug-in tranquilizer room freshener, New York Supreme would be the perfect testing site.

My clients, the Lopezes, an extended family of at least thirty people and two nursing infants, were already seated and I greeted them with a big smile. None of them speaks much English—they sit through the entire proceedings as if they're wearing Walkman stereos—but their impassiveness is easily mistaken for sadness, and hopefully will help us get treble damages.

This wrongful death suit against the City hasn't made me very popular with anyone. The police, the Corrections Department bureaucrats, doctors at the Bronx School of Medicine, some fellow litigators who now avoid eye contact in the hallways, even the elevator operators I've known for years, seem to prefer to shoot the messenger rather than accept that the police and the doctors screwed up big-time. Last week Sally slipped into our phone con-

12

versation that my participation in this case was negatively impacting (her words) her career as Deputy District Attorney. Total bullshit. We're getting divorced. She shouldn't have a problem bonding with her peers and dumping all over me.

The defense hadn't arrived yet. Who could blame them after last week's disaster when I'd made mincemeat of that pimply kid who must've been supplied by a temp agency? If they didn't send an experienced upper-level regular and I nailed Dr. John Winston, the City would owe my clients a pisspotful, which, for the self-insured City, would be a budgetary disaster.

Finally, they—attorney and witness—arrived. The City Corporation counsel fell outside the bell curve of my expectations. She was younger than I'd anticipated, as well as very pretty, though in the midst of one's matrimonial action isn't everyone? But what caught my attention most was her serenity. She brought forth no stacks of prior briefs, motions, transcripts, or anything else. I do not have to have a protective perimeter, she was declaring. She didn't even have an attaché case, let alone one that was overstuffed. Just a pen and a pad.

Sally had that same kind of certainty—in fact, that was what had first attracted me to her. Only later in our marriage did I understand that she had to wear emotional blinders to maintain it.

As we made ready for battle, opposing counsel in no way acknowledged my presence. However pathetic this may sound, I was hurt by this lack of interest. I let some moments pass, fussed with my legal ablutions, and then walked over to introduce myself. It was the right thing for me to do. "Hello. I'm Mike Malone for the Plaintiff. I don't believe we've met."

"Claire Baker," she said, extending her hand. "You know Dr. Winston, of course."

"Yes. Nice to see you again," I said. Winston nodded, but neither of us made any effort to shake hands. Totally correct, given the circumstances. Unlike his attorney, young Dr. Winston was quite nervous. He'd taken off his jacket and both armpits were already damp with sweat.

"This judge is always late," I began. "But who cares as long as he stays awake. Right?" Attractive women make me talk too much. "And even that doesn't matter. His law clerk tells him what to say." Ms. Baker's response was a thin smile. Polite. Ivy League. Icily confident. Then I caught a glimpse of something white between her fingers, a breath mint. Maybe not.

Judge Sherman arrived at the bench a half hour late. The stay of execution had in the meantime understandably made Dr. Winston more nervous. His fingers were drumming uncontrollably on the table and his right foot was tapping up and down so vigorously that Ms. Baker's pen rolled off the table several times. For Winston, unfortunately, the Chinese water torture continued as he suffered through another delay, this one caused by the court reporter's struggle with a package of transcribing paper.

Finally, the reporter was ready. She nudged her pocketbook under her chair and spoke to me and Ms. Baker. "Can I please have your business cards for the record?" I fished one out of my wallet and handed it to her. Claire Baker did the same.

"Everybody on the same page?" Judge Sherman asked, suddenly impatient to begin, as if we hadn't been sitting on our butts forever waiting for his honorableness. "Court officer, bring in the jury."

Six jurors and two alternates filed in through a door in the side wall. Even this early in the morning they looked bedraggled and put-upon. Eight angry men and women. Judge Sherman charged the jury, reminding them not to hold any opinion, form any opinion, or talk about the case with anyone until all the evidence was heard. His tone was bored, matter-of-fact, his mind elsewhere. The jurors looked equally preoccupied. When I rose to do my thing, I could only hope that I might entice some of them to return from fantasy land and tune in.

"Clerk, please swear in the witness," Judge Sherman commanded.

Dr. Winston walked over to the witness stand and stood there, fidgeting, as he promised to tell the truth, the whole truth, and nothing but the truth, so help him God. Amen.

Dr. Winston sat down heavily. "Good morning, Doctor," I said.

"Good morning," he mumbled. But I didn't ask him to speak up. With a professional person, it's better, at least at the beginning, to be gentle and not to hassle about minor imperfections. The last thing a jury wants to hear this early in the testimony day is unpleasantness.

"Please state your name for the record, Doctor," I said.

"John M. Winston, M.D."

"What is your address please, sir?"

"Nineteen ninety-one York Avenue, New York, New York."

I gave the witness a broad smile. "Oh that's great. We're almost neighbors." Ms. Baker looked up, wondering if I was up to something, but Dr. Winston seemed to relax a little, which is what I'd intended. "Doctor, are you represented by counsel?"

"Yes I am."

"And is your attorney present today?"

He pointed to Ms. Baker. "Yes, she's sitting over there."

"Now Dr. Winston, can you please tell me the name of your employer?"

"I work at the Rikers Island Correctional Facility Hospital."

"Let me be more precise. You receive payment for your

work?" Dr. Winston nodded. "What is the name of the payor on these checks?"

"The City of New York."

"So, Dr. Winston, is it not correct that you are employed by the Department of Corrections of the City of New York and are assigned by them to the Rikers Island facility?"

"Yes, of course," he answered, irritated. I wasn't making a big point, but it's always useful to keep everyone focused on the essentials, in this case the big bad government that hopefully would be able to scrape together enough money to relieve the pain and suffering of my client.

The law clerk whispered something to the judge and His Honor summoned us. "Counsel, approach the bench," he commanded.

I put down my notes and joined opposing counsel up front.

"Mr. Malone, I realize today is Monday, and that we've all had a restful weekend. But let's get on with it, don't you think? The Court has other things to do. We don't want to piss away the whole morning."

"I will, Your Honor."

You could take my answer either way, but Judge Sherman seemed unbothered by the ambiguity. "Fine. Proceed," he said.

I returned purposefully to my notes. There's no reason to upset the judge, not so soon anyway. "Dr. Winston, were you on duty the late afternoon and early evening of June twelve of last year?"

"Yes."

"And are you familiar with a patient named Arturo Lopez?"

"Yes, I am."

"Just for the record, Doctor, could you please describe your usual work schedule?"

"Twelve hours on, twelve off. Four days per week."

"And on average how many patients would you say you see during a shift, Doctor?"

"It depends."

"Depends?" I asked. "Depends on what?"

"On the time of year. More people are sick in the winter or during the summer if there's a heat wave, for example."

"What's the range, Doctor, of the number of patients you might see?"

"Fifty to two hundred."

"Two hundred," I exclaimed. "That's quite a lot of people to examine and diagnose and treat, isn't it?"

"Yes," he said and wiped his brow with the back of his hand.

"How much backup do you have?"

"It varies by shift. Anywhere from three R.N.'s and four aides to something less than that."

"Now, you indicated earlier you remembered the patient Arturo Lopez, correct?" Dr. Winston nodded. "Doctor, please answer with a 'yes' or a 'no' for the benefit of the court reporter."

"Yes."

"And do you happen to recall the time of day when you first interacted with Mr. Arturo Lopez as a patient?"

"Late afternoon."

"Can you be a little more precise, Doctor?"

"I don't remember the exact hour, if that's what you mean," he answered, annoyed.

"Was it close to suppertime? Or nearer the four o'clock shift change?"

"I can't recall."

"Is that the best you can recollect, sir?"

Claire Baker stood up. "Objection, Your Honor."

"Reason?" Sherman asked.

"Badgering the witness."

"Overruled."

It's always important not to crow in front of a jury, to show you're a good sport. In my kindest, most gentle voice I suggested, "Dr. Winston, if you like you can refresh your memory with the patient's file."

Ms. Baker stirred in her seat, her skirt riding up.

Whatever the reason, Dr. Winston was offended by my offer of help. "I don't need to, I have a great memory. I believe it was sometime after four o'clock."

Hadn't they prepared Dr. Winston? This was too easy. "You're sure you don't want to look at the patient record?" I asked with a solicitous helpful tone, like a kindergarten teacher.

"I'm sure," he answered defiantly.

Whether or not his recall of the time was accurate wasn't especially important. We had a written patient intake form available for all of us to review. I was just trying to get under his skin and I'd succeeded. I glanced quickly at the jurors—even the two at the end of the back row who'd been half-asleep were paying attention.

"Okay, good. Now, Doctor, let's turn to the patient, Mr. Lopez. When you first encountered him, can you remember what he said to you?"

"The patient was complaining of pain on his right side and in his right forearm."

"Did he make any statements about the etiology, the cause, of the pain?" "Etiology" was a deliberate word choice. Down the road I'd let the jurors know that I, too, was a doctor. Entitled to use big words and entitled to be upset on behalf of the Plaintiff about the care, or lack of it, that had been dished out.

Dr. Winston stared at the jury and said, "He claimed that two policemen had beaten him with their clubs on the way to Rikers."

"I take it from your tone that you didn't believe him."

"Objection."

"Sustained. Counselor, rephrase."

"Did you believe the patient's explanation?"

"No," he said sharply. "Prisoners often make those kinds of charges. He was agitated, upset at being incarcerated. Who wouldn't be?"

"So you didn't take his concerns seriously, did you?"

"I really didn't spend any time thinking about it one way or the other."

"Why not? Because you were too busy?" I asked.

"Objection."

"Sustained. Give the witness a chance to answer the questions. We want to hear his answers, not yours, Dr. Malone." He lingered on the "Doctor," somewhat disdainfully, but I noticed the mailman juror from the Village and the Macy's clerk looked at me with heightened respect.

"Of course, Your Honor," I said gratefully, now that I was relieved of finding the right moment to tell the jury about my medical background.

"Could you please repeat the question?" Dr. Winston asked.

"Certainly. Why didn't you think about it one way or the other?" I asked.

Claire Baker jumped to her feet. "May we approach, Your Honor?"

Sherman motioned us forward for a sidebar. *"Nu?"* he said, which is Yiddish for "What's up?"

"You broke my flow, it'd better be good," I added.

"We're willing to stip a lot of this," Ms. Baker declared.

I turned to her. "Sure, as long as the jury doesn't hear any of the facts. That's big of you."

"Talk to me, counselors, not each other," Sherman commanded. We both nodded, like chastened first graders. The judge's law clerk came up behind him and whispered something in his ear. "I'm reminded one of the jurors has a

doctor's appointment, so we have to wind this up sooner
rather than later. So, let's go for the beef, Malone, and
maybe after the break we can give a little, get a little, and
try to save the taxpayers some money and court time.
Okay?" He winked at Ms. Baker, which I found, at this
moment, particularly annoying.

"So, Dr. Winston, when you examined the patient, what
was his temperature?"

"He was hyperpyretic."

" 'Hyperpyretic' is the medical term for high fever, is it
not?" I asked for the benefit of the jury.

"Yes."

"And what was his temperature?"

"One-oh-four."

"And what did you do then?"

"I ordered some acetaminophen for the patient."

"That's Tylenol?" I asked. Medical testimony can be
excruciatingly tedious for a jury. It's important to keep
things simple and their attention engaged.

"Yes," he said.

"Did you also order restraints for the patient?"

"Yes, I did."

"Why?"

"I thought it possible his fever was caused in part by excessive activity, you know, thrashing about."

"Thrashing about?" I said skeptically. "What do you
mean by that, Doctor?"

"Flailing his arms, kicking off his covers, moving
around in the bed like a dog that can't get comfortable."

"Like a dog?" I repeated.

"Objection, Your Honor. Can we approach?" Ms. Baker
asked.

"You're trying my patience, Ms. Baker. What's up?"
Judge Sherman asked.

"Counsel's sarcasm is out of bounds, Your Honor. We're here to try the facts, not the witness's language skills."

"They're curious words for a physician, don't you think?" I said. "I was just underlining them for the jury."

"Noted," Judge Sherman declared. "Anything else bothering you, Ms. Baker?"

"No," she said.

"Okay, let's see if it's possible to move on without any other interruptions."

"I'll do my best, sir."

"I'm sure you will," he said and winked again at Ms. Baker. Or maybe it was a nervous tic. "Objection sustained," the judge told the courtroom.

I picked up my notes and resumed. "Now, Doctor, after you gave the patient Tylenol, did his fever go down?"

"Somewhat."

"Please be more specific."

"His temp dropped to one-oh-three."

"How about his agitation? Was he still thrashing about?"

"Yes."

I took a step closer to the witness stand. "And that's why you gave him Demerol? For his agitation, right?"

"Yes," he answered too quickly, before Ms. Baker could object, looking downward at an imagined speck of floor dust.

I always coach my witnesses. Don't hurry. Don't let yourself be provoked. This isn't a race. The wheels grind slowly here. Never let your Irish show.

"Foundation, Your Honor."

"I'll rephrase," I generously offered.

"Did you order Demerol for the patient?"

"Yes."

"Why?"

"Because he was agitated."

"And, hypothetically speaking, if Mr. Lopez, your patient, had told you he was taking Nardil, would you have prescribed Demerol?"

"No. It was contraindicated," Winston replied.

"Which meant it was very dangerous for him, right?"

"Yes."

"In fact, it might even kill him?"

"It might. Though I don't think it did."

I raised my voice. "You don't think so? Why don't you think so? Because you don't want to feel responsible for his death? Is that what you mean, Dr. Winston?"

Ms. Baker jumped to her feet. "Objection, Your Honor. The jury will decide if Dr. Winston was responsible."

"Sustained."

I looked down at my notes, paused somewhat melodramatically, and said in a low, very sad voice, "Yes, they will."

"Please repeat. I couldn't hear the last words," the court reporter asked me, but I never answered her question because the judge was loudly adjourning us for the day.

The jurors filed out quickly, making beelines to the bathroom, while the court reporter flitted about like an escaped parakeet, shaking out her fingers and tidying the pile of steno output. Dr. Winston, however, was inert, slumped deep into the witness chair, as if trying to find a place to hide.

# CHAPTER 3

I followed Ms. Baker through a wooden door in the middle of the wooden wall behind the bench to Judge Sherman's chambers.

"Coffee or tea, anyone?" the judge asked pleasantly, but both of us declined. "So where are we on this *thing*, counselor?" he asked Ms. Baker.

"We're willing to stipulate that the combination of the two medicines was contraindicated," Ms. Baker declared and rocked on her heels as if she'd made a creative and meaningful offer, seemingly oblivious to the fact she'd offered nothing.

"So? That's it," I said pointedly. "I don't need to stipulate what's been proven already. This is bush," I said, discarding the lawyerly civility. And the truth is I wasn't acting. I was truly pissed.

Claire Baker was taken aback by my anger. Upset flashed across her lovely blue green eyes, but it quickly disappeared and was replaced by more neutral corneal screens, activated by an unseen button somewhere in her brain. "We're also prepared to offer a generous settlement."

"How much?" the judge asked before I could.

"Three hundred fifty thousand dollars."

"You must be kidding. Don't insult us," I said.

"We feel that's very generous."

Sally had a similar outlook when it came to presents for Jess's friends. It wasn't a good idea to be "too generous and send the wrong signal," she always argued, as if any child would ever be concerned.

"A twenty-two-year-old dies a wrongful death and—"

"We can't afford more," she said sadly. Bring on the handwringing.

"And I can't afford to waste any more time."

The judge gave Ms. Baker a warm smile. "Well, counselor, given the facts of the case, I think it's a good beginning." Ms. Baker relaxed her shoulders, returning his smile. "But perhaps we can do better. What do you think would be fair, Dr. Malone?"

I considered his question for twenty seconds at least, without saying anything. I wanted to appear thoughtful, appropriately judicious. "Three and a half million, Your Honor." Opposing counsel made inarticulate sounds of nonacceptance.

"Well, Ms. Baker, with all due respect, maybe you should sleep on it." His tone was avuncular, though I'm sure he was wondering how she looked asleep, in bed, undressed. "Nine-thirty tomorrow morning in chambers."

"Yessir," we both said, the echo lost amidst the law books and the stacks of case files.

Sometime during the morning, while I was hitting my litigational stride, I'd realized that the trial meant I'd probably miss the partners' lunch. Now, with the unexpected early recess, I had almost two hours to kill. I called Arnie Glimcher, my divorce attorney, and squeezed in the mini-meeting he'd been hounding me about.

The Number 4 Lexington subway ride to his midtown office was sweet. I visualized the heavies from the City Corporation counsel's office, from the mayor's staff, from the Police Department doing their own thrashing about, trying to resuscitate their failed strategy, trying in vain to protect their asses.

Arnie's messy office matched his rumpled, overweight appearance. It's amazing he finds anything and even more amazing that cases aren't getting mixed up with each other, but so far they haven't.

He greeted me with his usual, "How're they hanging, kid?"

"Just fine. What's the urgency?"

"The court wants the financial disclosure forms and I don't like getting this judge upset," he told me.

"I haven't had any time."

"Look, kid, face the music and make some. They're required by law. This is New York, the Equitable Distribution State. We can't fart around about this anymore. Especially since Sally's submitted hers."

"She has?" I said. Arnie pushed a thick document over the paper hill and dale toward me.

I started reading. The first thing I noticed was that Sally had squirreled away a tidy sum. My nest egg was another story. Because she'd managed everything, I had no idea whether mine had hatched or flown away. That's why, despite a big income last year, I'm not exactly living high off the hog. After I pay temporary child support, temporary maintenance, plus my share of the mortgage payments and Jess's tuition, about the only thing in positive territory was my frequent flyer mileage. Which is why I chose Arnie.

Originally a high-profile prosecutor who had successfully tangled with many lowlifes and slime buckets, Arnie had taken the traditional exit, becoming a high-profile defense attorney, representing other lowlifes and slime buckets. Ten years ago, Arnie switched to family law after a client, out celebrating his "not guilty" verdict on a man-slaughter charge, raped a college coed who was working late-night at a club.

Though he mostly represented women, it would proba-bly be a mistake to characterize Arnie's law practice as atonement, for his clients were more likely to be the wives, mistresses, and one-night stands of the rich than the downtrodden in need of nurture. Last June I'd seen Arnie on television, Charlie Rose's show, detailing how he went about his business of extracting the maximum. Since in my case the tables seem to be turned, I hoped that this one time he could even the score for a fellow male.

"Let's do a little of this together," Arnie suggested. "Maybe all you need is a little momentum."

"Okay," I agreed.

He took me through the entire twelve-page form of sav-ings and checking accounts, expenses, sources of income, loans, IRA's, Keogh's, mortgages, penciling in answers to most of the questions, and putting big red circles around the items I couldn't recall. At the end of the interrogation I was glad this former prosecutor was on my side. It's funny, when the shoe was on the other foot, how much I didn't like being asked a lot of questions.

# CHAPTER 4

MARTIN BADGER, a creature of habit like most of us, and the named partner of Badger, Weissberg, Smith, a law firm specializing in medical malpractice and negligence, pushed his chair away from the table, stood up stiffly, and convoked the partners' lunch with the usual joke, or at least what passes for one among litigators. "A judge recently told me that med-mal lawyers were pre-meds who flunked chemistry." We waited for the punch line, and when none arrived, each of us somehow knew to laugh politely.

Badger didn't seem to notice the lack of enthusiasm. On the contrary, proud of his offering, he continued to grin almost idiotically. Once he must have cut an impressive figure, this tall, thin, gray-haired man, now shortened by failing muscles and curving bones into a dead-weight version of his former self. Deeply set eyes that previously twinkled were now so flooded with fluid that the skin folds of his lower lids resembled wadded-up paper towels. He sat down heavily, but continued to talk, while everyone else, having glimpsed their future, resumed eating the cold poached salmon with extra gusto.

These genteel gatherings were a self-indulgence of which I was totally unaware when the firm recruited me. Quite a contrast from hospital conference cold cuts. I'm a lapsed Catholic, but with enough fibers of hair shirt

27

remaining to explain why, in the midst of eating French wonderfulness, I'd think about former patients and feel sad I hadn't found the way to shake the sense of futility—that I was nothing more than a highly skilled mechanic, helpless to prevent the recurrent failures of the human body and soul.

The firm's three-star chef had been recruited from London of all places by a partner who was there on behalf of a deep-pocketed liability reinsurer. The fact of the chef's employment particularly galled Sally. In her mind no amount of pro bono—we all did quite a bit—could justify such group self-indulgence. No one would disagree, least of all me, that the firm spent way too much on unnecessary superficialities and, as a result, was billable hours rich, but cash poor.

Though Sally's criticism was somewhat accurate, it didn't explain everything. Her rage grew from envy, pure and simple, our marriage declining as my partnership income rose. Notwithstanding the above, I still managed to feel guilty, which is what motivated me to suggest Sally handle all our finances. When I'd mentioned the arrangement to Arnie at our first meeting seven months ago, he'd shaken his head in disbelief and called me a "piece of work."

Sally's career was hardly without its shining moments. Fresh out of law school she'd begun as an Assistant District Attorney while I was still a house officer at Bellevue. And after the mandatory two-year stint ended she'd migrated to the Vera Institute of Justice, where she'd attracted sufficient attention to be chased by the legal headhunters, who eventually transported her, courtesy of a hefty search fee, away from helping others, to a major salary at Williamson Communications. The whole family enjoyed her economic well-being—Jess acquired a full-time nanny and I signed on with a medical marketing publicist who promised the moon and delivered fifteen new patients within one year. If anyone had asked me at the time, I would have said Sally was very happy, fulfilled even. But I must have been wrong: otherwise why would she have chucked it all and rejoined Donald Gramb's team?

Perhaps Gramb, the District Attorney, knew her better than I did, for he'd given her something she couldn't refuse, a return to glory as Deputy District Attorney and first head of the newly formed Sex Crimes Unit. I just didn't like Donald Gramb. A lightweight through and through. An empty briefcase going nowhere.

The power and the glory were accompanied by a substantial cut in pay that didn't affect our lifestyle because by then my practice was going great guns. All that aside, I believe Sally's job change was the seed of our troubles. So long as I was on the short end of the unequal incomes equation, or even later, when I'd gained the advantage and everything was copacetic, the disparity could be explained away by our very different careers—prosecutor versus Park Avenue cardiologist. But when I switched over to the law, and worse started to reel in the big settlements, our marriage started to unravel. Two years ago we were supermarket shopping together, each with our own cart, a metaphor no doubt. I'd stopped on the periphery of gourmet foods in front of a caviar display, curious to know price and origin, while she'd gone off in search of milk, juice, eggs, bread. I was still dreamily considering the label when she returned with the essential food groups and a look of exasperated disdain that even now makes me feel lousy.

Badger was talking still, but I hadn't been listening and can't tell you what he said. Only the taste of the salmon sauce, a Eurasian flavor more sweet than sour, registered on my present. Sally had put a ton of money together for

herself. She had more IRA's and Keoghs and sub-Keoghs
than the Dublin phone book. No wonder she'd pushed for
the divorce: all her golden geese were in order. But what I
hated most was her hypocrisy. She'd never admit she
cared about money. Not my Sally. She was just prudent,
sensible, public-spirited, while I was somehow a parasite
sucking off hefty contingency fees. From my ten years
living with a Deputy D.A., I can tell you that public prosecutors are genetically incapable of admitting less noble
reasons for their behavior.

The Sutton Place duplex was her idea. "It'll be easier to
entertain" (we never did), "nice neighborhood for Jess"
(he spends most of his teenage time at school, in his room,
or on the phone), and "we're buying at the bottom of the
market." The country house. Also her purchase. Two years
ago. We needed "a place to unwind." We'd spent a total of
six days and two nights there.

Arnie was right about me, I was a piece of work. I
hadn't thought things through. Turning over control of our
money had definitely made matters worse for me: I have
zero leverage. Sally has me by the short hairs and she
knows it.

While most people like to forget their mistakes, I have
this way of torturing my soul and body with mine. Here I
was enjoying a perk for which I'd taken so much abuse
and now my mouth was going dry on me, so I couldn't
swallow the food, and I was breaking into a cold sweat.
Typical Mike Malone, owner of the world's most reactive
physiology.

I tugged at my shirt collar, breaking the water bond between cotton and skin. Maybe the cold sweat was my TB
acting up—I had forgotten to take the INH last night. In
my wallet, sandwiched between VISA and American Express, I found my emergency supply. I washed down the
little white tablet with sauvignon blanc, thinking, *No good*

*deed goes unpunished.* If I hadn't done pro bono work last year for the Midtown Homeless Shelter I wouldn't have been exposed and wouldn't have to take prophylaxis for the next seven months. The damned stuff is dangerous—liver problems, especially in the over-thirty-five age group. My group.

Badger finished talking and Jim Smith rose to speak. He was a Midwesterner, shy in private meetings, but excited, totally extroverted, in larger, more public forums.

"Well, everybody, I'm pleased to report we've got three new goodies. First we've landed on the right side of the wrong-side-of-the-brain operation done at Farley. Open and shut. Heads are going to be rolling there." This time the laughter was genuine, but I felt sorry for the brain surgeon, whoever he was. The poor bastard would never get his day in court. He'd have to take the fall for the foul-up because the insurers would insist upon a settlement and the public relations types would throw him to the wolves. All the years of neurosurg training wasted. If he was lucky, he'd end up doing appendectomies in Saskatchewan.

"Second. We've got an action against an HMO for denial of benefits. We're asking four million in damages plus punitive. Treble there. Looks like a solid bankable one. And third, the best for last, we're going to be pushing the envelope past the cutting edge on this one," Jim Smith declared. He paused melodramatically, scanning his peers' faces, hoping to maximize the attention level. I smiled. It never fails to amuse me when lawyers start confusing their tiny baby-step conservative efforts with true social or technological change.

"Our client's wife was concerned about Huntington's chorea, which ran in her family. A fatal genetic disease with a late onset, between the ages of thirty-five and forty-five. Right, Dr. Malone?" I nodded. "A disease with a lot of emotional problems—severe depression, suicide, anti-social behavior. Nothing glamorous here. The chief resident takes it upon himself, during the hospital admission for the removal of a uterine cyst (a particularly vulnerable moment given this woman's fears), to tell her about all the progress occurring in the biotech/genetics world, strongly suggesting now's the right time to get tested. 'It'll make your life better if you know one way or the other,' he says to her. Only problem is he forgets to have her sign a consent. And worse, he doesn't mention there's still no cure. The test results come back positive, the woman goes off the deep end, and we've got a winner." Jim Smith leaned over to whisper something in Mr. Badger's ear—Badger grinned broadly.

"Oh, one other point. The client's name." He stopped and circled the opening of his mouth with his tongue, like a woman fixing her lipstick. "Her name is Gail Graham," he added. A handful of faces lit up with recognition, while most partners, including me, sat there unimpressed, daring Smith to win his case. "You've all seen her on TV, right? She's the hot redhead in that sitcom. And now she's in that movie with John Travolta. You know the one, don't you?"

I didn't, and maybe my partners didn't either, but we lawyers are good at faking, and so in an instant the empty looks were replaced by sugarplums filled with daydreams of reflected stardom. Appearances on *Court TV*, *Larry King Live!*, *60 Minutes*, profiles in *People*, *Penthouse*, and *Playboy*, maybe even guesting on *Oprah* or a visit to the White House clouded their collective thinking.

Smith stared intently in my direction. He expected me, as the only physician in a med-mal firm, to take the lead on this case. My plate is full, thank you very much. The client's name didn't make a bit of difference as far as I was concerned. I was in the midst of the Lopez trial, I had to administer the silicone settlement claims for the court, and I knew with complete certainty that my personal legal problems would soon be increasing as our acrimony worked its way through State Supreme Court. What's more, genetics cases were like watching paint dry atom by atom. They drive juries nuts. And judges. And lawyers—even those of us who went to medical school.

Jim Smith, undaunted, disregarded my inner thoughts. "Regardless of who ultimately manages this case, I want you all to remember we have an invaluable in-house medical resource who will be an important part of our full-court press on behalf of our client." One thing I've noticed that both medicine and the law have in common is that whenever a male authority figure employs sports metaphors, you're in big trouble.

The salmon was drying out so I showered it with lemon, some of which dribbled down my palm under the butterfly bandage and stung. I dipped a napkin into ice water and rinsed the wound. It was still oozing. I should have gone to the ER Saturday night and had it stitched by the surgical resident, but, as the honored speaker at the silicone claimants' testimonial dinner, I didn't want to be late. I was lucky the jagged glass wedged into the door lock hadn't cut a nerve or a tendon.

I excused myself and went to the bathroom to wash my hand. All the faucets were turned on, as Badger stood there, looking miserable, unable to coax out any urine. I looked away, trying not to add to his embarrassment.

"Old age is so unfair. We don't have this kind of time to waste," he said to me.

"It happens to all of us. If you just relax, it might help. Think of something else," I advised him. "Breathe in slowly." He followed my advice. "Good. That's good," I said gently. Soon he passed some urine and was greatly relieved.

"Thanks, Mike. You're a good doctor. We're all proud of you."

"I hope so."

"By the way, Mike, I wanted to ask you something."

"Yes, sir," I said.

"How's that case, you know, the one involving the jail?" he asked casually.

"You mean the wrongful death at Rikers?"

"Yes, that one."

"Pretty good. I think they'll settle."

"I hope so. I hear it's taking up a lot of your time. I'd like to see you move on to something else."

"Some cases take time."

"We can't afford to tilt at windmills."

"I'm not. I've got 'em by the cojones. Trust me."

"This Graham case should be right up your alley."

"I don't like any case where genetics is even mentioned. Juries can't stand all that scientific evidence."

"It's a good case for the firm. Lot of visibility, unlike your jail case."

I wondered what was prompting this non sequitur of negativity. "There're some important issues here. The Lopezes are a nice family. We're doing the right thing helping them. And we're getting good coverage."

"It's not going to win us any friends. Or clients. Wind it up, Mike. Take less, just settle." I'd lay money he already knew of, had approved, and maybe even suggested, the City's settlement offer.

"I'll do my best, sir," I said.

"How 'bout the silicone monies? You on top of that?"

"Yessir," I answered brusquely and walked out, leaving Badger to tidy himself.

Before I had time to get pissed about Badger's pressure, Lydia, my frizzy-haired secretary who looks like an overage flower child but calls me Mr. Malone, though I've told her I prefer Mike, collared me outside the men's room. "Oh, thank heaven, there you are." Her voice was upset.

"What's the matter?"

"I don't know. First, a Dr. Feldman called. He's sending over a TRO and has to talk to you. Then *she* called twice in the last five minutes. And said it was urgent. A-S-A-P. She has to talk with you."

Lydia had an hysterical undertone. I put my hand on her arm. "Who're we talking about?"

"Sharronn."

"My wife's secretary, Sharronn?"

"Yes, of course. Who'd you think I meant?"

# CHAPTER 5

WE walked back to the office suite together. I tried to hide my apprehensiveness. ASAP meant bad news. Something about Jess. Sally shouldn't have let him go on the school trip in the first place. If she wanted to communicate that she didn't give a shit whether or not I celebrated our son's birthday during the appropriate time period, there were other ways, aside from agreeing to this nonmandatory excursion, to do it. All this approach did was upset me so much that I'd taken out my frustration on Jess and blamed him for going, proving that parental neediness doesn't help anyone.

Why had Sharronn called? This wasn't the kind of thing Sally should have delegated. We're both his parents, even if we're divorcing. For the rest of our lives this was going to be our fate. Even happy events—when Jess graduates from high school, then college; marries, has children—my grandchildren; accepts a professional award: all would be contaminated by regret and loss. Normal families can wall things off from others and from themselves. Divorced families can't. The truth is, as long as Jess was okay, I could handle anything.

The District Attorney's phone lines were busy and I died a thousand times before I connected with Sharronn. "Ms. Hager didn't come in this morning. It's not like her.

We have interrogatories at three o'clock. I've tried your house and your country house and all I'm getting are answering machines. I thought maybe you might know something."

I almost answered with a sarcastic, "I'm not my soon-to-be ex-wife's keeper," but I didn't, and instead allowed myself to feel relief that Jess was okay. "I don't know. We are in the midst of a divorce. I haven't talked to her since Wednesday night. And that was mostly about Jess's school trip." As soon as I said the words aloud the anxiety returned. "Have you called his school? Maybe there was some . . . ?"

She interrupted. "I've called. They know nothing." Instantly, I felt my heart rate slow.

"I don't know what to say. Connecticut's a possibility. She could be stuck somewhere." But we never went there, together or separately. "I'd call the downstairs neighbors, but Jess mentioned they're away in Europe, so that wouldn't do any good. I still have the keys to the house. Maybe I should meet you there."

My offer wasn't a good idea—if Arnie heard about it he'd flay me alive. Even though I hadn't initiated the divorce action, I'd come to accept and even anticipate its early resolution, a hope based mostly on my naiveté in these matters. One of the first truisms Arnie Glimcher had told me was that there was no such thing as an amicable divorce, only the false appearance of one; his second point was never to appear weak and overly concerned, or else, he'd said, my wife and her attorney would carve me up and eat me for breakfast. But I was raised to keep my word regardless of the consequences.

"Okay, that's what I was thinking," Sharronn answered.

"It'll take me twenty minutes. How about you?"

"Half hour."

*  *  *

A pesky swirling wind blew along Sutton Place, scattering the litter the homeowners had missed. I could feel a thousand eyes to whom I'd said "hello" and "good afternoon" watching. To my surprise, Sharronn soon arrived in an unmarked police cruiser driven by a burly detective ("Detective Harper, pleased to meet you, sir; Sharronn asked me to come along") and the three of us climbed the steps to the parlor floor entrance. I unlocked the two Medeco's and the Yale dead bolt. Heavy protection. Sally's idea. All the years in the D.A.'s office had made her skittish about crime and violence.

Inside, the house looked the same, yet I felt like a home-grown burglar—on edge, out of place, and excited. I hadn't been back in nearly seven months, soon after the court, in response to an early motion by the plaintiff, had awarded the mother, on a temporary basis, possession of the marital residence.

It sounded strange when Sharronn called out loudly, "Ms. Hager." No answer.

"Sally," I yelled. "Hello! Sharronn and a detective from your office are here with me." Still no answer.

I guided the two visitors to the kitchen at the back of the house. It was spotless, not a dirty plate or abandoned half-filled glass or cup. Sally was one of those people who couldn't leave home without first putting everything away in its right place. Out of restlessness or acquired habit, I opened the dishwasher. It was filled with dirty dishes. That wasn't like Sally at all, but I kept the thought to myself.

"Let's try upstairs," I suggested, and we trooped to the bedroom floor.

Jess's bedroom was visible and as messy as ever. The door to the master bedroom was partially open, as if someone hadn't been sure whether or not to close it, and from the hallway I could see that our bed was unmade and in the next moment, as if every image was projected simultaneously, I took in the large area of redness fanning out through the fibers of white shag carpeting and soiling the entire area beneath Sally's nightstand.

My heart was racing as I entered our bedroom and headed to the far side of the bed, my side, where I came upon nothing, and perversely felt disappointed, let down. I walked into the bathroom suite. The shower curtain rod was on the floor; the translucent waterproof version of Monet's lily pond had been removed.

"Don't touch anything, Mr. Malone. That's a good surface to lift prints," Detective Harper warned, referring to the greenish marble our fancy-shmancy decorator had special-ordered from Pietrasanta, Italy. I remember the town name because she'd gone there, courtesy of our fee, and sent an insipid postcard about how good the pasta tasted.

A few minutes later, how I got there I'm not sure, I stood in the middle of the living room and watched Harper and his peers, donned in plastic gloves, explore every nook and cranny of my house, a house now overrun by crackling walkie-talkie noise and purposeful, unsmiling people, a D.A.'s office party without food or drink or conversation. Finally, I heard someone shout, "Hey, Jack. Get over here. Look at this," and the spell was broken.

The detectives crowded into the large utility closet off the kitchen that we used for storage. As if in worship, they stood silently around the opened freezer that was our last major appliance purchase before we started to fight over every decision. The group seemed unbothered by the cold air chilling the pantry. I nudged between them to see what they'd found, half-knowing already. Wrapped in the plastic robe of French lilies, covered with an unseasonal pinkish crystalline frost, was the frozen body of Sally Hager Malone, no longer my soon-to-be ex-wife.

# CHAPTER 6

WHEN they began questioning me, I felt that the detectives were being insensitive—they'd started too soon, not allowing me a moment to crawl away, even the tiniest of distances, to a shelter where I could begin to take in the awfulness that had happened in my home. But I'm no longer certain of this. For a great shock can trivialize life and cast one adrift on a sea of misery where nothing is as it seems.

"Dr. Malone, could you please tell us when you last had contact with your wife?" a male voice had asked. Contact? What kind? Verbal? About a week. Emotional? Not lately. Sexual? Years ago.

"Wednesday," I'd finally answered.

"Do you recall what time that was?"

"Evening." Why'd it matter?

"What'd you talk about?"

"Our son Jess's school trip."

"When did your son leave on the school trip?"

"Early Saturday morning."

"Do you know the exact time?"

"No, goddammit. Ask the school."

"You said you last talked to Mrs. Malone Wednesday. Have you been out of town since then?" he'd asked disingenuously. A classic interrogation technique: shame the witness, remind him of his past failures. Our impending

**40**

divorce had been reported in the *Daily News* and *Post* months ago. "Sally Hager, deputy D.A., who heads the hugely successful Sex Crimes Unit, and her husband of eighteen years, famed doctor-lawyer . . ." they'd written. Gossip columns were required reading for homicide detectives. Everyone who worked in Manhattan law enforcement, unless blind, deaf, or head stuck up his ass, knew.

"No," I said loudly, annoyed.

"Where'd you talk? Here?" *Of course not, you asshole. I don't live here anymore. Ask Judge Oberman. He'll confirm. He'd ordered the change of scenery.*

I glared at him. "Nowhere. On the telephone. She called the office."

"She called the office," he repeated my sentence slowly, method-acting skepticism, trying to give the words more importance than they could possible deserve.

"Have you talked with your son since Wednesday?"

"Yes, I called him Thursday evening."

"What time was that?"

"Midnight."

"Was it something very urgent?"

"No."

"Why'd you call so late?"

I looked away, pretending to dislodge an errant eyelash. Jess hadn't placed much importance on my celebrating his birthday. Tuesday evening Sally had taken him out to dinner, Wednesday school friends had arranged something, Thursday I was tied up in a deposition on Long Island. And the midnight phone call, filled as it was with teenage grunts and mumblings, had only lengthened the distance between us.

"His line was busy for chrissake," I shouted, surprising myself by how angry I was, and upsetting the detective's interrogatory rhythm as well.

The pause prompted me to face the unstated theme behind these questions. As the estranged husband of the deceased I was the ready-made prime suspect, the standard of alleged culpability against which any others would be measured. Maybe Jess had said something that had made me kill Sally in a jealous rage? The detectives would never know unless they asked, poked, annoyed.

Now that I was alert, engaged, I wanted the questions to cease, I wanted to be left alone. Do whatever you must to secure your crime scene and then get the hell out of my home. My home, which would no longer have to be equitably divided. Now I could see Jess all the time. No more schedules and no more bills from Arnie Glimcher. Best of all, no more wasted time in fucking court. Murder can be liberating, I thought, and smiled somewhat inappropriately, though I'm sure a psychiatrist, unlike a suspicious detective, would suggest that under horrific circumstances a person often needs to find the proverbial silver lining.

"What're you smiling about, Doctor?" one of the detectives, ever predictable, asked, as I watched his butt involuntarily slide off the slippery surface of the blue-and-white-striped satin-covered side chair we'd purchased against my wishes at a Nineteenth Regiment Armory Antiques Show.

"I was remembering how I'd told my wife that these chairs were unsittable and the best she could do was to say there was no such word in the English language." A perfect example of the trivial, ridiculous competitions we allowed to define our marriage.

The detective pushed himself back up. "What did you and your son talk about?" I wished he would shut up. Ask, don't answer, questions. Litigation 101.

"I don't remember. Just father-and-son small talk. Nothing significant."

"Please, Doctor, let us be the judge of that."

Us? Who's us? Across the room two other detectives leaned against the wall of my living room, looking at my books on the shelves above my entertainment center. Nothing gave them the right to invade my privacy. But of course that wasn't true, this wasn't a civil liberties issue, they were doing their job, maybe even protecting me—the sooner they found the killer, the easier it would be for me and Jess to let go of the horror and rebuild our lives.

"His school trip. His computer. Have you looked at her cases? She put away a lot of bad people. Any one of them—"

"We'll be checking that, Doctor. Did Mrs. Malone ever mention any specific threats to you?"

"A few years ago there was one. A rapist who preyed on the women who cleaned office buildings."

"Do you remember his name?"

"You can find it out, can't you?" I snapped. "Sharronn knows this better than I do." Sharronn was seated in the white chair next to the couch, her head in her arms. For the moment, she didn't look like she'd be of much use. The detective ignored my outburst and continued to scribble on his pad. I heard my whine going round and round, a factory disgorging word waste. "Detective, I'm exhausted. Do you think we could continue this later? I really need to find my son at school."

Before he answered, and with no apparent direct stimulus, I began to cry. For Jess, for me, and for the woman with whom I'd shared my love and most of my adult life.

"Of course," the detective said, embarrassed as tough men can be by a distraught male. "If you think of anything else, call us." He handed me his card. "I might not still be on the case. They'll probably assign someone from the D.A.'s office. This is a special situation. I'm sure you understand. But you can reach me at this number and if I've been reassigned I'll leave instructions about who you should to talk to, okay?" He gave me a light pat on the shoulder. "Keep your chin up, Dr. Malone. Things'll get better, you'll see."

"Thanks," I replied.

The only reason things had to get better was because, as the cliché goes, they couldn't get any worse. Who the hell did this? It had to be some perp she'd put away. No one else would have had a reason, but I'd overheard a cop say there was no forcible entry. How could that be? Sally wasn't the type to let a stranger into our house, especially a menacing one. Nothing added up. I couldn't think straight, my head throbbed and was numb at the same time. I couldn't imagine what I was going to say to Jess.

As I dried my cheeks on my shirtsleeve I realized I'd better call Arnie Glimcher and tell him what'd happened before he heard about it on the evening news and thought I was a wife-murderer.

"One other thing, Dr. Malone. It'd probably be better if you and your son stayed somewhere else tonight so that the crime scene boys can finish up. Okay?" the detective added.

I nodded. I didn't want to stay here anyway. Suddenly I realized this wasn't my home anymore. Not now. Even if I threw everything out, I would always see the red-brown stains and the pinkened freezer frost. Blood where it wasn't supposed to be. Escaped blood. Like many a doctor, I'd always been a little squeamish about blood.

In contrast to the elementary school years, when the sidewalk was crowded with expectant parents happily chattering away with each other, as if they'd gone on the trip, no one else was waiting at the disembarkation site in front of the school for the bus from Montreal bearing adolescent sons and daughters. Ten minutes before the scheduled arrival, a teacher I didn't recognize came out from the old stone building, acknowledged my existence with a minuscule shake of his head, but, mercifully, kept to himself and made no effort to intrude.

Nothing in my professional life in court or at the bedside of dying patients had prepared me for this moment with Jess. How ironic that what I most needed now was a wife or even an ex-wife to stand beside me and relieve my impotence as I told our son that he'd returned to a funeral.

The teenagers alighted from the long ride looking scruffy, most carrying backpacks and sleeping bags, a few with poster tubes and other detritus from their adventures. With his face framed by long sideburns, Jess looked older, or maybe I just wanted him to be, so that he could be of help to me. Our eyes connected and he gave me a wary look, understandably confused by my presence. I moved steadily toward him, weaving through the others, giving him a big hug for both of us.

He disengaged quickly and greeted me with a typically terse, almost uncivil, "What're you doing here?"

Perhaps he'd assumed I'd come to continue our phone conversation (my monologue is more accurate), or chastise him about some school-related indiscretion, and was just trying to set up his defenses. "Can we go somewhere and sit down? You want something to eat? You must be hungry," I said rapidly, not giving him time to answer, as I tried to postpone the unpleasantness.

"I have a lotta stuff to do. Why're you here?" the son of two litigators asked again.

I sighed deeply. "We need to talk. Just you and me. Privately. It won't take long."

He wanted a guarantee. "How long?"

"A few minutes, Jess. Please, let's just go somewhere." It took all my willpower to hold myself together.

"Okay," he said, resigned, and then he steered us to an enclosed play space in the lot between the lower and upper schools where there were several comfortable wooden benches. I sat down next to him, my jacket lightly brushing against his backpack.

"Jess, I have some bad news to tell you. Someone broke into the house over the weekend while you were away."

"Did they steal anything? Any of my stuff?"

"I don't think so. But your mother was attacked."

"She's in the hospital?"

"No, I'm afraid not. It was more serious."

"What do you mean?" Jess asked, his voice suddenly tighter, higher pitched.

I twisted to face him squarely. "Mom's dead, Jess. She was murdered."

Jess looked stunned. I reached out for him, but he pushed my arm away. "I'm so sorry," I said.

"No you're not, you two were getting divorced," he screamed, consumed by anger, another inheritance we litigators had passed along.

"We loved each other for a long time, maybe not anymore, but we did, and regardless of our problems your mother's always loved you."

"That's not true. Save the bullshit for the courtroom," he screamed.

"I know you're upset, but how can you say that about your mother?"

He brushed away an imaginary fly from his face and in a measured shit-eating tone said, "Because she isn't my mother."

I was dumbstruck. "Who told you that?"

"None of your fucking business," he screamed, stomping off to take care of his stuff, leaving me alone to deal with mine.

# CHAPTER 7

"YOU never told him?" Arnie Glimcher asked, incredulous.

"I wanted to. Sally didn't. So we didn't," I answered, though in all fairness to Sally I'd accepted her position as legitimate. On some level I still do.

"You're some piece of work, Malone," he said, tapping the cleft of his chin so forcefully with the eraser end of his pencil that his jowls jiggled.

Why single me out? Everyone does things that in hindsight, under a tragic microscope, don't make sense. "We did what we thought was right. You weren't there."

Arnie sighed, puffing out his middle-aged belly. "I don't understand either of you. But people are like that. Especially men. I see it all the time. They follow their dicks and don't think things through. Then they spend the rest of their lives hiring guys like me to clean up the consequences." Arnie opened the bottom drawer and rummaged around.

I sat there, silently agreeing with him, the last part anyway, but I'd rather be incarcerated on Devil's Island than tell him. Arnie found whatever he was looking for.

"Hey, bottom line is, it's water under the bridge. But we still have a big problem."

"What's that?" I asked, relieved we were moving into problem-solving mode.

"The court, kid. Here we've been asking the judge to intercede in the custody issues and he's finally on our wavelength. Now we're going to have to tell him we haven't all been on the same page. And as sure as shit he's gonna make a big fuss that you never told him your kid didn't know the story of his creation."

"Why should he care? Custody's moot. The divorce action's moot. The whole friggin' situation's moot."

"Get real. With Sally's murder you're a megastar now. Everybody associated with you is going to play for the cameras." Did that include Arnie? I wondered. "Every two-bit publicity seeker. Everybody. You've been around the block, you're no virgin, you know judges. Do you know any that'll turn down free advertising in an election year? I sure as shit don't. You can count on it. His Honor will be more sanctimonious than Pope Pious at your expense, kid."

"Maybe he won't care," I suggested.

"Yeah. Right. Trust me, he will. Some grandstand play. Maybe a guardian for Jess. Or a temporary custodian until the dust clears."

"He can't do that."

"Oh yes, kiddo, he can and he will. How does he know you didn't do it? He's gonna protect his ass. You know any judge that can't suck up to the police and the D.A. with the best of them? Hey, even I've done it and I'm no trustee of the Authority Benevolent Association. Plus, in your case, Malone, you can probably count on the fact that a lot of guys in the so-called judicial system already hate your smart-ass guts."

I was wrong. Things could get worse.

I'd sought out Arnie today for help and wise counsel, not so he could make me feel lousy. Too many painful moments in my divorce had made me feel lousy enough already. Who was he to be upset with me? After all, I was the client, I was paying him. I'd never made a patient whose heart was failing feel as if he, not his defective motor, was the problem. Never chastised a client for not being sharp enough to prevent a doctor from performing medical malpractice on his or her body. I'm rationalizing, I know. Forget the big speech, Arnie's disappointment in me made me feel uncomfortable. I'd hired him as much for his gentle avuncular qualities (Gorbachev with curly hair and without the birthmark) as for his legal skills, and therefore his disapproval gnawed at me. "I'm sorry you're so upset. It wasn't my intention to—"

Arnie jumped up to a standing position, as if something on his chair seat had bitten him, and walked over to the window. I couldn't help but notice he was favoring his right leg. He'd do himself wonders if he lightened up and lost forty pounds. From the window, without turning, showing only back and butt, he waved me off with a flapping right arm. "Cut the mea culpas, counselor. Why don't you just give me a refresher course on your son's biological heritage as you remember it? I assume you can recall the facts?"

"What's the point?" I snapped, continuing to play the aggrieved party.

He returned to his desk. "Humor me." He sat down heavily.

I cleared my throat and began tentatively. I felt like I was making an opening statement to a one-person jury of my peers.

"Sally and I married during internship. She'd already graduated from Columbia Law and was working as an Assistant D.A. She was anxious to start a family before her workload geared up, but I wanted to wait. My residency training years were still ahead. We had lots of debts to repay. You know, the usual. But she was persistent. No, that's not strong enough. Relentless. Driven. Obsessed. She's always been like that. Her certainty obliterating my doubts. Finally, I agreed and we started trying."

I looked quickly over at Arnie, afraid he'd be scowling, certain he'd blame my difficulties on giving in too often and too easily to a woman, but he was rifling through his junk mail and paid me no notice.

I know I'd been a pushover or, more accurately, conflict-aversive, with only myself to blame. Yet I was happy during our early married years. I loved Sally, especially her forcefulness, though, at times, she went too far and pushed us onto the edge with psychotics. Once a cabbie had nearly run us over in a crosswalk and she'd smashed his rear signal light with my tennis racquet. The Bay Ridge butcher she'd accused of short-weighting in front of all his other customers. The landlords she'd driven nuts over running toilets, wet plaster, doors and windows ajar, roaches, defective ovens, or refrigerators.

She could be a ballbuster, but I must admit that her intensity was exciting, even when, as often happened, it was directed against me. Which didn't matter anymore—murder had canceled the relationship dynamics.

"After two first-trimester spontaneous abortions we consulted a specialist who discovered a uterine abnormality, double uterus, which required surgical correction, but postop she had two more abortions and by then her body was building up antibodies. Everybody we saw said the odds were she'd never be able to carry a pregnancy to term." Arnie said nothing while I laid out the whole story.

"I thought we should adopt, but Sally wanted a baby that was more connected to us. She said medical students donate their sperm all the time, so why not use some of mine to artificially inseminate someone on our own behalf. It sounded logical even then, when surrogate pregnancies were only in their infancy. No pun intended. After a lot of screening and negotiation Sally chose Mary Jane Willabrand, a Dutchess County divorcée with two young children, both healthy and attractive in every sense, and we contracted with her to be inseminated with my sperm, carry the fetus to term, and, upon delivery, to renounce all biological and any other claims to the baby in exchange for a payment of twenty-five thousand dollars, a lot of money way back.

"Everything went well except . . ." Arnie looked up. "Except after the birth, Mary Jane changed her mind and wanted to keep the baby. So we went to court. Sally litigated the case herself, for nearly nine months. All her biological frustrations were poured into the case. I understood and accepted and lived with her litigious fervor as her chance to produce what her body couldn't, and when she won we brought 'Baby S' home as our son, Jess." I paused to relubricate my mouth.

Arnie thought I was finished, though I wasn't, and impatiently asked, "Let's cut to the chase. I really haven't heard any compelling reason why you and Sally didn't tell Jess about his surrogacy."

"When Jess was little we were just never able to find the words to explain it well, and more recently, Sally thought it would drive a permanent wedge between them, that Jess would feel as if he were some kind of commercial product that Sally and I had created because we were selfish, self-centered, concerned about manufacturing a baby no matter what, and mostly that we would be hated as high-tech, highly educated slavers who'd taken advantage of a woman from a lower social class, forcing her, his natural mother, his *own* mother, to sell him to us. It wasn't the kind of confrontation you'd want to have with a sullen teenage son."

"Pandora's womb," Arnie declared.

I smiled faintly. "I guess so."

"And you just went along with that position?"

"Jess and I shared biology, while Sally felt she was a genetic stranger who'd be blamed, which I thought was irrational, as she was in every way Jess's mother, and a good mother, and with time I knew he'd understand, but it seemed insensitive on my part to cavalierly disregard Sally's fears because I accepted that she had the most to lose. Anyway she simply refused to tell him—the subject became a nonnegotiable nonmentionable that infected everything. Even the divorce proceedings."

"The fact that something can be done does not mean it should be done," Arnie said, his tone emptied of anger, warmer. "I wasn't speaking of the surrogacy," he added.

"Yes, I understood what you meant." In the midst of this dreadful afternoon the restoration of the lawyer-client relationship somehow made me feel a little better.

"Let me be devil's advocate, okay?" Arnie asked.

"Sure," I answered too quickly, hoping Arnie was changing the subject.

"Jess said he knew your wife was not his natural mother, correct?"

"Yes."

"Are you aware of any break-ins at your house?"

"No, but I had a robbery a few months ago at my apartment," I offered, eagerly still trying to curry Arnie's favor.

"Was anything taken?"

"A Rolex Sally had given me for my fortieth."

"Your keys?"

"No. They're always in my pocket."

"Why, when it happened, didn't you mention it? This is the first I ever heard that you were burgled."

"Why should I? What did it have to do with divorce?"

"And the marital residence? Any burglary there?"

"None that I know about."

Like a good prosecutor, Arnie backed off, shuffling some papers, letting my defensive tone hang in the air. "So you think someone let the perp in, maybe with my keys? Is that what you're getting at? But they were on me the whole time."

"Let me ask the questions, counselor, okay? And Jess didn't tell you how he found out about his parentage," Arnie said.

"Right. I asked him. He didn't answer. He told me to fuck off."

Arnie's expression seemed genuinely sorry to hear that. "And you have a housekeeper?"

"Part-time."

"And she has keys?"

"No. One of us always waited to let her in."

"Maybe Sally changed the procedures since your departure."

"No. Sally's an idée fixe kind of person."

"I'll check it out anyway."

"Aren't you being a little presumptuous?" I asked.

"About what?"

"You're handling my divorce, not any future criminal action."

Arnie disregarded my comment and continued. "So to the best of your knowledge you, Sally, and Jess are the only people with keys to the house?"

"Yes."

"So assuming you're telling the truth and you had nothing to do with your wife's murder, and don't tell me if I'm wrong, and for the moment assuming your wife let the assailant into the house because she knew him or her, or the assailant actually was already there—" I started to protest, but Arnie signaled time out with both hands. "Be-sides the other possibilities, do you think your son could have murdered your wife?"

"What?" I shouted. "Are you fucking crazy? He wasn't even home. He was away on a school trip." Why is no one listening?

"I didn't say he actually committed the murder, but he might have hired the person. That's a possibility we'll have to consider. And, unless I missed something, we don't actually know the time of death, do we?"

"No way. No fucking way," I said.

"We have to consider all the possibilities. She wasn't his mother, and he was pissed big-time."

"It's ridiculous. Impossible," I shouted, the words mixed with a very audible and high-pitched wheeze.

"Do you want some water or something?" I shook my head. "I'm sorry to have upset you. We're just exploring reasonable doubt."

I inhaled deeply, trying to get under the bronchial con-striction and cough through it, which I finally did. "More like unreasonable doubt," I declared.

When Jess was little he and Sally were so close I'd often felt left out, superfluous. Until puberty arrived he'd been open, communicative, happy, but in no way, shape, or form was he the type then or now who'd be capable of murder. Yes Sally had been concerned about Jess in Feb-ruary. She'd sidled up to me at a school benefit and had started talking. Our only amicable conversation of the year. She'd felt he was seething, becoming distant. I'd told her with certainty, but upon no authority beyond a Dear Abby column, that he was probably upset about the di-vorce, which we both agreed was understandable. Sally suggested family counseling. I'd said, "Fine." She'd of-fered to broach the idea with Jess and get back to me about the arrangements if it was okay. But in the interim, someone told her about Diane, the *new younger woman* in my life, and the friendly opening froze over. All communications were soon routed through secretaries and attorneys, and the subject of family therapy disappeared off the radar screen.

"Something else bothers me," Arnie said.

"What's that?"

"Your emotional demeanor. Except when we're talking about Jess, it seems off. Your estranged wife has been brutally murdered, and from where I sit you come across as too calm."

He paused, no doubt to heap more insults on the pile. I replied coldly, "Is there one official way to react?"

"No, but you're a lawyer. You damn well know how someone reacts, whether or not they appear guilty, contrite, smug, whatever, can have a big impact on the legal outcome, regardless of the triable facts."

"It's the best I can do. I didn't realize I had to convince you of my innocence as well."

"You didn't hear me ask if you did it, did you?"

"Do me a favor," I yelled. "Spare me the sanctimonious see-no-evil, hear-no-evil, officer-of-the-court, criminal-lawyer bullshit. Okay?"

I spent the rest of the afternoon and early evening oscillating between anger and anxiety. I was angry at Arnie for the third degree he'd put me through, angry at Sally for getting murdered, as if it was a decision she had participated in, anxious about Jess. Where the hell was he? It was already six-thirty. What if Arnie was right? Was he running away? No, it was impossible. I couldn't start thinking like that or I'd have nothing, no one. Things were bad enough, I didn't have to make myself crazy. That's what Sally would have said to me. She'd have stopped my morbid descent. She believed in action, but she was dead. I'd have to do it myself.

By seven o'clock when he still hadn't come home, to my apartment that is, I thought of calling the police. I went so far as to take out the investigating detective's business card from my wallet, where it was sandwiched between VISA and Blue Cross, and put it by the phone.

But I did nothing. Emotional fatigue had finally settled in, benumbing every neuron. Thoughts, images repeated endlessly: Jess sitting alone somewhere grieving in his own way; Jess in danger, the murderer stalking him; Jess and me running. Only the obligatory dinner hour junk call broke the spell and in gratitude I listened to the complete explanation of AT&T's long-distance plan. Reconnected to humanity, it dawned on me to telephone Tommy Shea, Jess's friend and classmate since kindergarten.

Tommy wasn't home yet either, but his mother, Sandy Shea, surely unaware of the day's events, for which I was grateful, reassured me. "These kids—they're so mysterious. Can't get boo out of them. I know there was a chess practice today, but Tommy couldn't go because he had a JV baseball game. Do you know Mr. Reynolds, the new chess advisor? All the kids are crazy about him. Maybe he knows where Jess is. Jasper's his first name and I know he lives in the Bronx because we once drove him to the subway. You could get his number from information."

"Thanks, I'll try that," I said.

But information had no listing for a Jasper Reynolds anywhere in the metropolitan area. Action hadn't helped me. My futile efforts had served only to intensify my worst fears and leave me bathed in a cold, smelly sweat.

Jess called while I was in the shower and left a message on the answering machine. Tommy's mother was right— Jess was hanging (his word) with the chess coach and he'd see me tomorrow. Not much, but better than nothing. I slept fitfully, hurt that Jess had turned to a stranger and had once again shut me out, missing Sally—wishing she was next to me in bed reading a brief into the early hours of the morning.

# CHAPTER 8

I was awakened in the early morning by the extra-loud ringing of the bedside phone. Margrit, my occasional Eastern European cleaning lady, must have inadvertently turned up the bell volume. I grabbed the receiver, expecting to hear Jess's voice. Instead a woman's. Unrecognizable.

"Dr. Malone?" she said. It sounded as if she were overseas. I wished it had been Diane, calling from Switzerland, because I desperately needed a long confessional conversation.

"Yes," I answered warily.

"Hope I didn't wake you. My name is Detective Ellen Levine. The reception's breaking up."

"I didn't say anything."

Between the audio gaps, she told me that she was now the lead detective investigating Sally's murder and that she needed to see me and Jess and "go over some things."

"Yes," I told her, "I'll be here." What choice did I have?

"We're five minutes away." And they didn't have to worry about finding a parking space.

I jumped into the shower, shaving and brushing my teeth under the spray to save time, and toweled off. Two and a half minutes. An Olympic record, and with no razor nicks. I hurried, like a man possessed. I chose some casual clothes, laid them out on the bed, and started dressing until I remembered I had a nine-thirty conference in the judge's chambers on *Lopez* v. *City of New York*. I quickly switched to an inexpensive dark blue suit I'd bought on sale because Justice Sherman was a man of the people who couldn't help but give well-heeled lawyers grief.

Avoiding the news programs, I flipped on the sports channel, knotted my dull blue tie during the NBA playoff highlights, and waited for the inquisitors. They arrived during the Play of the Day.

"Ellen Levine," she said with a smile more like a social worker's than a cop's. Perky, tall, friendly, she reminded me of someone. "And down there is my partner, Detective Johnson"—he was panting, like a heavy-coated dog in summer, from the four flights of stairs.

"I thought all doctors were rich. Even the projects have elevators," Johnson rasped.

"It's not so bad, you get used to it," I said. In fact, I ran up and down several times a day. A poor man's Stair-master. Don't misunderstand, I'm not really poor, just the temporary victim of a court-induced infection.

"Can we come in and talk?" Detective Levine asked.

"Oh, sure," I exclaimed, remembering where I'd seen Levine and Johnson. I'm not a statistician, but the chance of two detectives who were processing Figlio's floater Sunday being accidentally assigned to this case seemed pretty low. According to Sally, a homicide was handled by detectives from the local precinct. Though Sutton Place and Wall Street were surely inhabited by the same people, precincts were drawn geographically, not socioeconomically.

"We're so sorry about your wife," Detective Levine said.

"Yes. Find anything out?" I asked. Why beat around the bush?

"No, not yet," she said.

"Can I get either of you something to drink?" I wasn't

trying to be gracious, I wanted a minute alone to compose myself.

"Have any Diet Coke?" Johnson asked.

"Causes osteoporosis, you know. OJ, bottled water, coffee."

"OJ."

"Okay. Anything for you?" I asked Detective Levine.

"Coffee if it's no trouble."

The kitchen sink was a mess. The dirty dishes from Saturday's hurried lunch with Diane, before she rushed off to JFK, and Monday morning's breakfast with myself were still there, unwashed. In the house-cleaning department Diane and Sally were very different. While I washed some cups and glasses I wondered if the detectives were twiddling their thumbs or inspecting my things.

I placed the drinks on the round pedestal-style Formica-and-wood dining table and sat down.

"Is your son here, Doctor?" Detective Levine asked.

"No. Off early," I said, omitting his place of embarkation.

"He was able to go to school today?" Levine observed. "That's remarkable."

"Life goes on, Ellen," Johnson pontificated. Detective Levine, resentful of his patronizing sexism, shot him a disdainful look, but Johnson probably missed it, as his whole face was pressed into the glass of orange juice, slurping at high speed.

"Don't you have any leads yet?" I asked.

"We're developing a few," she answered. "How *is* your son handling it? A teenager in this kind of tragedy. Poor kid."

I hesitated. "I hope okay. I don't really know. He was very upset when I told him yesterday."

"These things take time," she said.

Maybe it was her seeming sincerity, maybe I just wanted to off-load some of the stress, but I proceeded to violate the first law of witnesses and volunteered information. "Last night he stayed with friends in the neighborhood, so I don't actually know how he's doing."

Detective Levine wrinkled her brow but said nothing. "How old's your kid?" Johnson asked.

"Fifteen," I answered, relieved neither one of them had asked for the names of Jess's friends. During a murder investigation, the last thing you need is to be caught in a lie, even a teeny-tiny white one.

"That's hard. I lost my mom when I was fourteen," Detective Levine confided. "Maybe it's worse for a daughter."

"I suspect it's lousy regardless," I said, as I sipped the coffee and spilled some onto the saucer because my hand was shaking, imperceptibly I hoped.

"We'd like to talk to him when you feel he can handle it." I raised my eyebrows. "Routine questions," Detective Levine reassured me. "We're assuming he can tell us everything was okay when he left Saturday morning. But he might have seen something unusual or something else in the past few weeks that can help us."

"Is there something specific you're referring to?"

"Not at this time. At this point, we just need to verify times," she stated.

I nodded, "Of course."

"And—" she paused "—I hope you understand, we'll also have to do the same for you."

"I can give it to you now," I said, always the good student anxious to be helpful, the second son who couldn't stop pleasing the grown-ups.

"Okay," she said.

"From when?"

"Start with Friday," Johnson piped in.

"Friday I was in court till four, before Justice Sherman, New York Supreme, Sixty Centre. Where, by the way, I have to be by nine-thirty. Then afterward back to the office. I returned here about seven. Had dinner with a friend, also here. And I guess I didn't leave until late the next morning to pick up a rental tux on Eighty-sixth and Third." Levine looked perplexed and I assumed it concerned the tuxedo. "You're wondering about the tux. Mine was at my wife's house. We're getting divorced, so I thought it'd be easier to rent."

"No, the friend," she replied. "A sleepover?" Today's cops, especially in domestic situations, never know what they'll find.

"Yes."

"And the afternoon?" Levine asked.

"After lunch, rollerblading along the Carl Schurz esplanade," which brought a smile to Johnson's face, as he imagined, from his perspective as a middle-aged male, how ridiculous I must have looked. Though I must say that everyone is amazed how lithe I am, even Jess, who undoubtedly would prefer that his father's leisure activities be less youthful.

"By yourself?" Detective Levine asked.

"No, with the same friend."

"How long did you skate?" Johnson asked.

"An hour or so."

"Does your friend have a name?" he asked.

"Diane Forster."

"We'll need a statement from Ms. Forster," Detective Levine said.

"No problem." I censored my tongue and didn't volunteer that Diane, who's an associate at the firm in the international division, was doing depositions in Switzerland for the next two weeks.

"And where'd you go after?" Johnson, the bird dog, continued.

"Her place," I said, hoping that the clarification would

satisfy what seemed like prurient rather than investigatory interest. "I helped her pack and waited with her
for the limo, which came about five. Then I went home,
showered, and dressed. Saturday night I was an honored
speaker at the silicone settlement dinner at the Waldorf.
After the testimonial I returned home, slept until quarter to
six Sunday morning, and then took a cab to Pier thirty-one
to meet the police launch. I saw you guys there. Did you
see me?"

"What were you doing out there, anyway? You're not
authorized," Detective Levine stated.

When challenged I slip into haughty, imperious mode.
"As a matter of fact I am. I've been an honorary police surgeon since before you joined the force. Lieutenant Figlio
and I go way back."

"How did you cut your hand?" Levine asked, glancing down.

"On my car door. Some friendly felon wedged a jagged
piece of glass into the keyhole, after they broke in."

"When was that?" Johnson wanted to know.

"Saturday night."

"Was Ms. Forster with you then?" she asked, somewhat
snidely.

"No, I told you. She was already on her way to the
airport."

"You didn't actually say that," she pointed out. "You
said you helped her pack—"

"And waited with her for the limo. Come on, guys,
gimme a break," I said, exaggerating my irritation. I could
see where she was heading and it made me uncomfortable.

"Where was Ms. Forster going?" Detective Levine
wanted to know.

"Switzerland," I answered.

"Why?" she continued.

"Business."

"Oh," Detective Levine said, as if she'd deduced some sinister meaning to Diane's trip.

"Do you at least know what the cause of death was?" I asked Detective Johnson, hoping to derail the interrogation.

Johnson looked at Levine, who nodded it was okay. "Multiple knife wounds," he replied.

"Did you find a weapon?" I asked.

"Not at this time," she interjected.

"None of the kitchen knives match the wound?" I asked.

"Are you asking or you know that?" Detective Levine answered.

"Asking."

"We're still doing forensics. Where's your car now?"

"Back in the garage."

"We'd like to take a look. The window still broken?" asked Johnson.

"No. I had it fixed."

Levine turned to Johnson. "No point, then. Get a statement from the garage."

"You don't have a fix on time of death yet, right?" Again they wordlessly consulted each other. I felt less anxious. I was regaining some momentum.

"Why do you say that?" Johnson asked me.

"Remember the jumper? Same problem."

Detective Levine wrinkled her nose. "Really?"

"Yeah, really. Body temp is the most reliable measure of time of death, but in this case it's useless because my wife was frozen, so you guys were just fishing when you asked all those questions about where I was, weren't you?" I asked.

"There are other ways," Levine declared.

"Not with Sally." Both detectives simultaneously widened four eyes and elevated four eyebrows, as if they thought I'd confessed. Arnie Glimcher was right, appearances matter, and I was being a little too logical and talkative where I should have been emotional and introspective.

"Why do you say that?" Levine finally asked.

It was too late to take back what I'd said, so I had to risk saying more. "She must have been murdered sometime between Friday afternoon, and most likely, Saturday night or else you'd have told me when exactly."

"And how are you so sure of that?" Johnson wanted to know.

"Like clockwork, Sally always ate a late lunch on Friday, and then fasted up until Saturday night, sometimes for special situations all the way through to Sunday morning. She said it helped her stay grounded. You didn't find any stomach contents, did you? And that's why you can't fix time of death." Even in death, Sally's compulsiveness was helping her.

Detective Levine was mulling over Sally's nutritional schedule and couldn't quite make something about it fit with other facts she might have had in her possession. "We will need, Dr. Malone, I hope you understand, because of the nature of the crime, some tissue scrapings, blood samples, hair samples, and fingerprints from both you and your son. It's totally routine—we're in the process of doing the same with Mrs. Schmidt, the housekeeper, and anyone else who might have visited the house recently."

"Of course."

"It's totally voluntary," she added.

"I'm a big boy. I know my rights. Where do I go?"

She handed me a card. The lab was located in the heart of Police Headquarters, near the courthouse. "Perhaps you should first consult with your attorney," she cautioned.

"I don't have a problem."

"Great, we appreciate your help. Can you do it this morning?" she asked.

"I'd like to oblige, but I have a court conference and trial."

"You're working today?" Detective Levine asked.

"Yeah, they can't be postponed. But if we finish early, I'll do it. How's that?"

"That's fine."

"Same goes for your son if you hear from him," Detective Levine reminded me.

I stood up and nudged the two detectives closer to the front door. "I understand. I'll tell him. Sorry to rush you guys, but I'm going to be late for court if I don't."

"Thanks for your help. Catch you later," Detective Levine said. Bad choice of words, I hoped.

"Oh, one other thing, doc," Johnson said from the hallway side of my front doorway.

"What?"

"Who else, aside from your son and you, knew of your wife's eating habits? That's kinda personal stuff," Johnson added. It was obvious he thought they'd found the murderer.

"Lots of people."

"You mean like the guys at the D.A.'s?" he asked.

"Yeah. Come to think of it, probably everybody."

"Everybody? Who's everybody?" Johnson persisted.

I smiled, but not too conceitedly, for I'd successfully maneuvered him. There was no need to rub his nose in it. I'd let his own plodding weight spring my exculpatory escape hatch. "At least a million people."

"You pick that number off your lottery ticket?" Johnson asked.

"It was in the *Times* profile last year on Sally. Didn't you *catch* it?"

Johnson looked crestfallen and Levine muttered something under her breath. Now they'd have to scratch around a lot longer and deeper if they wanted to find a replacement prime suspect. Good.

My satisfaction didn't last. It dawned on me that someone, I don't want to believe it's anyone we knew, had taken a great interest in Sally's life and her habits. From the *Times* vanity piece, the centerfold of Sally's media campaign, they had found the most opportune moment to kill her, which meant they also knew too much about Jess and me. Prime suspect or prime target? Both sucked.

# CHAPTER 9

AFTER the two detectives departed, I finished dressing, microwaved a factory-sealed croissant for a quick breakfast, picked up the newspapers at Son Ya's convenience deli, and headed downtown to fight for truth, justice, and the American way.

There was nothing about the murder in *The Daily News*, nothing in the *Times* Metropolitan Section, and only a small two-inch story buried in the middle pages of the *Post*. Sally's media insignificance pissed me off—a crusading Deputy D.A. was entitled to decent coverage. Alive, she'd rated better. Of course, she'd had the double misfortune to be competing with horrendous floods in the Midwest and the cloning of a cow.

At the courthouse where justice often limped along, word of Sally's death had spread quickly despite the newspaper nonevent. Judge Sherman's clerk, who'd read the story, said, "Sorry, doc. Ain't the world a mess," while the judge's law secretary told me, "I worked with your wife at the D.A.'s a few years ago. Great lawyer." Even the judge tried to be supportive. "Why are you here, son? We'll give you a continuance for as long as you need," as well as, "Time heals, trust an old man, maybe something good will come out of this." Only the opposing counsel, who arrived late, hadn't heard, and she seemed honestly shocked and upset when the judge explained why he thought it would be a good idea, for my benefit, to put Lopez over until next month.

I confounded all of them by wanting to proceed, for I viewed the defense of the Lopez family as my defense, too, and hard work as the most accessible, lowest cost, and quickest therapy available for my troubles. "I appreciate your comments, Your Honor. Thank you, everyone. They'll give me strength in the weeks and months ahead, but right now, I'd prefer to discuss the case."

There was silence—I'd upset the preconceived mourning ritual, and Claire Baker was looking at me strangely—but finally the judge said to opposing counsel, "Has the City reconsidered its offer and is the City prepared to improve the offer?"

"The City has, Your Honor. We are prepared to offer the Plaintiff three quarters of a million dollars."

"And you desired," the judge asked me, "if my memory serves me, three point five, correct?"

"Yes, Your Honor."

"Counsel, do you think the City would be receptive to splitting the difference?"

"Between three-fifty and three and a half million?" she asked.

"No, Ms. Baker, the three-fifty was yesterday. Between today's offer and Dr. Malone's."

"But, Your Honor, you're splitting the difference between my second offer and Dr. Malone's first and only. Wouldn't it be fairer to split between my first and his? That's a difference to the City of two hundred thousand dollars."

"In terms of the facts in this case, it is my opinion we're being reasonable. Of course the City has the option available, if they disagree, of letting the matter go to the jury."

"If we were to accept this offer," she said, "and this is a hypothetical" (though it was obviously a carefully scripted one), "the City would also like a stipulation that this agreement does not constitute an admission of guilt, and furthermore, that the Plaintiff will not pursue any corollary action in this matter."

We were back to their vulnerability again. Somebody was willing to authorize a lot of money so that the Police Department could sweep this under some inaccessible rug.

"Dr. Malone, is that acceptable?" Justice Sherman asked.

"Offhand I doubt it, but of course I'll have to talk with my clients."

"Dr. Malone," the judge suggested, "why don't we adjourn this until a week from today, during which you can discuss the stip with your clients. How's that? And of course if you need another date, I'm sure we can all accommodate you, right, Bernie?" Bernie, his law secretary, holding his chin in the palm of his hand, nodded vigorously.

"Okay," I said. The judge walked me to the door, a heavy protective arm on my shoulder, and then climbed the steps to the bench.

I motioned to the nuclear members of the Lopez family to follow me to the hallway, and in a primitive Spanish, learned from nurse's aides and Ecuadoran cleaning women, discussed the City's offer with my clients. They wanted to accept. Who could blame them?—$2,125,000 was a lot of money. A whole lot. Even after deducting my contingency fee, two-thirds of the money would last forever in some Latin America country—no one said they had to care about police misconduct just because I did. Let's wait until next Tuesday, *martes,* I'd said, and see if the nervous City brass comes back with an even better offer. They agreed.

\* \* \*

With a Vacutainer inserted into my right forearm, the police lab technician withdrew three tubes of blood, two lavender-tops and a red-top, which was the appropriate amount for an annual checkup, but too much for forensics, though I said nothing about this excessive bloodletting to the technician or to Detective Johnson, who was witnessing the specimen collection for the purpose of establishing the chain of custody. Johnson escorted me to another room for digitized fingerprints, no more messy ink, and to a third location where a technician plucked hair samples from my scalp with tweezers and scraped cells from my buccal mucosa, the inside of my cheek, with a sterile tongue depressor. They now had enough different sources of my DNA to clone me.

"Thank you, Dr. Malone, we'll be in touch should we need anything else," Detective Johnson said. *Like what? An organ biopsy? A donation? A signed confession?*

At my office, all eyes stared at me as if I were a masked intruder, not a rising partner whose name would one day be stenciled on the glass door and the faux cherrywood paneling behind reception. Of course I was, in a way, alien, a formerly common man now transformed by an unspeakable act into the surviving spouse of a murder victim, and no one, least of all me, knew exactly how to relate to this metamorphosed individual.

My secretary, Lydia, who's been with me almost two years, said something comforting, followed by, "Mr. Badger asked that when you arrive, you stop by his office. And Dr. Feldman has called twice. He messengered something to you this morning—I put it on your desk." Lydia hadn't ever met him, but Abe Feldman was one of my oldest clients.

Out of nowhere, my arm started thumping, a belated protest against the venipuncture, and I suddenly felt very tired once again. Should I call Detective Levine and see if they've found out anything? Was Mrs. Schmidt at Sally's? The police would have been happy to let her in. Maybe the chess teacher's phone number was posted somewhere? Or I could do the obvious—call the school and see if Jess had arrived, but I didn't because I knew Jess wouldn't like me checking up on him. No one answered at Sally's. I'd wait a half hour, then try again.

Martin Badger steered me to the very soft leather wing-back chair he reserved for himself when meeting with clients. He was uncharacteristically quiet, at a loss for words, his eyes wet from concern and from glaucoma.

"Barbara and I are so shocked."

"Yes, of course. Thank you," I said.

"And how are you bearing up?"

Oh, I'm just having one old-fashioned bearing-up kind of time wondering about Jess, hoping he's really all right, nervous in my new role as sole surviving parent. "I'm fine, sir."

"Is there anything we can do for you here at the firm?" I shook my head. "Take on some of your caseload?" I waved off the idea. "You're certain?"

"Yes," I said firmly.

"Are you up to discussing a professional matter?" he asked.

"Definitely," I said with enthusiasm, which seemed to please Badger.

"I received a call this morning from a friend of ours, Mal Snyder." Badger cast a sideways glance to see if I recognized the name, but I didn't. "Mal has been very helpful to the firm for many many years. A lot of our success we owe to Mal. A decade ago, before you joined us, we roasted him with a gold-and-pearl-inlaid umbrella we'd commissioned to honor his rainmaking."

"Is he still a rainmaker for us?"

"Oh yes. Smith's big case for the medical society, that's through Mal."

"Is he of counsel?"

"No no. Mal's not a lawyer."

"He isn't?" I said.

"Mal's a facilitator." Why do I think of zippers and garments when I hear that word? "He knows everybody. And Mal is concerned about one of your cases."

"One of my cases."

"Yes."

"Which case?" I asked.

Badger pretended to fumble through the papers for the name of the case, finally unearthing a scrap of paper. "*Lopez* v. *City of New York*."

I was incredulous, but stanched my anger. "About what is he concerned?"

"The parties, we're told, would like to see the matter settled, and Mal is under the impression, and I told him he must be mistaken, that you're somehow an obstacle to that resolution."

"Mr. Badger, what exactly is Mal's relationship to this case?"

"I don't think that's germane. As I've said, much of our success we owe to Mr. Snyder. We're not of the mind to bite the hand that has so loyally fed us."

"I didn't say we should. I'm simply trying to understand why Lopez is of any concern to anyone except the parties. Why it's so important to keep bringing it up. First yesterday, then now?"

"Yesterday?"

"In the bathroom. You called it the 'jail' case."

"Oh yes, I remember," Badger finally said, perturbed. At least he didn't have Alzheimer's. "And *we'd* like it settled." The upset was making his eyes water more.

"We're not very far apart," I said.

"I'm aware of that. Just accept the settlement so we can move on," he said. "Understood?" Move on to what?

I looked at my watch. "Mr. Badger, I've got to make some calls. I'll think about what you said."

Badger said nothing, but his angry glare, its intensity magnified by the excess watery film washing over his eyes, more than made up for his silence.

# CHAPTER 10

"DO you know who Mal Snyder is?" I asked Arnie.

"Of course. This is the urgent call that my secretary drags me out of a deposition for?" Arnie asked over the speakerphone.

"I'm trying to put things together. Who is he?" I persisted.

"You have enough problems already. Don't add to them by playing detective."

"Skip the sermon and just tell me, dammit."

"The mayor's power broker. A mover and a shaker. He knows everybody."

"Maybe I should ask him to find Jess."

"Where's Jess?" Arnie asked, clearly concerned.

"He didn't come home last night. He stayed at his chess advisor's."

"He didn't come home, he stayed at his chess advisor's," Arnie repeated. Even over the phone I could see his scowl. "And what have you done about it?"

"What's there to do?" I asked.

"He's your son. Why isn't he with you? It doesn't look very good, that's for damn sure, kid."

"Feels worse."

"I'm sure it does," Arnie said. "Have you talked to the police?"

"I mentioned it to the two detectives this morning."

"What two detectives?"

As a lawyer I understood how I was making Arnie crazy. Withholding information from your attorney was bad enough, but in the middle of a capital investigation it was really stupid. And I haven't yet met an attorney who can advocate effectively on behalf of a stupid client.

"The investigating detectives. Levine and Johnson. I deliberately didn't make a big deal of it. Given your suspicions—"

Arnie interrupted, "About Jess's involvement."

"Exactly. Discretion seemed like a good idea. I don't want the police poking into every aspect of my life before I have a chance to assess the situation."

"Well, at least you have a few self-protective instincts still working on your team. How 'bout your friend? Uhh. You know the one who . . . I'm blocking. Gimme a second, don't help me. Mental aerobics. Control panel check. It's coming. Starts with a G. No, that's not it. Shit, I have to do the alphabet. A, no. B, no. Figlio. F. That's the one. He'll help, won't he?"

"I've got him on auto-redial. His line's been busy for forty-five minutes. The SOB has it off the hook if I know him."

"He lives someplace weird, right?" Arnie recalled.

"Right."

"So go see him, then."

"I was just about to."

"Don't let me stop you," he snapped. "What does Mal Snyder have to do with anything?"

"Nothing. He's a non sequitur," I said.

"Don't let him hear that. He's supposed to be the angry type. After you talk to Figlio, if there's a problem, or anything turns up, I want to know right away. We're a team here. You share everything with me. No surprises. Is that clear, kid?"

"Yes, I hear you," I assured him, but I knew he wasn't one hundred percent convinced.

Before I could make it to the door, Lydia buzzed me. "Dr. Feldman's on the line. He says it's urgent. Should I tell him you're in a meeting?"

"No, I'll take it." I reached for the unopened package Feldman had messengered. "Hello, Abe, how are you?"

"I'm sorry about your wife. Is there anything I can do?" Abe asked.

"Nothing, thanks. I know you've sent something over, but I haven't had a chance—"

"Of course."

"Can it wait?" I asked Abe.

"I don't mean to sound insensitive, but no."

"One of my partners can help."

Abe sighed, "I want you."

There was no point in arguing. Abraham J. Feldman, M.D., Ph.D., was one of the most stubborn, single-minded people on the planet.

"How's tomorrow morning?"


During my time in the empty descending elevator, then walking through the busier office building lobby and especially among the jostling elbows, shoulders, and bodies of the more crowded sidewalks, the phrase "endangering the welfare of a minor" resonated within my head. I shouldn't have been so brusque with Arnie. This was my usual reaction to stress—mistaking stubbornness for true self-reliance.

I fast-walked across Central Park. The air was cool yet moist. The walkways were littered with the pale, friable, dried-up dappled bark that looked like a massive

accumulation of third-degree-burn skin, an image rein-
forced by the newly exposed patches of raw, dark, trunk
wetness, which, in the early spring of tiny green buds,
made the plane trees appear shorter, stubbier. Sally's
murder and Jess's absence exposed the morbid sinkhole
all around me and, most frightening, suggested how much
farther we could still sink.

The traffic light changed on the nearby drive and the ex-
hausts of acceleration made me cough, but they were
redolent compared to the dank odor of urine in the stone
tunnel under the West Side Highway, the subterranean entrance to the Seventy-ninth Street Boat Basin, a place
Figlio called home. (Why would anyone? But Figlio told
me there was a long waiting list for permanent mooring
space.)

I found him polyurethaning *Annabelle,* the houseboat
he'd lived on for several years. At least since Election Day
1993, when as his only mate on the police tug, we'd towed
the rickety metal box across the river from Hoboken
through choppy waters. I'd thought at the time, *Why
bother? Why not let this rusting piece of tetanus contamination, with its kelly-green Astroturf carpeting stained by
coffee grinds and wet cigarettes, sink? If you're going to
live on a boat, why not buy a brand new one?*

But I'd never asked him to explain his thinking, or his
financial situation, and instead spent most of that day, after
the boat was secured, cleaning up the mess from the several swells that had washed over the sides into the living
area. I still sing the praises of the Sears wet/dry vac Figlio
specially purchased for the move, but even so, ninety-
three was the only election, since I came of age electori-
ally, that I didn't vote.

I believe *Annabelle* has something to do with Figlio's
former married life, though I'm not certain he ever had a

wife or family. I'm probably speculating about his demographics so I don't have to think about mine.

He greeted me with, "Grab a brush. They're in the jar by the sink, soaking." I grabbed one.

Figlio had taken up the Astroturf, and in its place had installed interlocking rectangular pieces of tongue-and-groove oak (probably oak veneer) over the metal floor in a very domesticated basket-weave pattern familiar to any Manhattan apartment dweller. I wondered who or what was provoking these interior changes.

"Looks great," I pronounced.

"It's an improvement."

"Your phone's not working," I said.

"I threw it overboard last night."

"Why?"

"It's a long story. What's yours?"

"Where should I start?" I said, twirling the brush.

"In the corner by the window. And at the beginning." He must have sensed my confusion. "Since brunch Sunday," he clarified.

I recounted the events concisely, with professional dispassion, a skill learned twice, first as a doctor, then as a lawyer. While my summary of the forensics would have made a good case presentation for Pathology Grand Rounds, my description of our family life, especially the rift between Jess and Sally, was less certain. I hoped the comparative uncertainty didn't send the wrong message to a police detective, even one I called a friend. Figlio listened in silence, his painting stroke undisturbed by the summary, as I completed my story and the corner area.

"How 'bout a beer?" he asked me.

"Sure. Thanks."

Figlio took two bottles of Red Dog from the tiny refrigerator in the galley, set them down on the white lawn table that was his dining room, and pulled off a sweat-soaked T-shirt with the slogan,

MAKE AN ARREST, NOT LOVE
DETECTIVES' BENEVOLENT ASSOCIATION 19TH ANNUAL PICNIC.

His Italian-American upper chest was well muscled (but also somewhat barrel-shaped: early emphysema?—maybe), covered with clumpings of curly gray-speckled hair that wound around both upper arms and grew thickly, especially on top of his shoulders—wild, wispy, permanently rooted epaulettes. Even while slumped in his chair, his abdomen remained taut, unaffected by too many beers.

Unlike most cops who, by nature or as a consequence of the kinds of things they do and see, tend to be suspicious, Figlio trusted people and was just as likely to view fellow detectives and prosecutors with hostile skepticism as the accused, even in situations of egregious probable cause. Among police types his support for the underdog was uncommon. I'd always attributed it to a fundamental antiauthority devil-may-care streak until he told me his tales of childhood discrimination in a Philadelphia mainline suburb, where his father made pizzas for rich private school kids while they in turn dished out unpleasantness to him. Except for that one moment, he's never again spoken of his unrequited bitterness toward the privileged and the powerful. To his credit, he's somehow managed to pigeonhole the hurt. He's never, for example, said anything that indicates he resents my status as a high-profile lawyer or my previous incarnation as a fancy Park Avenue cardiologist. He mustn't have been as successful at containment with others: when he was young and eager, the departmental brass said he needed more seasoning; when he was older, in his early forties, they said he was too late for a promotion, so I concluded, though Figlio and I have never really talked about it, that he wasn't well liked by the higher-ups because he was, for want of a better word, difficult.

"You know what I can't figure?" he said, clearly the afterthought of some lengthy interior monologue.

"What's that?"

"Why's there no one fuckin' in your story."

I could feel my face reddening, the temporal and maxillary arteries shipping extra blood, emblazing me, a lapsed Irish-German Catholic, with a Hester Prynne tattoo. "It wasn't relevant," I finally said, lamely.

"Cut the B.S., Malone. You're in so deep you can't even smell *it* anymore. Maybe *that*'s the problem."

I wasn't sure what the *it* or the *that* referred to, but this wasn't Syntax 101, and a minute or two later, when a strong smell of tar wafted across the deck from somewhere, I ignored the odor: the health and welfare of my greater being, not the acuity of my cranial nerves, was the issue before us. "You're asking about our sex lives?"

Now it was Figlio's turn to act dumb. He played tic-tac-toe in the condensate of river air on the cold beer bottle and with a series of shrugs, grunts, and tugs at bodily skin coverings, refused to answer or even acknowledge the question. An undoubtedly practiced interrogation technique designed to annoy most people who, like me, were made uncomfortable by the silence, and who reacted to it by hurling themselves into the auditory void before they could avoid self-inflicted injury. But I'd learned to wait. I was good at that, but once again, what would be the point of making a pathetic show of strength, of character? Who'd be the loser? Me.

"I told you I put Diane in a limo. No, I didn't say I was screwing her, but I am, so what? I'll anticipate your next question. Diane's in Switzerland now. She's an associate

of the firm, hoping for partnership. She handles the leg-
work for the international cases. She's bright and a tough
negotiator, but she's not pressing for marriage or kids or
commitment.

"If you're asking about Sally's sex life, I know nothing.
Jess certainly never said anything, but I guess that doesn't
mean much. You can't expect him to, right?"

My last comment lighted a neuronal path. I watched
Figlio process a memory. "No. Of course not, he's a good
kid."

"He is. He really is," I said. How much effort Sally and I
had always expended on his behalf. From day one. From
breath one. Even before. To give him everything. And we
did. Except recently. "He's always liked you, too."

"Is he freaked? Is that why he's AWOL?" Figlio asked
with concern.

I didn't know. You can't encapsulate all that someone's
going through with one word, "freaked," and expect
you've come to any meaningful place. I can't do it about
myself. Even in regard to Sally, who filled so many years
of my life and whose soul was at times clearer to me than
my own. The divorce action was expected, wasn't a guerrilla attack on my life, and yet its effect was to undermine
all my assumptions about our lives, so much so that I
wasn't really certain about anything. There's a part of me
that wants to scream at her today, right now, and say something like, what goes around comes around, or don't start
what you can't finish, or even, you got what you deserved.

I'm not proud to be so mean-spirited, but everything
that's happened seems like an intrusion in what could
have been, with more effort, nice, fulfilled lives. I was able
to change directions, and if I didn't want to divorce, at
least I went along, passively perhaps, with the process. In
my heart of hearts I knew Sally was right, an ironic final
concordance between two adults who no longer wanted to

share even breakfast cereals. So I stayed at the office longer, let Sally by default direct the dissolution, buried my head in dreaminess, and managed to ignore the pain of others. Especially Jess. Nothing to be proud of here.

Was Jess freaked? More important, did he have something to do with Sally's death? I don't think so, but this is a hope, this is a wish, this is a prayer because I don't really know.

"He's very grounded and sensitive," I finally answered.

"What the fuck does that mean?"

They were Sally's words, a mother's language, her description of our son, and she was dead and couldn't elaborate. "It's the best I can answer," which was unfortunately the accurate, whole truth. On Figlio's face there was a mix of snarl and exasperation. On my own I imagined he saw contrition, sadness, guilt. "He's a level-headed, normal kid. He likes his computer, the Mets, and his music. He tends toward the quiet side of things."

"Could he have killed your wife?"

The provocative "your wife," rather than "his mother," made me shudder. "I don't see how—"

"Trust me. Based on the facts it's possible."

If he hadn't interrupted, I would have said, *I don't see how you could think that.* Instead I responded to Figlio's version of reality. "He was away. On a school trip from early Saturday morning to Monday afternoon."

"Uncertain time of death. No forced entry. A fugitive, perhaps. Et cetera, et cetera. You know the speech better than me."

"And the motive?" I asked disingenuously.

Sarcastically he replied, "Malone, do you really think this quiet boy wasn't really very angry about finding out about his parents?"

I waved him off. "I'll grant you Jess was pissed. But enough to murder his mother?" Figlio opened his mouth to say something, and anticipating his rebuttal, I added, "Okay, at least the only person he knew in that role. No. No. No way."

"Let me tell you somethin', Buster. If I were your kid and you did that to me, and never told me nothin', I'd stuff the two of you into a freezer so fast you wouldn't know what hit ya."

"Yeah. Because you guys are sociopaths," I said.

"I see why a lot of the dickheads don't like you."

In my experience as a trial lawyer the exchange of insults between two people usually occurs because one person's subterranean guilt has been drilled into and exposed by the other party. The hopeful part is that the release of the below-ground energy is often the first step toward reconciliation. I was an unwilling accomplice to Sally's determination to keep the facts of Jess's conception from him, but an accomplice nonetheless, and Figlio was right to toss the two of us into deep freeze, which didn't prevent me from saying, "Same goes for you. That's why we're buddies, right?" and making a very transparent attempt to resuscitate the bond between us.

Figlio let it pass. "Though you haven't come right out and asked me to, I know you're scared shitless, and I'm goin' to get a line on Jess and have a little talk. That's a numbah one," mimicking immigrant dialect, "and then I'll see if I can find out what the Department knows, numbah two, and then we'll go from there. Numbah three."

Hardly an imaginative or reassuring plan, but the only one offered to me.

The sun was still a few hours from setting so I headed north along the river promenade, asking nature, such as you find it in New York's parks, mingled with the detritus of humanity, for relief from the problems closing in on me. The river moisture had caused some of the tree buds to open early and start their journey to full-sized leafiness. In some places even the grass was sprouting. Looking up the light green hill punctuated by sharp splashes of blooming yellow forsythia toward Riverside Drive with its massive apartment buildings, and knowing that these impressionist images had remained the same year in and year out, I offered myself the solace that maybe all my difficulties would eventually right themselves.

I felt a little better because I'd reached out to Figlio and done something vis-à-vis Jess, so by the time I reached Broadway I was starving. For my metabolism, worrying's better than any of the commercially available dieting drugs, but after the worry eases, I'm ravenous and can easily pig out if I'm not careful.

All my favorite corner diner-style luncheonettes were long gone, replaced in the early years of West Side gentrification by banks and most recently by an oversupply of trendy coffee bars serving croissants, muffins, and finger food that was expensive, fattening, and, late in the day, too crumbly. I cruised the Korean vegetable stores, their produce spilling out onto the broad sidewalks in carefully stacked crates, surveyed gently rising slopes of Granny Smith apples, plums and peaches from Chile, Florida citrus, and five-dollar flower bouquets for errant spouses and cheap dinner guests, and finally settled on a plain, unbuttered bagel because I had an uncontrollable urge to grind and chew. The gratification lived up to my expectations.

The nearby chain drugstore had a sign in the window behind the stacks of scent-free Charmin family packs offering free aromatherapy (yes, one word) consultations. Trust me, try masticationtherapy instead. The aroma advertisement reminded me I needed a new good-for-three-months tray of roach motels for the upcoming summer months. I made the purchase immediately, as if the road back to domestic tranquillity was dependent on household hygiene, rather than on the trapping and disposing of real difficulties.

# CHAPTER 11

I went home with the idea of setting out my bait traps, ordering in an early dinner for two from the new burrito place on York (on the assumption Figlio would have a positive impact on Jess) and reviewing Abe Feldman's still unopened packet. Nothing in life ever works out that easily.

My sublet is on the fourth floor. From the front street–facing living room slash part-time bedroom for Jess you can, if you crane your neck, see the mayor's house, Gracie Mansion, through the open balconies of the high-rise apartment house. There's also a central dining room plus kitchen and a rear bedroom with an adjacent full bathroom complete with a claw-footed porcelain bathtub long enough for me to stretch out my six-foot frame without bumping up against the faucet. The bedroom overlooks a south garden, which my friend assured me receives "tons of sunlight" by the middle of May. I hope so because the trees out back are very spindly, like anorexic giraffes, their only branches near their tops. The place is furnished in post–grad school eclectic—lots of found objects (wine-box end tables, an electric company spool for dining), covered with nice cloths, small but expensive area rugs, a leather recliner facing a futon couch/bed, sagging particle-board bookcases, a stereo sitting on an antique cherrywood washstand—all in all perfectly appropriate for the exposed brick and polished hardwood floors.

There are two apartments per floor, mirror images of each other. We have a nonresident Eastern European (Albanian, I think) super who lives somewhere in the area, but everything's worked just fine so far, and I've never called him. Nor have I interacted with anyone else in the building. I attribute my neighbor noncontact to an almost continuous trial calendar since January, though it's possible other residents have atypical schedules as well. Most important, I want to declare I've been quite happy here, I haven't felt as if I've fallen down the apartment class ladder, and only occasionally have I missed my more luxurious marital digs. Now I plan to miss them permanently.

The entry hallway smelled of lemon; even the mailboxes had been polished. On the other side of the lace-curtained glass door, the shiny plastic hallway runner and the black-rubber staircase risers repeatedly reflected the bare ceiling light above. Homey. I climbed the four flights taking two steps at a time to increase the aerobic benefits. I unlocked the front door and stood in the middle of the kitchen and in that moment immediately sensed that something was different, that someone had been in my apartment while I was away. Jess has keys. Yes, that was it, and I felt relieved, happy that he was ready to come home. It had to be Jess. Wait a second, there were no telltale junk food crumbs on the countertops, no carelessly discarded papers or stuff, no disturbance whatsoever of the visual order, which ruled him out and made me feel lousy again.

*Come home, Jess. Make as much of a mess as you like. I'll never say another word on the subject. I promise.*

Maybe it was the super? He might have needed access to fix something, I have no idea what, nothing was broken, but no, I'd changed the cylinder on the top Medeco and never gotten around to making him a new key, and he would have left a note somewhere for me. Maybe the lock was picked. After all, this is New York.

A quick visual inspection suggested that nothing was amiss. I sat down on the recliner, suddenly tired, and closed my eyes. Diane came to mind, though I hadn't been thinking of her. She had a complete key set, she could have dropped them somewhere, at the airport, for example, and an arriving traveler, down on his or her luck, taken advantage of her departure to Switzerland to catch a few hours of undisturbed sleep.

I heard a distant household noise whose origin I couldn't localize, but it was soon followed by a creaking sound that I knew came from my bed: I had a visitor and it wasn't Goldilocks.

As quietly as I could, I tiptoed to the rear of the apartment, my nervous system primed for fight or flight. I'm more cautious than brave, which I don't fault myself for, and I entered the room slowly. There, to my amazement, I found Diane, sprawled out on my bed, asleep in all her clothes except her outerwear, which she had carefully draped over the chair by the window. She lay on her side, her knees pulled up to her chest, cuddling the calfskin attaché case I'd given her as a birthday present last month in a demonstration of extravagant affection that was as much about my needs as it was for her.

I gently tried to pry loose the case so she would be more comfortable. I made a game of it, a variant of pickup sticks, which I'd lose if Diane waked. Finally, after much carefully sustained effort on my part, her fingers released a bit and the soft leather yielded, offering no resistance as it slid over the cotton bedspread and onto the floor. Through it all Diane had remained soundly asleep, wrapped in her

jet-lagged dreams, my first success of the day. I turned off
the ringer on the bedroom phone, covered Diane with the
afghan she'd given me for Christmas, and retreated to the
living room to wait. For Figlio to call. For Jess to come
home. For someone to talk to.

In the several afternoon hours before the phone rang at
five, I hadn't done much except worry and go over the
same ground. Even knowing that Diane was here with me
didn't help. In some ways her comatose presence made it
worse, for she had now become in my mind the official
lady-in-waiting and a testimonial to the reconciliations
that would never happen. Were I a drinker, which I'm not,
I would have drunk quite a few whiskeys, passed out, and
missed the phone call.

"Hey, doc. I'm up here with them. Can you believe that
the little pisser beat me with a Ruy Lopez?" Figlio shouted
into a pay phone.

"Where are you?"

"Soundview. The Bronx."

"Is everything okay?" I asked.

"Yeah, why shouldn't it be?" Figlio answered.

"Who's this Lopez?"

Figlio laughed. "A chess opening." Figlio never fails to
surprise. "I'm bringing them both down. Great guy, taught
me a few tricks. Depending on the weather we should be
there in about two hours."

He hung up before I had a chance to ask him what the
weather had to do with anything. The little bit of sky outside the living room window looked blue and cloudless.
Far away, a toilet was flushed, then the sound of footsteps.

Diane was once again under the covers, but this time
only half-asleep or half-awake, depending on your perspective. I lay down on the bed next to her and nuzzled in
closer, running my finger along her cheekbone, circling

the hollow of the skin below, coming upon a dark pig-mented area in the shape of a question mark, which I'd never noticed, behind her left ear on the sterno-cleido mastoideus muscle that ran downward supporting her head. She responded to my inspections by sinking further into sleep and snoring—the heaving respirations coming from the roots of her bronchial tree—but before she could attain a regular rhythm a heavier snort occurred, which broke the pattern of raucous breathing. This was followed by gurglings and dribble on the corner of the pillow, now in her mouth, as if she was a hungry baby at the breast.

The relief having quickly given way to fatigue, I was in danger of falling asleep myself, which would have made me angry because I very much felt entitled to a late matinée–early evening lovemaking. With Jess on the way, we needed to hurry. I yanked sharply at the covers, hoping the sliding movement of bedding underneath would waken her, as a sleeping sunbather is suddenly roused when the tide sucks the sand to the sea.

Diane responded by rolling onto her back. Saliva trickled out the corner of her mouth, irrigating the tempo-rary fabric lines that crisscrossed her face and dripping onto her neck. Her carotids pulsed noticeably. If they were cut, how far would they really spurt? As far as Sally's had? Sally always used to say how much I missed by always making comparisons where none was necessary. It was a stupid thought. Definitely untestable. You couldn't do a controlled experiment. Diane swatted at the wetness and smeared the dribble farther afield. Then she swallowed hard, moved her tongue, smacked her lips.

In the most self-serving way I took all this activity to be an amorous invitation. I kissed the soft area directly below the thyroid bulge. Her first verbal response was an unintel-ligible mumble, which emboldened me. I pursed my lips and sucked in, creating a tiny vacuum that, applied to her skin tissue, pulled it between my teeth, leaving the area reddened, angry. I released the tension on my lips and her skin and switched over to planting a trail of kisses northward along her neck. At the intersection of her straight squarish chin and the underside of her lower lip, I offered quicker feathery kisses that made her nostrils flare, her brows furrow, and finally caused her eyes to open and stare at me for a few seconds, before the heavy lids came down. I did not say anything—she was not yet enough of a coparticipant to distinguish my foreplay from unwanted sexual advance. I watched as familiarity replaced tension (even if it was pleasurable) and when she was totally re-laxed I shifted my weight, swung myself astride her, and planted a full-mouthed kiss, which told her semiconscious being I was engaged in a predocking maneuver.

Unexpectedly, Diane grabbed my upper arms and pulled herself to an upright position.

"What the hell's going on?" she asked.

I rocked onto my knees. "Just welcoming you home to America." I leaned forward and with my arms encircled her waist.

She pushed me away. "Cut it out. This is serious. What's happening?"

"I missed you. I didn't mean to be presumptuous. But you are here."

"I just want to know one thing," she said, her voice qua-vering. "Did you or did you not murder your wife?" She whispered "wife" as if that might make the crime less real, less likely.

Her question immediately deflated my ardor. "No. Of course not. You can't believe I did. Or you wouldn't be here."

My spirited defense transformed my lusting state into a

sad hangdog demeanor and Diane now looked gently upon me. I am a litigator, a lawyer trained in impression management, able to leap tall gaps of logic in a single bound, but I am not so calculating that I can change my emotional appearance on command. Whatever was written on my face was unintentional and unplanned, which is not the same as saying I'm a spontaneous, natural, or honest kind of person, though in point of fact I am.

And before you become too cynical, you need to know that Diane is no shrinking violet ready to believe any crock someone tells her. She's one tough litigator herself—a real juror of my peers, and she wasn't going to accept whatever I said just because of emotional things between us. She is perfectly capable of putting two and two together and coming up with her own conclusion. Just like Sally.

"Why would I? What would have been my motivation?"

"That's why I was so confused, but I didn't know what to think," she said, starting to cry. "I've never been this close to a capital crime and it's scary."

"That's okay, I understand," I said, trying to comfort her. "I haven't been either. I'm hoping, as my cardiology professor used to say, 'The condition will take care of itself.'"

"Do the police have any leads?"

"They haven't said so."

"Why not? People just don't get murdered on Sutton Place South all the time. There must be a witness."

"There are problems. They're doing the best they can."

"What kinds of problems?" Diane said, the edge returning to her voice.

"With the forensics."

"Listen, Malone," she shouted, "I came home all the way from Switzerland to be here, to help you. Don't parse out the info like you're feeding me tiny spoonfuls of baby food. Give it to me all at once. *Okay?*"

"Fine," I yelled back. "No one's been trying to *parse* anything out. I don't enjoy this any better than you and in fact probably a whole lot less, so don't start lecturing me. I've had enough of everybody acting as if I'm some piece of work, when all I am is a crime victim who's doubly unfortunate to be in the midst of a divorce action. Instead of receiving the status of 'grieving husband,' the suspicion first falls on me because everyone's got their heads up their asses. How do you think that feels?"

"Okay, I hear you. Calm down," she said. Diane didn't say she was sorry. In a perverse way that was one of the things I liked about her.

"The pathologists can't determine the time of death."

"Why not?" she asked.

"You know how they usually do it?" Diane shook her head. "By body temp or stomach contents or both."

"So?"

"The murderer put Sally into our freezer. The M.E. couldn't even begin the post until a day after they took possession 'cause the body had to thaw. And as for stomach contents, I already knew they'd find nothing." Diane knitted her eyebrows. "Sally's a fanatic about weight, about appearances in general. Every weekend after a big Friday lunch, she fasts until Saturday night or sometimes Sunday morning. She even used to take high colonics after some quack convinced her of their 'therapeutic' benefit. At least she had the sense to stop that. So all she ingests is Gatorade or something similar the whole day and a half to keep up her electrolytes. It's absorbed right away, and for timing purposes won't be very helpful."

"Why is it a problem for you more than anyone else?" Diane asked.

"I didn't say it was," I answered, testily.

"But you were pretty sure her stomach would be empty."

"Not sure. High probability. Almost half the weekend she's running on empty."

"How do you know it didn't happen on Friday?"

"I suppose it could have, I wish it had. But Jess will know that. He probably saw her when he left Saturday morning."

"Why do you want Friday?"

"Because I was in a court-ordered deposition all day at New York Supreme and then I shared a ride uptown to meet you at that Italian restaurant and then we went back to my apartment and . . ." I paused to remember the night of lovemaking. "I.e., I had no opportunity in addition to having no motive."

Diane smiled. "And all day Saturday you were with me, and then you had the silicone gel claimants' dinner, right?" I nodded my head. "You went. You were visible." I mouthed a "yes." "And afterward you went on the police boat with your buddy like you said you would, didn't you?" I nodded again. "So that only leaves Sunday. What did you do Sunday?" she asked.

I gave Diane an accurate, detailed accounting of my activities. She seemed pleased.

"Great, so there're only two very narrow unalibied windows of opportunity—Saturday, after you put me in the limo and before you appeared at the silicone dinner, and Sunday afternoon-evening, when you left the office, and presumably someone would have seen you go into your wife's house in broad daylight, if you had. Not much exposure," she said.

"You're talking like my lawyer or lover?"

"Both," she said.

She reached over, loosened my belt, and began to undo my pants.

"So how are you feeling?" she asked.

"Lonely. Confused. Angry. Scared. All of the above."

"I understand. It must be terrible. Maybe this will help a little." She reached over and started playing with my cock. The contrast—cool hand on warm penis—was perfect and for a moment allowed me to forget my problems.

After sex I usually sleep. Tonight I was all revved. "There is one other big problem," I said.

Diane sat up in bed. "What's that?" she said sharply, the postcoital spell broken.

"Arnie thinks Jess may have something to do with Sally's murder."

A darkness enveloped her Minnesotan blondness as rapidly as a tornado crossing the cornfields. "Oh that's not possible. It can't be."

"I don't believe it either. But he'll be here in an hour or so. Figlio found him. He's been incommunicado."

"Where's he been?"

"At his chess teacher's."

"Mike, let's both try to stay calm. This must be terrible for Jess. We have to help. Even if he shuts down, we have to."

"I know. Maybe I should ask Arnie to be here."

"Why? He's your divorce lawyer. What does he bring?"

"His kind cuddly-bear presence. It might make it easier for Jess. He was also one hell of a criminal defense lawyer. One of the best, everyone says. Maybe he'll pick up on something we'll miss."

"Let's keep it simple."

"Okay," I agreed. "We'd better get dressed."

"What's the food situation?" she asked.

"I was thinking burritos."

"No way," Diane declared.

"I don't think we have much else. I feel like I shopped a million years ago."

"That's what you always say."

# CHAPTER 12

DIANE and I cobbled together a giant tomato-cheese-mushroom omelet—about all our stomachs could handle.

After eating, Diane showered while I washed the dishes, tidied the kitchen, swept the wood floors (Sally would have been proud of my improved housekeeping), and did the kind of general penance expected of any good half-Catholic awaiting the arrival of a painful situation.

Soon thereafter I was opening the front door to the three of them: Figlio, Jess, and a tall skinny guy with a ponytail. An aging hippie. I hugged Jess tightly. His clothes and skin felt clammy, a sure sign of inner turmoil on an April night.

Yesterday's anger was replaced with formality as Jess introduced Jasper to everyone. "I'm very sorry about Mrs. Malone. I'm sure she must have been proud of Jess," Jasper said.

"Yes, she was. We are," I said to Jasper. *It would have been nice if you'd told me what was going on,* I thought, *so I didn't have to die a thousand deaths wondering if Jess was okay.*

Figlio headed straight for the fridge, taking out a cold beer, then introduced himself to Diane, who had hung back in the shadows, perhaps not wanting to add to Jess's discomfort.

Amid all the adults, Jess seemed sheepish, shy, though

at least he gave Diane a nice smile. I was a nervous host, uncertain what to say to break the ice, my supply of chitchat prematurely depleted.

In spite of myself I tried. "Did you guys get caught in the Yankee Stadium traffic?" Jess looked at Jasper and they smiled conspiratorially. Not wanting to appear too interested in their little secret, I didn't press for more.

"We came by boat," Jess answered. "It was really neat."

"On a launch?" I asked Figlio.

"Yeah. We tied up at the mayor's. Only way to find parking in these fancy neighborhoods," Figlio replied.

"Is anyone hungry? I can whip up something. It's no trouble," Diane announced.

"Nothing for me. We ate on the way," Jasper said. "Nice place you have here, Doctor." Jess shrugged, but said nothing.

"It works out. No complaints." I smiled. My tone, to my ears anyway, was cold and unfriendly. Instead of being grateful that Jess had an adult he could turn to, I was wallowing in this pathetic jealousy.

"My wife and I are separated. It was tough at first. You give up so much," Jasper said.

"Yes," I said through clenched teeth. I was supposed to be the grown-up here, I had to do better. "Mr. Reynolds. I want you to know how much I really appreciate everything you're doing for Jess."

"My pleasure, really. Keeps me off the streets," he said. "It's getting late, I'd better be shoving off—it's a long subway ride."

"Why don't you come for dinner sometime?" I suggested.

"That would be great. Whenever is fine. I don't have a busy schedule."

After Jasper left, Jess paced around the apartment, unable to stay in one place for more than a few minutes.

Maybe it was Diane's presence that made Jess uncomfortable. Or it could have been simply that he wasn't ready to be left alone with me.

"Malone, I promised Jess he could sleep on *Annabelle* sometime. How would you feel if we did it tonight?" Figlio asked.

Given the household atmosphere it seemed like a wonderful idea. "Yeah, that'd be fine. If Jess wants to." He nodded his agreement.

On the stairs I heard Figlio tell Jess, "We can leave the launch here and take a cab, or go by boat. Which do you prefer?" I didn't hear Jess's answer, only Figlio's "me too," so I assume they went by water.

Diane and I went to sleep around midnight. I dreamed Sally and I were both on-call, doing an OB-GYN externship at Bellevue, and together we delivered a baby boy who looked like Jess to a young Puerto Rican woman who screamed during, and after, the labor.

A loud rapping on the door interrupted my REM cycle. A neighbor in distress? My mailbox did say M.D. and heart attacks often occur in the predawn hours. "Yes," I called out from bed.

"Dr. Malone. This is Detective Johnson. Could you please open the door?" I recognized his grating voice, an irritating mixture of Queens and Long Island, the urgent undertone further intensifying the unpleasantness.

"I'll be right there," I said. I hope it's not something bad about Jess. What else could it be? And I broke out in a cold sweat. Instantly.

I opened the door. Detectives Levine and Johnson stood there, unsmiling. You could even characterize their expressions as grim.

"Sorry to bother you, doc," Johnson began.

"What's up?" was the best I could do.

"May we please come in, Dr. Malone?" Detective

Levine asked. I moved out of the way wordlessly. Johnson closed the door quietly and remained near the entry. "I'm very sorry to have to do this, Dr. Malone." She reached into her jacket inner pocket for something. "Michael J. Malone, M.D., I hand you this warrant for your arrest, on the charge of murder. I have to caution you, anything you say may be taken down and used against you. You have the right to remain silent and have a lawyer and if you can't afford a lawyer, the court will assign one. Can you please get dressed and come with us?"

It's strange how in the midst of awful situations you sometimes worry about the silliest of things. "Do you mind if I just dry those dishes and put them away?" I asked.

Johnson was about to say something predictable for a tough guy, but Levine shut him off. "That's fine. Take your time." Perhaps she was glad to meet a man who took an interest in household chores as opposed to the sexist dogs with whom she probably had to live and work.

At least they'd come for me, not Jess. "Ms. Levine, would it be possible for you and the detective to step outside for a few minutes while I tell my friend about the change in our plans."

"That's against regs, doc," Johnson informed me.

"It'll be okay," Detective Levine decided. "Just make it snappy."

In the bedroom, Diane was awake, tears streaming down her face. "I guess you heard. Nothing's changed, you know that. We know it's impossible. Call Figlio. His number is in my sock drawer. (I hoped he'd replaced his phone.) Try to get some sleep. Don't worry about me. And, if you're up to it in the morning, go over to the marina and check up on Jess. I'll be all right." I gave her a peck. "Hey, at least this is one unpleasant memory Jess won't have to delete."

*  *  *

Despite all my litigation work, I've never spent much time in police stations (because, I like to think, I represent the good guys): once to return a thick envelope of fresh twenty-dollar bills I'd found on the floor of a cab, and a second time, six months later, to claim them when no one else did. Perhaps the sergeant who'd applauded my act of good citizenship could vouch for me to his colleagues.

Detectives Levine and Johnson shepherded me through the procedures, hovering as I was booked, photographed, and fingerprinted. Within hours, or minutes probably, members of the media, via the grapevine, would hear and use my predicament to boost their careers, as I'd used them to help mine. The firm would discreetly but speedily distance itself from me, as would clients, outside lawyers, and judges. Unless expunged completely, this felony indictment would hang over everything and erode my life. After a while it wouldn't matter that I was innocent—the wheels of justice would grind over me.

Detective Levine allowed me to wait for my attorney to arrive (I'd made the one call to Arnie Glimcher) in a locked interrogation room rather than the chain-link cage at the rear of the station house where the other "felons" of the day marked time. She meanwhile busied herself filling out arrest report forms and assorted ziplicate paperwork that needed to be disseminated throughout the law enforcement bureaucracy. Detective Johnson came and went several times, often returning to whisper something in Levine's ear, which from my perspective looked like a lot of amateur theatrics.

Most of the time we were alone, Ellen Levine seemed uncomfortable, even ill at ease. I guessed the charges against me disturbed her, for I sensed she liked me and was upset with herself for misplaced affection. Too often she'd probably been told that she picked the wrong men.

But attractive professional women actually have a harder time separating the wheat from the chaff because of all the jerks who hit on them. I couldn't help but steal glances at her. Lustrous, long auburn hair framed a face whose main feature was widely set large eyes, a Jewish Jackie O. She was tall and in her blue tailored conservative suit over a white silk blouse exuded a deep harbor of femininity. I made a promise to myself: after I was successfully extricated from this mess I would introduce her to some nice young lawyers or, even better, to a few equally attractive and good-guy former medical colleagues.

Arnie Glimcher, ushered in by Detective Johnson, entered in his usual rumpled state, made worse by the circumstances—he'd had to schlepp down from Westchester without much time to pull himself and his wardrobe together.

"Are you the detective in charge?" he said to Ellen, without bothering to acknowledge my presence.

"Yes," she answered softly, and I must report because it confirmed my speculation, with sadness, as if to say, *I'm sorry we have to be here, I'm sorry we've charged your client, I hope there's some innocent explanation for all this, but I know there won't be.*

"I'd like to see the warrant if you don't mind."

Ellen ruffled through her papers, pulled a sheet out from the bottom of the pile, and handed it over. Arnie read the document slowly, his lips moving the whole time. "Everything seems to be in order," he pronounced.

"Yes, it is," Detective Levine answered. "Would you like to confer with your client before we bring him down to arraignment?"

"Of course."

Detective Levine pushed her chair out from the solid maple-colored wood table. "We'll be outside if you need us for anything."

"Detective, one other question." She stopped midstride. "The arrest warrant refers to evidence gathered on a search warrant as the basis for being bound over, is that not correct?"

"Correct," she answered, warily.

"Do you have a copy of the search warrant?"

"I can get it if you'd like," she answered.

"Do that," Arnie said gruffly in the best tradition of the abrasive marital attorney. She glared at him, her hackles up. I personally never begin an adversarial relationship antagonistically—Detective Levine was only doing her job—but I wasn't representing myself, and decided to shut up. A good idea, as I hadn't even wondered about what evidence they had, where and when they'd obtained it, or any of the other particulars I was entitled to know.

Just as she was closing the door behind her, Arnie called out, "Detective," and she did an about-face and stuck her head into the room. "I was wondering, Detective, if you could tell me where the search warrant was executed."

"At the accused's residence," she said.

So I wasn't paranoid. Someone had been in my apartment today without my knowledge, though with the permission of a judge. As an officer of the court I had no basis to complain and take offense. What they did was certainly legal, yet I felt violated, which in fact was an entirely appropriate response.

"And there was probable cause?"

"The magistrate believed so."

"I'll need to review everything before we go over to arraignment. Is that understood? And . . ." he paused, "is there a D.A. assigned to this case yet?"

"I was told they're sending one over."

"When he or she gets here, I'd like to meet with him or her before we go before the judge."

"I'll tell him or *her*, okay?"

"One other thing, Detective." Levine shot Arnie a very exasperated look. "I don't want to find that this room was bugged," he declared. Ellen Levine slammed the door loudly. I could hear the sound of her disappearing down the hallway for a long time.

"Arnie, don't you think you're being a little too aggressive? She's only doing her job."

"You know, kid, one of the things I've learned in all my thirty-plus years of being a lawyer is never listen to anyone who, in the presence of a pretty woman, thinks with his dick. We have to establish some ground rules here. There have to be some lines drawn in the sand, across which they don't move, so that they know I'm not a schmuck, and by extension, that you haven't been a schmuck for hiring me. Is that understood, kid?"

"They've got nothing, Arnie. They can't make it stick."

"Kid, the jails are filled with people who've said that. They've got enough or they wouldn't have dragged you in."

"Arnie. There's nothing in my apartment relevant to Sally's murder. I'd stake my life on it."

"You might have to," Arnie said.

According to Arnie, the Assistant District Attorney for New York County sneezed during most of their meeting. "It's an allergy, not a cold," he'd reassured Arnie. Very unlikely. Few antigens are activated this early in the year. He was probably allergic to early morning work.

"What do they have?" I asked Arnie.

"Who knows? That kid doesn't know a rat's ass about the case. He hasn't seen any files. Nothing. He's just a body they suited up for the occasion, someone to say 'ready' when the clerk calls the case." A thought flickered across Arnie's face. "He ain't ready for shit," he added.

"So. You can take advantage of that?" I declared.

"Hope so."

Not exactly the kind of response that leaves me with full faith and confidence.

We, myself and some other alleged felons collared by the precinct, ambled downtown to the Criminal Court Building on Centre Street in a converted school bus operated by the Department of Corrections. The dark blue vehicle had no working interior lights. Heavy metal grillwork covered the windows and rear emergency exit. And the shock absorbers had long ago died or been stolen. Instead of seat belts, which would've been useful, my fellow passengers and I were handcuffed to the metal bars of the seat in front. Even at this demeaned level of travel, everyone had taken a window seat.

When we reached Lower Manhattan the driver picked up the pace dramatically, racing through the deserted streets as if he was being paid by the head. I was relieved to arrive at the curb in front of One hundred Centre in one piece. One of the advantages of a 4 A.M. arraignment is that the disembarkation and procession into Criminal Court occurs in the absence of sidewalk gawkers.

As we entered the building the guards removed our handcuffs so that we could pass through the metal detectors without triggering the alarms and on the other side they recuffed us and marched us down a dingy hallway to the courtroom, or more accurately a side room nearby, where we waited on benches, graffitied with gashes carved by those who'd sat here before us. Five other prisoners had accompanied me from the station house. All were male, four Black, one Hispanic or Italian. Most appeared scruffy, down on their heels, and definitely, their luck. None of them seemed particularly apprehensive, though a slightly better dressed Black man spent an inordinate amount of time buffing his loafers with his shirtsleeve.

Our two guards, looking very bored, chewed gum, read dog-eared pages of magazines they'd picked off the floor, and, a lot of the time, stared at nothing apparent.

At this node of the criminal justice system efficiency flourished. The arraignments moved swiftly, averaging about four minutes per person. Whether procedural justice was being dispensed, I don't know, but could only hope for the best. As the waiting room emptied with the other accused going through the door into the courtroom and disappearing, I became very anxious. A tic started in my right upper eyelid. Was I to be the last presented because I was somehow presumed the most guilty? Were the facts amassed against me so overwhelming? Was I already being declared an outcast from society, an unmentionable they had to hide for fear the social fabric would come undone if my story were revealed to others?

Finally, my turn came, and I passed through the portals into a large high-ceilinged room, whose very size by comparison felt like freedom. The guard nudged me to the defendant's table.

The court clerk looked up, noted my presence, and called the case. "*People of the State of New York* v. *Malone.*"

Arnie and a younger, shorter person came forward out of the shadows in the rear of the room and parted at the low railing before the bench. Arnie stood beside me, while the other attorney stood next to the table reserved for the prosecution. I glanced quickly at opposing counsel and the only thing I noticed was his red bow tie—I wondered if it was a clip-on because he looked no older than Jess. The clerk handed the thin file to the judge.

"Both sides ready," the judge intoned.

"Ready for the State," the young kid said.

"Defense," Arnie stated.

"Counsel, state your names for the record, please, and leave your cards with me afterward."

"Henry J. Wilson the Third, on behalf of the People."

"Arnold Glimcher, for the Defendant."

"Okay, what have we here, gentlemen?" His Honor asked.

"The Defendant, Michael J. Malone, M.D., is held on a charge of first degree manslaughter in the death of his wife, Sally Hager Malone, on or about April eighteenth or nineteenth of this year, Your Honor. The People do reserve the right to amend the charge before pretrial."

"How do you plead, Dr. Malone?" the judge asked me.

"Not guilty," I declared, but not as forcefully as I would have liked because my mouth was so dry.

He asked the D.A., "Any mitigating circumstances, counselor?"

"Not that we're aware of," Henry number three answered.

"If it please the Court, Your Honor," Arnie began, "my client is a member of the bar. And also a physician. A man with an impeccable record and no priors of any kind. He has cooperated totally in the investigation of this tragic incident without regard to his own grieving and pain. We ask that the Defendant be released on bail on his own recognizance."

"What kind of practice are you engaged in, Dr. Malone?" the judge asked.

I swallowed hard—negligence lawyers aren't particularly popular. "Med-mal primarily, Your Honor."

"Solo?"

"No, Your Honor. I'm a partner at Badger, Weissberg, Smith."

"I'm not offhand familiar with the firm."

"We don't have many cases down here, Your Honor," I offered.

The judge didn't even smile. In fact, he winced a little. "Mr. Wilson?"

"Yes, Your Honor?"

"Are the People offering bail?"

"Your Honor. The People feel that, because of the heinous nature of the crime the Defendant is accused of, he not be released on bail at this time."

Arnie rose to object, but the judge motioned for him to sit down. "Mr. Wilson. The Court is mindful of the serious nature of the crime alleged in this matter. The People could have gone with murder one but instead chose man one. And as counsel for the defense has reminded the Court that the Defendant is a most unlikely person to flee this jurisdiction . . ."

"But," Henry Wilson started to say.

"Don't interrupt, sir," the judge scolded, and the Assistant D.A. sat down like a reprimanded schoolchild, sulking, looking down while the judge finished. "The Defendant is unlikely to flee this jurisdiction. In the interests of justice and economy the Court remands him to the custody of his attorney. Bail is set at five hundred thousand dollars."

Now it was Arnie's turn to rise and complain. "Your Honor. We believe the bail is excessive."

"If your client is unable to make the bail, the correctional facilities of the City of New York will be placed at his disposal. Your choice, counselor."

"I understand, Your Honor," Arnie conceded.

"Any objections?" the judge asked.

No one said a word.

"So ordered. Bail is set at five hundred thousand dollars. Defendant is remanded to the custody of the Department of Corrections until the bond is secured." The judge banged his gavel and the court clerk called the next case, *People of the State of New York* v. *Martinez.*

"I'll have you out in a few hours, kid. Don't worry about a thing," Arnie told me.

"That's easy for you to say."

"I'm glad about one thing."

"What's that?" I asked him.

"At least you've finally woken up to the seriousness of this whole meshugaas. I was beginning to worry if you were compos mentis."

"Thanks for the compliment," I said.

"Relax. My criminal defense juices are flowing. This'll be fun, kid. It's lucky I was handling your divorce."

"How's that lucky?"

"I've got copies of all the deeds and bank records. Five hundred K is no problem with your family's assets. Would you prefer to pledge the Sutton Place property or Connecticut?"

I answered quickly, "Sutton Place."

"Great. I'll be back to you very soon."

"You know where to find me," I said.

# CHAPTER 13

THE ride uptown, back to my apartment, in the stretch Arnie had thoughtfully ordered for me (for which he'll bill me as a disbursement, of course), was a thousand times more pleasant than the earlier government-sponsored bus trip. I felt grateful, strike that, exhilarated; I was a force field sucking in every aspect of the slowly awakening city. I was prepared to seize the day over and over and over, never again to waste another moment. If Diane was keeping our bed warm, I would tell her until she told me to stop how much I cared for her, how much she meant. I would love her until my body gave out.

At 6:41 A.M. the limo driver dropped me off at the all-night newsstand a few blocks away from my apartment so I could satisfy an uncontrollable urge to read all the morning papers. It was something I had to do to confirm the world was still round and everything in order despite the Sturm und Drang that had descended upon me. I bought three croissants at Mansion Diner, where the mayor goes when he wants to be alone, and quickly leafed through the papers at the counter. There was nothing yet about my arrest or the murder investigation, which made me feel even better.

My street was sleepy quiet. No birds awake, only one basement apartment alit. Even the double-parked vans at the end of the block, across the street from my house, were still, their motors turned off, waiting for some morning mayoral media event to begin.

In front of my building I retrieved a garbage can cover and replaced it on the container that had toppled over in the night, and it was only afterward, when I'd had some time to reflect, that I was able to separate that physical act from the furious change that occurred simultaneously. It was as if a large fuse switch had been thrown. The street was suddenly high noon bright, the façades of the buildings glaringly floodlit. The curtain went up and act one—beginning with the all-too-familiar choreography of reporters sticking mikes and cameras in my face—began. In retrospect I am most amazed by my revulsion, for I was someone who lived by the media and it was only fair that one day I face the other side of the sword.

"Did you kill your wife?" *Eyewitness News* asked, not wasting any time or demonstrating any restraint. I don't remember answering, though I probably said, No comment, automatically.

"If you didn't, who did?" a talk-radio interviewer inquired. I shrugged, threw up my hands, rolled my eyes. How should I know? I have no burden of proof. Ask the prosecutor or the police, not me. Which of course is bullshit. If I didn't serve up to the People an alternate suspect no one else would, because no one else really gave a damn.

And then there was Marcy Lewis of Channel 2, to whom, over the years, I've leaked many facts advantageous to my side of a case. She was a reporter with perspective and common sense, someone who could separate the substantive from the self-serving drivel. On this cool grayish predawn, where I could still see my breath and hers, she asked me a question that shattered my protective shield. "Dr. Malone, a police source says they've identified your ex-wife's blood on your property and yours on hers. If, as you say, you're innocent, do you have any explanation how that might have happened?"

The sinking feeling was so strong it was amazing I was still able to stand, though I do remember self-protectively slipping my right hand into my pocket to hide the bandage on my finger. This was the first I'd heard about blood evidence (though I wasn't going to let an outsider, even one I'd worked with, know that; how queer that I worried about image when my very life was being threatened). While one mystery was solved—they'd arrested me because of the lab tests—another had surfaced: I couldn't, for the life of me, think of any way our blood could have become interwined. "It must be a mistake, Marcy. They couldn't have done DNA this fast. No other explanation is possible."

Before any other questioners could catch me off guard I retreated into my building, slamming the inner door so hard the glass panes rattled and the outbound rush of air sucked Chinese restaurant menus and throwaway circulars off the hallway table. I was suddenly so tired, I sat down on the soon-to-be threadbare carpeting to pick up the mess.

Mistake. Yes, that was the only possibility. Marcy was misinformed. There was no DNA match. Of course not. She hadn't said anything about DNA. This wasn't, thank the Lord, Los Angeles. I was jumping ahead. Hadn't I called some lab people as expert witnesses in my cases? Hadn't I given them generous honoraria? We were colleagues. There was going to be no rush to judgment here. Sure, I'd been on the opposing side a few times, but that's the nature of the game. We're all professionals. I prided myself on equitable dealings with everyone. I've stepped on toes, pushed hot buttons on behalf of a client, who hasn't? But it was never personal and nobody's ever seemed particularly upset. Certainly not enough to deliberately lie to the media. Or tamper with the forensics.

Unless those two detectives from Rikers were behind this. They were pissed big-time, yes, but they didn't seem smart enough to fool with DNA. Yet there was simply no legitimate way the lab guys could be so certain so quickly that I'd murdered Sally.

Steve Kim's name floated forward in my head. I should see my old med school buddy, ask for help. We hadn't talked in a year. Under the circumstances he might refuse; in his shoes I might do the same, but it was worth a try. Steve knew more than anyone in med school about DNA. It was such an obsession that everyone had called him Gene. One night during third year he was helping me, translating, while I took care of a Korean gunshot victim also named Kim. Steve told me that 20 percent of Koreans have Kim as their last name and that Korea has a centuries-old ban on marriages between two people who have the same surname, a primitive protection against inbreeding that had forced Steve's parents to emigrate to the U.S. so that Steve wouldn't be created out of wedlock, an unacceptable identity in Korea. Or anywhere.

Steve was a good guy. He'd level with me. He'd never be part of a frame. On the other hand he was, after all, Deputy Chief Medical Examiner, and this could get messy.

Not messier than Marcy's words: "Dr. Malone, a police source says they've identified your ex-wife's blood on your property and yours on hers." Identified. What was she talking about? She'd called Sally my "ex-wife," throwing me off, dredging guilt silt. We were "in the midst," we were heading there, but we were still married. The other surprise word was "property." What property? My furniture. My dishes. My sheets and towels. They all came with the apartment.

I took a deep breath and counted to twenty. The answer I gave Marcy was accurate. There hadn't been enough time to do DNA. Someone at the Police Department, if they'd said anything, at most had told her about a presumptive match—standard red blood cell typing, which didn't prove a damned thing.

I can, however, understand even without DNA testing why the police believe they have meaningful evidence. I'm blood type B, which isn't too common (among Whites, one in ten), and Sally has an infrequent Rh (one in twenty-five), something we'd learned only after several spontaneous abortions "suggested" to her OB-GYN man the need for a complete infertility workup. The odds for both being found in the same place are very low. Not, I hope, low enough to convict, but easily low enough to indict.

I put the throwaway menus back on the table and dragged my leaden legs up the four flights. *It's not DNA. Relax, kid,* I could imagine Arnie saying.

*But Arnie, one in twenty-five multiplied by one in ten means this blood could only be found, associated with two people like Sally and me, once in two hundred fifty times. Those odds aren't too good either,* I'd tell him.

*Don't sweat the small stuff, we've got plenty of exculpatory,* he'd counter.

*Sure, Arnie, anything you say,* I'd respond. Why not? There was definitely no percentage in being my own lawyer.

I unlocked the door to my apartment. Déjà vu, intensified by sleep deprivation. However, this time my nervous system was too zonked to worry about intruders. I just wanted to sleep. The front room was aglow from the news lights below and as a result the whole apartment was too bright. I went over to the windows, closed the Levolors, and started to undress in the middle of the living room. A diluted exhibitionistic flaunting of my freedom. When I was stark naked I plunked myself down on the velour-covered couch, scrunched my feet and hands as deeply as possible into the pleasurable softness, and allowed myself to feel superior to all those news people in the cold below, but in the end I was unable to find a position that would make me unaware of the electronic bracelet I wore around my right ankle, a gift from the court and a condition for bail. The court officer had not said anything about showering. In this state-of-the-art technological era, it was probably okay. If it wasn't, and it set off all their alarms, tough shit for them. All it would mean for me was I'd have to get dressed in a hurry once again.

Diane's telephone call awakened me several hours later.

"Oh, you're home. How'd it go?" she asked, as if she were asking about an athletic event at Jess's school.

"Okay, I guess. Arnie was good."

"They dropped the charges?" she asked.

"No."

"But you're out."

"On bail," I said.

"Bail! You can be bailed on a murder charge?"

"Seems so. I didn't escape, I'm not a fugitive."

"I never heard of that. What if you killed again?"

"That's not funny, Diane. I was expecting to rot on Rikers for months. And it's not as if I could trust the medical care there."

"How much bail?"

"Five hundred thousand," I answered.

"Wow. That's a lot." I suppose she hadn't really thought of me as rich.

"Not really," I answered, proud that the material assets I possessed might temporarily salvage some of my self-respect vis-à-vis Diane. "It's secured by the town house. And my jewelry—I'm wearing an ankle bracelet. Totally ridiculous. It's not as if I can go anywhere with all the reporters camped out front."

"Oh, I almost forgot. Your buddy Bill Figlio called before I could get to him."

"Does Jess know? What'd he say?"

"Sorry he missed you, but he'll be in touch."

"Real illuminating. What time is it?"

"Eleven. Malone, I've gotta go, a client's hanging on the other line."

"I'll see you later," I said, not knowing if that was possible.

When I left a few hours later, there were no reporters lurking outside and I was able to hail a cab without being hassled.

Why did I go to the office? What choice did I have? If I stayed home, I'd have to take the phone off the hook, and I didn't want to do that in case Jess called. I suppose I could have put on dark glasses and strolled the City or treated myself to an all-day multiplex movie experience, except I'd have felt dissolute taking in a pop culture cocktail before the happy hour.

I went to the office because I thought I could relax there, as my professional plate was, conveniently, empty. The wrongful death suit against the City of New York was in continuance until next week. The silicone gel breast-implant class action, except for a few minor issues that needed my attention, was for all intents and purposes settled. Under my control the checks for the plaintiffs, for myself, and for my very hungry partners, living well beyond cash flow, would soon be rolling in. So, I could put my feet up on the cherrywood desk, handcrafted in Denmark, that Sally, despite all her protestations about the materialistic values of the firm, had bought for me to mark partnership, survey the view over the East River and

Long Island, talk to Figlio and Arnie, and be thankful I wasn't still stuck in jail. I hoped not too many of my colleagues would invade my privacy with their support or worse, their tentativeness, their *is he? or isn't he?* kind of thinking.

Lydia was not at her desk or in secretarial support, but she'd left me a ton of messages. Condolence calls from out-of-town mutual friends of Sally's and mine unaware of the local gossip. John Ames, to whom I'd sold my cardiology practice. Call Dr. Feldman X 3. Shit. I'd forgotten our ten o'clock and I'd never even opened his envelope.

Sally had always liked Dr. Feldman, though at a distance. To Sally, born as she was to older parents and orphaned as a young girl, Feldman must have seemed like the father she'd never known. I remember how proud of me Sally was when I successfully defended Abe and his fetal tissue research before a congressional committee of know-nothings in '91. And I know that at the time the trust passed to her, four years ago, her first major disbursement was an anonymous gift to Memorial in honor of Dr. Feldman. The rest of the money, by the way, we used for the down payment on the Connecticut country property. Would she have wanted to be buried there? Except for me and Jess, she was alone in the world, which meant it was my decision. Even in the best of circumstances, clearly not the case, I wouldn't have looked forward to handling this. Who does? For all I knew the M.E. might not release the body during a homicide investigation. I should ask Arnie. Or, better, Steve Kim, because it would give me an excuse to talk to him.

Someone carefully placed down the phone on a metallic surface and yelled out, "Dr. Kim." Water was running somewhere near the mouthpiece. I heard the snap of plastic gloves being stripped off, then the sound of feet padding across the linoleum.

"Kim here."

"Steve. Mike Malone. How are you?" The long silence was unmistakable. There was no way I was going to ask him about DNA and no way, had I, that he would have answered.

"Fine, Mike."

"I'm sorry to bother you. I hope you're not put off after such a long time. About Sally, I have an administrative question, nothing more." I heard him suck in his breath and try to think of a way out, but he said nothing. "Can you find out if her body's been released, so my son and I can make the arrangements?"

"Can do," he said, relieved. "Where can I reach you?"

I gave him my direct number. "Thanks, buddy. I owe you a dinner someday, whenever."

"Not necessary, Mike. Sorry about everything," he said and hung up quickly, as if I were the Black Plague, leaving me to speculate about what other damaging forensic data he knew.

Then I called Figlio's voice-mail service and left a message. Deedee, Badger's secretary, buzzed to say his holiness wanted to see me right away. Only a fool, which I assured myself I wasn't, would imagine he had good tidings.

Deedee showed me in to the large sitting room where Badger conferred with our important institutional clients, the hospitals and insurers and drug companies he chose to defend. I'd rather represent the little guy, the one abused by these same organizations. Outsiders are always amazed the firm can handle such disparate interests without a schizophrenic breakdown. The partners, however, were color-blind. All green was treated equally. In fact, my class actions were very lucrative. Especially the silicone. Complicated, generous, and long-term, stuffed with fees of all kinds for administration, contingency, you name it.

If the settlement went as expected it would support the overhead of Badger, Weissberg all the way to the millennium. Even for these high-end consumers, it takes a lot of purchases to spend seventy-five million dollars.

Martin Badger entered stiffly and sat behind the Louis XIV antique desk that Napoleon had once used. Badger was jacketless and as a result he looked overstuffed, his abdomen protruding past the plane of his red suspenders. For a man in his late sixties, who prided himself on his fitness and cardiovascular status, it was totally out of character. He must have eaten too much breakfast this morning at the club where he hosts a daily rainmaking event. Above his upper lip he wore a pencil-line thin mustache of sweat beads.

"What's up?" I said cheerfully.

"Michael," he began, his visage wavering between its usual avuncular, serenely confident demeanor and an atypical half scowl, finally landing on the latter. "This whole situation with you pains me terribly." *Not as much as it does me.* "I'm not sure how we should react. I've given it a lot of thought and I'm still not sure what to do." *Why do you have to do anything? Your wife hasn't been murdered. You're not accused. Your son isn't treating you like a pariah.* "We do have to think of the firm's best interests, which I'm sure you understand and agree with."

*Oh yes, the firm. The whole is greater than the sum of its lawyers.* "Of course," I said.

It was all understandable. Badger was the head of a business, a very large, very profitable, revenue-generating operation. As such he had a fiduciary responsibility to the stockholders, the partners, to prevent profit erosion, put a stop to employee distraction, reassure our clients that my problems wouldn't somehow redound to their disadvantage. Preserve, honor, and protect till death do us part.

"We need to create, I know you understand, a judicious

appearance, at least, of some distance. I want to do everything I can to protect partnership equity, yours included, and our ability to help our clients. I think that's paramount, that's what we can do best to help you through this."

"What exactly did you have in mind?" I asked, not because I was in a hurry to know, but because I was tired of the unctuous explanations.

"A leave of absence until your personal affairs are settled."

"Who would handle my clients?" I asked.

"You're on wind-down from the silicone gel, right?" I nodded. "And the wrongful death we can do a stipulation."

"A stip saying what?"

"Long-term continuance, for one."

"A continuance. We're in the middle of a trial," I protested.

"If you prefer, one of the associates could pick up the baton. I'm sure Judge Sherman will, under the circumstances, agree to a change of counsel. I'm told they could be up to speed in one day," he declared.

He probably heard that from his friends in the Police Department.

"I'd consider a cocounsel. As long as any stips or negotiations are approved by me," I said.

"Fine, we can do that," he quickly said. But he was too eager to please and his tone wasn't sincere. My gut told me they were throwing my client to the wind. The powers that be in the universe were taking advantage of my personal plight to screw Roberto Lopez, my client.

"Okay. Memorialize it in writing," I demanded.

"Excuse me," he said, clearly taken aback, unused to anyone impugning his word.

I ignored his upset. "One other point we need to discuss." Badger looked at me warily. "I'd like an early down payment of my partnership income. I don't want to wait for the June thirty regular distribution. I have a lot of costs ahead of me to get out of this mess."

As I spoke Badger's face became so red I wondered if he might be having a cardiovascular incident. "I thought you understood. The leave of absence from the firm is without remuneration. Your share will be held in escrow for you. It'll look better as far as the media is concerned if we do it that way."

"I'll tell you what, Martin. I've changed my mind. A stipulation in the Lopez case won't be necessary." Badger smiled, sure I'd capitulated. "I've decided I'll continue to handle the case myself." I stood up to leave. "Nice seeing you again."

"You can't do this. The partners will vote you out and more," he stammered.

"Try. It'll be a wonderful litigious diversion from my problems. Give it your best." Under my breath I added, "asshole," and stormed off.

# CHAPTER 14

I hunkered down in my office and called Arnie a few times. "He's still not returned from a pretrial on the Island. When he does, I'll tell him you called, Mr. Malone." I reached into my desk, pulled out the dog-eared twenty-fifth anniversary issue of *Rolling Stone*, and escaped.

The phone rang. "You got a TV in your office?" Figlio asked.

"Yeah. Does Jess know about my indictment?"

"Turn on *News One*."

"Why?" I said. I've disciplined myself never to watch television during the daytime because I fear I'd waste the whole day but it was, after all, almost time for the early evening news.

"Just turn it on."

A news conference. Police brass, led by the Chief of Detectives, one James McIlhenny, walked onto the stage. The chief read a prepared statement. "The Department has placed in protective custody Jess Malone, son of Dr. Michael Malone and the late Mrs. Malone, who was murdered sometime last week. Mr. Malone, a minor, is being represented, at his request, by a Legal Aid attorney, appointed on his behalf. No further information is available at this time. Thank you."

"They can't do that," I shouted.

"Wake up. They can. They have. Get your attorney's ass down there."

"How'd you hear about it?" I asked.

"Some buddies tipped me. They rousted him at the Javits Convention Center. Some kinda techno-nerd convention. They had a warrant out for him as a material witness. A private dick recognized him."

"Wasn't he with you at the boat?"

"I'm not a baby-sitter, Malone. The captain sent over a cruiser this morning 'cause they needed me to fill in on the day shift."

"Why didn't you tell me? I would have sent someone over to the boat to stay with Jess."

"I called."

"Yeah, Diane told me. But you didn't tell her anything."

"I didn't know how permanent she was."

"Why didn't you call that teacher, Jasper what's-his-name?"

"Didn't have time."

"Did you know they had a warrant out?" I asked Figlio.

"No. I'm not downtown too much, you know that."

"Maybe you should be," I said, irritated. "The big guys are out to fry my ass. The fix is in."

"Stop feelin' sorry for yourself. I'll see if I can find out what's going down. You call Arnie," he commanded.

It took Arnie and me three hours before we caught up with Jess. The cops had been deliberately moving him from precinct to precinct on orders from above to keep us apart. After I telephoned a friendly columnist who in turn called the D.A., the dance stopped and we were able to regain custody. In the meantime, however, Jess had been allowed to sit for an interview with a reporter from the *Post*, the transparent purpose of which was to throw down the media gauntlet, spin the case in their direction, and send a message that the D.A.'s office was going to use every tactic to destroy me. By tomorrow every Tom, Dick, and Jane would know Jess was the teenage version of Baby S and every moralizing SOB would say, *I told you so. Not a good idea to fiddle with the natural order of things. What goes around, comes around.*

I never should have let Sally talk me into keeping Jess's identity hidden from him, especially since now, with her death, I'd be the one taking all the shit. Of course, I could always sell out Lopez and I'd bet my firstborn some of this would stop.

Arnie didn't want to listen to my rantings on prosecutorial venom. "I know you, kid. First of all, if they believe that you're the embodiment of the rich, successful, attention-grabbing, fun-loving legal hotshot then they're really fucked and we should get them some professional help," he said and laughed a little too heartily, which I didn't appreciate.

"And how about the Lopez case?"

"They're unimaginative, not stupid. No way they mix and match 'em."

Jess was standing by himself, leaning against the wall near the water fountain, and gave me no acknowledgment when we entered the Thirty-eighth Precinct community room, though I smiled broadly in his direction. At a distance, he looked okay. He'd changed his clothes. Dressed in the semiofficial standard urban high school uniform— black T-shirt, tucked in, under a plaid unbuttoned L. L. Bean Black Watch flannel shirt, hanging out from his black jeans, black shoes with very thick soles, he looked the part of the disaffected scion of professional parents. At least he had no baseball cap on backward.

I went over to him directly and gave him a big hug. He stiffened. A deeper version of Monday's post–school trip sullenness had set in. There were so many possible explanations I decided there was no point in pursuing any of them at this time, in this police place. It could wait.

"Jess, this is Mr. Glimcher, our attorney. Arnie, my son, Jess." Arnie extended a hand to Jess, who glared and shook hands limply.

A thirty-something young woman stepped forward to introduce herself. "Dr. Malone, I'm Barbara Golden, Legal Aid. How do you do, sir?"

"Fine. Our attorney, Arnie Glimcher." We all shook hands.

"May I talk to you privately for a second, Dr. Malone?" Ms. Golden requested.

"Sure," I answered, and we walked to a far corner of the room, which was empty except for a blackboard hiding a stack of folding chairs and the watercooler.

"I'm worried about Jess," she began. "He seems so upset, so within himself." Who else could he be within? I thought, but who could argue with someone whose tone was so heartfelt? She rubbed her hands together, looked deeply pensive, worrying whether she should say more. In a less socially unstable era, Ms. Golden could have been a settlement-house social worker, a matron in an orphanage, maybe even a pioneer woman raising her children alone as her husband went off to fight the rustlers or locusts or some other demon, but today in our sink-or-swim, tough-love society she was a person with a crippling dosage of portable social consciousness, thus out of step with her clients' realities.

"A lot has happened," I said.

"It's good to let the rage out," she said with such earnestness I almost forgot how banal, how patronizing her psychobabble was.

"Is that why Jess gave an interview to the reporter?"

She blushed. "It was his choice."

"His choice?" I raised my eyebrows. "His choice?" I

raised my voice. "Aren't you supposed to represent him, buffer him from his choice? Aren't you supposed to protect his rights and his interests? Aren't you there to stop others from pushing him into self-destructive situations? Or am I just from Mars and that's somehow inconsistent with what attorneys are supposed to do on behalf of their clients?"

I watched Ms. Golden as she tightened her body, drawing her bodily armor around her. "It . . . was . . . what . . . ," she stammered, "what he wanted." Slowly, deliberatively, her words and manner enhancing her ineffectualness, she continued, "I considered it his first step. One step at a time to find his moral center—"

I cut her off. I'd heard enough. "Look, Ms. Golden, moral centers are luxuries for your clients. Keep your self-help–codependency–victim crap to yourself. If you can't, and you want to be a missionary, find another job."

Ms. Golden was the type of person who allowed the system to victimize her clients and afterward became upset and self-righteous about it, without having the slightest clue she was an accomplice, a cocreator of the victimhood in the first place. It was one of the reasons I'd left cardiology: I was sick of patients who ate too much, smoked like chimneys, didn't exercise, and then asked me to find a way to prevent their problems. Prevent? Forget it. Damage control was all I could do for them. Which was the same situation Arnie and I found ourselves in with respect to Jess.

"Ms. Golden, were you present for the whole time the police interviewed Jess?" Arnie asked.

"Yes," she said, but I detected uncertainty.

So did Arnie. "Was she?" he asked Jess.

"Sorta," he said.

With hand motions, like a partner in charades, Arnie encouraged Jess to elaborate. "Like how?"

"Not in the police car. The detectives asked me questions then."

"Had they read you your rights?" Arnie continued.

"You have the right to remain silent. Everything you say can be taken down—" Jess started.

Arnie clapped Jess on the back. "Chip off the old blocks. Yeah. Did they?"

"Nooo," Jess shook his head.

"Great, kid," Arnie said and playfully jabbed at Jess. I realized I didn't know much about Arnie's personal life except that he lived somewhere in Westchester and commuted by Metro North into the City. He must have had kids. I hope so. He was good with them. At least he was with Jess, who wasn't easy. Not now, anyway.

"It almost doesn't matter," Arnie said to me, "what they talked about. He wasn't Mirandized, so screw them and their info."

"Maybe not in terms of admissibility, but—"

Arnie interrupted me. "You're right, kid. Smart as your son. Now, Jess, tell me exactly what these bozos asked and what you told them."

"They asked me stuff about Dad and Sally."

It made me sad to hear that our son had replaced "Mom" with "Sally."

"What kind of stuff?" Arnie asked.

"Whether they got into fights. Whether Dad had a girlfriend. Did he spend a lot of money? That kind of stuff."

"Whadidya say?"

"Nothing, really. Just average family stuff. I don't think Dad spends a lot of money. I wasn't sure if Diane was a girlfriend, but I told them about her."

I kept quiet, but it was starting to piss me off. Who gave those jokers the right to pry without me and Jess having any protections? Screw those bastards.

"Did they ask for a blood sample at any time?" Arnie asked.

Jess's face lit up. "Yeah. They said I had to. I didn't want to, but they wouldn't listen and brought a nurse down to the room. They told me it was routine police procedure and I had to do it. Didn't I want to find out who killed my mom? one of them said. What kind of son was I? a lady cop asked me. They asked me if I knew what contempt of court was. They said I could be put in jail by a judge if I didn't let the nurse take my blood. When I still refused, they started yelling at me."

"So you didn't let them take your blood?" Arnie asked.

"No."

"You knew they didn't have the right. That's great, kid," Arnie declared.

"No, that's not why," Jess said. "I'm afraid of needles, right, Dad?"

"Guess what, Jess. Even though I'm a doctor, so am I." I hugged Jess as hard as I could. This time he didn't stiffen. "They didn't have the right to your blood, Jess. Period."

"Dad," Jess began, "if you don't mind, I'd like to spend another night on the boat."

"You don't know if it's all right with Lieutenant Figlio."

"He said it was. Please, Dad."

"Okay," I agreed. At least he hadn't called me "Mike."

# CHAPTER 15

EVEN though Sally had worked there for many years, that early Thursday morning was only the third time I'd visited the Office of the District Attorney on official, or even unofficial, business.

Donald Gramb, the District Attorney for New York County, was first elected by the people in 1964, the year Johnson won the presidency in a landslide. Because he was the only Republican to triumph in any contest of importance, he was immediately proclaimed the fair-haired, future savior and in 1972 was nominated by the muck-a-mucks to run for governor. He was, however, handily defeated by the incumbent Democrat who, though lackluster, was a man of the people, rather than a patrician snob. His loss was particularly galling because Nixon's victory was even more one-sided than Johnson's, which goes to show, if you didn't already know, how unpredictable and totally silly politics is.

Hurt by popular rejection, Gramb never again sought higher office, and for the past twenty-plus years had been content to hold on to his first and only elected position. As a young D.A. his efforts could best be described as energetic, and his prosecutions as trendsetting. In contrast, today's atmosphere at the department was stale, running on habit rather than creative juices.

There was, ironically, one extremely relevant exception. To his credit, Gramb had the foresight to create the first sex crimes unit in any county in the U.S.A., a model everyone emulated, and to hire Sally away from Williamson Communications, where she'd been Vice-president, Legal, and the architect of their anti–sexual harassment programs (also widely copied throughout the corporate world), to head the S.C.U. Most people would have gone the other way—from the S.C.U. to W.C., but not Sally. As far as she was concerned, this was the job to die for.

Given how complicated my situation was (grieving estranged husband or accused spousal murderer), Don (Gramb's nickname, the only residue of his populist campaign) greeted Arnie and me affably enough. "Nice to see you again. Sorry about the circumstances," he said for my benefit.

His handshake was firm and he still looked fit for a man on the upside of fifty, though I did notice a slight hand tremor, which may have been the result of age, anxiety, disappointments, or too much alcohol. Probably booze, because his complexion was rubicund, with many tiny arterioles fanning out, like windblown hair, along both cheekbones.

He put his feet up on the corner of his desk. Hand-crafted, mahogany-colored wing tips that spoke of England and horses and solidity—soft, pliant leather resting against perfectly pressed woolen slacks. Gold cuff links on white cuffs, white spread-collar divided by a red Valentino silk tie, blue-striped shirt making him look even thinner, fitter—the whole package giving Gramb an effete undertone that clashed with his job description, but maybe he felt he had an inalienable right to shop. Hardly a crime just because I'd deliberately made Bloomie's, Barneys, and Bergdorf's distant marital memories. He shifted in his swivel chair, no longer facing us head-on, showing his left profile. "Your dime, gentlemen," he said, age and socio-economic disconnectedness revealed.

Arnie began haltingly. He seemed tentative, a little rusty perhaps, in the presence of the D.A., which was understandable. "We're concerned," Arnie paused to clear a throat frog, "that in the inimitable words of Johnnie Cochran, Jr., there seems to be a rush to judgment here. I've represented Dr. Malone for some time, most recently with his divorce, a proceeding that has been not without legal skirmishing between the parties, but when all is said and reviewed, was basically amicable. We have no priors of any kind. In fact, another point that needs to be underlined, this action was begun by Mrs. Malone. We're not dealing here with a rage situation, a woman or man spurned kind of thing." Gramb tightened his neck muscles at that point and made a microscopic adjustment of his collar. "If anything, just the opposite."

"We have strong probable cause, Mr. Grimcher. I'm sure you understand that it isn't appropriate for me to discuss the evidence at this time, but I know the lead prosecutors will be happy to sit with you and see if we can't find some common ground."

"If you're talking plea, forget it. We have no intention whatsoever of going down that road," Arnie bristled. "You don't have motive."

"We believe we have more than enough. So, too, I might add, did the Grand Jury."

Gramb's last remark broke Arnie's ice. "Let's cut the bull, okay, Mr. Gramb?" The Arnie I know and loved and hired was launched. "Grand Jury indictments mean squat. You guys could use them to nail the pope if you wanted to. Big deal."

Gramb interrupted, "We have," and here Gramb lifted

both arms, as if he was bestowing a blessing on the St. Peter's faithful or lifting a massive beach ball, "a lot."

"I don't wanna get into a pissin' contest with you, Gramb. We all know how mountains of evidence can turn into piles of slush and go right down the toilet. Let's get down to business."

"Which is?" Gramb raised his left eyebrow, the only one I could see.

"We want full access to your department—which we're entitled to. We're going to need to interview all the people on Mrs. Malone's staff, look over the cases she's been handling. And we'll also need a full accounting of any and all problems associated with the dirtbags she's prosecuted."

"We'll cooperate, of course. But there's no requirement or reason I'm aware of why we have to do so on your timetable, Mr. Grimcher," Gramb said as he turned into his right profile.

Arnie caught him between sides. "To make your life easier."

"Yours, and your client's, you mean. We're not about to turn this department upside down and jump through hoops and put our efforts in jeopardy just because you ask us to."

"You're missing my point," Arnie began, sounding more patient than I suspected he felt. "I fully anticipate you can raise objections to some of this on the grounds of confidentiality. No one wants to jeopardize any of your pending investigations. We're all lawyers here, all officers of the court, including, may I remind you, my client, Dr. Malone. The issue is: will you make this access easy for us or will we have to bust balls and drag it out of you, which, as you know, we will ultimately be entitled to do in our search for exculpatory."

"You're not entitled to a fishing expedition," Gramb growled, the blood flow reddening the facial butterfly.

"Look, my client can affirm and attest that on many occasions his wife came home troubled about some of the characters she was prosecuting, necessitating, in fact, unlisted phone numbers, and on two occasions police protection for the family, all of which can be corroborated."

"We don't have the staff or the budget or the time to do all you seem to want," Gramb said limply. It didn't take much, it would seem, to make our Beau Brummell public prosecutor back down.

Arnie panned Gramb in all his Easter finery with an intense glare. "I'm sure you have enough."

"We doubt there's a link here to Sally's murder," he said.

I was struck by the "Sally." Gramb, though he'd directly hired her, wasn't one of the names from the office Sally bandied about, almost as if each had forgotten about the other's existence. At the department's annual dinner dances, I couldn't recall the two of them having contact. If anything, Gramb seemed stuck at his table, waiting beside his thin plastic surgery–correct wife for the members of his team to make their obeisances. Which Sally, to her credit, never did.

"Have you investigated that possibility?" Arnie asked Gramb.

"We've looked at lots of areas. I'm not privy to all of them, obviously, but I'm satisfied we've been thorough."

"But on a limited budget, of course," Arnie tweaked.

"Is that it? Are we finished? We seem to be circling La Guardia—I do have other matters to attend to."

"Do we have an agreement then?" Arnie asked.

Gramb took his feet off the desk, I suppose to signal the meeting was ending, and stared intently at both of us, full face, and for some reason I had the impression that no one was home, and hadn't been for a long time. "We can work something out. Next week I'll have my secretary call yours."

"Forget it. That's unacceptable. Any first-year law student knows now's the time in a criminal case to look for leads," Arnie protested.

"That's the best we can do, Mr. Grimcher," he said, rising up behind his desk, mangling Arnie's name once again, and trying in vain to substitute stubbornness for decisiveness.

"It's not good enough," Arnie replied, angry.

"May I remind you, Mr. Grimcher, this is a murder indictment, not one of your usual high-profile matrimonials, and we, not you, dictate the pace and terms of the investigation and the cooperation."

"First of all, it's Glimcher. Second, let's get something straight right now. Dr. and Mrs. Malone have some rather substantial joint assets. Now that she has been murdered, my client intends to avail himself of them, as his right, in order to defend himself against this asinine indictment and hopefully uncover who the real murderer is. As you may know, both Dr. Malone and myself, on behalf of our clients, are skilled users and abusers of the media. We might start with the clear abuse of prosecutorial power with regard to Dr. Malone's son. Then, of course, there's the Lopez case. No big deal to raise the specter of police cover-up and how it relates to your actions. I'm sure our own East Coast dream team can uncover all kinds of nice things about this case and your department, so if you or any of your flunkies obstruct or obfuscate or otherwise become a pain in the butt you're gonna be left with one big hemorrhoid."

"Are you threatening me?" Gramb shouted.

"You bet, kid. But I'll tell you, just to show you I'm really a nice guy, I'm gonna send over a stip this morning, outlining what will be in our mutual interests, and you know what, I'd be willing to bet you a pair of Ralph Lauren slippers you'll think this approach makes a whole lotta sense."

"And what do the People gain from this?" Gramb asked softly, his voice unsteady.

"Confidence," Arnie replied. "Confidence that their elected public law enforcement officers aren't wasting public money and aren't as stupid and as prone to acting outside the law as they might otherwise appear to be."

We left, none of us bothering to be so disingenuous as to shake hands. "Is that guy or isn't that guy a wuss in fancy clothes?" Arnie observed.

I wasn't so certain about writing Gramb off. Some of the wimpiest people can be, if you push them past their personal envelopes, the roughest, meanest, most tenacious opponents.

I helped Arnie with the stip and we sent it over in the late morning. A bicycle messenger returned it two hours later, signed, validating Arnie's "wuss," eradicating my "tenacious," but mostly arousing litigational suspicions. "I always worry when someone's being too cooperative too quickly," I said to Arnie.

Arnie adjusted his glasses, which had slipped down his short, almost childish nose. "I have an insight," he said. "I see why Sally was divorcing you." He paused for the punch line. "You're suffering from occupational paranoia." I started to defend myself, but stopped. He was right. "Look, kid, trust me. I know how this profession makes us too cynical. It's hard not to be when one hears all the awful things people do to each other, about the secrets they hide, not to mention the assets, about lives turned against themselves. No one—not you, not me, not the president, not the D.A.—wants his personal life or even his professional life and activities examined. In our society only an exhibitionist would. So instead of sinking into that swamp of suspicions, why don't we try to focus on the facts? What the D.A. has? Where he got it? Whether it's accurate or contaminated? If there's mitigating evidence they haven't considered? That kind of thing. Okay, kid? If the D.A. wants to cooperate, let's just take it as a sign of practical maturity and not waste our time analyzing his motives. You were a cardiologist, not a shrink, right?"

"There could be something Gramb doesn't want us to find out," I said.

"Yeah. So? I don't mean to be a ball buster, kid, but the bottom line is we don't have the resources to find out. We're basically in defensive mode. We have no choice 'cept to leave the investigatory stuff to the police, and use our wits to shoot holes in their shit. I know what you're thinking—forget my fancy speech to Gramb—if we could really put together a dream team we'd send them out looking for who killed your wife, right? 'Cause the cops aren't gonna bother—their minds were made up long ago."

"That's what I'm afraid of," I said.

"Good, we agree. Now, how 'bout your police buddy?"

"Figlio."

"Yeah. See what he's found out," Arnie said.

I wanted to linger, unwind, and share my thoughts with Arnie, but his phone kept ringing, interrupting both of us. With each successive call, Arnie was becoming more impatient. I edged myself to the door, realizing it was up to me to leave. For all his brusqueness, Arnie was an excessively polite pussycat and would never have suggested I go.

"Do you mind if I call my office?" I asked.

"*Mi casa, su casa.* Just press eight first."

Lydia reported that Badger was frantic to meet with me. "Tell him I'll be able to see him some time after noon as my schedule's looking good." I smiled, impressed with my breeziness.

Lydia greeted me with a sour face, as if she'd rushed lunch and it hadn't agreed with her. "Between Mr. Badger and Dr. Feldman I'm going to lose it."

"Anything else?" I asked, trying to ignore Lydia's gloom and doom and by so doing make the reason for it evaporate.

"No, but Dr. Feldman is really driving me nutso."

"What did you tell him?" I asked sharply.

Lydia blushed, unsure if she'd done the right thing. "That you're sorry you forgot the appointment, but that you're all booked up today, and we'd have to get back to him later this afternoon."

"Fine," I said and walked into my office.

"But he keeps calling. Every twenty minutes. He says it's a 'stat' situation." She looked at her watch. "He'll be calling in four minutes. You want me to say you haven't returned and aren't expected?"

I considered her suggestion, but if it were truly an emergency, I'd be calling every twenty minutes myself. Maybe Dr. Feldman's legal problems, whatever they were, would distract me from mine. "No, I'll talk with him."

I closed the door behind me, sat down, and waited for the phone to ring. The internal intraoffice, interpersonal communications channel had probably already notified Badger I'd arrived. He'd said nothing good to me yesterday; a second meeting could only be worse. Yet in all fairness to him my nameplate hadn't been removed, the locks

were unchanged, and my secretary hadn't been transferred
to the suite of a more viable partner. Even so I felt isolated,
abandoned, unwanted. Perhaps my impassioned performance had impressed Badger and stopped him from im-
plementing his cowardly plan. More likely, he couldn't
raise a quorum of partners to certify his faithlessness. But
it might be, and when I think about Badger and his
bottom-line brain I favor the following mental scenario:
he remembered the disbursement protocols for the silicone settlement and decided to leave me alone. Because
the one thing you could bank on with regard to Badger
was that he never acted out his self-destructive impulses.

I don't want to brag, but the arrangement the court im-
plemented for the administration of the silicone settlement
was a stroke of genius. It wasn't luck and Arnie should
give me credit for more than a little farsightedness. After
I'd told the court that our firm wanted to avoid even the
appearance of comingling, the court had agreed to my
suggestion that the monies be disbursed through a special
trustee account of which I, on behalf of the plaintiffs, was
the only signatory. In view of the pain and suffering the
plaintiffs had suffered, we didn't, Your Honor, want them
to worry about how the settlement monies sitting in a
Badger Weissberg–controlled account would be disbursed.
"They have no relationship with Badger Weissberg, nor
need they," I'd said.

"Refreshing," "paragon," "moral gold standard" is how
the judge characterized the plan. Best of all, the defendants, through their lawyers, who were still in shock from
the size and finality of the settlement, didn't raise any objections to the disposal plan.

Of course I never told the judge about my divorce proceedings, and there was no reason I should have. He didn't
have to know about the angry argument Sally and I had

had about equitable distribution, and of my desire to shield as much of my assets as I could from the beady eyes of her attorney. Badger approved the arrangement, gleefully in fact. I remember thinking he must have had a bad divorce once upon a time.

Abe Feldman's call interrupted the self-praise. What struck me first was that I'd forgotten how high-pitched Dr. Feldman's voice was. "Mike, have you read the file?"

"No, I haven't had a chance. Abe, I really can't help you, whatever it is."

Abe wasn't put off. "I need your help to get a temporary restraining order as soon as possible."

"TRO for what?" I asked.

"To restrain University Med Center from shutting down our facility at midnight."

"What kind of facility are we talking about?"

"Oh, I'm sorry, it was in the papers, I thought you knew. I'm the director of the Center for Human Biology."

"When did that happen? I thought you were at Memorial."

"I've been here three years."

"What's the Center do?" I asked.

"You don't know?" Feldman sounded surprised. "We're a lab and diagnostic facility in the human fertility and vital fluids areas."

"After I worked so hard for you, and won, why'd you leave Memorial?"

"The Center made me a great offer."

"And this is about an eviction?"

"On the surface."

"Abe, don't you have a lawyer who's been handling this?" I asked.

"I fired them Monday. That's why I've been calling."

Bad planning. No wonder everyone says doctors are lousy in business. "What's your connection to University?"

"We're sponsored by them. Many of us have faculty appointments there. We have a standard affiliation contract, like what you had at Mount Zion."

Under normal circumstances, I would have asked him why and how this dispute came about, and why the university was so intent upon shutting them down, but I knew the answer would be long and largely irrelevant, and that it wouldn't change my mind. "Abe, with all due respect, I sense your case may well be very complicated, and I'm not sure I'm the right person to sort this all out at this point in time. What you need is a landlord and tenant lawyer."

"You're a physician, Mike, which means we can get to the real issues faster. Trust an old man's judgment. You're the man to help us."

"Abe, I can't. I need help myself right now. You need someone who can give you more than I can."

"I know this isn't a very good time for you. I sympathize with your predicament. And, for whatever it's worth, I don't believe the charges. Time will vindicate you." Feldman paused, perhaps to allow me to demonstrate my gratitude, but I was in a quirky mood and withheld it. "And like you," he resumed, "we have the same kind of difficulty. Forces arrayed against us, unfairly. I just need you to get us the TRO—it's breathing room until I can marshal our defenses."

"Even if it's granted, which sounds like a long shot, the university will move for an immediate stay and appeal. That means more papers will have to be filed. There'll be another court appearance, and I honestly just don't have the energy to devote to this, that's the big problem. It's not fair to your case. Why not let me recommend some other lawyers who'll do a fine job for you?"

"I'm an older man, Mike, a little stubborn perhaps, but I really want you. Even with your distractions, you're the most appropriate attorney for this situation. You did a great job for me the last time."

"That was different. It was more up my alley."

"I saw you on *Court TV* with the silicone case. You did a helluva job. And this situation here is similar."

This time I acknowledged the compliment. "Thanks. Listen to me, Abe. I think you can do better at this moment in terms of legal representation. I'm under siege myself. It's a mistake for you to think I'll be able to devote anywhere near my full resources to solving your problem. You've got a midnight deadline and I haven't read the file or anything. I just can't do it." I heard my voice becoming a little shrill. Add additional stressors and I'd be hysterical. Feldman deserved a calm, reasoned advocate, not me. Why didn't he understand this?

"I can walk you through the crux. Please, Mike, spend an hour with me. I know this case inside out. If, after the one hour, you want to walk away, I'll hire whoever you say. How's that? One hour."

There are some people, we all know them, who refuse to accept a turndown, even if the rejection benefits them. I could argue until I turned to dust and he wouldn't change. "Let me ask you this, Abe, will the other side consent to hold it over till tomorrow or the next day?"

"No, the university's coming under a lot of pressure."

"Let me take a different tack," I said. "Is there any reason why you don't just break the affiliation contract and move your operations elsewhere?"

"In the current social environment it might take a while to find a replacement medical center with the courage to affiliate with us. And then there's the fragility of the biological materia to consider, as well as the move being very disruptive and expensive. We don't have a lot of flexibility given that the university has frozen our bank accounts."

"How were they able to do that?" I asked.

"They're joint accounts. They've alleged, I think under state RICO laws, you know the law they use against the Mafia, really ironic, that we've engaged in conspiracies to defraud the public through, in their words, unauthorized transplanting of eggs and embryos, failure to maintain adequate records on blood and other bodily fluids we store, and conducting research without our clients' knowledge or consent."

"Have you?" I asked.

He chortled, "I'll answer you this way. Last year I was nominated for the Nobel for Medicine. I'm a scientist, a careful scientist. These charges are a smoke screen."

"Aren't you licensed by the Health Department?" I asked.

"Yes."

"If it's a smoke screen, why won't they intercede on your behalf?"

Feldman laughed, "Without trying to be clever, let's just say there's a lot of bad blood between us. The Health Department is one of the parties behind this. They want to kill everything."

"Why?" I asked gently. Maybe Abe was going senile. The last thing I needed was to walk into a paranoid-conspiratorial swamp.

"We've stepped on a lot of toes."

Instead of feigning another call and terminating the conversation, I stupidly asked, "Whose specifically?"

He answered indirectly, "Political. The whole pro-life crowd, some of whom are big donors to the university. Tobacco interests. I've done much of the research on the effects of smoking on the unborn fetus. The Red Cross."

"The Red Cross?"

"They're one tough organization. Did you know they earn revenues in excess of one billion dollars from their blood products? They don't like competition from any source. And they have lots of friends in high places, hiding as they do behind their Clara Barton image."

"Come on, Abe. Aren't you carrying this a bit far? The *Red Cross*?" If he were younger I would have asked, *What're you smoking?*

"Mike, I can hear you're starting to think I'm pre-Alzheimer's. I know it sounds far-fetched, but if you'd come over to our offices and I could show you the documentation, your skepticism would disappear. You'll see we're in the same boat."

"How's that?" I asked.

"We've both been falsely accused of something," Dr. Feldman declared.

I almost blurted out, *How're you so sure about me?* but caught myself. Innocent flippant remarks can be twisted and recounted one day, out of context, in court. "Okay," I said, one beleaguered worn-out soul helping another, "I can you give an hour. What's the address?"

Lydia caught me on the way out. "What about Badger? He's waiting for you. What do I tell him?"

"He'll have to wait a little longer."

The Center for Human Biology, Incorporated, was located in a small nondescript building that, from the outside, didn't look as if it was even remembered by the university: the white brick façade was in desperate need of pointing and cleaning and was defaced by a natural graffiti of auto emission grime and pigeon droppings. The protective paint on the metal window sashes had bubbled up and peeled, exposing deep scabs of rust. The sidewalk out front was much littered, as if a tightly focused tornado had sucked up the waste collecting against the

Soleil de Provence restaurant to the west, and the University Nursing School to the east, and dumped the whole mess at the entrance to the Center.

A dented metal box loosely attached to the wall housed an intercom. Aside from the Center the only other tenant seemed to be John Guzzilli Photographers on the second floor. I pushed the Center's button and was immediately buzzed in without anyone checking my bona fides. To my surprise the lobby was spiffy with black marble flooring and walls, and must have been a beneficiary of the recent short-lived period of inflated real estate values and commercial optimism.

The Center occupied the third through sixth floors. The dreamy-eyed receptionist announced my presence to Dr. Feldman, who quickly appeared. "Mike, how nice of you to come," he said, as if I was an unexpected guest at a lawn party. This short, bald, elderly though sprightly man led me to his office past many laboratories staffed by white-coated technicians who seemed purposeful and, more to the point, uncontaminated by any threat of imminent unemployment.

The first thing I noticed about Abe's office was the art. Like many older, financially successful physicians, he was an afficionado—every available surface was filled with statuary, primitive wooden sculpture mostly of pregnant women or women nursing babies or women with other women, while figures of men were absent, which I thought strange, as we males, even in an age of high-technology alternatives, were the necessary precursors for fertility. Abe sat down behind his highly polished wood desk, its intricate inlaid pattern clearly the work of a master artisan. Behind him were matching bookshelves, filled with books carefully arranged by size, spine color, and subject. The other walls of his office were covered with diplomas and honors of all kinds. Abe was a serious scientist, a man of significant achievement and social connectedness—a photo of Abe and the president taken in the White House Rose Garden, a gold key to some city or state or country resting in an open velvet-lined box, a laminated newspaper story about a benefit at the Metropolitan, framed congratulatory letters from distinguished people—Henry Kissinger's florid signature caught my eye, as well as signed photos of celebrities whose households had been populated with the help of Dr. Abraham Feldman.

The Center for Human Biology was a deep-pocketed, plugged-in enterprise that should have been able to weather anything and should not have been in this defensive position in the first place. As Abe had correctly pointed out, the same could be said for me.

Forget the similarities, disregard the bonding, I reminded myself. This was a sinkhole. Others could help Abe, others could minister to him and handle his legal troubles. He had to understand I had my own personal deadlines. He had to find someone else or restore his relationship with his previous attorneys. If I were in his legal shoes, that's what I'd do. "Who were your attorneys?" I asked.

"John Stevens at Gorham Grant and Hayes. Do you know him?"

"Not personally," I answered, which was true, though if someone had wanted to hire the quintessential white shoe, Waspy, big law firm partner, many lawyers would probably suggest Stevens. "But he's supposedly a great litigator. I *do* know the firm."

Their name anyway. The only place that never bothered to give me an interview when I was third-year law review and job prospecting, living up to their reputation as anti-Irish, anti-Semitic, anti-Catholic, anti-everybody who wasn't exactly like them. All these years later, it still bothered me.

"They're very influential. It doesn't make sense you'd fire them."

"I had no choice. They were trying to sell us out to the university."

"John Stevens?"

"Gorham Grant. I don't know if John knew."

"Did you ask him?"

"Yes and no."

"Which means?" I asked.

"He hemmed and hawed inappropriately."

"And?"

"That was all I needed," Abe declared. I exhaled loudly. "I know how it sounds. You feel I've acted prematurely, that I've been unfair to John. But I am a scientist. I made a reasonable deduction based on the evidence."

"I haven't heard any. But be that as it may and more to the point, from where I sit it appears you've only hurt yourself. You have a drop-dead deadline tonight and no attorney. If your body was about to be hammered with a virulent infection, would it make sense to you to remove all your white cells from your blood?"

"Yes, if they were contaminated. Gorham Grant's in bed with a lot of the trustees of the university. Technically, there's no conflict. No representation of these people, but John should have known this and talked it over. Here, let me show you something." Feldman handed me a fax, the thermal paper curled into a thick roll. "He should have damn well reclused himself, don't you think?"

"Recused," I corrected.

"Yes exactly."

"You know, Abe, I look around your office and I see all these pictures and awards and I remember how distinguished you are and I say to myself, 'Abe and his Center are pretty well connected themselves.' Wouldn't you agree?" I asked.

"We've been fortunate. We've made major contributions in infertility research. We've helped many people, some of them important. Yes."

"At a certain social level, Abe, and I'm sure you've encountered this more than I ever have or will, New York is a very small town. Some might say incestuous. Everyone who's anyone knows everyone else and is involved with everyone else. You're represented by a top lawyer—he has lots of important clients. He wouldn't have taken you on if you weren't also important. Right?" Abe nodded. "So that there's cross-contamination isn't really surprising and certainly isn't a justification for removing your attorney at the eleventh hour."

"Read the fax."

I uncurled the memo, which was addressed to Dr. George Phillips, President and Chief Executive Officer, The University Medical Center. It seems a certain anonymous major donor had expressed a strong interest in bestowing an "unprecedented" donation upon the university for the purpose of medical genetics research. There were, however, "preconditions," which the letter writer did not feel were "too onerous" and which would be handled "by the donor's attorneys, Gorham Grant & Hayes," et cetera, et cetera.

Feldman was impatient to present his case and interrupted me at the bottom of the first page. "By accident, a member of my staff was being recruited for a position at the Medical Center and a friend of his at the university strongly suggested he take the offer because our Center's future wasn't looking too bright. This comment surprised Brian, who like many of my people is very committed to this organization and its welfare. We were able, it's not important how, to obtain this memo and further determine that our closure is one of the 'preconditions.'"

"Do you know why the big donor wants you shut down?" I asked.

"As I told you, Mike, powerful forces don't like the work we do and the choices we've made. So be it. I'm not afraid of them as long as it's a fair fight out in the light because our ideas will eventually prevail. But this sneaky underhanded stuff makes me very angry."

In all honesty, it sounded to me as if Abe and his organization were getting a shabby deal and had a legitimate right to be pissed. In other circumstances, this is a fight I would have willingly joined. But not now, not when I had to defend myself against a possible charge of first degree murder. "Abe. Believe me, I'm very sympathetic to your position. I'd love to help you. But I feel I have to stand by what I said earlier. That is, you need a good lawyer who's not dealing with personal distractions and who knows something about landlord-tenant stuff."

Abe got up from his desk and walked over to retrieve a photograph at the far end of the credenza. I anticipated he was warming to a Churchillian lecture about duty, truth, and responsibility, so idly, defensively, I took shelter in the printed word, and finished reading the fax.

"Oh my God," I said to myself.

To Abe, whose back was to me, I said, "I'll take the case," catching him off guard. He flashed me a big smile, which reminded me of my grandfather in whose eyes I could do no wrong, and the two of us did a geriatric version of high fives.

I wrote Son Ya's address on my business card and handed it to Abe. "Messenger the whole file, everything your attorney sent you, to this address. It's a Korean grocer's near my house. She'll hold everything for me. I'll work on your motion from home. We should be able to put in a show cause tonight."

I know he wanted to ask me what had changed my

mind, but he didn't. It was a good thing, because I wouldn't have heard him, lost as I was in speculation about what it meant that the fax memo had been written by Victoria (Mrs. Donald J.) Gramb, the wife of the District Attorney.

# CHAPTER 16

IT was Figlio's idea to meet at the Roosevelt Island tram station. Not the most convenient place, and not the warmest either. Briny ocean air had attached itself to the rising East River tide, wrapping the homeward-bound commuters in layers of aromatic coldness, making everyone, with their arms folded tightly against coats, seem stolid and depressed. I thought about how Figlio always arranged our interactions on or near or, in this instance, above the water. If someone were to ask me what was my defining nature symbol, I wouldn't have any idea.

The packed tram cab descended past the gridlocked cars on the Fifty-ninth Street Bridge and landed smoothly at the station. After the other passengers had scattered hurriedly like a frightened school of fish I saw Figlio standing in line at the bus shelter across the platform. He motioned to me with a small movement of his hand to join him.

We sat in the rear away from the other riders on seats overly warmed by the diesel engine underneath. "Is the cloak-and-dagger stuff really necessary?" I asked Figlio.

"What do you mean by necessary?" he shot back. Figlio can be, because he's testified in too many trials, legalistic, which, when combined with his basic stubbornness, is yet another reason why his career has plateaued: the police brass concluded he's an arrogant know-it-all, best avoided. Which is too bad because in fact the opposite is true. He listens, he considers all reasonable opinions, is honorable, has good common-sense judgment, and on behalf of what's right, is fearless. You'd think his superiors would appreciate these traits, but bureaucracies aren't always sensible.

"Is this standard operating detective procedure? That's what I mean."

"It is for us."

"How's Jess?" I asked.

"I dropped him at school this morning, if that's what you're asking."

"Thanks. I'm in your debt big-time."

"I know. I bet you've never been to Cetona, the four-star northern Italian buried out near Shea. Maybe when the dust settles we'll give it a try."

"Deal."

"The Lopez case. You asked me to check up on Mal Snyder. Friend of your boss. Friend of the mayor. Friend of the police chief, the D.A., anyone with real power and a few bucks. Malone, you've done me one better—you've managed to piss off a whole lot of important people. I usually stick to the slobs."

"Okay. So what's new?" I said quietly, but I could feel myself becoming angry, very annoyed, agitated that everyone was butting into my case.

"My usual sources are shutting down. The word's out that I'm your buddy, and not that I give a flyin' fuck about bein' falsely associated with you. . . ." I smiled. "But somethin's rotten in Sweden." It was Denmark, but I got the point.

"I told Arnie there was a connection. What with Badger pressuring me to settle."

"Someone wants blood. Payback. They'll do anything to get it."

"What're you saying?" I asked.

"Subornation, counselor. Manufactured evidence, counselor. Tainted evidence. Is that clear enough?"

I couldn't see my reflection in the windowpanes. Had I, I'm certain I would have looked crestfallen, disbelieving, shocked. And not because I'm naive and idealistic. I wasn't born yesterday. I have a law school classmate, Tom Miller, a poor kid from Chicago, who's a Legal Aid lawyer, and from him as well as from my own skeptical observations I know Figlio's story is business as usual rather than the exception. So why am I upset? Because I consider myself a powerful, skilled litigator, a well-known advocate with the resources and the ability to fight back. But these people have me pegged otherwise; they're filing me in the impotent box without my permission.

"How'd they do the frame? They tampered with the blood specimens somehow. How secure is the chain of custody? It's the only way. You have any friends in the police lab?" I asked.

"Not really."

"Is there any way we can prove any of this is going on?" I asked.

"I can't. That's what I'm telling you. I can't get close enough."

"So why're we having this clan-des-teen meeting in this desolate dump if there's nothing you can do? I already know something's screwy. This whole friggin' indictment makes no sense. I *know* I didn't do this. There's no reason for me to kill Sally. There never was. Some SOB had to be framing me all along. That's what's kept me sane. I know they can't have evidence that'll stand up. But if the cops are involved, anything's possible. But you know what, the world's fucked, no argument there, but excuse me if I don't believe it's that fucked. This is too big a risk for them to take to eliminate a small irritation like me. Mal

Snyder's supposed to be smart. Too many people have to be involved. All these guys are too smart."

"Who said it had anything to do with Mal Snyder?" Figlio declared. "Maybe it's the dickheads from Rikers."

"That's what I thought at first. But do you really think that they could pull this off with Internal Affairs watching them?"

"Somebody could be helping. It's possible. Maybe they got something on someone. There aren't enough garbage trucks to pick up all the dirt in this town."

"Can we go past the 'maybe' and find something concrete?"

"I don't know," Figlio answered.

"You're the detective. I mean, can't you detect? Do something. Pay off a snitch. Do whatever you do, you're no friggin' virgin. We're talking about my life here. You think I want to spend the rest of my life, like Harrison Ford, telling Jess and everyone I'm innocent? Half the guys in Rikers probably say that. No one believes them, either."

"Calm down, doc. That was the bad news," Figlio replied.

"Oh. You have some good news, too?" I asked.

"Yes," he said.

Figlio fidgeted. He seemed uncomfortable. Out of character. What next? I thought. "I'm listening."

"You might find it upsetting."

"Cut the preamble. There's not much left that can shock me."

"Okay," Figlio said, resigned almost. "Your wife, your estranged wife that is, was being bopped by the District Attorney."

"Donald Gramb?"

"None other," Figlio said.

"Can you prove that?" I said. My voice cracked.

"Yes."

"Will it hold up in court?"

"It will," Figlio said and looked down at his shoes.

Figlio's information was a lightning bolt. Palpitations thumped into both carotids. I felt hot. I loosened my collar. *Relax. Relax. RELAX*, I yelled inwardly and sighed outwardly, embarrassing Figlio, who'd known the good news would be painful. *Inhale slowly. Slowly. Exhale even more slowly. Be happy. There's light at the end of the tunnel. You have them behind the eight ball. The District Attorney made a big mistake, a newly licensed lawyer mistake. He should have recused himself. No one would have cared.*

When did this relationship start? Did they cuckold me? They'd taken me for a fool. Gramb had insinuated himself into my bed and my family. Fucker. A district attorney who'd pretended to represent justice and fairness at our meeting when he'd already stuck his sticky fingers into the deck and hopelessly stacked it against me. What could Sally have possibly liked about you? You arrogant pathetic politicker, you shameless plea-bargaining panderer. There's the mystery the Grand Jury should investigate. You screwed Sally on silk sheets my Great Aunt Emilia gave us. How many of your pubic hairs have you shed on my property? I'll bet you didn't mention that to the forensics guys. Watch out Gramb, I'm going to drag your skeletons behind my wagon so completely you're going to experience your autopsy while still alive—I'm going to indict your life.

I licked my lips. "What can you find out about the D.A.'s wife?" I asked Figlio, my voice, surprisingly, strong and under control.

Figlio smiled. "The killer lawyer's alive and well. You figure if he wasn't porkin' her she might be upset, full of vengeance. Or porkin' someone else. If you're thinkin' maybe the missus stuffed your wife, that's a reach. Not by herself anyway. She'd kill the hubby first."

The bus stopped at the new subway stop on Roosevelt. "I gotta go," he said, "unless there's somethin' else you wanna say."

"See if you can encourage Jess to come home. I miss him."

"I'm no fuckin' therapist, Malone."

"Nobody said you were," I said.

"Why don't you stay on another round? Just in case someone's watchin'."

"Fine," I said. I needed some time to myself. Figlio got up and strode to the exit without saying good-bye, as if we were strangers. "Hey," I called out. He paused at the bottom of the bus steps. "Her name's Victoria."

"How'd you know that?" he called to me from the curb.

"A little birdie told me," I yelled through the closed window, my breath fogging the pane. Figlio made no comeback and walked quickly away, down the stairs and into the darkness of the subway.

Why did I withhold information from my friend? Attorney-client privilege? That would be bullshit. Maybe— I think this is honest—for a few hours I wanted to have an old-fashioned one-upmanship over the rest of the world. Something, given my inner turmoil, I needed. And, I believe, deserved.

I picked up the Center for Human Biology's litigation file from Son Ya, the Korean grocer on Eighty-eighth Street who's kind enough to act as a depository, purchased some necessities, and headed home. As I climbed the four flights of tenement stairs, hungrily anticipating the Spanish omelet I would make, my load—a dozen eggs, quart of milk, orange juice, bread, and legal papers—seemed disproportionately heavy. By the top landing I was convinced

I was a candidate for an MI. (The degree of my hypochondria is an accurate indicator of my emotional state.)

I never got to eat the eggs. Diane was in my kitchen, very involved in the preparation of an elaborate dinner. I planted a rather perfunctory kiss on her beautiful neck. "Hello. What's the occasion?" I tried to sound cheery, even if I didn't feel it.

"Dinner. Can't really talk now. I have to concentrate on what I'm doing." She was measuring out olive oil, not exactly rocket science.

I put away the perishables and sat myself heavily at the table and watched her, so full of effort and purpose. She looked great, "fetching" is the word that came to mind, but I never hear anyone say that anymore.

"I'm dead. All this is too much," I said to her back, as she vigorously whisked ingredients.

"I know. It seems so unfair after all you've done for them."

The meaning of her words escaped me. Only after she dried her hands on the dish towel and patted me on the shoulder in a motherly fashion, as if to say, buck up you'll be okay, did I realize she was the bearer of more bad news.

"What's unfair?"

"They didn't tell you? Just like them. Those cowards."

"Diane, please put me out of my misery and tell me. I can handle it."

She turned away, unable to look me straight in the eye. "The partnership held a special meeting this afternoon and they've put you on indefinite leave of absence. They've even sealed your office."

Somehow, compared to Sally's murder or her secret love affair with the D.A., or a serious injury to Jess, this development didn't grab me.

"Fuck 'em," I announced.

I picked the Center file up from the floor and hoisted it to the table.

"That's it? That's your reaction? Aren't you going to do something?" she said.

"Like jump up and down. Or cry to the gods of partnership. What did you have in mind?"

"Something. I don't know, I'm not a partner."

"The rules are simple. The partnership can suspend anyone if they feel his or her actions do or may bring harm to the partnership. It's their call."

"You can ask them to reconsider," she implored.

"They will on their own," I said, and started to review Abe Feldman's case. "What're we having for dinner or am I not supposed to ask?"

"How can you be so calm? They're taking everything away from you. How're you going to be able to mount an adequate criminal defense if they tie up your partnership income?"

"They can't," I said.

"They just have."

"Not really. In fact, they're the ones in trouble."

"I don't see how you can say that."

"Trust me. They'll soon be crawling back."

"How can you be so sure?"

"Because unless I'm disbarred, which by the procedures would take many months and would have to await a felony conviction, I'm the only person authorized to disburse the silicone monies to all parties, including attorneys. The firm's been salivating a long time about the settlement dollars and my fellow partners are going to be real unhappy when they realize I hold the key to their financial well-being. It'll be diverting to watch them grovel. Trust me."

"Do they know that?" Diane asked.

"Sort of."

"Sort of?"

"Badger never really paid attention to the details. He doesn't understand how airtight the arrangement is, and how much it favors me. And I doubt he ever mentioned any of this to the other partners. And if he did, they all would have been so fixated on the humongous amount—seventy-five million dollars buys lots of perks—they would've missed the disbursement procedures. So what're we eating?"

"Not crow," she said with a smile.

A big noisy horsefly landed on a sweetened spot of the university's motion for a final notice of eviction, which had been granted almost seventy-two hours ago in State Supreme Court. In my experience the New York Appellate Division rarely, if ever, heard expedited appeals, which meant, my confidence and moxie notwithstanding, I couldn't really deliver a TRO for Abe Feldman in a timely manner. The fly took off and buzzed around my head. I shooed it away, but like everyone else today, it paid no attention and continued to bother me.

"Go to Diane, stupid, that's where the food is," I exclaimed.

"Who're you calling stupid? They ought to sue for discrimination," Diane advised. She was talking about the fly no doubt, but the suggestion triggered my legal tactic. Yes, what a brainstorm. Federal court. I can expedite there. The university was invoking the state RICO statutes, we'd counterpunch with an antidiscrimination action—the university was deliberately, willfully, violating the civil rights of the infertile. All I needed from Feldman was a John Doe or Jane Doe who'd be willing to swear out an affidavit in support of their abused civil rights. Take that and stick it, Mrs. Donald Gramb.

I called Abe and suggested he first contact several of his patients, preferably Black or Hispanic. Find two who'd waive their rights to medical confidentiality and be willing to talk with me and then sign an affidavit. It might not be easy—a lot of people, no matter how committed they are, don't like to become involved in a legal situation. Given the venom these social-ethical cases arouse, who would?

Abe called back within twenty minutes and gave me the names and phone numbers of seven patients. The first two patients I telephoned were very ready, willing, and gung ho. Two points for our team. I outlined their affidavits. They loved them. What's even better, they lived in the neighborhood. Two more points.

"I knew you could help us, Mike," Abe said.

"Thanks for the vote of confidence. But hold off on the gratitude until we see if this flies first," I cautioned. "I'll keep you posted. Stay within reach."

I put down the phone, feeling very proud of my efforts. "I'm really hungry, Diane. When's dinner? I have a lot to do tonight."

"Soon. We're waiting a little bit," she answered.

"For what?" I asked, as the intercom, as if on cue, buzzed. "Who's that?"

"Clear all your stuff off the table and set it for three," she commanded and opened the front door. I heard someone bounding up the stairs. In a few seconds, Jess, with no evidence of shortness of breath, was in our kitchen, making himself at home.

# CHAPTER 17

A family that files a legal brief together is a family that . . .

My son, Jess, the chess and computer maven, king of the word processor, banged out the motion and the affidavits in record time, downloading precedents from the ends of the judicial universe, expertly collating the required six duplicate packets of exhibits and affirmations, all while giving half his attention to a Knicks play-off game. Malone & Malone. Sounded good. If that didn't happen, so be it. At least he'd have paralegal skills as a career backup.

I didn't press him about the last few days, the TV interview, life on Figlio's boat, his chess teacher, Jasper. I handled him as if he were a post-trauma victim, which in fact he was. I was loosey-goosey, self-effacing, warm, and friendly without any edge. His cooperativeness bears testimony to the value of the approach. I recommend it to all parents who have an urge to confront their teenagers head-on about real or threatened transgressions.

Throughout our legal effort Diane cooked, deliberately downplaying her law background as she suffused the apartment with oven heat and sweet vapors of baking brownie mix. She promoted, by her distance, a long over-due father-son collaboration. I wonder, and I know there's no simple answer or even a way to test this hypothesis, how much of our recent estrangement is attributable to our particular family history and pain and how much is just your everyday, normal, typical tension.

Because Ricky Rodriguez, my good-luck process server, has a beeper and a cell phone, but mostly a wife who listens to his telephone answering machine messages and responds with action, I was able to locate Ricky and serve upon Clyde Wickersham & Goldberg, attorneys for the Defendant, the University Medical Center, an expedited show cause motion for a preliminary injunction to be heard on an emergency basis by a federal district court judge no later than eleven-thirty this evening. After some telephone calls among us, the motion was set down for the eleventh hour (I'm not being cute, the night clerk made the suggestion), at which time oral arguments would be heard at the courthouse in Foley Square.

Jess wanted to watch the end of the basketball game and Diane, a new convert to fastidiousness, suddenly couldn't imagine leaving without first cleaning up the kitchen. As I was uncharacteristically impatient and concerned about being late, but really fearful of the wrath of a federal judge put out by an off-calendar emergency hearing, I went downtown alone. I did, however, first call a car service, taking the advice I'd always given my cardiac patients, "do something nice for yourself every day," and treated myself to a medium stretch with a phone and a television. If I successfully argued the motion, Abe wouldn't begrudge me the ninety-dollars-per-hour disbursement, especially if the extravagance helped maintain the confidence I needed to strut my lawyer's strut and prevail over the university.

Even at this late hour, security was tight at the magnificent new federal courthouse hidden behind the crumbling classic Greek façade of the New York Supreme building. Metal detector, body search, two pieces of ID, a call to the judge's chambers, and voice confirmation of my identity by the law clerk. And an armed guard who accompanied me to chambers. Would I need a signed permission slip from the judge to use the bathroom?

From the hallway, through the glass partition, I could see two Clyde Wickersham lawyers sitting in the reception area. One was meticulously dressed, gray-haired, very calm, self-contained, probably a partner; the other was younger, perkier, full of nervous energy, his right foot tapping away, a ready-to-do-battle associate who'd done all the grunt work, knew the case six ways to Sunday, yet never got from the client the recognition he deserved.

I entered the outer offices. The nervous associate jumped up. "Ted Wickersham. Pleased to meet you." I could only hope my take on the legal issues would be sharper. "John Albert," their other attorney added.

All I remember saying is, "My pleasure," and being struck by its oxymoronicness.

The door to the inner sanctum opened and the law clerk appeared. "Everybody here?" We nodded. "Okay. Let's get on with it," and he beckoned us inward.

Judge Roderick Stein came out from behind a large pedestal-style polished granite desk and headed toward an equally modern motorized leather recliner, the kind you only notice in the Christmas catalog of Neiman-Marcus, while the clerk steered us to the comfortable array of couches nearby. We sat in a semicircle, each facing a part of the bay window, which afforded a breathtaking view south of New York harbor, a not too subtle reminder of the power and prerogatives of the judicial officeholder.

No one said a word as the judge played with the controls of his chaise, adjusting the headrest and the height of the foot support. Dressed in a cardigan sweater and wearing alligator slippers, all this self-indulgent pampered middle-aged man going on ninety needed to make himself comfy was a lap blanket.

There'd been a lot of controversy when President Reagan appointed Stein to the bench. In his thirty years of practice, mostly representing the rich and famous, he'd managed to offend everyone with whom he'd come in contact. Though he was Jewish, at least by birth, every major Jewish organization, liberal and conservative, most of them headquartered in New York, opposed their native son. It was said at the time that his obnoxious self-promoting representation of Rabbi Kahane and later Roy Cohn had united Jewish philosophical enemies for the first time since the diaspora.

While the judge continued to adjust himself, I scanned the office furtively. To my right, but mostly behind us, on a red eight-by-ten Persian, were row upon row of pairs of slippers, precisely arranged, I'd guess by season. At each of the four corners of the rug stood a mahogany hatrack overloaded with hats from around the world, which made me recall that President Reagan had originally intended to make Stein ambassador to Trinidad and Tobago, perhaps to help him expand his slipper and hat collections. But when the Senate failed to confirm Stein, Reagan had been forced to switch gears and, in a fit of pique, had nominated him to the federal bench, which tells you all you need to know about the administration of justice. The Senate Judiciary Committee, the same gentlemen who would later distinguish themselves in the matter of Clarence Thomas and Anita Hill, approved the nomination, as did the full Senate, in both instances by voice vote, for no one wanted to be on record as having supported Stein, which was of course understandable. What wasn't understandable was my hope for positive judicial intervention on behalf of my client, dependent as it was on the goodwill and right thinking of a jurist with a slipper and hat fetish.

"Gentlemen, can we get you something to drink?" Stein began.

"No thank you," we three said, in unison. Tired robots.

"Okay, then let's proceed forthwith. Mr. Malone." Stein craned his head in my direction, and despite the disparaging recollections I've just reported, I was instantly impressed by the lively laser-beam eyes focused on me. "I've read your papers. Why don't you give us your best arguments in a nutshell as to why the court should grant an injunction with regard to this matter?"

"Yes, Your Honor," I said. I cleared my throat and swallowed hard. "My client, the Center for Human Biology Incorporated, asserts in this motion that the University's termination of the affiliation contract and their desire to remove forthwith the Center from its facility constitutes a discriminatory action against a class of people, herein minorities, who would not otherwise have access to infertility therapies, and that furthermore, the effect of such a termination, should it not be enjoined, would be to cause irreparable harm. We believe, Your Honor, that with regard to the issue of irreparable harm, there can be no mitigating argument on the part of the Defendant because of the unique biological materia with which we are confronted. And therefore, we assert that the two criteria meet the required standards for a preliminary injunction under the federal guidelines."

The judge turned his head. "Mr. Wickersham."

"Yes, Your Honor."

"Your best shot."

"We are of the belief and opinion that the Plaintiff has not made a showing consistent with the requirements of Title VI of the Civil Rights Act. There has been no demonstration that a racial class per se has been or will be discriminated against as the result of the Defendant's assertion of its rights and obligations to maintain strict standards, which the Plaintiff agreed to as part of the original affiliation contract."

"Are you saying, Mr. Wickersham, that the Plaintiff has breached the contract?"

"Yes, Your Honor. And unilaterally."

"I trust that the Plaintiff disputes this. Is that correct, Dr. Malone?"

"Yes we do, Your Honor." I opened my mouth to say more, but the judge raised his palm and made a stop sign.

The judge turned back to Wickersham. "And in your papers you're basing this claim of a breach on the legal premise that the RICO statutes have been violated?" Stein asked.

"Yes, Your Honor. It is the Defendant's contention that these standards, which are commonly accepted throughout the scientific and health communities, have been violated as part of a criminal conspiracy."

"That's in dispute, Your Honor," I interrupted.

"Not by anyone credible," Wickersham responded.

"Stop, gentlemen. We are having a hearing; you'll address your arguments to me, not each other. Now, Mr. Wickersham, since the Plaintiff's motion concerns the violation of Title VI, and that is what this hearing is addressing, not the merits of your other arguments, are you asserting as your defense, Mr. Wickersham, that the RICO statutes supersede Title VI and therefore any civil rights violation is subsidiary to RICO?"

The judge, it seemed to me, had set a nice trap for Wickersham.

"No, Your Honor. Just that Title VI is not germane, nor valid, as the Plaintiff has failed to prove an injured racial class." Impressive escape. Whatever the University's legal bills, Clyde et al. was worth it. Wickersham winked at his associate and knew he'd scored a direct hit, but like most people he wasn't content to savor his success and pushed too far. "And RICO has been proved, as you can see in our papers."

A quick flash of anger crossed the judge's face. He looked down and riffed through the motions. "We're not here, Mr. Wickersham, to decide the merits of the RICO . . ."

"But Your Honor," Wickersham scrambled to regain his advantage, "as you can see from our appended exhibits, we have a consensus of regulatory agencies that have investigated this matter and come to this conclusion."

"Stop," he cautioned Wickersham, and with a lot of will, Wickersham was able to quickly put a lid on himself, a skill he must have learned in law partner academy. "Now I'm sure both sides will agree with Mr. Malone that the issue of whether or not irreparable harm will result from this midnight closure is not in dispute."

"We don't agree, Your Honor," Mr. Albert said.

"And why not?" the judge asked, the right corner of his mouth fixed in a sarcastic curl.

"The Plaintiff has had sufficient time to make alternate arrangements. It should not be the Defendant's burden to redress that failure," Albert declared authoritatively.

Roderick Stein disregarded the comment with so much disdain that Louis XVI would have been proud of him. "Mr. Wickersham, I have not heard you directly respond to the Plaintiff's contention that closing this facility impacts unevenly, unfairly, on a particular racial class that would otherwise be denied fertility services and therapies."

"The University's position is that we do not and did not control or mandate to whom the Center chose to provide services and that therefore our actions in regard to closing this facility and severing the University's ties are independent of and have nothing to do with the demographics of the Center's patients whatever they may be, and we should therefore not be held accountable for the choices the Center itself made." I bet he was a tough-love parent you always hear about, but never actually meet.

"You are aware, Mr. Wickersham, that if the Center receives federal funds, it must comply with Title VI?" the judge asked.

"Yes, of course," Wickersham conceded.

"Okay, we're making progress. I'm sure you're also aware the courts have held that to win a case under this section it is not necessary to show intentional bias, only a discriminatory outcome. I think you will agree, regardless of how this came about, there exists the possibility of a discriminatory outcome in this situation."

"Excuse me, Your Honor, you're saying that if an organization somehow, accidentally or maybe even deliberately, chooses to focus its efforts on a racial group, it has the legal right to avoid legitimate regulatory and contractual obligations by invoking protection under this statute. I don't think that kind of loophole is the intention of this statute," Mr. Albert opined.

"No one says it is, but I don't see anywhere in your documents that you're saying you believe that this was a deliberate strategy by Dr. Feldman and his staff to evade legitimate regulatory oversight."

"No, but—" Albert started.

The judge cut him off. "That's what I thought. You're fishing, gentlemen. And at this time of the evening, no matter what you put on your hook, nobody's biting. Is there anything else anyone wants to add?"

This hearing was going well, unbelievably well for me, so I saw no reason to respond. Wickersham and Albert looked as if they'd given up the ghost, their blood drained out of them.

"All right. Let's wind this up. Take notes, Bob," the judge called to his clerk. "Having read the papers and after hearing the arguments from both sides, I'm going to rule in favor of the Plaintiff and issue a preliminary injunction. I trust you will inform your client, Mr. Wickersham, not to do anything to interfere with the order of the Court. A written copy of my decision will be available from my office tomorrow morning."

"Will you stay the order pending appeal?" Wickersham asked.

"In other cases I would. We both know it would cause irreparable harm in this instance."

"But my client is anxious to keep to their timetable."

"Mr. Wickersham. Let me give you a word of advice. No judge likes to be rushed. I think your client would be well advised not to involve three Appeals judges at this late hour on a matter that can wait until the morning. You're not likely to get a sympathetic hearing from the panel."

I felt like leaning over and saying to Wickersham, *He's right, you know. I prevailed because my arguments are so strong. Which means you'll need better arguments if you expect to win a late-nighter. Otherwise, you're probably going to get clobbered again. Give it a rest.* But of course, as all lawyers know (and Wickersham would be correct to caution me about gloating), the outcome of this case could be reversed several more times before it was finally concluded.

The judge swung his legs off the recliner and pushed himself to a sitting position. "Good night, gentlemen."

# CHAPTER 18

EN route uptown I called Abe Feldman's home number but no one answered. Maybe he'd gone over to the Center to man the barricades (he'd told me he lived nearby), or possibly somehow he'd heard the good news and was out celebrating. Oh I hope not, for then I'd feel deprived of a litigator's payoff, the delivery of wonderful, liberating, happy information to an anxious client. I considered asking the driver to swing by the Center, but if Abe wasn't there I'd feel foolish and emptier, so I chose the less risky option of a solid sleep at home as the safest way to avoid an all-too-familiar postsuccess letdown.

I must say I found it incredible, unbelievable really, that no one at the hearing had mentioned, even indirectly, my personal legal difficulties, although for all I knew the judge might have ruled in our favor because of some uncon-scious compassion toward me. For the next few months, permabonded to trial publicity, passersby would see me in supermarkets or in lines at the post office or in restaurants and have this dim impression that they knew me, and only later, if at all, would the recollection of an accused mur-derer crystallize. A dark star by any other name was still a dark star, forever and ever.

My street was quiet and remained so, but inside my apartment lights were ablaze with Diane sprawled out across the comforter on top of the bed and Jess on the couch, also asleep, still clutching an American history textbook. Except for the kitchen oasis, which Diane had dutifully cleaned, the place looked like a dorm room.

I turned off the lights, threw the afghan over Jess, undressed down to my undershirt and boxers, and laid claim to some bed surface area. I slept soundly until the morning, when Figlio called.

"It's for you, Dad," Jess said as he handed the portable phone to me over the body of the semisleeping, fully clothed woman whom he might be viewing as a stepmother candidate.

"I didn't hear the phone ring," was all I mustered.

"It didn't, I intercepted it, I'm late for school, see ya."

And he was off before I could ask him, *Intercept? What are you talking about?* Or take care of household business: *Will you be here for dinner?* Or the more important: *How are you* really *doing? Will you come to Mom's cremation ceremony? What are you thinking about? Do you believe I killed your mother?* Questions that were getting swept under every rug every one of us could find.

"Hello," I hoarsely whispered into the mouthpiece.

I heard water sloshing around inside a big tin drum. "Counselor, you may be on to something."

"How so?"

"Victoria Gramb. The D.A.'s wife. She works for your buddy, Mal Snyder."

I sat up. "Really." A foghorn blared in the background.

"That's not all."

"Spill it, Figs, it's too early for a tease." Diane stirred, rolling onto some of the space I'd vacated.

"Hey, I'm the one who's been up all night," Figlio protested.

"Your choice. Last I heard you volunteered, so I'm not buying the load. Now what do you have?"

"Victoria's got a secret.

"Yeah."

"She's been bangin' a lotta guys."

"Mal Snyder?"

"Not sure about him," Figlio answered.

"Oh," I said, deflated. "Another dead end."

"But you must suspect somethin'. Why else did you ask me to check out this Gramb broad?" Figlio declared.

"I had my reasons," I said.

"Don't be cagey, doc. Not a good time in your life cycle."

"I'm not being cagey. Has to do with a client, that's why. Attorney-client privilege. You remember that from the academy?" I tend toward the snotty when I'm confused or scared.

"Fuck you, Malone."

"I'm sorry," I apologized. I thought of invoking privilege again, but Figlio would chew me up. "There's a memo a client showed me that would have impacted negatively on him."

"Scrape the shit off your words and spit it out," Figlio demanded. "Listen, doc. This ain't some constitutional issue. Let me remind you, you're gonna be on trial for murder for which, thanks to the electorate and the dickhead they elected, the prosecutors could change their charge and ask for death. So if they've got the DNA evidence they say they have, and you know better than me how compellin' that shit is, it's gonna be finito, doc, because this ain't L.A. All your efforts and all your years of higher education are gonna go up in smoke. They're gonna fry your ass and make your son a fuckin' orphan in order to showcase an example to everyone of how fair the system is. Hey, we even zap the rich and famous. Do you get it or do you still have your head stuck up your ass?"

I was hot, my skin felt clammy. "You made your point. You're right. But guess what, it *is* a constitutional issue."

"Really," Figlio snickered.

"I'm representing the Center for Human Biology. Have you heard of them?" I asked.

"No."

"They do infertility research among other things. They're affiliated with University Medical Center. They're down on Thirty-third. UMC's been trying to terminate the relationship and evict them, which was supposed to happen at midnight, but it didn't, because I got a preliminary injunction in federal court last night on a civil rights discrimination. . . ."

"What's this have to do with Victoria Gramb?" he asked, impatient.

"An anonymous donor's been promising a shitload of money to the university, but with one caveat."

"Let me guess. Mr. Big Bucks wanted to ace the Center."

"How'd you know?"

"I'm Italian and Catholic and a cop. One way or another I'm bumpin' into that kinda talk on a daily basis. We've got a lotta right-wing Christian types on the Force and believe me they never shut up about all this stuff and how it's an evil. At least for other people anyway. You know if they couldn't produce an heir to carry on their life's shit they'd try anything. Do anything. So where's Victoria fit in?"

"She wrote the memo."

"Wait a second. Correct me if I'm wrong. You were only interested in Victoria because of her connection to your client, not because she was the wife of your wife's boss, the one and same who was out to prosecute your ass? You weren't trying to get a line on her for some leverage on the hubby? Is that what I'm hearin'?" Figlio declared.

"I guess sorta. Though, under every rock . . ."

"You just backed into this half-assed and got lucky."

"I don't feel lucky," I said.

"Who's your contact at this Center?"

"Why?" I asked.

"Maybe I should talk to the guy about Victoria. See what he knows. You haven't done that, right?" Figlio guessed correctly.

"There's no reason to."

"Doc. You do your lawyerin' and you let me do my detectin'. How's that as an arrangement between friends?"

I agreed. What choice did I have? "But let me call him first and tell him you'll be contacting him and why."

"Fine. What's his name?" Figlio asked again.

"Dr. Abraham Feldman."

"The famous doctor whose ass I saw you rescue from the open mouths of those D.C. dickheads?"

"You watched me on TV?"

"You know, you're almost as good a lawyer as you were a doctor."

I smiled. Coming from Figlio, a backhanded compliment was the best you could hope for.

# CHAPTER 19

AFTER several days of discussion Arnie and I decided on a legal strategy. At first I thought it was too risky, but faced with the stagnant reality of my life, I reluctantly agreed it was the safest course of action.

"Look, kid, it'll never get any better. Let's strike while the iron is cold. We've got Figlio's stuff on Gramb and Sally. We've got your case against the two Rikers Island cops. The two together give us the possibility of police and prosecutorial tampering. We'll bring on the usual experts, I'll do a withering cross of all the lab people involved in collecting your blood sample. So much mud will stick to the chain of custody, it'll become an albatross, and the DNA testing won't mean squat, and then we'll have reasonable doubt up the wazoo. Kid, because we have nothing new, we take the initiative. And if we do it now, we're gonna catch them by surprise. Trust me."

"Don't you think," I protested, "we should investigate more? Or at least wait to see if anyone comes forward?"

"It's been three weeks since the murder. No one's coming. By waiting we're only playing into Gramb's hands—he'll leak the DNA test results strand by strand, he'll leak your financials and audio bits of Jess's 'conversations' with the detectives. By the time they're finished there won't be a person left in the jury pool who doesn't think you're just some rich snot who didn't want to go through all the meshugaas. That's Yiddish, kid, for madness."

"But if we find who really did this. . . ."

"We could have a zillion dollars and a thousand private dicks and if the cops have fucked with things how're we going to find anything? What if we wait three months, six months, spend a lot of effort, and come up with zip? That makes you look even worse. But, now, if we go early, then the playing field is leveled. Nobody's gonna hold it against us if we don't have an alternate suspect. In fact, if I'm crafty enough, which I am, we'll plant the impression with the jury that this whole rush shows how weak the prosecution's case is. They were in a hurry, they didn't give this investigation their best shot, because they'd made up their minds to nail you from the get-go. And if we go now, the prosecution might not be so ready to counter us. You've seen Gramb—do you really think they run a tight-ass operation?"

I couldn't fault Arnie's logic, so with some trepidation, a diver standing on the ten-meter springboard, I jumped. Or, rather, we jumped.

Arnie made a motion for an expedited pretrial hearing, which was granted and set down for two days hence.

On an atypically cold May morning we, Arnie and I, appeared at 111 Centre, Room 535, with the prosecutor, Janet Weinstock, Acting Deputy D.A. and acting head, Sex Crimes Unit, Sally's job, before the Honorable James J. Miller, justice Supreme Court.

"Don't you think we should object to Weinstock's involvement as prejudicial?" I whispered to Arnie.

"No. Not now. Maybe at some point, if we need it, we will," he answered.

One-eleven Centre was originally designed as an administrative support facility for the main Supreme courthouse two blocks south. As a result, the whole place, including the cannibalized jerry-rigged courtrooms, had from the beginning a cheap, utilitarian, vending-machine quality, now made worse by chronic budget cutting. In addition over the years, the administrators had packed other courts into the building in a futile attempt to prevent the system from slipping into permanent intestinal obstruction. During the daytime, the lower floors heard Landlord and Tenant, and in the evening, after six, they became Small Claims Court. Both are regularly featured in Dante's circles of legal hell and I've never had any business with either one.

Justice James J. Miller turned out to be a pleasant surprise. Based upstate, Miller was designated a circuit justice, randomly assigned by the chief administrative justice to different jurisdictions as the need arose. With an out-of-towner presiding, Donald Gramb and company could not count on having their usual dose of inequitable political and practical advantage in their prosecution of *People* v. *Malone*.

Because we'd asked for an expedited ruling, we were, according to the perverse logic of the system, placed at the end of the motion calendar, forced to listen to pleadings in twenty-two other cases, most of them criminal actions. My practice is almost exclusively civil, where the rules and procedures are very different, so I took advantage of the wait to reeducate myself.

The two most relevant differences between the civil and criminal concern the rules of evidence and the jury.

As Arnie had repeatedly told me, we're not interested in the truth. "I don't give a flying fuck about the truth" were his actual words. "Let the cops find out, if they can, who cut your wife's throat. I'm a reasonable-doubt farmer," he'd said, during one of our arguments about strategy.

"And I'm gonna push it by the bushel under the jury's nose so they'll have no choice but to acquit."

In a civil case, by contrast, the standard is weaker—preponderance of evidence instead of reasonable doubt.

The other big difference is the jury. In a criminal case there're twelve jurors and two alternates; civil needs only six and two. The criminal verdict has to be unanimous, but only five civil jurors have to agree to a verdict, which always made a lot of sense, especially now, since the civil defendant can only be found liable for monetary damages, while all criminal defendants, myself included, can lose their freedom or even their lives.

Finally, just before the noon lunch break, a bad time to decide anything, the clerk called our case.

The judge greeted us pleasantly. "Madam. Gentlemen. Good morning." Everyone responded in kind and introduced themselves.

"What do we have here, Ms. Weenstock?" he asked, mispronouncing the unfamiliar name.

"Your Honor, if it please the Court, this is a capital felony. The People allege that the Defendant, an attorney, did willfully murder his estranged wife, a deputy district attorney. The Defendant has made an application to waive pretrial discovery and to have this case marked ready for trial. We strongly object, Your Honor. We don't see what the hurry is. The People have an extraordinary caseload and we were not anticipating, and don't see any reason for, such an expedited timetable. Thank you, Your Honor."

"Mr. Glimcher," the judge said.

"Thank you, Your Honor. And welcome to Manhattan. Your Honor, as Ms. Weinstock indicated, the Defendant is an attorney, indeed a distinguished civil attorney, practicing here in New York County. He, too, has a pending caseload but, unlike the People, he has, hanging over his head, a charge of murder, to which he's entered a Not Guilty plea.

"We find the People's argument against speed more than a little disingenuous, Your Honor. The People indicted my client two days after the murder was discovered, rousting him from his home in the middle of the night. Surely, on both counts they could have waited for a more reasonable moment. If they rushed then, and as a result did not take adequate time to assess their evidence and witnesses, the Court should not be asked to give them now what they implicitly waived three weeks ago, prosecutorial restraint and deliberativeness.

"The defense has waived the right to depose any of their witnesses and we intend to present no witnesses, so there'll be no time needed for the People to examine defense witnesses. We have submitted, it's Appendix B in our motion, a list of potential expert witnesses. It's a broad list of mostly DNA experts. We've contacted none of them, interviewed none of them, have no notes whatsoever to disclose, and will only call some, or maybe none, as rebuttal expert witnesses, for our case-in-chief, dependent of course on the case presented by the People.

"Dr. Malone, Your Honor, believes so strongly in his innocence that he's willing to forgo some of his legal rights and safeguards so that a jury of his peers can have the opportunity to hear the whole story and render a verdict. He believes that his right to a speedy trial, given his circumstances, is most important, and he is literally willing to put himself on the line, in front of a jury of his peers, right now, and begin the trial as soon as the jury is impaneled. Dr. Malone believes that this represents the fairest and best way to erase this heinous accusation and, in so doing, best help his teenage son, who has suffered grievously these past weeks. Thank you, Your Honor."

The judge looked at me. "Dr. Malone, are you in agreement with your attorney?"

"Yes, Your Honor," I answered.

The judge grunted something to himself but said nothing, drumming his fingers on his front teeth. Big teeth. Bordered by incisors slightly rotated inward, which gave the judge's smile a mischievous quality. I watched his silent deliberations. His eyes, twinkly behind rimless wire frames, the kind worn by Robert McNamara, whom the judge resembled mostly in the way he slicked back his steel-gray hair, offered no clue as to his decision.

Judge Miller cleared his throat. "I find your motion, Mr. Glimcher, to say the least, very strange. Especially given that the Defendant is himself an experienced trial attorney. Certainly, this country boy feels you're tilting against caution, here, and that Ms. Weenstock's arguments should by reason of my experience prevail. Giving full weight to the People's arguments and yours, and also your client's wishes, and mindful of the Court's duty to move along cases appropriately, I see no reason, however, not to grant your motion. So ordered. Clerk, set this down for a trial date. Can you both proceed with voir dire at this time?"

"Your Honor, I can't this morning," Ms. Weinstock implored. "And I'd also like to make another motion in view of the Court's ruling."

"Just a moment. Mr. Glimcher, can you be ready for voir dire, tomorrow at ten?"

"Yes, Your Honor."

"Now, Ms. Weenstock. Is tomorrow okay with you?" She nodded. "What's your motion?"

"Yes, Your Honor. The People were in the midst of considering whether or not this crime and the Defendant's alleged involvement fell under statute in terms of mandating that we ask for the death penalty. By your granting of the Defendant's motion for a precipitous start to the trial, the

People will not have had enough time to complete these deliberations. The People request a delay to allow this determination to occur."

"Mr. Glimcher, do you have anything to say about this?"

"Your Honor, may I confer with my client?"

"Fine, we can come back after lunch recess. Is that enough time?"

"Five-minute recess is all we need, Your Honor."

"Granted."

Arnie gripped my upper arm firmly and guided me to the rear of the courtroom. Though we had expected this move, he could see that I was shaken by its public announcement.

"Okay, kid. We've been over this."

"I know. The reality is worse. I can't stop shaking."

"It'll never happen. We'll never lose on reasonable doubt. If anything the jurors, knowing that this is a death penalty situation, are gonna be more reluctant than ever to find you guilty and kill two professional people."

"Two?"

"A doctor and a lawyer. Well, at least not the doctor."

"I'm going to need a doctor after all this," I said.

We walked back to the front of the room. Ms. Weinstock rose from her seat, certifying the gravity of the decision.

"Mr. Glimcher, have you and your client conferred about Ms. Weenstock's motion?" the judge asked. It was more a caveat than an official motion, but nobody, except me, probably cared about the semantics.

"Yes, Your Honor. Dr. Malone is willing to put his fate in the hands of the jury. If the People wish to ask for the death penalty, which is their prerogative under the law, then that is their decision. We ask only that they inform us of their decision before we begin voir dire."

"Any objection, Ms. Weenstock?"

"No," she said softly.

"Please be at the jury assembly area tomorrow morning, nine-thirty. The clerk will give you the directions. Court adjourned."

# CHAPTER 20

I spent the rest of the day outside, walking, all the way uptown from court. When you're being threatened with the death penalty, the darkness of the subway is the last thing you need, and the city's cacophony and chaos acted as perfect antidotes to the claustrophobic dread I was feeling.

Home by five-thirty, I waited for Jess to return from school.

"How'd your day go?" I asked.

"Great," he answered, though his subdued tone more accurately reflected his inner turmoil.

It didn't seem fair, given all he'd been through and his effort to project good spirits, to mention my day in court. Tomorrow, regardless of his mood, I'd tell him.

"What's for dinner?" he asked.

"How's order-in Chinese?"

"Fine with me. Whatever."

"You want the usual?"

"Sure. Should we order for Diane?"

"No, she's in Switzerland, taking a deposition. She'll be back tomorrow, so tonight's a guys-only night in."

The chicken lo mein, orange-flavored shrimp over Thai noodles, and sautéed string beans in sesame sauce, Hunan style, never tasted better, though the slight tremor in my hands made it difficult for me to use the chopsticks with accustomed proficiency.

"So what did you do today in school?"

"Nothing special," Jess answered as he tried to straighten a bent tine on the serving fork. "But, afterward, we had a chess meet, and I really creamed the guy. Jasper said what I did was really imaginative."

I reached for another helping of the noodles, spilling some on the table. "Well, the court case is gearing up. And to tell you the truth, I'm getting a little nervous. It's a lot different being on the other side, facing a jury. I still can't believe this is really happening. This whole thing is just incredible." Jess kept eating and didn't say anything. "Arnie would like you to be there, you know, to send the right message, that kinda thing. Can you do that?"

"How 'bout you?" he asked.

"I have to be there, I have no choice," I snapped.

"Do *you* want me to be there?"

"Yes, of course. Why wouldn't I?"

"Don't know," he mumbled.

"This isn't easy for you, I understand that. I hope no one at school's been bugging you. I want to tell you again, even if no one else believes me, I hope you can. I had nothing to do with the murder."

"I know that. You don't have to convince me."

Right. Just the jury.

The pool of potential jurors was assembled in a large high-ceilinged room on the top floor of the main court-house. There, given the new law that no one could be excused except in person by the court, a sample of citizens ladled from the melting pot read their newspapers, munched junk food, did office paperwork, inputted data to their computers, or sat around, bored, waiting to serve, or trying to dream up an excuse that a skeptical court would accept. Much money had recently been invested in the restoration of the wood panels and the murals of old New York history that encircled the room, so that the setting, though not the Met, was aesthetically pleasant.

When I arrived Ms. Weinstock and Arnie were already there, chatting amiably, but listening with one ear as the jury clerk spun the wheel and filled panels—eighteen people at a time.

"Will the following people please bring their possessions up to the front when called," the clerk said over the PA system.

When he'd reached the eighteenth name, the clerk told the group to please follow the attorneys to the courtroom in 635, where each of the potential jurors was asked to fill out a juror questionnaire and then answer questions posed to them first by Ms. Weinstock and then Arnie. The point of the voir dire was to find those jurors who we hoped would be fair-minded to our case, and eliminate those who might not.

While the jurors were filling out their questionnaires, Arnie informed me that the People had decided not to ask for the death penalty. While I understood the reasons for his disappointment, the prospect of a long jail sentence, as opposed to a lethal injection, or whatever they do now that they've restored the death penalty, seemed infinitely preferable. It certainly made it easier for me to tell Jess that the trial was about to begin.

Most lawyers and every legal commentator believe as an act of faith that you win or lose your case during voir dire. Thus the proliferation of jury research companies and jury experts and strategies about whom to pick and whom to exclude. But when all is said and done, the working rules are simple, and probably apply to every kind of case: avoid professionals, never pick an attorney, get blue-collar types, and try for women because they're more sympathetic. From our perspective, given that the case involved the murder of a woman professional, I wasn't sure which of the rules, if any, would help us.

When Arnie's turn came in the voir dire he did what I usually do—chatted with the jurors about their interests and activities, trying to see which of them would be sympathetic to his courtroom style and the facts of the case.

We went through four panels of eighteen, creating a pool of thirty for Justice Miller to interview. After the judge's questions, ten more jurors were dismissed and from the remainder we were able to select the nine women and five men, twelve of whom would decide my fate.

Arnie was happy with the result. "We got lucky, kid, gettin' all those guys on the jury." Yeah, I said to myself, I feel real lucky.

The speediness of the proceedings had caught New York's media flat-footed. I saw none of the usuals lurking about. At this point in the case, the weakest for us, we had no reason to alert them, but I was surprised the D.A. hadn't. Maybe Arnie's strategy was a smart move after all. Time and testimony would tell.

When the judge asked if there was any pretrial business that had to be addressed before he swore in the jury, Ms. Weinstock said she wanted to introduce her co-counsel. From the back of the courtroom Will Washington came forward. Tall, skinny, with thick glasses, he looked anorexic, a Black Abraham Lincoln. When the two of them stood side by side, each seemed softer, becoming kinder, gentler versions of Marcia Clark and Christopher Darden.

I was one step ahead of the judge, as I'd met Washington earlier, in the bathroom. A seasoned prosecutor with a high conviction rate, District Attorney's Office Prosecutor of the Month three times in the last year alone, Washington confided that just like me he'd started his professional life in the health care industry—as a licensed practical nurse at Bellevue.

All in all the prosecutorial team was cleverly designed, offering the predominantly African American jury a second chance to do justice on behalf of a murdered wife, though it's possible I'm being overly cynical, since convicting me, a White man, wouldn't do anything to help anyone in California.

"Pleased to meet you, Mr. Washington," the judge said. "Mr. Glimcher, any requests?"

"Two, Your Honor. As it's late in the day, we wonder if we could put off the jury swearing until the first thing in the morning for continuity purposes."

"You were, as I recall, in quite a hurry to begin, Mr. Glimcher." Arnie opened his mouth to say something. "Request denied. Next."

I whispered to Arnie, "What was that all about?"

"I wanted the jury's first courtroom snapshot of you to include Jess."

"Mr. Glimcher, what else is there?" the judge asked.

"Sorry, Your Honor. While the defense has nothing but respect and profound admiration for the prosecutor, Ms. Weinstock, we feel that because she is the acting head of the Sex Crimes Unit, the position formerly held by the deceased, her very presence in this prosecution will unwittingly be a constant and prejudicial influence on the jurors, and we ask that she be removed from this case."

"You might have made this argument earlier, Mr. Glimcher, before you moved to trial, and it would have had more weight, but having failed to do so in a judicious manner, if the Court were to grant your request at this time, the Court would be placing an unfair burden on the People. I'm sure the Court can and will monitor and protect the jury from any unfairness. Motion denied.

Anything else, anybody?" The counsel stood mute. "Good. Officer, please bring in the jury."

The court officer opened a door in the side wall, between the jury box and the witness stand, and ushered in the voir dire survivors. Arnie jabbed me in the side to make me rise, which I did on rubbery legs.

Instead of the excitement and anticipation I'd experienced so often as a litigator ready to take on the lions, I was, on the other side of Justice's shadow, terrified. If my mom were standing next to me I would have buried myself in her bosom. Each of the jurors paraded stiffly past the rail as if their posture was being evaluated. When they entered the jury box several seemed to lunge for their seats, no doubt trying to duck under the glares of the audience. When all fourteen were seated, we sat down, but I continued to stare at these men and women and worked hard to present a relaxed yet concerned demeanor. Most met me with impassiveness; a few sat tensely, vigilantly, like guard dogs protecting their turf. Why would these people care about me and my problems and my fate?

"Good afternoon, ladies and gentlemen," the judge said, and they responded in chorus, "Good afternoon, Your Honor," sounding like a class of kindergartners.

In a too-loud voice, the court officer announced, "The Court is now in session. The Honorable James J. Miller presiding. Supreme Court, State of New York, County of New York." I stared intently at the judge as he made himself comfortable on his perch, trying to squeeze his long frame into the high-backed swivel chair. I noticed that the buttons on his robes were fastened askew and hoped his administration of justice would not be as careless.

"In the matter of the *People* v. *Malone*, are both sides present and ready for trial?"

"Yes, Your Honor," both sides chanted in unison.

"Officer, please swear in the jury."

The court officer approached the jury box, asked everyone to rise, and then administered the oath. Fourteen "I do's" resonated throughout the room.

That done, the judge motioned for counsel to approach the bench. Arnie pushed his chair back noisily, unwilling to raise his butt until the last possible moment, making four scrape marks on the green linoleum. The two deputy district attorneys made their way forward more quietly.

I didn't like being out of earshot, forced to imagine what he was saying that brought tiny smiles to the attorneys' faces.

Maybe: *I want this to be a good clean fight. No kidney punches, nothing below the belt. When a lawyer is down, go to a neutral corner and wait till the count is done.* But Judge Miller didn't look like Teddy Brennan and this wasn't Madison Square Garden, no matter how ferocious the legal fisticuffs.

The sidebar ended and on cue the court officer declared, "The Court is now in session in the matter of *People* v. *Malone.*"

Judge Miller swiveled to face the jury. "Ladies and gentlemen of the jury. I want to thank you at the outset for exercising the most important civic duty in a democratic society that a citizen can perform by agreeing to serve on this jury. The matter before us is serious and I want each and every one of you to understand that you are to make no judgment, form no opinion, or in any way come to any conclusion until such time as you've heard and considered all the evidence.

"You will hear opening and closing statements from the prosecution and from the attorney representing the Defendant. What they say is not evidence, it is their version, their story of the events and facts. Testimony of witnesses and documentary evidence—papers, recordings, et cetera—this is the only evidence you must consider.

"You are admonished not to read any newspaper or magazine article, watch any television program, listen to any radio program or anyone in regard to this matter, and to hold no discussion among yourselves or with anyone else until such time as you retire to the jury room for your deliberations. Any violation of these prohibitions will be treated severely. At this time I am not ordering your sequestration, but should these rules not be followed, I will have no choice except to do so."

The jurors stared back impassively, giving no sign of whether they were listening or whether they intended to follow the guidelines.

"As the hour is late, we are going to adjourn at this time. Court will resume promptly at nine-fifteen tomorrow. Officer, please escort the jury from the courtroom."

Arnie leaned over. "Make sure Jess is here tomorrow."

"I'll do my best. He does have school."

"He'll learn more here."

# CHAPTER 21

BEFORE the judge arrived on the bench and before the jury was called, Arnie shamelessly asked the front row people to shift their seats so that he could place Jess behind me and to my left. Every time a juror looked at me, they'd see Jess in the near background.

The judge's early-morning demeanor was growly. Maybe the city pace was getting to him.

"Good morning, everyone," he said, unsmiling. "Clerk, will you call the jury."

The judge waited until everyone was seated. "Good morning, ladies and gentlemen," he said, his tone more pleasant to the citizenry. "Clerk, will you read the charge."

"*People* v. *Malone*, Index Number 97-8027. The Defendant, Michael J. Malone, is charged with murder in the first degree in the willful, premeditated murder of Sally Hager Malone, his wife, on or about the eighteenth of April in the year 1997, in violation of Section four-oh-three of the Penal Code of the State of New York." The clerk stopped and pushed his glasses back up onto the bridge of his nose.

"And how does the Defendant plead?" the judge asked in my direction.

With appropriate demeanor, sadness mixed with confidence, I rose, slowly, exactly as Arnie had rehearsed me, and said to the jury clearly, loudly, and without hesitation,

"Not guilty." Then to the judge, "Your Honor," but he was already distracted, writing something on a pile of legal papers his law clerk had handed him.

"Are the People ready?" the judge asked.

Ms. Weinstock sprang to her feet. "Yes, Your Honor."

"Proceed, please, with your opening arguments. The jury is reminded that opening statements are not testimony."

Ms. Weinstock picked up a thick three-ring leatherette binder and carried it to the podium, which was in the no-man's-land between the tables for the defense and the prosecution. In her tailored, gray, iridescent suit she was quite attractive, with a figure much like Diane's, who, in case you're wondering, was asked by Arnie to stay home.

"Your Honor, members of the jury, with an especially heavy heart I stand here before you today. Every murder is awful and that is why we have strong laws, prohibitions, to punish those who commit this horrific crime. The victim, Sally Hager Malone, if she were alive, would be here today, in my place, for her job, ladies and gentlemen, was to bring to the bar of justice and prosecute people who committed crimes of passion like this. That was her specialty and she had great success at it. If Sally were alive she would be telling you that no person, whoever they are, should be allowed to escape their punishment. If Sally were alive she would tell you that her husband, the Defendant, Michael J. Malone, must and should, if convicted, answer for his crime.

"The People will prove, ladies and gentlemen of the jury, beyond a reasonable doubt, that Michael J. Malone did willfully murder his estranged wife. We will demonstrate that the Defendant had the opportunity and, in the midst of an acrimonious and financially threatening divorce, the motive to commit this crime.

"The People will present unassailable scientific evidence, so much so that afterward, when you retire for your deliberations, you will have no reasonable choice except to convict. Thank you."

I thought her performance perfunctory, but the jury seemed to listen intently. Arnie elevated his rumpled self and ambled to the podium. Consistent with his casual unhurried style, he brought no notes. No one on the jury would ever guess he was a high-powered divorce lawyer who could get down and dirty with the best of them.

"Good morning ladies and gentlemen, Your Honor," he began, reversing the prosecution's greetings sequence, which was entirely appropriate, for it was the jury, not the judge, who'd vote on my innocence or guilt. Better to curry their favor.

"This is, ladies and gentlemen, a simple case. The People will try to show that my client, the Defendant, Dr. Malone, murdered his wife. They have no witnesses who saw the murder committed. They, as Ms. Weinstock said, are going to rely on scientific evidence. In other words, this is a circumstantial case.

"The People will have you believe that Dr. Malone committed this terrible crime because he and the deceased were in the midst of a bitter divorce. You will be the judge of that.

"Keep an open mind. Listen to all the evidence—not just scientific evidence—and ask yourself, Does this make sense?

"Every divorce is acrimonious. Every divorce stirs up unpleasant feelings. But, you must demand, you must insist, that the People show you overwhelming evidence, beyond a reasonable doubt, that the Defendant, Dr. Michael Malone, had so much uncontrollable rage that he could have committed this horrible crime. Ask yourself why the People will present no witnesses who can so testify.

"The People will try to make you believe that Dr.

Malone committed this horrible crime out of financial necessity. Ask yourself why the People will present no witnesses who can testify to the doctor's financial difficulties. Not surprising, as he didn't have any.

"Ask yourself, Does this allegation make sense? With no unusual motivation, why would the Defendant have committed this crime?

"Ladies and gentlemen, this case makes me feel humble. Why? Because there's no possible explanation of the facts that accounts for what's happened here and such overwhelming lack of certainty makes me feel inconsequential and humble.

"The only incontrovertible, scientific fact in this case is that Sally Hager Malone was murdered. Why and by whom are conjecture, at best pathetic guesses.

"For Sally Hager Malone we all grieve, most especially my client and their son. But if you keep your mind open, as I know you will, if you follow the judge's injunction and don't form an opinion prematurely, as I know you will, perhaps all of us together can walk down this path of mystery, reason together, and find the truth, which is what my client wants, what his son wants, what you want, and what everyone else gathered here wants, for closure for this family will only occur when the real perpetrator or perpetrators of this terrible crime are apprehended by the police and punished. Thank you."

Arnie sat down heavily and patted my forearm. Everything will be all right, you'll see, he was telling me and the jury. The jurors remained stone-faced, though I had a big lump in my throat and, if asked, would have given Arnie's overall performance a B/B+ (an A for presentation and a C+ for substance and syntax).

"Are the People ready to call their first witness?" Judge Miller asked.

"We are, Your Honor," Ms. Weinstock replied. "The People call Officer Willems."

A young man popped up in the row behind the prosecution table and strode to the witness stand. He looked vaguely familiar. The court officer held the Bible like a waiter carrying a tray. "Do you swear to tell the truth, the whole truth, and nothing but the truth, so help you, God?"

"I do."

"Please be seated," the judge said.

Ms. Weinstock began, "Will you please state your name for the record, officer?"

"My name is John, everyone calls me Jack, Willems."

"Could you please spell Willems?" the court reporter interjected.

"W-I-L-L-E-M-S."

"Officer Willems, can you please tell the jury how long you've been on the force?"

"Two years."

"And where do you work and what are your duties?"

"I've been with the Nineteenth Precinct since January first of this year and I mostly ride patrol."

"By yourself?"

"No, with my partner."

"Now, Officer, can you tell the Court and the jury what happened on the afternoon of April nineteenth of this year?"

"Yes, ma'am. We received a ten-eighty-five to go to Sutton Place and we hurried—"

"Excuse me, Officer," Ms. Weinstock interrupted. "What's a ten-eighty-five?"

"I'm sorry," he blushed, "a ten-eighty-five's a call to provide backup at a crime scene on a stat basis."

"Thank you," she said. "Please continue."

"We received a ten-eighty-five and we hurried over to Twenty-two Sutton Place."

"How long did it take you and your partner, from the time you received the ten-eighty-five, to get from where you were to Sutton Place?"

"About six or seven minutes. We wouldda gotten there sooner, but First Avenue was all gridlocked 'cause of some U.N. bigwig's security," he apologized.

"And when you arrived, can you please tell the jury what happened?"

"Detective Watson told us this was a potential crime scene. To put on rubber gloves and for the two of us, me and my partner, to start searching the basement and the garden, and after that the first floor."

"Did he tell you what you were searching for?" she asked.

"I don't remember if he did."

"Okay, now will you tell the members of the jury what you found?"

"There was nothing in the basement or the garden, but when we got to the kitchen my partner opened the fridge. I think he said somethin' like, 'Beautiful ain't it, but empty,' and that's why, I guess, when I saw the freezer in the pantry off the kitchen I was curious to see what was in it, so I opened it."

"And what did you find?"

"The body of the deceased."

"And what was her state?" the D.A. asked.

"She was frozen solid."

I looked over at the jurors. So were they.

"She was dead, correct?" the D.A. asked.

"Absolutely. Her face was covered with white frost."

"And what did you do then?" Ms. Weinstock asked.

"I shouted to the detective to come to the kitchen."

"And he did?"

"Yes, ma'am."

"Did anyone else come?"

"Two other officers who were checking the upper floors."

"Anyone else?"

"Objection, leading the witness," Arnie shouted.

"Overruled," the judge said.

"Was anyone besides the officers in the room when you discovered the deceased's body?" Ms. Weinstock asked.

"The Defendant."

"By the Defendant you mean Mr. Malone sitting over at the defense table, correct?"

"Yes."

"Had you ever met the Defendant before that moment?" she asked.

"No. Never."

"And how would you characterize his demeanor?" she asked.

"Objection, Your Honor. Calls for a conclusion. The witness has already testified he'd never met the Defendant, so therefore his appraisal of the Defendant is without basis."

"Sustained," he said and turned to the jury. "You are to disregard that question. Counsel," the judge beckoned.

Arnie stood up and joined Ms. Weinstock at the bench. The meeting was short.

"What was that about?" I asked Arnie.

"He told her to establish a foundation. Big deal. He shouldn't be letting this shit in."

"Thank you, Your Honor," Ms. Weinstock resumed. "Officer Willems, have you been at other murder scenes with close family members?"

"Yes."

"In your experience, Officer, can you please characterize the state of family members upon discovering a loved one is dead?"

"They're very upset."

"Would it be fair to say there's lots of crying?"

"Yes."

"And fair to say you've seen many loved ones being very emotional?"

"Yes."

"Isn't it true, Officer Willems, that on the afternoon of April nineteen, when you were able to observe the behavior of the Defendant, that he was not very emotional?"

"Objection, Your Honor."

"Rephrase the question, Ms. Weenstock," the judge ordered.

"Officer Willems, did you observe the Defendant crying?"

"No, ma'am."

"Did you see the Defendant being very emotional in any other way?"

"No, ma'am."

"Thank you, Officer. Your witness, counselor."

I thought the testimony was effective. When Arnie'd shown me the prosecution witness list, I'd expressed surprise he was their leadoff witness. Not the more experienced detective who'd come to our house with Sharronn, my wife's secretary. Not the one likely to be comfortable on the witness stand, which is what they'd intended. A rookie's sincerity to counteract the presumed defense—police conspiracy and wrongdoing.

Arnie stood up in place. "Officer Willems, in your two years on the Force, can you please tell the jury how many murder crime scenes you've been on?"

"Lots."

"Twenty?"

"No, not that many," he said.

"Half that, ten?" Arnie asked.

"Maybe a little less."

"Let's say, for the sake of argument, eight. Is that fair?"

The patrolman nodded. "You have to say yes or no for the court reporter."

"Yes," Willems said.

"And on how many of these eight were you the first person to actually discover the victim?"

"This was the only one," he answered.

"So this was a very special crime scene for you, is that not correct?"

"Yessir."

"Isn't it a fact, then, that you don't really have any similar experience with the emotional state of loved ones?"

"Objection, Your Honor, counsel is badgering the witness," Ms. Weinstock asserted.

"Sustained. Mr. Glimcher, let's try to stick to what the witness knows, rather than what he doesn't."

Arnie nodded, said nothing to the judge, as if disturbed by his ruling, but out of view of the judge and jury he winked at me. Despite the judge's admonition, His Honor had certified Arnie's contention—Willem's impression of my emotional state was lame evidence.

"So, Officer Willems, is it fair to say that this particular crime scene, on which you were the first law enforcement officer to discover the body of the deceased, will probably live in your memory a very long time, correct?"

"Yessir," he said with relief and pride. "It's as if it just happened yesterday."

"Good," Arnie said. "So, Officer Willems, if I were to ask you details about your discovery you could recall them, to use your words, as if it just happened yesterday?"

"I think so," he said, but nervously played with his shirt collar.

"Good." Arnie paused, lifted up a stack of documents, removed a piece of paper from underneath, and stepped out in front of the Defendant's table. With the document he made small figure eights in the air around him. Finally after his long theatrical intermission, which probably lasted only twenty seconds, Arnie continued, holding the paper behind his back, standing there as if he was Prince Philip on a state visit. "So, Officer Willems, with respect to the freezer chest where you found the deceased's body, can you please tell the Court and the jury whether or not there were any other items in the freezer?"

"You mean, like food?" the witness asked.

"Exactly," Arnie answered.

"Some frozen vegetable packages, a package of bacon."

"Was there any frost on any of these?"

"Yes," he answered quickly.

"Was the frost also white?"

"Yes," he said, certain.

Arnie brought the paper out in front, and briefly seemed to read it. "Are you sure nothing was pinkish?"

"Yes I'm sure," he answered, a pink blush spreading across his face.

"So, you're certain, there was no blood that had touched anything in there as far as you could tell, is that correct?"

"Yessir."

"Thank you, Officer. You may step down."

Arnie turned, pirouetted almost, and walked back toward our table, smiling. He seemed pleased with himself; I had no idea what was the purpose, if any, of his cross.

"What was that all about?" I whispered in his ear. "And what's on the paper?"

Before he could answer, Ms. Weinstock rose to call her next witness, but the judge interrupted. "We seem to be close to the time for our midmorning recess. Why don't we adjourn for fifteen minutes? The jury is admonished."

The judge left hurriedly, I presumed on his way to the men's room.

"What was on the paper?" I asked Arnie again.

"An old trick I learned in the fourth grade," he said.

"What the hell does that mean?" I asked angrily.

"Calm down, tiger. I'll tell you. In the fourth grade I had chicken pox. During the week I stayed home I watched the Army-McCarthy hearings. Are you too young to remember them?"

"I know what they were. So?"

"McCarthy liked to wave papers around while asking people if they were Commies as if the paper had something to do with that. 'I have a list here,' he'd say. I tried it once in the fourth grade, worked great. Every once in a while at the right courtroom moment I use it."

"If I'm not mistaken, didn't Joe Welch catch on to McCarthy's trick?"

"Correct," Arnie answered.

"What're you going to do when that happens to you?" I said.

"It won't. At least not this morning, anyway," he replied.

"Do me a favor and let's stick to the facts. Okay?" I said.

"Disdain isn't very useful, kid. When the facts are on our side, I'll go with them. When the law's on our side, I tilt that way. When both are stacked against you, you gotta be creative."

I rose to anger quickly, upset that even my own lawyer didn't believe me. "You think I could have done this?"

"Shut up, kid, I didn't say that. But it doesn't matter what I believe, it's what the jury believes. I'm just sowing seeds of doubt. We've got the damn DNA to deal with. We have no way to explain the match. Figlio has turned up diddly."

"Yes," I said. I did know that. "I've gotta take a leak. Jess, do you need to use the bathroom?"

"No," Jess mumbled, looking away, as if he believed I was a murderer.

# CHAPTER 22

THE courthouse restrooms reflect the state budget cuts; the floors were so sticky and dirty I feared my rubber soles would bond to the tiles. I washed up with cold water, the hot-water faucets having been removed, and dried my hands by shaking them vigorously while watching a balding lawyer position his comb-over. My world was so topsy-turvy that only if I was lucky, and Arnie somehow convinced these fourteen citizens of reasonable (I'd even settle for unreasonable) doubt, would I have the opportunity to be bald in public.

There was a line for the single phone booth on the third floor, so I rode the elevator down to the lobby.

"Pack of breath mints, ten dollar bill, a dollar in quarters if you can, please," I said to the blind owner of the newspaper and candy concession, whose presence attests to the public best behavior of the legal crowd. He quickly, as well as if he were sighted, gave me the correct change.

With quarters in hand, I called my home answering machine. Forcibly barred from my office, there wasn't much I was expecting. Three hang-ups, followed by Diane's, "Keep your chin up. I love you," and an unintelligible lengthy message in Spanish and English from Roberto Lopez, my client.

Roberto answered on the first ring. *"Tio abocado. Que pasa?"* I said in my best New York Puerto Rican Spanish.

*"Mucho,* Meester Malone." He sounded half-asleep.

*"Que?"* I said again (my Spanish vocabulary is very limited).

"De juuudge telephone me."

"He did," I said, surprised at this ex parte communication.

*"Si."*

*"Porque?"* I asked.

"He want stop trial," Roberto said.

"Judge Sherman said that?" I shouted.

" 'Ee's *secretaria.*"

"No. Juuudge. *Secretaria?* Okay?" I asked.

*"Si,"* Roberto answered, but by now our dialogue was so confusing, I, for one, had no idea to what the *"si"* referred.

"Okay. I go see judge. I telephone you, okay?"

*"Quando?"* he asked.

I said, *"Ocho.* Tonight."

*"Muchas gracias."*

I wanted to give myself some time to wind down and would have preferred after ten, but eight was the only Spanish number I was confident about.

When I returned to the noisy courtroom Arnie and Jess were talking about privacy issues and the Internet. I didn't put my two cents in because, right now, it was difficult for me to care about anyone else's constitutional rights.

The court clerk was once again loudly dispensing calendar dates and other administrative details to various supplicants. Along the back benches, groups of spectators were animatedly engaged in conversation, discussing, I hoped, matters other than my guilt or innocence.

Only the prosecutors, who were holding a deep tête-à-tête with each other reviewing a motion, seemed to be focused on the task at hand.

I was impatient to resume; waiting hurts everyone, but mostly defendants. The hour hand on the clock above IN GOD WE TRUST was stuck on the nine. According to my watch the judge's fifteen-minute break was stretching into thirty-five. There's no reasonable excuse for the wasted time that flattens the tires of justice.

His Honor returned five minutes later. "Officer, please bring in the jury." The hypocrisy of his curt self-serving take-charge manner, after he'd been gone almost forty minutes, offended me, but I did my lawyerly best to hide my disdain. The jury at least seemed ready—several sat poised with pen and notepad.

"Ms. Weinstock, your witness," the judge said. He seemed to have learned how to pronounce her name during the recess.

"The People call John Eng."

A tall pencil-thin man in a gray suit, too short at the sleeves as if his growth had recently spurted, was sworn in.

"Good morning, Mr. Eng," she began.

"Good morning," he said and smiled at the jury, a professional witness.

"Mr. Eng, can you please tell the Court and the jury your occupation?"

"I am a criminalist for the New York City Police Department."

"Would you briefly, sir, describe for the jury the duties of a criminalist?"

"Yes. I collect evidence at a crime scene for testing and analysis." No one would ever accuse Mr. Eng of being a big talker.

"And are there standard procedures that you follow?"

"Yes, the Department has a manual which we follow. We also follow the FBI lab guidelines and the ABC's."

"ABC?"

"I'm sorry. American Board of Criminalistics."

"That's an association of professionals, is it not?" she asked Eng.

"Yes."

"And you received many years of training in order to become a criminalist?" she asked.

Arnie popped up. "If it please the Court, the defense, in the interest of moving forward, is willing to stipulate that the witness is an expert in the matters he will testify to as a criminalist."

"Any objection, Ms. Weinstock?" the judge asked.

"No, Your Honor. Thank you," she said, but her smile was wan. In front of the jury Ms. Weinstock did not want to appear ungrateful or upset, even if she was, by Arnie's intrusive meaningless gesture of helpfulness. Only from my angle could you see how hard she'd tightened her facial muscles in order to maintain her composure. The judge should have called a sidebar and cautioned Arnie not to disturb the prosecutor's rhythm with gratuitous interruptions, but he didn't. In my experience if a judge doesn't rein in the attorneys early on in a proceeding, he or she runs the risk of the trial disintegrating into a circus, which could be very useful to the defense strategy.

Ms. Weinstock riffled through her notes, looking for a new starting place. "Mr. Eng, how many evidence tags did you collect at the crime scene?"

"I believe eighty-five."

"And, in connection with your investigation, did you collect any evidence anywhere else?"

"At the apartment of the Defendant," he answered.

"And when was that?" she asked.

"The following day, April nineteenth."

"And that was after the Department had obtained a search warrant for the Defendant's premises, is that not correct?"

"Definitely."

"And how many items did you tag there?"

"Maybe forty. I'd have to refer to my notes if it's important to know the exact number."

"No, that won't be necessary. Mr. Eng, can you please describe for the jury the kinds of evidence you collected?"

"Blood evidence, hair samples, carpet fibers, fingerprints, swatches of clothing, shoes."

"And where did you find blood?" she asked.

"At the crime scene and at the Defendant's apartment."

"At the Defendant's apartment," she said, feigning surprise. "Can you please tell the Court how you determine if something is blood rather than a food stain or paint or whatever?"

"We do a BSP presumptive test."

"What is that exactly?"

"It's a chemical test that tells you if a sample is or is not blood," Eng said.

"And when you did this test at the Defendant's apartment you found blood, is that not correct?"

"Yes we did."

"Just in one place?" she asked.

"No, it was in the sink traps in the bathroom basin and the bathtub, on a shirt in the laundry bag, and I found some on both heels of a pair of shoes. And also the kitchen sink trap."

"Really," she paused for dramatic effect. "And what did you do with those samples?"

"Of blood?" Eng asked.

"Yes, of blood," she clarified.

"We sent them first to our lab for ABO typing, and then we sent them out for DNA testing."

"To where?"

"A lab in Philadelphia," he answered.

"And what were the results of the DNA?" she asked.

"We came back with a match," he answered.

I nudged Arnie. This seemed to be the right place for an impassioned objection. Eng wasn't a DNA expert. Why let him testify as if he was? Arnie brushed me off with a whispered, "Not now. I have a plan."

"In terms of this case, could you explain in layman's terms what a match is, Mr. Eng?"

"The blood of the victim at the crime scene matched, was identical to, in terms of its DNA, the blood found at the Defendant's apartment."

"Was that the only match?" Ms. Weinstock continued.

"No. We found some blood at the crime scene that matched the Defendant's blood."

"And did you have a comparison sample of the Defendant's blood?"

"Yes."

"Where was it obtained?" she asked.

"A Police Department lab technician drew a sample from the Defendant at our lab on April nineteenth."

"So you know for a fact, with all possible certainty, that the Defendant's DNA that was provided to you is the same as the DNA you found in blood evidence at the crime scene?"

"Yes we do."

"Thank you. No further questions."

Eng reached for a glass of water, took a sip, and apprehensively waited for the cross-examiner to commence firing. So did I. Weinstock's direct was a bull's-eye. No wasted time, unlike *People* v. *Simpson*, on the tedious boring details of lab techniques. Right to the heart of the matter, leaving us not very much wiggle room.

In contrast to his cross of the first witness, Arnie did not begin behind the cover of the defense table. He walked over and stood in the wide open space near the jury box. "Good morning, Mr. Eng."

"Good morning," Eng answered warily.

"We have stipulated that in terms of your skills as a criminalist you are an expert, Mr. Eng."

"Yes," Eng said.

"Is it fair to say, Mr. Eng, that criminalists like yourself are primarily experts in gathering evidence?"

"I suppose so."

"And isn't it also fair to say criminalists are not experts in DNA?"

"Objection," Ms. Weinstock proclaimed.

"Basis?" the judge asked.

"Calls for a conclusion."

"Overruled. The foundation has been established by calling him an expert and then asking him about DNA. I'll allow the question. Please answer, Mr. Eng."

"Can you please ask the question again?" Eng asked.

"Let me make it simpler. Are you an expert in DNA analysis, Mr. Eng?"

"No. Not if you ask it that way."

"What way, Mr. Eng?"

"If I'm an expert. I know something about DNA, that's what I mean."

Arnie was barely able to withhold his sarcasm. "That's good, Mr. Eng. We appreciate your comments, but for the record you are not an expert, is that a reasonable characterization?"

"Yes."

"Good. So it is possible, you will agree, that someone else, reviewing the data, someone with more training and experience than you, might come to a different conclusion about the so-called DNA match, is that not correct, sir?"

"Yes, it's possible."

"Good. Now let's turn to another area you testified about, the collection of blood evidence from the crime scene. Are you with me?"

"Yes," Eng answered, looking uncomfortable.

"Aside from the crime scene and the Defendant's apartment, did you check any other sites for blood evidence?" Arnie asked.

"No."

"So you never tested the Defendant's automobile?"

"No."

"You were never told by any of the detectives handling this investigation to test the driver's-side door handle or the inside of the automobile for blood?"

"Objection, Your Honor. No foundation on direct for this line of questions."

"Ms. Weinstock. I'm going to allow it because this is a murder charge and some latitude is in order," the judge decided.

"I strenuously object for the record," the prosecutor said.

"So noted."

"Therefore if I were to tell you that the Defendant's auto had spots of the Defendant's blood, but not the decedent's, would that in any way influence how you interpret the facts of this case?" Arnie asked.

"May we approach the bench," Ms. Weinstock demanded.

"Yes."

While they held their rather heated conference, I watched the jury. They were very attentive. Arnie was managing to attach skepticism to police procedures and thus was indirectly devaluing hard-core facts. The meeting broke up and the judge declared, "The jury is advised to disregard the last question. The witness cannot testify to that which is hypothetical." But the damage had been done, a seed of doubt sown.

"One further question, Mr. Eng. You testified earlier that you recovered blood at both locations and specifically from personal items at the Defendant's apartment?"

"Yes."

"Now, Mr. Eng, you testified that you found blood at multiple locations in the Defendant's apartment. Quite a few, correct?"

"Yes."

"In fact, wouldn't it be fair to say that every place you might expect there to be blood did in fact have it, almost as if someone had been very careful and methodical about laying out this evidence?"

"Objection, speculation."

"Sustained. Strike the question," the judge said to the court reporter.

*Not bad, Arnie,* I thought. Seed of doubt number two successfully planted.

"You are aware, of course, when a blood sample is drawn, there's a preservative, EDTA, in the tubes, to prevent clotting, are you not?" Arnie asked.

"Yes."

"Did you test for the presence of EDTA in these samples you recovered?"

"No, but—"

"Just answer yes or no, Mr. Eng," Arnie ordered.

"No."

"No further questions, Your Honor," Arnie said.

"Any redirect, Ms. Weinstock?"

Ms. Weinstock stood up. "Yes, Your Honor."

"Mr. Eng, you said you didn't test for EDTA, correct?"

"Yes."

"But you can say there was no EDTA in the samples, correct?"

"Objection, Your Honor," Arnie called out, "his testimony's conflictual. He's already testified he didn't test for it."

"Ms. Weinstock, I assume you're heading somewhere?" the judge asked.

"Yessir."

"Then do it quickly. Your objection is overruled, Mr. Glimcher."

"Was there any EDTA in the samples?"

"No."

"How do you know that?"

"We tested them," Eng said.

"And what you meant to say, in answer to Mr. Glimcher's question, was that you personally didn't do the test, but that someone else in the lab did. Is that an accurate statement, Mr. Eng?"

"Yes."

"No further questions," and she sat down, smiling.

"Mr. Glimcher?" the judge asked.

"No further questions," Arnie answered, which was the best thing to do.

"Your Honor," Ms. Weinstock said, "as it's close to the noon hour, perhaps it would be a good time to take our noon recess." Smart move. Send the jury off to lunch on your high note. I would have done the same thing.

"Good idea. The jury is admonished. Court will return at one-thirty," he said, and immediately huddled with his law clerk about another case.

"Not exactly a dream team moment," I said to Arnie.

Briefly Arnie seemed taken aback. "Maybe their victory will come back to smack them in the face, you never know." He was someone in whom optimism flowed naturally.

"Sure," I said, a skeptical nonbeliever. "I have to go see a judge on the fifth floor about a case of mine. Jess, do you want to come? Afterward we could catch something to eat. I know a good Thai place. You like spicy," I said.

"No, I've gotta get to school. They only excused me for the morning."

Arnie wanted to add something but I cut him off. "Okay, thanks for coming," I said to Jess, hiding my disappointment, and giving him a big hug as much for myself as for him.

The stairs to the fifth floor were covered with spackle and paint droplets; the painters had propped open the windows to let out the fumes and as a result I found myself climbing upward against a strong cool breeze that was kicking up plaster dust all around me. Nevertheless, I felt exhilarated, temporarily liberated from my third-floor role of defendant. For ten minutes I could advocate on behalf of Mr. Lopez and resume my professional life. As I reached the top landing the heavy metal fire door opened and the officers who were essentially the defendants in *Lopez* stood there, blocking my way.

"So how's it going, counselor?" Detective Jennings said.

"Fine, thanks. Excuse me, I'm in a hurry."

"Sure," Jennings answered, but neither moved, and his partner, Detective Garcia, let the unpainted door close behind them.

"I wanted to ask you somethin'," Garcia declared.

"What's that?" I bristled.

"How's it feel to be facing the big D, *maricón*?" Garcia said.

"You mean, unlike you guys, *D* for dismissal of all charges?"

The two of them laughed. "You're going *D* for down, Mr. Lawyer man, count on it," Garcia declared.

I answered imprudently, "I want to thank you guys for giving me an added incentive to be acquitted so I can return to what I do best, frying your asses," but neither took offense.

"Whaddya think, Garcia, they're gonna use lethal injection or they're gonna bring back the chair for the doc?" Jennings asked.

"Tough call," Garcia decided. "Which costs less?"

"Sorry to disappoint, but the D.A.'s not asking for death. You guys ought to try to keep up with the news."

"I betcha he's gonna tell everyone, right up to the last minute, how he's innocent. But no one's gonna believe that shit, right, Garcia?"

"You bet. Not one fucking person. Not even his kid."

I'd had enough. "Get outta my face," I shouted and tried to push past, but they were both built like brick shithouses and didn't give an inch. Garcia backed me up against the wall, doing a Canadian isometric exercise on my sternum. My heart was racing, heavy thuds of blood shot out, so much so that my ears heard the carotid vibrations.

"What's the hurry?" Jennings said. "You're a snake of the system. Wouldn't be right if a cold-blooded lawyer got away with a murder, or wasted the taxpayer's money living the life at Attica. You've been fuckin' with public safety, which we're sworn to protect. You stirred up a lotta bad blood, lawyer man, and from what I listened to you're gonna drown in your own."

"Don't count your chickens, assholes."

"Tut, tut, tut," Jennings clucked. "Shouldn't call people names. Not very professional. Educated man like yourself. A doctor and a lawyer. I'm real ashamed of you," Jennings said.

Counterintuitively, Garcia relaxed his pressure on my sternum and I was able to move away from the wall. Jennings straightened my tie and brushed white dust off my lapel. "Looks smooth, doesn't he, Garcia?"

"Sure thing."

My pulse was slowing and my adrenaline was spent as Jennings hit me in the solar plexus with so much force that I would have thrown up if I'd eaten anything. While I was doubled over, trying to catch my breath, Garcia, not to be outdone, landed two vicious rabbit punches to my left kidney, which made me straighten up and unfortunately gave Jennings a perfect target for a second assault on my abdominal muscles. This time I crumpled in a heap to the ground.

"Do you think we should call nine-one-one, doc, or will you be able to self-medicate?" Jennings asked.

All the way down the stairs the two of them couldn't stop laughing.

# CHAPTER 23

IT took awhile, but eventually I staggered to an upright position. Dizzy. Nauseated. Everything hurt. Especially my kidneys. Bloody urine and a G-U consult were in my future. As a teenager I'd stuffed envelopes for Bobby Kennedy. "Don't get mad, get even," he'd said. Didn't do him much good. Maybe I could improve on it.

Mercifully, Judge Sherman's office was adjacent to the stairwell. I remember his secretary, I think Mindy is her name, asking, "What happened to you?" before I passed out.

I don't know how long I was unconscious.

The parameds were asking me the usual questions. "Who's the president?" *Of what?* I thought, and stared blankly. "His pupils react. Not an overdose." *Exactly, and, I could add, I didn't have a stroke or a heart attack. Someone beat the living shit out of me.*

"Who's the President of the U.S.?" the paramed repeated.

"All the way with Kennedy," I answered. I wasn't trying to be a smart-ass. I couldn't for the life of me remember.

"What's your name?" a second medic asked.

"Malone."

"Where do you live?"

I answered too quickly, "Twenty-two Sutton Place." My marital residence. "Where am I?" I asked.

"Judge Sherman's chambers. You passed out," the second paramed informed me.

"How long?" I said, agitated.

"A few minutes."

The ugly faces of the two detectives flitted across my memory. I tried to sit up, but someone gently pushed my shoulders down. I protested, "I have to be back in court. I don't want to be late, it won't look good."

"Easy does it, Mr. Malone, you're not going anywhere. Now let's try again, who's the president?"

"Clinton," I yelled. "Now let me up."

The hand on my shoulder remained. The other paramed asked, "Someone said you're a doctor, Mr. Malone. Is that correct?" I nodded. "What's your usual blood pressure?"

"Ninety over sixty. Why? What's it now?"

He heard the concern in my voice. "You're okay, it's almost normal."

"What is it?" Quantification is one of the ways I handle stress.

"Seventy systolic. Fifty diastolic."

"And before?"

"Sixty–forty."

"Wow," I said, genuinely surprised. If those bastards fucked up my kidneys, forget getting even, I'd strangle them with dialysis tubing. I'd kill them if it was the last thing I ever did.

"Do you remember what happened?" the first paramed asked.

"I fell on the stairs," I answered, without elaborating, because I wasn't ready to press charges and thereby become involved in a second criminal proceeding.

"That's what I thought," I heard a woman telling someone.

"No seizure or fainting spell first?"

"No, nothing like that. I've gotta get to court on the third floor."

Judge Sherman's secretary, Mindy, leaned over, "Don't worry. I've taken care of it. They know. It'll be adjourned."

"Where's Arnie, my attorney? I need to tell him something."

"Everyone's at lunch. I'll see he gets your message," Mindy assured me.

"Okay, doc. We're gonna be taking you to New York Downtown for observation," and before I could protest they hoisted me onto a gurney, strapped me in with two sturdy leather belts, and quickly wheeled me to the elevator.

The ambulance sped through the busy streets of Wall Street world. In the space of a day I'd been transformed from an accused murderer to an ICU inpatient. Either way a prisoner. "Your body has the right to hurt. However, anything that goes wrong will be taken down and held against you," I rambled to myself. If I vocalized my fears, they'd mothball me in Neuro or Psych and never release me.

The look of the ER-ICU hadn't changed much in the ten years since I'd practiced cardiology at Lenox Hill and Mount Zion. There was some equipment I didn't recognize, everything was more computerized, but the basic gestalt wasn't different, nothing I couldn't understand and master if I'd wanted to.

The resident took a rather perfunctory short medical history, for which I was grateful, did a quick, complete physical examination, and drew blood samples. He was young enough that he reminded me of my son. I told him I was a retired cardiologist. Under these vulnerable circumstances I omitted any mention of my current career in medical malpractice, not wanting to make him nervous when he was about to insert a urinary catheter. "It's routine for the ICU," he'd assured me. Given the nature of my recent bodily insults it was entirely appropriate and medically indicated, even if it hurt like hell.

All orifices connected to tubes, they sent me upstairs for X rays and a total-body CAT scan to look for broken bones and internal bleeding. Grossly, they found nothing. Hallelujah, my luck was turning.

The aides were parking me and my gurney back in the ICU when Arnie arrived.

"What happened, kid?" he asked.

The nurse was busy tidying so I told Arnie I'd fallen down the stairs.

I know Arnie was sorry to see me in the hospital. Nevertheless he couldn't stop talking about the positive benefits. "This'll help us, kid. Good for sympathy. And breaks the flow of their case." He was right, yet the flow I was thinking about was urinary, and how painful it might be.

"No one'll remember their last witness, you'll see. The dream team is alive and well." But not as a result of anything we'd done.

When the nurse departed, I told Arnie what'd really happened and I think, for the first time, he started to believe in my innocence and the possibility of a police-orchestrated frame. "Those fuckers," he said over and over. "We're gonna nail them to the floor." I wondered, however, if he had any particular strategy in mind.

Another nurse arrived to chart my urine output and Arnie excused himself to go to the bathroom.

"Call Figlio," I told Arnie when he returned.

"Just did, kid."

"What did he say?"

"Something about getting even," Arnie reported.

Great. I hoped he wouldn't make matters worse. How could he? What could be worse?

Diane arrived and I dutifully introduced her to Arnie and vice versa.

"He'll be all right. Just a clumsy fall," Arnie told her.

"Some fall," she answered, unconvinced.

"I've gotta be goin'," Arnie announced. He gave me a hug and whispered in my ear, "She's a real looker."

Diane had never seen me in a physically weakened state and she seemed genuinely upset. I pride myself on my good health and youthful energy, and here I was covered in white, connected to an IV, with a tube sticking out of my pecker and running down to a plastic bag that was slowly filling with very yellow urine. I hoped, should I survive this situation and my legal troubles, she wouldn't be put off by the memory.

"Oh, baby," she said, "I'm soo sorry." "Baby" was a new term of endearment. "What happened?" she asked.

"I slipped on the stairs at the court. There was some construction going on." I didn't tell her about the two detectives. No need to worry her more. "How was Switzerland?"

She ignored the question. "Is everything okay? What do the doctors say?" she asked.

"No broken bones. No internal bleeding."

"Then why're you here?"

"Routine. Observation. I had an episode of low blood pressure. It's no big deal," I reassured her.

"Why'd you have low blood pressure?"

"It happens. A little shock to the system. Don't worry about it."

"You think they're doing everything? Is this a good hospital?" she asked me.

"Good enough."

"You're being shitty, you know. Patronizing. I'm worried about you. I know a little about this." I raised my eyebrows. "My dad's a surgeon."

"Really," I said. She'd never mentioned her parents' occupations and for some reason, probably irrational, I'd assumed her father was a lawyer. "Did your dad used to take you to the hospital to see his patients with him?"

Her face lit up. "Yes, all the time. I loved it."

"How come you didn't become a doctor instead of a lawyer?"

"I wanted to. I sucked in chemistry. Hopeless."

I held out my arms and pulled her to me. "Sorry. I was being a shit. I guess this whole thing's freaked me. Doctors make the worst patients, you know that, I'm sure."

"Yes," she answered, not trying to stop the tears that were running down her cheeks and dirtying the sheets with mascara residue. "What's going to happen with your trial?"

"Two-day adjournment, Arnie says. Probably longer if the doctors don't let me out of here tomorrow," I sighed. "How's the office?"

"Everyone's really being awful. They can barely talk to me. They mumble, look away, as if I'm communicable. I wanted this to be over," and she started to cry more.

"So did I. Maybe it's for the best. That's Arnie's take anyway. He believes in breaking the prosecution flow," I explained.

Diane raised her head off my chest. "That's his strategy? That's it?"

"No. It's a technique. Not a strategy. He's doing a good job. I've done more litigation, trust me," I said. I had my doubts several times this morning, but basically he was okay. The last thing I needed was to change lawyers in midstream.

On her own, without any further advocacy on my part, as if we were meeting after a joint therapy session in which she'd just accepted that you had to allow the other person to run their life, Diane announced, "All right. I have to get back to the office. I'll try to come again in the evening." Perhaps the discomfort of seeing me lying in a hospital bed had finally hit her.

Soon after Diane left, the nurse arrived for the Q 1H vital signs check. BP, temp, and pulse were all stable. Good, they'd have to discharge me soon.

A gaggle of house officers dressed in white followed the nurse to my bedside, surrounding me on all sides. How I'd always hated afternoon medical rounds—at the end of the day patients and doctors were united only by their fatigue, boredom, and hunger.

The Chief Resident picked up my chart and flipped through the lab slips. "Dr. Malone, I'm Dr. Aswami. How're you feeling?" she asked.

"Better. Ready to leave. How much longer are you going to keep me?" I asked.

"We're not sure. Have you donated any blood recently?"

"No. Not since years ago. My wife's employer's program."

"What color have your stools been?" she asked.

"Regular. Brown. My crit's always low normal if that's what you're worried about."

"Thirty-five?"

"Usually. It's why I don't give blood. Look, I don't have internal bleeding. My urine's clear. There was no blunt trauma or puncture wounds. You didn't find anything on the CAT scan, did you?"

"No, but as a precaution we'd like to keep you over-night, just in case, and see where we are tomorrow."

"There's no 'just in case' here. I'm going to sign myself out tomorrow if you don't."

"Dr. Malone, with all due respect, that's not advisable. If you don't object, sir, I'd like to ask the Attending to come and talk with you before you do that."

"Fine by me. I don't mean to be a pain in the butt, I just know I'm okay," I asserted.

I must have dozed off because I don't remember the crowd leaving. Mostly, I was aware of birds singing. Not unusual—it was spring—but the tone was tinny, artificial almost, and there were no outside windows in the ICU. Whatever its origin, I tried to enjoy nature's noises, drifting in and out of sleep until Jess arrived in the early evening accompanied by Jasper.

"You're okay, right? The doctor said you were and all that stuff."

"I'm fine, nothing but a clumsy accident. A just punishment for not playing more sports with you and staying agile," I said, though the reality was that Jess, no matter how enthusiastic I was about tennis or baseball or soccer, really didn't like sports. Some kids are just that way. "So what's been happening with you?" I asked Jess. "And how are you, Jasper?"

"How 'bout the trial? Is it—" Jess asked.

"Adjourned," I interrupted. "Everything's gonna be okay," I added. "You'll see." Why should he believe me? Everything wasn't okay. "What did you do at school?"

Jess's face lit up. "We had another match today. Metro division. That's why I'm late. They said you were okay. I aced two guys. Tell him, Jasper."

"He was super, fierce, Dr. Malone."

I raised my left arm, which wasn't attached to anything medical, and exchanged high fives with Jess. "Great," I said.

"You shouldda seen me, Dad. My opening really froze the second guy." My father had taught me chess. The few times I beat him he'd made certain I knew he wasn't trying too hard, which was a real demotivator, and as a result I have trouble getting excited about the game. "Jasper says

I'm ready for the statewide level. And look, Dad, he gave me this ring. Isn't it neat?"

I admired the gold ring designed from a chess pawn. "That's wonderful."

"It's also a late birthday present," Jess added.

"That's very nice of you, Jasper," I said.

"Dad, when the trial resumes, is it all right if Jasper comes to court? I don't like coming by myself and I can't really ask any of my friends."

"No, that's fine." Jess needed all the support he could muster. We all did.

"Do you want to eat dinner with Diane? She's planning on staying the night at the apartment."

"I don't need a baby-sitter. I'm fifteen."

"You can't stay by yourself," I said.

"I'll stay with Jasper. Is that okay?"

"Do me one favor and stay at home tonight."

"Why?"

"Because I said so. I don't have the energy for this, Jess."

"Jess, your dad's right. That's where you should be. You know that."

"Okay, you guys win."

"If you'll excuse me," Jasper said, "I have to make a telephone call. I'll wait outside, Jess. Take care, Doctor."

Alone with Jess, I decided now was as good a time as any to tiptoe through the daisies on stilted language: "How're you really doing?" I asked. He shrugged his shoulders and said nothing. Jess swallowed hard, making his newly protuberant Adam's apple slide up and down, but remained mute. Silence drives me nuts, especially in situations where I'm already nuts, making me talk more. "It helps to talk, you know."

Jess made a mini-frown and maintained verbal deep freeze. He was acting so much like Sally it was unbearable. We used to have these arguments where she'd retreat into her shell, say nothing, and leave me alone in the conversation to compromise with and negotiate against myself. Only in the last few years when I'd understood the pattern had I been able to prevail or at least not make things worse for myself. I hoped Jess hadn't Xeroxed the whole ball of interpersonal wax we'd performed on his childhood stage.

"What're you going to do for dinner?" I asked, deliberately switching away from our Mexican standoff. More shrugging. "All right, Jess. Enough is enough. You're pissing me off. We need to make plans, I'm not exactly in a mobile mode. How 'bout cutting me a little slack for a few minutes? I can't really handle your moodiness now. I'd be happy to later, when I'm outta here and feeling better, but not now, okay?" Good speech, except I shouldn't have ended on "okay," as if I needed his permission to ask something of him.

"Give me money, I'll get something. Enough for Jasper and me."

"You can't eat alone?" I said in a pique of mean-spirited cheapness.

"That's what I usually do," he said, glaring at me with the memory of hundreds of solitary dinners eaten as babysitters watched the clock and waited to be relieved of a burden that rightfully belonged to Sally and me. We were so busy prosecuting and defending the rights of others, we couldn't afford to see how we were denying basic constitutional happiness guarantees to our child.

"My pants are over there." I pointed to the wall hook on the other side of the monitors. Jess walked over and carried the dusty trousers to my bedside. "Take a twenty out of my wallet."

"You do it, I don't want to."

"What's the big deal. Just do it," I shouted.

"No," he said defiantly.

By some temporary lightness of being I was able to realize that Jess's reluctance might have more to do with an unwillingness to encounter another parental secret than with any rebellious stubbornness. "Okay, give them to me, please." I fumbled through the pockets, but it wasn't there. "Look in the drawer of the nightstand," I suggested, which is where Jess found the worn Italian leather wallet, a Christmas present from Sally years ago, so thick with receipts and miscellaneous items it looked like a triple-decker deli sandwich.

"How 'bout forty instead?" Jess asked. "Good food's expensive." Jess smiled for the first time since we'd gone off on this tack.

"Fine," I agreed. A twenty-dollar extortion isn't much when you consider the self-esteem and good cheer it brought my son.

Figlio arrived as Jess was collecting his backpack and stuff. Between the hourly monitoring by the nurses and all the visitors, it's amazing anyone can recuperate in an ICU.

"Hey, sport, how're ya doin'?" Figlio asked.

I wasn't certain if he was addressing me or Jess, though I chose to respond. "Looking better," I said.

"Hey, Jess, looks like your dad ain't such a tough guy after all."

"He never was," Jess said, a little too willing to bond with Figlio against me.

"Well, I'm making a little progress finding your mom's killer," Figlio told Jess.

"She wasn't my mom," he answered, and hurried off before anyone could engage him in further conversation.

"Teenagers," Figlio declared.

"No, it's more than that. He's got a lot of justifiable reasons to be pissed."

"Even if she wasn't his natural-born mom, she's

someone he knew a lot who loved him and who he loved. Right? Her gettin' snuffed's gotta be hard on him. You don't have to look elsewhere for a lot of fancy-shmancy explanations."

"I know, and I don't know how to deal with his pain. What progress did you make with Sally's murder?"

"Nuthin'. I thought it'd help the kid."

"Yeah. Thanks a bunch. How about the goons in uniform?"

"Not much, but I put some sand in Jennings's gas tank. He's not gonna make it home tonight without a tow."

"That's a little childish, don't you think?" I said.

"Yeah. So? Hey, ya never know. Maybe he'll start gettin' a little par'noid, then we can really go to work on him."

"He already is and forget the 'we.' I've got enough trouble without asking for more from the Disciplinary Committee and the medical licensing people."

"How'd it go in court today?"

"Shitty. The D.A. is about to nail us with the DNA. The criminalist testified there was no EDTA in the samples, which means Arnie's going to have a tough time blaming my mess on chain of custody, but I know those goons have somehow stuck their fingers in my blood," I said.

"You know, I know they're dickheads and I know more than ever you're sure they're framin' you, but those two guys aren't smart enough to pull this off. Yeah, they hate your guts, but I think they're bluffin' about nailin' you."

"We've got no better possibility," I declared. "Why don't we go on the basis they're behind it somehow. Because if they didn't set me up with the blood, then who did?"

"Maybe someone above those dickheads is behind all this."

"You really think so?" I asked.

"That's what we gotta find out," Figlio said.

"Let's do it before my DNA ends up in formaldehyde at the M.E.'s."

"Do you know anyone down there?"

"Yeah. Steve Kim, the Deputy M.E."

"He likes you?"

"If you mean, do I think he would think I could've killed Sally, the answer's no. He'd believe me, I hope."

"You're not positive?" Figlio asked.

"The problem is last year one of our classmates at med school was convicted on Long Island of spouse murder. Maybe Kim thinks there's an epidemic."

"I'll go see him. He's worth a try anyway," Figlio said.

"He'll help if he can," I said, which, given the forces arrayed against me, wasn't saying a lot.

# CHAPTER 24

ABE FELDMAN came to see me at six-thirty in the morning.

"What's this, Grand Central Station?" I asked.

"The Chief Resident asked me to stop by. I hear you're being a typical doctor patient."

"You're the Attending? I didn't know you had privileges here."

"Yes, thanks to you and the TRO, they're still stuck with me. Downtown's an affiliate of University. So, what's your medical story?"

"I'm fine. I'm not having an internal bleed. I just have a low crit. It runs in my family. My mother always said our family's blood was thinner than water."

A bemused smile crossed Abe's face. "It wouldn't hurt to stay an extra day or two. We'll step you down to a transitional room so you won't be bothered by anyone and can rest."

"I can't. My HMO—Help Me Outta here—wouldn't be happy. Neither would the jury."

"I know a good attorney who can put in a temporary restraining order for you," Abe suggested.

"I appreciate your concern, but, right now, the best thing for me, medically and otherwise, is to get on with the trial. If I lose, I'll have plenty of rest days ahead of me. I'm leaving tomorrow morning, Abe, regardless."

"I give up," Abe declared. "It's your life."

* * *

The ICU head nurse was kind enough to send my suit and shirt and tie to the dry cleaners and I was therefore able, upon early-morning discharge from the ICU, to go directly to my conveniently located trial without first having to go home.

As soon as she noticed me, Janet Weinstock came over to assess my damages. "How're you feeling?" she asked. Her interest seemed sincere.

"Better, thanks," I said.

She studied my face. "You were lucky. No visible cuts, no bruises." I thought she was really thinking how lucky she was that the jury wouldn't get to see any injury and feel sympathetic toward me. Sally always said that litigators, in contrast to doctors, couldn't help becoming mean-spirited, untrusting, lonely people, and why did I want to do that to myself? While I'd protested, some of the profession's shabbiness seems to have rubbed off on me.

"The nonvisible ones really hurt," I said.

"If you need a recess, whenever, just say so. Okay?"

Ms. Weinstock patted my shoulder gently, almost lovingly, then returned to Will Washington's side to marshal the People's case against me.

"So, kiddo, how're ya' doin' today?" Arnie asked me.

"Okay I guess. Except my dick's killing me from everybody poking around in there."

"Where's Jess? I left him a message on your machine last night to remind him to be here by nine."

"He's not coming. They're taking the PSATs."

"Shit," Arnie muttered.

"Who's their witness this morning?" I asked.

"Tough day, kid. Sorry about that. First the Medical Examiner, then your housekeeper, Mrs. Schmidt, who'll be followed by a doctor from the DNA lab."

"Mrs. Schmidt? She can't have anything material. She's off Friday through Monday," I exclaimed.

"She goes to motivation."

"We didn't have any big fights or anything. Sally and I were more the silent miserables."

"Maybe they're just setting the table. There's no point speculating. We'll see soon enough and we'll be ready," Arnie declared.

Arnie was right about speculation. It was litigational masturbation and not even pleasurable. About our readiness, with my body aching, I wasn't so confident.

"Once Mrs. Schmidt found a love letter under our bed," I blurted out to Arnie.

"From whom?"

"It's not relevant."

"Humor me. Tell me and I'll decide."

I did and afterward he wanted to use it.

"No, I don't want you to."

"Kid, listen. You're facing life. This letter will work wonders. It always does in my domestic cases. Don't fight me on this. You'll get over the embarrassment."

The People's leadoff for the second day of the trial was Dr. Mustapha Cole, a youthful, mid-thirties deputy medical examiner who was spiffily dressed in a double-breasted suit that he couldn't have bought on a pathologist's salary.

"Dr. Cole, good morning," Ms. Weinstock greeted her witness. He smiled at Ms. Weinstock, and despite his haberdashery, looked uncomfortable. "Doctor, you are a deputy medical examiner for the City of New York?"

"Yes, ma'am," he said. His accent was American with only a hint of India or England.

"And you performed the autopsy on the decedent, Mrs. Malone, sir?" I wanted to shout out, "No one called Sally Mrs. Malone. Either Sally or Sally Hager. Occasionally

Sally Hager Malone," but I would have risked a stern warning from the judge.

"Yes," he answered, and he seemed to blush, though it might have been the way the fluorescent light hit his lightly pigmented skin.

"And when was that, Doctor?" she asked.

"On the morning of April twentieth of this year."

"And for the record, sir, is that the same day the Medical Examiner received Mrs. Malone's body?"

"No. Mrs. Malone was supposed to be posted on April eighteen." I know I might seem cruel and insensitive, but I closed my eyes and visualized a mailman trying to weigh and stamp Sally's body. The jury probably thought I was overcome by emotion.

"And why was that?"

"We received the body in a frozen condition and we had to wait for it to thaw out before we could do the post," Cole answered.

"Can you please describe for the Court and the jury, Dr. Cole, the external appearance of the body of Mrs. Malone?"

"Both carotid arteries were severed, probably by a knife with a serrated edge. There were many scratches and bruises on Mrs. Malone's face, upper arms, and upper back, between the scapulae. Excuse me, shoulder blades."

Ms. Weinstock asked the judge, "May I approach the witness, Your Honor?"

"Counsel, please approach the bench."

Both sides huddled with the judge for a few seconds. Everything seemed amicable.

"He told us to hurry things along," Arnie told me. "All this oversolicitousness is getting on his nerves."

"The People would like to enter these photographs taken at autopsy as People's Exhibit Numbers one twenty-eight through one forty-five." Ms. Weinstock handed them to the clerk, who affixed labels to each item. "Now, Doctor," she said, showing him the items, "do these accurately reflect what you saw on the morning of April twentieth?"

"Yes, they do."

"If it please the Court, I'd like to show these photographs to the jury," Ms. Weinstock asked.

Arnie was immediately on his feet, protesting. "Objection, Your Honor. Highly inflammatory and prejudicial."

"Sustained," the judge ruled, and to the jury he said, "The Court will hold these photographs and will take it upon itself to confirm the accuracy of the witness's testimony."

Ms. Weinstock frowned, but made no further comment. "Do you have any way of knowing, Dr. Cole, for how long Mrs. Malone's body was frozen?"

"No we do not."

"In your opinion, what was the cause of Mrs. Malone's death?"

"Trauma to the neck resulting in massive blood loss."

"Not hypothermia, not being frozen?" she asked.

"No, Mrs. Malone sustained this blood loss antemortem. If she had been placed in the freezer chest against her will while still alive or at least conscious, she would have died of asphyxiation, for which we have no supporting pathological evidence."

"So it's your testimony that Mrs. Malone died from the blood loss resulting from the severing of both of her carotid arteries and that when she was placed in the freezer she was already dead, is that correct, sir?"

"Yes."

"And under those circumstances, Doctor, would you expect to find blood contaminating other items in the freezer?"

"It's possible, but not highly likely."

"As a forensics expert, Dr. Cole, do you have any ideas

why the assailant might put Mrs. Malone's body in the freezer?"

"Objection. Calls for a conclusion, Your Honor."

"Overruled. I'll allow it. Please proceed, Ms. Weinstock."

"Forensically speaking," Cole sighed, "about the only reason might be to blur body temperature."

"What do you mean by 'blur'?"

"One of the ways to measure time of death is by core body temperature readings. A freezer environment is going to override the biological system."

"Is this a commonly known fact?" she mused.

"About freezers?" he asked.

"I'm sorry," she apologized. "About the forensic usefulness of body temperature?"

"Certainly within the medical community, but I don't know about the public," he answered.

"So in your opinion, Dr. Cole, a graduate of a medical school, a person with medical knowledge, would probably know how time-of-death determinations are made?"

"Most definitely."

"And a medical school graduate would also, in your opinion, Dr. Cole, know how to 'blur' the time-of-death calculation?" she asked.

"Of course."

"Now Doctor, you testified that Mrs. Malone had bruising and scratches over her face and other areas, I presume consistent with a struggle to save her life?"

"Yes."

"Did you find any blood under her fingernails?"

"Yes we did."

"Could you please describe it?"

"There was a mixture. Type A sub one and type B."

"Do you know Mrs. Malone's blood type?"

"Type A sub one," he answered.

"So how do you think her blood got under her fingernails?"

"Objection. Calls for a conclusion."

"Overruled. Proceed." Arnie, I assumed, was simply trying to disturb flow again, as the prosecutor had every right to ask an expert witness to offer an opinion.

"Let me rephrase the question," the prosecutor offered magnanimously. "What are the possible ways a victim's blood would come to be found under her fingernails?"

"Through direct trauma to the nail bed during a struggle or passively as she lay in her own blood."

"Thank you. Now Doctor, how about the type B blood? Where'd that come from?" she asked.

"Presumably, the assailant."

"No further questions, Your Honor," Ms. Weinstock said and sat down.

Her strategy was interesting. She wasn't going to provide answers for the jury at this juncture. Despite the judge's admonitions, she wanted the jurors to speculate, to let the issue dangle in their heads. Later, when she was ready, she'd call another witness, probably the DNA expert, who would state unequivocally, with more authority than anyone on the planet, that I, the Defendant, was type B.

Arnie ambled to the front of the courtroom and stood beside the witness stand. "Dr. Cole, I wonder if you were surprised, I certainly was, that Ms. Weinstock did not ask you to give an estimate of the time of death?"

Ms. Weinstock must have noticed, I did, that Arnie's question struck a responsive chord with several members of the jury. "Objection, Your Honor. What the People do or do not ask is their prerogative."

From the bench the judge looked down and sternly said to Arnie in a measured, deliberate tone, "Counselor, I'm sure you can rephrase the question."

"Dr. Cole, were you able to determine the time of death as a result of your autopsy of the decedent?"

"No, we were not."

"Why, Dr. Cole, were you unable to?" Arnie asked.

"As I said to Ms. Weinstock, the state of the body made temperature readings meaningless."

At the hospital the previous night, Arnie and I had talked about time of death, a fitting subject given the ICU surroundings. If Ms. Weinstock failed to explore the subject fully, we decided we would and see if she fell into the trap. "And is that your only way of determining time of death, sir?"

"No, it is not," Cole replied.

"What other techniques do you have in your arsenal?" Arnie asked (a poor choice of words).

"We test the stomach contents."

"In what way, Dr. Cole?"

"Degree of digestion, essentially," Cole stated.

"And did you perform those studies, Doctor?" Arnie asked, his tone skeptical.

"No."

"Why not?"

"Because there were no stomach contents," Dr. Cole said.

"In other words, Doctor, there are two standard ways to determine time of death, is that not correct?"

"Yessir."

"The digested state of food in the stomach, right?"

"Yes."

"And body temperature, right?"

"Yes."

"And both of these being unavailable, you have no possible way of knowing when the decedent died, is that not an accurate statement?" Arnie asked the doctor.

"Yes, but—"

"Now, Doctor," Arnie ignored Cole's attempt to clarify, "if, as you say, the decedent died from massive blood loss, would you expect to find some blood evidence from the decedent in the freezer or on the handles or the outside surfaces or anywhere nearby?"

"Not necessarily. Not if the body was moved after a sufficient period of time had gone by."

"You mean enough time for the blood to have clotted, is that what you're telling us, Doctor?" Arnie was taking the lead, trying to give the impression to the jury that he, too, was an expert.

"Yes."

"Now this kind of attack on a person would cause a lot of bleeding. I believe that's what you've testified. Doctor?"

"Yes, massive," Cole replied.

"So, it would take a long time to clean up all this blood, and maybe even wipe off the decedent's body, to avoid having too much extra blood land as evidence on the ice and the frozen food, for example, is that not correct?"

"Objection, Your Honor. The witness is a pathologist, not an expert murderer."

"Overruled. I'll allow it, Ms. Weinstock. The witness is a forensics expert. This is a reasonable question given his knowledge," the judge said.

"Repeat the question, please," Dr. Cole asked.

"It would take a lot of time to clean up this amount of blood, would it not?"

"Yes, I believe so."

"So the murderer would need a large window of opportunity to not only commit this crime, but also complete the cleanup, is that not correct?"

"Yes."

"Good. Now Doctor, you testified earlier that the body contained numerous bruises and scratches. Can we presume from your testimony that the decedent put up a valiant fight against her assailant or assailants?"

"Yes, she did," Dr. Cole agreed.

"And would you have a reasonable expectation that the perpetrator of this terrible crime might also be covered with bruises or at least scratches?"

"Yes."

"You testified that you tested for blood under the finger-nails of the decedent?"

"Yes, we did."

"And what did you find?" Arnie asked.

"As I said earlier, a mixture of type A blood and type B blood."

"And you indicated you knew the blood type of the decedent, correct?"

"A sub one."

"And how common is that type?" Arnie asked.

"Among Whites approximately thirty-three percent."

"And you also testified that you detected another type, type B, correct?"

"Yes."

"And Ms. Weinstock did not ask you if you happen to know the Defendant's blood type, did she?"

"No, she did not."

I sat up in my chair. I liked what Arnie was doing, taking the bull by its horns, making it appear that the prosecution had something it was trying to hide by not pursuing this line of inquiry.

"Dr. Cole, do you know what the Defendant's blood type is?"

"I personally didn't—"

"Yes or no, please," Arnie cautioned him.

"Yes."

"And what is it?"

"Type B," Dr. Cole declared.

"And how rare is the B blood type?" Arnie asked.

"Among Whites only one in ten have it."

"How 'bout among Blacks?" Arnie asked.

"I believe it's closer to twenty percent."

"Good. How 'bout among Asian peoples?"

He took a long time to answer, trying to calculate the frequency of occurrence. "One in four."

"Twenty-five percent, correct?" Arnie asked.

"Yessir."

Dr. Cole adjusted himself in his chair, his eyes darting over to the prosecution table, imploring them to help him before it was too late and he was trapped, but Ms. Weinstock, at least in this instance, was asleep at the wheel.

"So if a person of Asian descent committed this crime, you'd be almost three times as likely to find type B blood under the fingernails of the decedent, correct?"

"It's closer to two and a half."

"Objection, Your Honor. Counsel is deliberately confusing the jury by connecting statements that shouldn't be," Ms. Weinstock declared.

"Sustained. Strike the question and the answer from the record. The jury is admonished to disregard," but the damage was done. The judge should have called a sidebar and cautioned Arnie, but we lucked out—his clerk distracted him with a message.

"No further questions, Your Honor," Arnie declared.

"Redirect, Ms. Weinstock?" the judge asked out of the side of his mouth while continuing to talk with his law clerk.

"Yes, Your Honor."

"Dr. Cole, if someone wanted to murder someone and cover up the time of death, it would be useful, would it not, if they knew the personal habits of the victim, like for example, if the intended victim fasts every weekend?" she asked, falling for the bait and the hook and the line and the sinker.

"Yes, most definitely."

"And is it your opinion that Mrs. Malone hadn't eaten for at least twenty-four hours before her death?"

"At least eight," he answered.

"Now, you were not a close family acquaintance of the victim, Doctor?"

"No, I wasn't."

"You didn't know anything about her personal dietary habits, did you?"

"No, I did not," Dr. Cole said.

"If I were to tell you that Mrs. Malone regularly fasted from Friday afternoon through Saturday night, based on your autopsy findings that wouldn't surprise you, would it, Doctor?"

"No, it would not."

"No further questions, Your Honor."

"Mr. Glimcher, recross?"

"One question, Your Honor."

"Proceed."

"Dr. Cole, I have in my hand and let me enter it, Defense Exhibit Number one forty-eight, a copy of an article from the Living Section of *The New York Times* last year that described the decedent's weekly fasting habit. Did you ever read that article, sir?"

"No," Dr. Cole said.

"Do you happen to know the daily circulation of the *Times*?"

"Objection."

"Withdrawn."

We didn't need an answer from Dr. Cole. Millions of readers, some even from the D.A.'s office, presumably had read the story. And any one of them could have murdered Sally. Which is exactly what I'd told Detectives Levine and Johnson.

"No further questions, Your Honor," Arnie said triumphantly.

"The witness is excused," the judge declared.

Dr. Cole stood up, stretched, and walked out of the courtroom. I noticed that there was a dark, wet stain running up along the back of his suit jacket. I had to give Arnie his due for the cross. From the defense perspective this was a guaranteed no-win witness, yet Arnie had managed to make the jury speculate that an Asian was more likely to have committed this crime and turned the prosecutor's pathetic attempt to emphasize Sally's dietary habits to my advantage.

Crafty Arnie signaled to Ms. Weinstock that I needed a break, which Ms. Weinstock dutifully asked for, thus further undermining her witness.

Arnie was beaming. "Take a bathroom break and cover my ass."

I headed for the water fountain to give my kidneys a rinse. At the fountain a reporter from National Public Radio tried to induce me to be interviewed. I was flattered that I was on the cusp of national notoriety, but I kept my wits and steadfastly rejected her pleadings.

# CHAPTER 25

"WOULD you please state your name for the record?" Will Washington, the prosecutor, asked Mrs. Schmidt.

"Nellie Schmidt."

In all the thirteen years she'd worked for us, I must admit I'd never focused on her first name. She was simply Mrs. Schmidt. I don't think there was a Mr. Schmidt or little Schmidts, but I'm not certain, that's for sure.

"And where do you live, Mrs. Schmidt?"

"Do I have to tell everyone?" she asked him warily. Mrs. Schmidt, a large, heavy-boned woman and certainly no shrinking violet, was clearly uneasy in the presence of this tall, Black, head-shaved Deputy D.A. If she told him where she lived, you'd never know what dangers might follow. The prosecutors should have switched: Janet Weinstock doing Mrs. Schmidt and Will Washington doing Dr. Cole. But maybe their purpose was to arouse the fears of the women jurors—a man, especially a strong, fit man, could dominate, control, and kill almost any woman if he wanted to.

"Yes," Mr. Washington said, gently.

She whispered, "Five-one-one-oh Rivington in the Bronx."

"Thank you. Now Mrs. Schmidt, do you know the Defendant, Dr. Michael Malone?"

"Yes. I'm the housekeeper for the Doctor and Mrs. Malone."

"For how long have you worked for the Malones?"

"Thirteen years."

"And during this time, can you please describe for the members of the jury and the Court the atmosphere in the home?"

"I kept a very nice place. Mrs. Malone and Dr. Malone are very neat and organized. They're both professional people, if that's what you mean," she answered. The middle-aged juror in the back row who was a housewife and a retired substitute schoolteacher smiled.

"Not exactly. Let me help you, Mrs. Schmidt. Could you describe the mood between Mrs. Malone and the Defendant? Were they very friendly toward each other?"

"Yes," she said.

"They were affectionate?"

"Excuse?" she asked.

"They smiled and hugged?" Washington elaborated.

"I think so," she said.

"Are you certain?" he asked.

"They're not both home when I work." Three jurors laughed out loud. Arnie rolled his eyes. It's unusual to see an early witness so unprepared. If it were my case, I'd move to declare her a hostile witness.

"Mrs. Schmidt, how many bedrooms are there in the Malone house?"

"The master. Jess's room. I try my best, but it's such a mess. And there's a guest bedroom with twin beds."

"I want you to think back to the year before Dr. Malone was ordered out of the house—"

"Objection. Prejudicial."

"Sustained. Rephrase, Mr. Washington."

"August, ten months ago, Mrs. Schmidt, did there come a time, as part of the temporary separation agreement between Mrs. Malone and the Defendant, that Dr. Malone agreed to vacate the marital residence, do you remember that?"

"Yes, I helped Dr. Malone pack."

"Good, now in the months before the Defendant left, when he and Mrs. Malone were both still living in the house, a house you worked in for thirteen years, how often, when you arrived in the morning . . . Strike that. Let me start again. Mrs. Schmidt, what were your usual work hours?"

"Half past nine in the morning to seven in the evening."

"Can you describe an average day? What you did, that kind of thing?"

"When I come in I go right away to the kitchen and put the breakfast dishes in the machine. Clean up the kitchen. Then I make the beds and pick up in the bedrooms. Sometimes, I start a laundry. Every other day I vacuum. We have lots of rugs. In the afternoon I do the grocery shopping. Mrs. Malone leaves me a list or sometimes she says what they'd like to eat and I buy everything. They all like my cooking, even Jess, and I've been making their favorites for a long time," she said proudly.

"I'm sure they do. Do you work every day?" Washington asked.

"When Dr. Malone was living with us, every day."

"Saturday and Sunday?" he asked.

"No," she laughed. "Every weekday. But afterward, when Dr. Malone moved, she had me come in only Tuesdays and Wednesdays and Thursdays, which I didn't like."

"You didn't like it because you were paid less?"

"No, no. Mrs. Malone paid me the same. No, the house got so dirty by Tuesday, I had so much to do," she said.

"Did Mrs. Malone ever explain why she changed your schedule?"

"Yes. She said she wanted more time to herself." Sally

had given me the same explanation, which, quite honestly, never made much sense.

"Now Mrs. Schmidt, in the year or two before the Defendant moved out, when you'd arrive every weekday as usual to take care of the housekeeping, how often did you find that someone had slept in one of the guest room beds?"

Mrs. Schmidt looked at her hands, her face reddened, and she said sheepishly, "Every day."

"So when I asked you earlier if Mrs. Malone and the Defendant were on friendly terms and getting along, you can say, isn't it a fact, that they did not sleep in the same room together for a very long time before the Defendant moved out?"

"Yes."

"Thank you, Mrs. Schmidt. Your witness."

Washington sat down. For whatever it's worth, I wasn't particularly impressed by his examination. It seemed like much ado about nothing. So we didn't sleep together. That didn't compute that I killed Sally.

Arnie walked over to an imaginary spot in front of the jury box. His manner was friendly and very solicitous. "Good morning, Mrs. Schmidt. How are you today?" his voice rising on the "today."

"Fine, sir."

"Good," Arnie said. "Mrs. Schmidt, I can tell from what you told Mr. Washington that you are, were, very fond of Mrs. Malone and Dr. Malone. Am I right?"

"Oh yessir. They're both very nice. But they work too hard. I worry about them."

"You know what kind of work they do, right?" Arnie asked.

"Yessir. Mrs. Malone, she's a district attorney, and Dr. Malone, he's a doctor and a lawyer too."

"And they work long hours?" Arnie asked.

"Very long."

"And sometimes you'd have to stay late with their son when he was younger and they couldn't be home for dinner?"

"Many times," Mrs. Schmidt said.

"And in the morning when you arrived did Mrs. Malone or Dr. Malone let you in?" Arnie asked.

"Dr. Malone usually. Mrs. Malone leaves very early."

"And sometimes, because they're lawyers, one or both of them had very long trials, which required many long hours of work."

"Yes."

"So you didn't think, did you, when Mrs. Malone and Dr. Malone slept in different bedrooms, that they didn't love each other?"

"Objection. Calls for a conclusion."

"You did open the door, so to speak, to this line of testimony, Mr. Washington, so I'll allow it."

"Yessir."

"So isn't it a fact, Mrs. Schmidt, that you thought it was because of their work schedules that they often slept in different beds?"

"Yessir," she said, nodding her head vigorously long after she'd finished speaking. Her relief was understandable. Mrs. Schmidt was from the old school of household employees, which meant she'd never voluntarily say anything bad about an employer in public to anyone under any circumstances and whenever possible would paint an even rosier picture than the reality deserved.

"Mrs. Schmidt, one final question."

Arnie paused melodramatically, removed his reading glasses from his breast pocket, and sucked on an arm of the frame, as if it were a pipe, contemplating, prepared to measure his words carefully. I knew what he was about to ask, and I still disagreed with the tactic.

"Mrs. Schmidt, in the year before Dr. Malone moved away from their home, did you ever come across anything that made you think perhaps Dr. and Mrs. Malone did not love each other?"

Deep islands of red dappled her pale Germanic face, making her blond gray hair seem darker. She took a sip of water from the paper cup provided by the state of New York. "Do I have to answer?" she implored the judge.

"I understand your reluctance, but yes, Mrs. Schmidt," the judge told her.

"Yes," she said, so softly the court reporter had to ask her to repeat her answer.

"Can you please tell the Court, Mrs. Schmidt, about this incident?" Arnie asked gently, acting as if he too was unhappy to be mentioning all this. Janet Weinstock scribbled a note on her yellow legal pad and pushed it toward Will Washington, who, after reading Janet's message, shook his head.

"I was vacuuming under the bed in the master bedroom one morning when the machine sucked something up. Afterward the vacuum wouldn't clean. Dr. Malone was still home and I asked him to help me clear the hosing."

"Was he able to get the item out?"

"Yes."

"What was it?"

"A piece of paper."

"Do you know what was written on the paper?"

"I didn't read it, I wouldn't do that," she said, looking at me.

"But you know what it was?" Arnie asked.

"Objection," Washington declared. "She's already testified she didn't read it."

"I'll allow the question, subject to the proviso that you're going somewhere, Mr. Glimcher."

"I am. Thank you, Your Honor. Mrs. Schmidt, you know what the paper was, even though you didn't read it?"

"Yessir. It was a letter to Mrs. Malone."

"How do you know that?" Arnie asked.

"While Dr. Malone was fixing the hosing I got down and looked under the bed just so nothing else would cause a problem and I found an envelope addressed to Mrs. Malone."

"Was it a Number ten envelope?" Arnie asked.

"Excuse?"

"I'm sorry. Was it a business envelope, eight and a half by eleven, or a personal envelope?"

"Personal."

"Was Mrs. Malone in the habit of storing her mail under the marital bed?" Arnie wanted to know.

"No, that was the first time my vacuum had sucked anything from under their bed."

"Did you happen to observe Dr. Malone's reaction as he read the letter?"

"Yes. He looked upset."

"Did he say anything or do anything?"

"He told to me, 'Mrs. Schmidt, sometimes, no matter how hard you try, things don't work out,'" Mrs. Schmidt recounted.

"Did you take that to mean that Mrs. Malone was having an affair?"

Washington stood up, angry. "Objection, objection, objection, Your Honor. This is way out of line. Defense counsel knows this is inappropriate."

The judge, his finger in the legal wind, like most of his colleagues, protector of his butt, found his anger quickly. "Sustained. Jury will disregard. Confine yourself to the facts in evidence, Mr. Glimcher. Do you understand, sir?"

"Yes, Your Honor," a chastened Arnie answered. "In the months before or after this incident did you ever see

Dr. Malone get especially angry with Mrs. Malone or in any way physically abuse her?"

"No, never. He's a good man."

"No further questions, Your Honor," Arnie said.

"Redirect?"

"No, Your Honor."

"Mrs. Schmidt, you're excused. I see we're close to the noon recess. Usual admonitions. Court adjourned until two," Judge Miller intoned, and banged down his gavel with what seemed to me extra vigor.

Although the prosecutors seemed drained by Arnie's cross, I felt and still feel it was a mistake to open the infidelity can of worms, for it might ultimately help the prosecution by presenting them with motivation on a silver platter. Obviously, Arnie had disagreed. His position was that given the physical threat against me by the two detectives and the failure of the district attorney to have prevented such an outrage, we had no choice but to fire a shot across the prosecutor's bow and play hardball with Gramb.

"The letter wasn't from Gramb," I'd told Arnie.

"So what," he'd said. "He was also boffing her. That's what Figlio found out, right?" I nodded. "What we've done is put that fucker on notice: corral the police if you want to avoid your affair becoming breakfast cereal for New York's bulimic media."

"Doesn't seem fair," I'd said.

"Is it supposed to be?"

# CHAPTER 26

ARNIE was pleased with himself, busily giving interviews to the reporters who'd crowded around him. All I wanted to do was to crawl away as inconspicuously as possible—no man should have to defend his life by advertising to the world that he's been cuckolded.

The hallway outside the courtroom was in semi-darkness. During the second half of the morning session, maintenance workers had erected scaffolding and strewn cables all over the floor in the course of replacing the lighting fixtures. The place was an accident waiting to happen, which explains why I jumped when, from behind, someone put their heavy hand on my shoulder. "How are you doing, Michael?" I responded with an uncontrollable shiver to the mellifluous, avuncular, and mostly contrite tone of Martin Badger, rainmaker.

"Fine," I said warily.

Badger wasn't here because he cared about my fate. He wasn't here to express his regrets over my recent hospitalization. He'd come because, as I'd predicted, he'd have to make nice in order for the firm's share of the silicone settlement monies to reach the greedy little hands of the partners. The issue before me was whether I would be courteous and considerate and sensitive to his predicament or whether I'd be a mean SOB, in other words exactly what Badger had been. Go with the flow, I advised myself.

"Your lawyer's doing a great job," he wanted me to know. Did Badger mean to add, *given that you're as guilty as sin*?

I answered neutrally, "Yes, I think so."

My back was hurting, a residue of the police beating, so I steered us to a dust-covered bench by a window so filthy I at first thought it was frosted glass. "Are you finished with your newspaper?" I asked.

"Yes, of course." He handed the *Times* to me and I unfolded two seat coverings' worth of the Metropolitan Section.

"I assume this isn't a social call," I said.

Badger appeared uncharacteristically tentative—the twitch in his left cheek and the tremor in his resting hand were very apparent—and he seemed at a loss for the right words to begin his pleadings to me, the court of angry resentment. I should have said to Badger, *Just say it, you know I hate your chicken-shit guts, the words you choose are irrelevant, the best you can hope for is that some cosmic ray of forgiveness has landed on my soul, but if I were you, Martin, I wouldn't bet the Mercedes and the 401(k) and the subscription to the opera on such a mutational long shot.*

"The firm is concerned about your status," he finally began. *Really. Kiss my ass.* "Some of the partners feel we've acted too precipitously." *You're right about that.* "That we have not accorded you that most basic right of American jurisprudence." *Guilty until proven innocent, unless I've got something you want.* "We want to redress the wrong." What a nauseating illustration of the effect of impending poverty on a bunch of overeducated slimers.

"What did you have in mind?" I said.

"Restoration of full partnership rights and privileges

subject to the resolution, we hope positive, of your legal difficulties. You'll have complete use of the office and access to your clients until your case is concluded. How's that sound?" he asked, certain I'd be extremely grateful for such generosity of spirit.

"It's a beginning."

"What else do you want?" Badger asked me.

"A sign of your sincerity." Badger gave me the *how-dare-you-impugn me, what gives you the right to call a spade a spade* look.

"Which is?" he said.

"Have the mayor's man, your man, Mal Snyder, see to it that the City agrees to a five-million-dollar stip settling the Lopez case and that the two officers involved are indicted and placed on disciplinary leave without pay. Second, I want everything Mal has about his deputy, Victoria Gramb."

"The D.A.'s wife?" Badger squealed.

I short-circuited further protests. "Not the chicken-shit stuff. We already know that. All the deals, all the relationships, all the interconnections. And don't bother to come back to me with privilege this and confidential that. I don't give a shit. Everything. I'll be the judge of what I want. Is that clear?"

"We don't have that kind of leverage," he protested. "You're being unrealistic."

I loved that. I'm facing life without parole and I'm unrealistic. "It's gonna be harder and harder for you unless you act soon," I said.

"What do you mean?" he asked.

"When the firm goes under, because you haven't worked out a way to make me happy and thus no one receives a slice of the silicone monies, and every one of you is bankrupt, do you think anyone who doesn't have something better to do, which is everyone, will ever let you parasites suck up again?" He seemed stunned, staring off into the wilderness. Some dribble was collecting in the corner of his mouth and I wondered if he was suffering a TIA, transient ischaemic attack. Medicalese for a mini-stroke.

"You know where to find me," I said and walked away, leaving Badger's ass sitting on all the news that's fit to print.

In the more gentle world of medicine I can't imagine a situation where I could have gone as ballistic. If I had, they would have insisted I see someone before continuing my professional responsibilities. Anger restrained within, I'd always told my patients, wasn't good for the blood pressure, so all I'd done was follow my own advice.

One of the things I've noticed about lawyers is that many of them seem to have been kids who were always picked last, if at all, during schoolyard sports, so hardball posturing is the only game they know how to play.

I avoided my usual lunch haunts, I wasn't in the mood to be stared at, and bought two hotdogs from the stand in front of Police Headquarters. Junk food for a junky situation. Where could I go to hide and relax? South to Wall Street to the shopping malls? West to the World Trade twin towers and more shopping? East to the public housing projects? North through all the oppressive governmental and judicial buildings?

The early spring breezes, alternately chilly and warm, kicked up the street litter and beckoned me north to the Louis J. Lefkowitz State Office Building. I ducked into the expansive motor vehicles offices on the ground floor. If you're not there to conduct business or wait in any line, the DMV's the place to be to keep your mind off your troubles. The operations have been streamlined, the employees appear helpful and friendly, and if I continue along this line of thinking, I'll probably be appearing on their infomercials.

* * *

Court resumed promptly at two. The judge's manner was lively, frisky almost, as if his nervous system had been energized by a quickie. I hoped so—he'd be less likely to bust my balls if his were happy.

The prosecution was scheduled to call Dr. Jane Crandall from DNA Diagnostics in Philadelphia, but was requesting a change in their witness order. "Your Honor, Dr. Crandall's train was delayed. She's in the area, just eating some lunch, and rather than make the Court and the jury wait, we'd like to call the next witness first, Nurse Atkins," Mr. Washington asked.

"Any objections, Mr. Glimcher?"

"None, Your Honor," Arnie answered, always anxious to appear flexible and friendly on behalf of his client.

"Good. Officer, bring in the jury please."

"The People call Bernice Atkins."

Ms. Atkins lumbered to the witness stand and was sworn. She was extraordinarily overweight, in the three-hundred- to four-hundred-pound range (when someone's that obese guesstimates are very inaccurate), but a very nice lady. I'd enjoyed talking with her about her medical problems, as she'd filled one red-top and two lavender-top tubes from my right arm last month. Not surprisingly, she was diabetic, hypertensive, and suffered from poor peripheral circulation. "Lord, they have so much trouble findin' my veins," she'd told me.

"Ms. Atkins, you are a nurse assigned to the Police Department?" Will Washington asked.

"Yes."

"And for how many years have you been so employed?"

"Goin' on twelve," she said proudly.

"You are an R.N., a registered nurse, is that correct?"

"Yes."

"And drawing blood from a person is something you've done a lot in your life?"

"Can't count 'em, seems like I've been doin' 'venee-punctures' for ever and a day," she answered.

"Now, in terms of venipunctures for the Police Department laboratory, you've done many of them, and you're very familiar with the procedures, correct?"

Ms. Atkins shifted in her chair, almost losing her balance, but she averted disaster by grabbing the railing. "You mean the administrative procedures?"

"Yes," Washington clarified.

"Yes, I am very familiar with them."

"Would you please tell the jury and the Court what is meant by the term 'chain of custody'?"

Ms. Atkins turned her head and talked directly to the jury. "Basically what that means is we have a record-keeping paperwork trail to make sure we always know where a specimen is, who's handled the specimen, and what they've done to it, so that nuthin' and no one gains access who shouldn't without anyone knowin'."

"Now, Ms. Atkins, on the nineteenth of April of this year, did you withdraw any blood from the Defendant?"

"Yes, I did."

"How much?" Washington asked.

"I filled two purple-tops and a red," she said.

"Purple-tops?" Washington asked.

She swiveled to face the jury again. "Purples have an anticoagulant, so they don't clot."

"How 'bout the red?" he asked.

"They have nuthin'," she answered.

"Blood clumps and clots in the red tubes, right?"

"Yessir."

"Just like it does if it's outside your body, if you've been cut and it lands on your clothes or the carpet, right?" he asked.

"Objection, Your Honor, the witness isn't an expert here," Arnie said.

"Sustained. Jury will disregard the question."

"Now, Ms. Atkins, in terms of these purple-topped tubes, do you happen to know the chemical name of the anti-coagulant that's in them?"

Of course she knew. After *People* v. *Simpson* the whole world knew. But it was smart lawyering to make his witness appear both proficient and forthcoming. "EDTA," she answered.

"And what do those letters stand for?" Washington was milking this for all it was worth.

"Ethylene diamine tetra acetic acid." A Black female juror tapped her knee against the leg of a Black male juror seated next to him, as if to say, "Told ya so."

"Now, Ms. Atkins, when you withdrew this blood from the Defendant on the morning of April nineteenth, one day after his wife was found murdered—"

"Objection, Your Honor," Arnie said.

"Sustained. Mr. Washington, let's just stick to the question and try to avoid editorials, okay?"

Washington seemed taken aback by the judge's sarcasm, but let it go by. Antagonizing the judge wouldn't have been a good idea and it wasn't necessary—the mostly minority jury was probably on Washington's side anyway. "Ms. Atkins, when you withdrew the Defendant's blood on the morning of April nineteenth, were there any witnesses in the room?"

"Yes, Detective Johnson."

For the first time in the trial, I hurriedly scribbled some important comments on my legal pad. I could feel the jurors' eyes. Good. This is where we had to implant the idea that there were crucial lapses.

"And Detective Johnson saw you withdraw the blood and label the tubes?"

"Yessir."

"And you're pretty certain, are you not, from your many years of experience, Ms. Atkins, that from your professional perspective, everything in the chain of custody followed the correct procedures?" Washington asked.

"Yessir. The detective countersigned what I did."

I pushed the legal pad in front of Arnie, who played along, making skeptical eyebrow and facial contortions and nodding solemnly while reading my predictions for the upcoming NBA finals. *Wait'll you hear what we have to say,* we were telling the twelve men and women and two alternates.

"Thank you. Your witness," Washington said.

Arnie shuffled some papers, opened a medical textbook on the table so all the jury and Ms. Atkins could see the colored pictures, and began his cross. "Ms. Atkins, do you recall how much blood you withdrew?"

"Yes. I filled all the tubes to the top. Always do. Like to give the lab enough to work with."

"And how large are the tubes?" Arnie asked.

"The purple hold eight mil. The reds ten."

"So, Ms. Atkins, you're certain, absolutely certain, that the three tubes you withdrew and labeled, those that Detective Johnson watched you sign in at the beginning of the chain of custody, that the three tubes together would have contained approximately twenty-six mil., sixteen from the two purples and ten from the red-top, is that your testimony?"

"Yes," she said with certainty.

"Did you actually watch Detective Johnson the whole time you were in that room taking out Dr. Malone's blood, labeling it, filling out the paperwork?" Arnie asked.

"Not the whole time, no, I was doin' things."

"Of course, Ms. Atkins. So you don't know, do you, if

Detective Johnson was awake the whole time you were in that room together?" Arnie declared.

"I guess if you put it that way, no I don't," she said.

"And the same's true for you?"

"I don't follow."

"If he did fall asleep, he couldn't have seen everything you did or did not do."

"Objection, Your Honor. This is highly speculative," Washington declared.

"Sustained. Mr. Glimcher, please confine yourself to what's been testified to."

"Of course, Your Honor. No further questions."

"The witness is excused," the judge said. "Is the next witness ready?" he asked the prosecution.

"Yes, Your Honor. She's waiting outside," Washington informed him.

"Good, let's move it along."

Washington caught the eye of the court officer who was leaning against the wall next to the jury box, and he quickly left the room to find the next witness. Washington whispered something to Janet Weinstock that made her smile broadly. My one-track mind suspected a sexual interchange between them—it could have been a comment about Bernice Atkins, whose breathing was labored as she slowly exited the stand, and who was still walking up the aisle to return to her average everyday life as the court officer entered with the most attractive scientist I'd seen in a long time.

Jane Crandall was tall and full-figured, statuesque with the big cat intensity of Raquel Welch. One doesn't, at least I don't, expect to find such an African American woman functioning as the top scientific officer of a cutting-edge biotech company. All Arnie had to offer as our rebuttal defense expert was a balding, geeky guy who headed the genetics lab at Syracuse University. We'd have to find someone else with more sex appeal if we couldn't puncture enough holes in her testimony.

"Dr. Crandall, thank you for coming today," Washington began solicitously, as if she was doing the court a favor rather than being paid for her time. "Dr. Crandall, could you please tell the members of the jury and the Court what your occupation is?"

"I'm Director of the Laboratory for the DNA Diagnostics Company." I listened to her voice and thought of shiny satin.

"And how long have you held that position?" Washington asked.

"Since the start up of the company. That would be eight years next January," she said.

"You seem young for such an important position."

The comment brought a smile to her face. Dr. Crandall's teeth were perfectly aligned and so white they glistened. "I received my Ph.D. at twenty-three from Rockefeller, but I'm not so young, Mr. Washington." Was this the *Dating Game* or Supreme Court of the State of New York?

"Good genes, I guess," he told her. She smiled shyly and looked down at her lap. The jury, the judge, and the spectators were noticeably quiet and still. They were living vicariously, watching this soap opera between two very attractive people, yet the prosecution didn't realize (I've had this happen) that the evidentiary benefit of her testimony might be lost in the charismatic glow.

"Isn't it a fact, Dr. Crandall, that your doctoral thesis demonstrated how to use DNA probes to match blood samples?" Washington asked disingenuously.

"To match bloods by their DNA. Yes."

"Could you please tell the jury what the New York City Police Department laboratory sent you in the way of specimens with regard to this case?"

"Yes, of course. First we received five purple-top tubes,

each with approximately five mil. of blood, and several cotton swatches of blood that had been collected, as well as some items of clothing that were bloodstained."

"Were you told, Dr. Crandall, the origin or circumstances associated with any of the samples you received?" Washington asked.

"No."

"So before you tested these samples, you had no preconceived idea that would lead you to expect a match?"

"No, we did not."

"In fact, when you tested these items, didn't you discover that there were five different DNA's you were dealing with?"

"Objection. Foundation."

"Sustained. Rephrase, counselor."

"Dr. Crandall, how many distinct DNA's did you find?" Washington asked.

"Five," she answered.

"And did you find any matches?"

"Yes, we did."

"Could you please elaborate?" he continued.

"One of the samples of tube blood matched some of the cotton-swatch samples. Another tube blood matched clothing bloodstains," she answered.

"And this is what you reported?" he asked.

"Yes. It's in our report."

"Did the police identify, in any way, these specimens?" he asked.

"Do you mean did I know whom they belonged to?" she asked.

The judge interrupted, "Counsel will ask questions, Doctor. Rephrase, Mr. Washington."

"The police never told you where these specimens came from, who they belonged to, did they, Dr. Crandall?"

"No, they did not."

"And right now, as we sit here this afternoon, you still don't know the source of these samples, correct?"

"Correct."

"And therefore if anyone accuses you of any bias—"

"Objection," Arnie shouted.

"Withdrawn," Washington said quickly.

Unfortunately, the jury was following every word the impressive Dr. Crandall said. She was the Pied Piper of high technology and she was going to lead them to my destruction.

"Good, Dr. Crandall. Now, after you disclosed your results to the appropriate laboratory personnel from the Police Department and the prosecutor's office, what did they say?"

"The Director of the Police Department laboratory told me that some of the provided samples were controls."

"Doctor, can you please tell the jury what a control is?" Washington instructed her.

"A control can be anything that allows the lab to test the accuracy of its proceedings. In this matter, what it means is that we were given DNA samples that were in no way connected with their investigation."

Washington walked over to the jury box and placed his right hand along the railing, as if it was on a Bible. "And, you don't know, as you just testified, even now, which of the samples submitted came from the crime scene and which were controls, do you?"

"No, I don't."

The prosecution had played it smart. Their double-blind approach, where not even the DNA lab knew the identity of the samples, had torpedoed a potential defense strategy. It'd be tough for us to demonstrate bias.

"So, if you are asked whether the Defendant's blood from the test tubes matches any of the cotton-swatch samples or clothing samples, you don't know, do you, Dr. Crandall?"

"Yes, that's correct. I do not know," she declared.

"The People enter into evidence, and so mark, this report from DNA Diagnostics, which indicates which of the numbered, but otherwise unidentified, samples match and which don't. This is People's Exhibit two fourteen."

Washington gave one copy to the judge, one to Arnie, and then proceeded to show his copy to the witness. "Now, this is a copy of the report your company submitted, is it not?"

"Yes, it is."

"And you believe these results are accurate?" he asked.

"Yes, I do."

"Thank you. No further questions at this point, Your Honor, but the State reserves the right to recall this witness, should it be necessary."

Now it was Arnie's turn, and I prayed he could hold his own—the jury was so focused it was unnerving even to me, an experienced litigator. "I am pleased to meet you, Dr. Crandall. I'd just like to ask a few informational questions, if you bear with me."

"Of course," she indicated.

"Now, blood is made up of many components, is it not, Doctor?"

"Yes. There's the plasma, the liquid part, which contains nutrients and antibodies. And the cells—red, white, and platelets."

"And the DNA is everywhere?"

"No, DNA is located in the cell nucleus. Red cells don't have a nucleus, their job is to carry oxygen, so they don't have any DNA."

"So, in other words, most laymen who see a red-stained sample would think you're testing the red blood cells for a DNA match, but you're not, correct?"

"That's right. We use the white cells. They have a nucleus and they have the DNA."

"You testified earlier, Dr. Crandall, that you received five purple-topped tubes, each containing five milliliters of blood. Is that correct?"

"Yes."

"Ms. Atkins, the police lab technician, has testified that she withdrew blood from the Defendant and filled two purple-tops. Do you have any idea where the extra three milliliters in the tube went and whether or not they could have been sprinkled on the crime scene?"

"Objection. Objection, Your Honor," Washington shouted.

"Mr. Glimcher and Mr. Washington." The judge beckoned.

Arnie acted contrite before the bench, but I knew he'd proudly regale me, later, with the brilliance of his guerrilla question.

In the most serious tone he could muster the judge announced, "The jury is instructed to disregard counsel's question. There has been no evidence introduced to support the question. If counsel has such evidence, the burden will be on the Defendant to present it after the prosecution rests. Mr. Glimcher, please continue, on track, hopefully."

The judge's warning was especially stern, but from the prosecution's perspective probably too little, too late, to undo the damage.

A seemingly chastened Arnie resumed his cross. "Now, Dr. Crandall, we've heard testimony in this case from other witnesses about EDTA." She nodded. "Did you test for the presence of EDTA in any of the specimens?"

"Yes we did."

"And what were the results?" Arnie asked.

"EDTA was present in the tube blood, but not on any of the swatches or the clothing."

"You're aware, Doctor, of course, that EDTA is a

preservative that's used in breakfast cereal, mayonnaise,
even some laundry detergents, and it wouldn't be unusual
if on some of these samples, particularly the clothing, you
found EDTA?"

"Mr. Glimcher, this isn't actually my area of expertise,
though I know the EDTA argument—it's used often enough
in cases. But I can say first that we found none in any of
the samples, only in the tubes. As to the cotton swatches or
clothing, are you asking me if someone . . ."

Forget the Raquel Welch comparison, Jane Crandall
was closer to Muhammad Ali. I wanted to slink down in
my chair. Some of the jury members, particularly the retired pharmacist who'd seemed sympathetic during voir
dire, looked saddened by the testimony and appeared to
have given up on me.

The judge leaned over and with a twinkle in his eye said
to the witness, "There you go, again, Doctor. Let the attorney ask the questions."

"Thank you, Your Honor," Arnie said. "Dr. Crandall,
you testified earlier, I believe, that EDTA testing isn't your
area of expertise. If that's the case, why then did you test
for it? You're a DNA lab, not a chemical testing company?
Strike that," Arnie said. "Let me rephrase. When did you
perform your DNA testing?"

"May I refer to my notes?" she asked Arnie.

"If it'll refresh your memory, of course."

So the goddess didn't have a photographic memory, she
was a mortal like the rest of us. Maybe there was an
opening here for Arnie. "We received the samples on April
twenty. Preliminary testing was completed April twenty-
four and final testing, the beginning of this week."

"And when did you test for the presence of EDTA?"
Arnie asked.

"Two days ago."

"Is there a reason for the delay?"

"No," she said, but for the first time I could hear some uncertainty.

"EDTA testing isn't routine, correct?"

"Well, it's—"

Arnie interrupted, his tone impatient. "Yes or no, Dr. Crandall."

"No, it's not."

"And was there some reason . . . Strike that. Did someone ask you to do this test?"

"Yes."

"And who was that?" Arnie asked.

Arnie's question made Dr. Crandall uncomfortable. You could tell she felt like she was breaking some kind of confidence. "Mr. Washington."

"The prosecutor."

"Yes."

I had to give Arnie credit again. He was doing his best to make a logical preemptive request on the part of the prosecutor appear sinister. "And did Mr. Washington offer to you any explanation as to why, so late in the testing process, he wanted you to look for the presence of EDTA?"

"He said because of Barry Scheck every defense lawyer would ask about EDTA and try to explain away results, so we'd better be prepared."

"Okay. Now, Dr. Crandall, you are a distinguished scientist. You are aware of course that EDTA, like many substances, degrades over time?"

"Yes."

"So isn't it a fact, Doctor, that the absence of EDTA more than three weeks after the samples were collected and then tested by your company doesn't necessarily mean that EDTA wasn't present back in April when you first tested the samples? Yes or no, Doctor?"

"I see what you're saying, but—"

Arnie pounced on her. "Yes or no, Doctor?"

"Yes."

"So let's make sure we're all clear about this. When you initially tested the samples, two days after they were first collected, you agree there could have been EDTA present?"

"Yes."

"Thank you, Dr. Crandall. No further questions, Your Honor."

The judge peered over his bifocals. "Any redirect, Mr. Washington?"

"Just a few brief questions, Your Honor."

"Proceed."

"Dr. Crandall, when we called you to ask you to test for the presence of EDTA, did you take that to mean that we were demanding a particular result from you?"

"No," Dr. Crandall replied.

"Would it have mattered to you if you thought we had?"

"No, I'm a scientist. I report the results as they are."

"Isn't it fair to say, Dr. Crandall, that you didn't take the request to mean anything more than that the prosecution had confidence in its collection procedures and physical evidence and was certain nothing had been tampered with?"

"Objection, Your Honor. First of all the question calls for a conclusion and second the prosecutor is asking the witness to validate procedures the witness knows nothing about. If the prosecutor would like to testify as to his reasons for ordering the EDTA testing done, let him be sworn in and we'd be happy to examine him."

"Sustained. Are you finished, Mr. Washington?" the judge asked. I wasn't sure why the judge didn't like Will Washington, but it was clear he didn't.

"No further questions at this time, Your Honor."

"The witness is excused. We're approaching four-thirty,

gentlemen and ladies. Unless there's an urgent reason to continue, I suggest this is as good a time as any to adjourn." Arnie looked over at Janet Weinstock, they both agreed, and the judge quickly banged his gavel and court stood adjourned.

As the jury departed, some male members veered off the imaginary exit route to move closer to Dr. Crandall, the ultimate exercise in frustrated voyeurism because court procedures in the interest of fairness and justice precluded any contact whatsoever between them and the witness. But you couldn't blame them for trying.

# CHAPTER 27

MY college English professor used to tell us that several inches of concrete were all that separated civilized people from the jungle. I believe he'd agree that the divide between good and evil isn't especially wide either, which is why most of the other parents at Jess's school would have probably preferred if I hadn't come to the Annual Dinner and Auction and reminded them of their darker tendencies.

I would have gladly skipped the evening festivities, but Jess to my surprise had been insistent. For a teenage boy, usually embarrassed by innocent parental presence—here he was with a cloud, no a tornado, looming over us, flaunting his family. How could I not be supportive of his moxie? How could I, even with my thoughts flooded by EDTA, DNA, milliliters of purple-top tube blood, not put aside my doom-and-gloom terror and try to be as brave?

The food was atrocious—greasy overcooked chicken accompanied by a scoop of grayish-colored rice that was topped off with fluorescent-green frozen peas that were cold. I didn't know anyone at my assigned table. They in turn acted as if they didn't know who I was, which allowed me to remain apart from their school-related conversations without appearing aloof or unfriendly.

Jess and his chessmates were seated on the far side of the room. At a distance they did not look especially nerdy, though their response to the comedy skits performed by faculty and students was reserved in comparison with the other kids, who couldn't contain their belly laughs. During the refrozen vanilla ice-cream dessert, the chess team presented a chess takeoff of tag-team wrestling. It was too intellectual, not very funny, and their solitary female compatriot giggled before every punch line, undermining whatever timing the sketch possessed.

Afterward, before the auction began, everyone mingled.

Jasper caught up with me in front of the chicken remains. "Dr. Malone, how are you doing?"

"I've had better days." I remembered the cuckolding testimony and felt my cheeks warm instantly from the involuntary blush. "I wish my attorney didn't have to ask so many embarrassing, personal questions. I'm glad Jess didn't have to hear all that."

"I'm sure your attorney did what's best for you. As well as for Jess—it won't help him if he loses his father, too."

"You're right. I know you are. Thanks for reminding me of what's important. I'm glad you've been able to be there for Jess. Especially now."

"I don't want you to think I'm a saint—far from it. I've worked with the boys because it's also good for me. I don't have any kids of my own." Jasper looked away and swallowed hard. "Sometimes you have to find your own way, let things go that can't be changed. If I were you, Doctor, I'd enjoy the weekend and be proud of what you have. Sounds syrupy, but it works."

I suddenly felt dizzy. "The room's going round on me. I've got to sit down." Jasper grabbed my upper arm and guided me to a folding chair. "Thanks, Jasper."

"Should I get you anything?" he asked, concerned.

"No, I'll be okay. Just a transient hypotensive episode. Excuse me, low blood pressure."

"I've worked in hospitals. I understand," Jasper volunteered.

"Then you know how stubborn doctors can be," I said.

Jasper laughed, "You bet."

"Dr. Feldman told me to stay an extra day but no, not me. Instead of listening to one of the world's great hematologists, I had to rush back to court to get my daily dose of punishment. Anyway, I think I just need to sit down. It could have been an orthostatic drop." I put my hand to my neck. "My carotid pulse is strong. I just need to sit. If I pass out, you have my permission to call nine-one-one. Okay?"

"Let's hope that won't be necessary," Jasper said.

Jess joined us at that moment. "Hi Dad. Sorry I couldn't be in court. What're you not hoping for?" he asked Jasper.

"More of this food," I interjected.

"I told you their food sucks."

"How'd the PSATs go?" I asked Jess.

"I think I aced 'em." And we gave each other high fives. "Jasper said Arnie aced the DNA lady."

"She was still pretty convincing," I said.

"Jasper, did you tell my Dad about the new chess rankings?"

"No, I thought you'd want to."

"You do it," Jess insisted.

"The team's moved up, Doctor. We're now number two in the Metro New York region. Jess is getting really good. When you're out from under all this, you should come to a match."

"I'd love to. Too bad Grandpa isn't alive. He loved the game." The chess gene must have skipped me. "How long have you been playing chess, Jasper?" I asked.

Jasper's eyes widened. I steeled myself for a lengthy tedious history of his life in chess. "Since high school." He looked away, the sadness and resignation in his voice unmistakable. Chess must have replaced something more basic, something he'd lost and never recovered. Something he didn't want to discuss, especially with an outsider. No wonder he felt at ease with teenagers.

While I was noting, and judging, Jasper's sadness, Jasper's loss, I was not accepting my own. I was in danger of becoming the kind of person I hate the most—someone who deludes himself about his life and where it is going. The realization made me uncomfortable and ashamed.

The rest of the evening was uneventful, for which, given my dissatisfaction with myself, I was grateful. I bid on several items, not seriously, really to help the fundraising, though I would have been glad if I'd won the ten-day Mexican getaway.

The heavy food was weighing down both my stomach and consciousness. I said good-bye to Jess and left in the midst of the Mickey Mantle memorabilia bidding.

Plumes of carbon monoxide arose from the tailpipes of a black stretch limo parked in front of my house. Car doors opened, Mafia hit style, blocking the sidewalk. Out stepped a short man I didn't know, who was wearing a fur-lined duster that was too long and made him look as if he were sitting on a bar stool.

"I'm Mal Snyder. I understand you wanted to talk."

During the two years since I'd made partner at Badger, Weissberg, Smith, and for the preceding three, I'd never laid eyes on the man. Stealth was undoubtedly his style, smoke-filled rooms his habitat.

"What's your poison, my place or yours?" I said, always the wiseass.

He started up the front steps. "Let's go inside. We don't want to cause any more air pollution than's necessary."

"Are you sure?" I asked, suddenly unwilling to submit

my personal space (that is, mess) to his appraisal. "I'm on the top floor. There's no elevator."

"Let's go, it's late."

I ushered Mr. Snyder into the vestibule and led the way. Snyder climbed the four flights of stairs without wheezing or shortness of breath or any other sign of cardiac compromise that you'd expect to find in a fifty-five-plus overweight person. After I'd turned on the lights and fluffed the living room pillows, the place looked warm and cozy and did in no way undercut my negotiating position.

"Can I get you anything, Mr. Snyder?" I asked.

"Nothing thanks. Sit down." I complied with his command without a moment's hesitation. So much for the assertiveness training I'd taken after law school in preparation for trial work. "In exchange for your releasing control of one-fifth of the seventy-five mil silicone dollars to the firm, the City's prepared to offer three point five in the wrongful death. That was what you wanted, right? I'm sure your clients will be satisfied." No bush beater, our fat little rain man.

"And Detectives Jennings and Garcia. What about them?"

"Early retirement."

"No indictments?"

"For?" Snyder asked.

"You know damned well. Where do you think, because of those assholes, I'm spending my days?"

"Can't do."

"Can't or won't? You're supposed to be all-powerful."

"We don't control the courts. No one does," Mal declared.

"Don't tell me—you have a day job as a constitutional law scholar, and somehow obstruction of justice, assault, attempted murder, tampering with evidence, framing someone for a murder they didn't commit, doesn't bother you.

Of course, since it's not you they've done this to, why should it?"

"It's nonnegotiable."

"And how about your distinguished associate, Victoria Gramb?"

"What about her?"

"We want access to her real files. Not just the version you'll hand us on subpoena."

"What're you talking about?" he asked.

"Don't play dumb with me. We know about her connection to the medical center."

"What connection? You got nothing."

"Take a chance and find out," I said, raising the schoolyard pissing contest another notch.

"You've got till tomorrow morning at nine, Malone. Take it or leave it."

For what seemed like forever I remained silent. Snyder probably took this to represent some kind of face-saving posture before I accepted his deal. If I were stuck in a normal human predicament, maybe. But I wasn't. I could be in Attica for life and these guys knew that and thought they had me by the balls. Possibly it was already too late and I was kidding myself. But nothing ventured, nothing gained, or lost, or whatever fits. Go for broke, I told myself, how could it get worse?

"You know, Mr. Snyder, your position disturbs me." He shifted his butt on the couch, as if to say, *I don't see how that's possible.* "I was under the impression, as a result of your alleged work for the firm" (I was being deliberately provocative with "alleged") "that you were a pragmatic type, your finger always on the political pulse. Now I find that's not the case. So few people live up to their publicity, it's undoubtedly the source of some of the malaise affecting our society, don't you think?"

"You know, doc, it's not my problem, it's yours that

you've got some fantasy about my influence and power. Things don't work the way you think. We don't run the courts or the D.A.'s. With what I heard on the news about the DNA, you'd better wake up before it's too late, while you still have some leverage over the silicone settlement, because pretty soon whatever control you think you have isn't going to be worth shit."

"If you believed that you wouldn't be here," I said. "So if I were you I'd run to my masters and tell them I'm not going away and this isn't over until you guys give up Jennings and Garcia because we all know, including you, they're part of the frame."

With difficulty, arthritis or chronic fatigue, Snyder lifted himself off my couch. "We'll be in touch," he said.

"Make sure it's with something meaningful," I replied.

After he left, I was aware how sweaty and tired I was, perhaps even a little feverish. Maybe the TB had converted to an active case, so I took an extra INH tablet and went to bed.

Jess came home while I was drifting off and in the morning was still sleeping when I went out to buy the Saturday papers to see what had been written about the trial. I never did find out because I was too stunned to read past the tabloid headlines that announced the murder of Dr. Abraham J. Feldman.

# CHAPTER 28

THE police had cordoned off the area in front of the Center with yellow tape, restricting pedestrians to the opposite side of the street. A city bus, parked diagonally from curb to curb, blocked the street and appeared to be functioning as a field headquarters. Dr. Feldman's worldwide fame as a medical scientist hadn't protected him from his adversaries but at least, in death, he was receiving the large-scale law enforcement investigation his murder deserved.

I identified myself to a uniformed cop who moved the police barricade aside and pointed me in the direction of a bemedaled officer standing next to the door of the bus.

"Excuse me, Captain. My name is Michael Malone. I'm the attorney for the Center and for Dr. Feldman." I extended my hand. "The officer over there said you were in charge."

"Of the precinct, not the case. Jack O'Neill. Pleased to meet you. Detectives Scavone and Ianucci are the ones you want."

"Where can I find them?" I asked.

"They're upstairs with the forensics guys. They'll be down when the crime scene unit is finished and I'm sure you'll be able to talk with them then." He sensed my impatience. "It won't be long. We've got coffee and doughnuts in the bus if you'd like to wait in there. Little nippy, still."

"Sounds good," I said in my most upbeat tone. It would have been counterproductive to radiate the doom and gloom I was feeling.

I climbed aboard the bus, the old-fashioned model with vinyl-covered seats that only appears in the event of subway emergencies or transit workers' strikes. Despite my training as a cardiologist, which should have had a restraining influence on my behavior, I helped myself to black coffee (with two heaping teaspoons of pure cane sugar) and a double chocolate glazed doughnut. In this unpredictable world, I took comfort in the certainty that at nine in the morning I'd already ingested a significant percentage of the American Heart Association's suggested amount of daily saturated fat.

After only a few minutes of solitude, two gentlemen in shiny suits charged up the front steps of the bus. The first to reach the landing said to me, "Captain says you'd like to talk with us."

"I'm Michael Malone."

"Pete Ianucci. And my partner, Detective Scavone."

We shook hands and I handed each my card.

Scavone turned it over a few times. "Aren't you the husband of Sally Hager, the D.A.?"

"The one that was murdered?" Ianucci added.

"Yes. And I'm on trial in Supreme, just in case you missed it. Dr. Feldman was my client. Can we talk about what happened?"

The two detectives conferred nonverbally. "Sure," Scavone said. "Why not? Gimme a minute."

Scavone walked to the back of the bus, and returned with a clipboard of notes.

"We're all ears," Scavone declared.

Because these two detectives didn't know me and had no reason to reveal much, the burden was mine, the person who'd sought them out, to be as forthcoming as possible.

Candor about any matter, especially a murder, could only help my tattered reputation.

"As I said, Dr. Feldman was my client for many years. Last month he hired me to represent the Center in federal court."

"Against whom?" Ianucci asked.

"UMC. They were trying to shut him down."

"But they didn't?" Scavone pointed out.

"No, I won, we won."

"These aren't the kind of people who are sore losers?" Ianucci asked.

"I don't think so," I answered, but, honestly, I wasn't certain about anything, anymore.

"When did this happen?" I asked Scavone.

"We're not sure yet. Problem is we fished him out of the river, so you know it's hard to say." That's one thing I did know.

"The M.E.'s working on it," Ianucci added. "Sometime after nine."

"When did you say you last talked to him?" Scavone asked.

"I didn't. Thursday morning. He visited me in the hospital."

"Did he seem upset or worried about anything?" Scavone asked.

"Only me," I answered.

"Why?" Ianucci wanted to find out.

"Because I wanted to discharge myself from the ICU and he thought I should stay another two days to make sure I wasn't bleeding internally."

"Where was he shot?" I asked both of them.

"How'd you know he was shot?" Scavone asked, suspicious.

"It was on the news, Scav," Ianucci interrupted. "In the head."

"No, I meant where'd the shooting take place?" I clarified.

"Why's that matta?" Scavone insisted on keeping up the toughguy role.

"Listen, guys, I'm not tryin' to be a pain, but I'm a litigator. I deal with a lot of deaths, some wrongful. Not murder usually. But I've spent my fair share down at the M.E.'s, I was married to a prosecutor, and, if that's not enough, I'm also a doctor. Bottom line is maybe I can help you and my client at the same time. We're both interested in the same result, I presume."

"He was shot in the lab," Ianucci responded. "That's why the forensics guys are crawling all over the place."

"Is there anything else, Dr. Malone? Otherwise we gotta bust tail," Scavone said.

"Do you mind if after the forensics guys finish I go up there and look around, talk to some of the staff?"

Ianucci took the lead. "No, it's fine. What the hell, three heads are better 'n two. Here's our card. Call us if you come across anything."

"Thanks, I appreciate it."

And I did. Their downtown superiors might be after my ass, but here were these two nice detectives willing to be accommodating. All the more amazing given the charges I was facing. Maybe my police conspiracy theory was just that. A theory.


By noon, when Jess and I arrived, *Annabelle*'s aft-deck had been stripped down and Figlio was on his third Red Dog.

"How's it goin', kid?" Figlio greeted Jess.

"Okay."

"Can I get you guys anything?"

"Nothing for me," I answered. Jess picked up a paint scraper and never bothered to reply.

"Sorry about the doc."

"Yeah. He was a really good guy. Nobel Prize level."

"Sometimes those smart guys make a lot of people angry, or envious. I can tell you this, somebody definitely didn't like him," Figlio declared.

"Why do you say that?"

"This almost looked professional. It was no random, that's for sure. Any ideas?"

"There's the university. Victoria Gramb—"

"Oh, not her again. You're becomin' a nut case, Malone."

"And there's Abe's bugaboo—the Red Cross," I added.

"I'm startin' to worry about you. You're watchin' a lot of junk TV again. I threw mine overboard, you know."

"Every time I come here you've done something like that. You're the one who needs help before Environmental Protection arrests you. And may I remind you, you didn't believe the Rikers Island boys would do anything either!"

"Okay. You win that one. Want another Red Dog?"

"Figs, it'd be my first."

"Tell you what, Malone, how 'bout I poke around the Center and see what I can turn up. Maybe I'll get lucky and find Florence Nightingale on ice there."

"You mean Clara Barton," I told him.

"Who's she?" Figlio asked.

"The lady who founded the American Red Cross."

"I give at the office."

# CHAPTER 29

ARNIE grabbed my arm from behind as I passed the telephone booth outside the courtroom. "Hey, kid, where the hell've you been? I've been tryin' to reach you all weekend."

"Yesterday I was home and Saturday I was helping a client. Maybe you dialed the wrong number."

"No way, kid," as he reached into his shirt pocket to retrieve the number he'd written on the back of his Merrill Lynch statement, which he unfolded methodically and slowly, so I would notice how invested he was.

"You transposed the three and the seven," I told him.

Without so much as a microsecond of contrition or logic, Arnie said, "You know some of us can use a phone and shtupp at the same time."

I wondered what was eating Arnie—frustrations with the telecommunications superhighway or the mountain of chromosomes arrayed against me?

"So, *how* was your client?" Arnie continued.

"Dead," I answered, which deflated Arnie's sexual envy instantly.

"Natural or unnatural?"

"Bullet to the brain."

He didn't ask but I gave him the executive summary version anyway.

"Maybe we're dealing with a professional serial killer," Arnie mused.

"Serial killers are usually psychos," I said.

"No, I mean a serial killer who preys on professionals. First, Sally, a lawyer, then your doctor friend."

"I doubt it," I said. "The MO's not the same."

"I hope you're right because the guy could buy one get one free if he zapped you." I scowled. "Just kidding." The old lady therapist told me that behind every joke was a serious emotional grievance.

"So what did you need to talk to me about?" I asked Arnie in an attempt to move the conversation away from this dysfunctional path.

He shepherded me to an empty area of the hallway. "They want a deal."

"Who's they?" I asked.

"The prosecution," he snapped, the irritation once again surfacing. "And, by the way, it would've been nice if you'd told me about Mal Snyder's visit."

"There wasn't anything to report. Deal how?"

"They'll back off if you back off."

"Which means?"

"They'll drop the indictment to manslaughter two if you take Snyder's offer and give 'em access to the silicone money."

"So what's your recommendation?" I asked Arnie.

"I think we're doin' okay, but it's up to you to make the decision. Your ass is on the line, not mine."

"My first response is to tell them to stuff it."

"Good answer. I can't help but wonder why Gramb gives a shit about those stiffs at Badger Weissberg," Arnie said.

"My thought exactly. Trust me, Arnie, somehow Victoria Gramb and Mal Snyder are mixed up in my client's murder and Sally's too. She's involved with the Center.

My client, Dr. Feldman, showed me that. Hubby is screwing my wife. As a result you can bet your booties Gramb drags his Gucci's on the Feldman murder."

"Could be Gramb who's behind everything. He's the one with the opportunity to fuck with the chain of custody. He's doing jack shit with the Rikers boys—they could be in his debt and vice versa. And Gramb's the one pushing this deal."

"Who actually made the offer?" I asked Arnie.

"Pretty Boy Gramb. Called my cell phone. Right in the middle of my morning shtuppin'. Goddamn intrusive technology."

"When?"

"Saturday morning."

"When all their ducks were in order," I said.

"I tell you something, kid, and I know you'll say I'm contradicting myself, which I am, but I can see all these people involved with one or another of these murders, but not really the two connected. It really doesn't make sense."

"I asked Figlio to do some checking at the Center. See what he can turn up. Meanwhile, I think the best strategy for us is to diddle the prosecution. See what cards they're holding. I'm not ever going to take a plea, you know that. And I really want to see the trial through, all the way to the end—it's the best thing for Jess and me. Otherwise it's always going to be there as unfinished business, hanging over us, a living death sentence. But I'm also not about to fall on the sword."

"Now I'm really confused. So whaddya want me to do?" Arnie asked.

"Go in there and talk to some reporters and shuffle your papers and then tell the prosecutors very casually and very matter-of-fact, 'We'll think about it.' "

Lawyers and actors have a lot in common. While I sat

calmly at the Defendant's table reading, really skimming, *Race Matters* in order to impress the eight African American jurors who might notice the book when court resumed, Arnie played the role I'd scripted for him perfectly. I most appreciated the dismissive, cavalier way he rejected the plea bargain offer.

Weinstock and Washington, who no doubt had been led to believe the opposite would occur, looked stunned. Given the obvious strength of the prosecution's case, Gramb must have had to work overtime in the first place to promote the plea deal to his subordinates. And now that it was being consigned to the dustbin of uncertainty, the prosecutors had to be wondering what we had up our sleeves. It had to be something special or else how could we be so confident? Soon the word would reach the big boys at headquarters, compelling them to waste tons of time scratching their asses.

After several minutes of huddling, Ms. Weinstock departed, presumably to phone her superiors and seek help and guidance.

The court functionaries arrived during Ms. Weinstock's absence and the clerk called the court to order. Judge Miller had a spring to his gait as he climbed the steps to his perch and I suspected he'd been informed ex parte that a deal was in the works, which of course isn't supposed to happen but goes on all the time. "Where's Ms. Weinstock? Is there anything unusual holding her up?" the judge asked disingenuously.

"No, Your Honor," Mr. Washington replied, "she should be right back."

The judge smiled benevolently. "Is there any other business we have to conduct?" he asked his clerk, who readily produced a stack of legal documents for the judge's intervention.

"Anything else?" the judge asked, ignoring the thick

pile. Why distract yourself with paperwork while you're waiting to preside over a case settlement that was going to make a lot of important people happy with your performance? Miller had, so far, been fair and evenhanded. Who was I to begrudge him this temporary moment of job security. He'd soon, in a few minutes, be disappointed, and hopefully he wouldn't take it out on me.

"Should we call in the jury, Your Honor?" the court officer asked.

"No, no. Let's wait for Ms. Weinstock," he answered. "Mr. Green, how are you today?" the judge called to an attorney trying to file motion papers and open a package of breath mints at the same time. "Please approach the bench." The two of them chatted away amiably about an all-night poker game and shared mints together. I felt a little guilty that I would be responsible for bursting the friendly ambience, but, as far as I knew, I was the only person in the courtroom facing a long prison sentence.

The first thing I noticed about Janet Weinstock upon her return was the long run in her nylons, which extended from her right calf straight up toward the danger zone. Next I was struck by how much nervous anger she radiated—she fiddled with her hair, brushed imaginary lint off her clothes, and bit off the pencil eraser. I guessed Donald Gramb was a poor loser who'd blamed her for the negotiating turnaround. After all this was over and done, somebody, and I'm designating myself, needed to snap his suspenders.

"Ah, Ms. Weinstock, I see you've rejoined us. Good morning. And how are you today?" Judge Miller asked her.

"Fine, thank you, Your Honor."

Her gloom was unmistakable, but the judge managed not to notice. "I understand that both sides are considering a settlement in this matter, is that the case?" he asked.

"May we approach, Your Honor?" Ms. Weinstock responded.

Judge Miller waved everyone to the base of Mount Miller. "Okay, what's the good news?"

"I'm sorry to inform you, Your Honor, that the Defendant does not wish to accept our offer of a reduced charge."

The judge's lower jaw dropped as he watched his lifetime sinecure slipping away. "Is that true, Mr. Glimcher?"

"I'm afraid so, Your Honor," Arnie said.

"Is your client aware of the consequences?" Judge Miller asked. His tone was beyond cold. Antarctic.

"He is, Your Honor," Arnie answered.

"This is his decision, counselor?" the judge shouted. Shock was wearing off, replaced by rage. Arnie nodded. "Come here," Miller beckoned to me. I stood up, tugged at the bottom of my gray pinstriped suit jacket, and walked to the front, holding my posture as erect as I could, and took my place next to my attorney. "Is what I'm hearing correct, son, that you've turned down the People's offer?" Son. He wasn't much older than me.

"Not quite, sir. We said we'd think about it. We haven't actually rejected it, yet." I answered firmly. I wasn't some dumb slob who didn't know the way the law really worked; this sonofabitch in black judicial robes wasn't going to intimidate me just because he was disappointed and upset.

"The case is pretty strong against you. That DNA stuff's incontrovertible, don't you think?"

"Maybe it is, maybe it isn't. I've prevailed in more difficult situations," was the best I could come up with.

"Listen, son, this isn't a med-mal case where you can twist the court and the jury with fancy technical experts. We've both been listening to the same witnesses, I assume, and from what I've heard, there aren't going to be too many experts willing or able to impeach this testimony. Don't kid yourself that anyone buys the blood-tampering theory either. I thought the police nurse was pretty convincing, and so did the jury, as I read them. You're going to hang yourself with this chain of custody stuff if you don't watch out."

"No offense, Your Honor, but I fully understand the risks, and I'll take my chances," I declared.

"Okay, we tried, so be it. It's on your head, Dr. Malone. Officer. Please call the jury," the judge commanded, an omnipotent power in the courtroom, yet unable to stop the corner of his mouth from twitching and a little spittle from settling there.

"Your Honor, if it please the Court?"

"Yes, Ms. Weinstock."

"The People request a one-day adjournment," she announced.

"Why?" the judge asked.

"We would like the opportunity to demonstrate different options to the Defendant."

The judge's eyes widened as he considered the resuscitation of his career. "Any objections, Mr. Glimcher?"

"May I confer with my client?"

"Certainly. Take all the time you need."

Arnie walked me back a few paces. "So whaddya want to do, sport?"

"No reason not to be generous," I indicated.

"How's that?" Arnie asked.

"We just won Round One," I said.

"Really. I must've missed something."

"You have," I couldn't resist saying. "Let's go see their show-and-tell."

"Good, we're agreed," Arnie said authoritatively, as if my strategy was his idea.

"We're on board, Your Honor," Arnie affirmed to Judge Miller.

"Court stands adjourned in the *People* v. *Malone*. I have a morning conflict on Wednesday and something on Thursday, so let's set this down for Friday, nine-thirty. Make sure you come back with something. The Court doesn't like to waste its time and the jurors' time. Is that clear?"

"Yes, Your Honor," Arnie said.

Janet Weinstock ripped off the cover sheet from her yellow legal pad and handed it to Arnie. "Eleven-fifteen. This morning. I trust you can be there."

# CHAPTER 30

DIANE reached me via Arnie's notorious cell phone as the limo Arnie'd hired (he can't take public transportation, it makes him claustrophobic, he says) was detouring around a water-main break at Houston and First.

"Mrs. Schmidt left a message on your answering machine for you to call. She sounded upset. I didn't know if something was wrong with Jess."

"Thanks," I said and dialed Sutton Place without asking Diane why she was at my apartment in midmorning.

Mrs. Schmidt answered on the first ring as if she'd been waiting for my call. "What's up, Mrs. Schmidt?"

"I need to talk with you, Doctor."

A foreboding came over me. The last time I'd rushed there, we'd found Sally stuffed in the freezer. "Is anything the matter?"

"You must come."

"Is Jess there?"

"No," but I heard hesitation in her voice.

"I'm with my attorney, Mrs. Schmidt. We're on our way to an important meeting. Can it wait till later?"

"It'd be better now. I have to leave early to visit my sister in Greenpoint who's sick."

"Okay," I said, giving in to her timetable.

I wasn't anxious; I resisted playing the doom-and-gloom scenarios in my head. For all I knew, I reassured myself, Mrs. Schmidt's urgency was merely German efficiency, not an indicator of more bad news.

The house was immaculate. Why shouldn't it be? No one, except Jess, occasionally, stayed there. I'd kept Mrs. Schmidt on because I didn't have the heart to let her go (it wasn't her fault Sally was dead), and because I thought it might be good for Jess to have his childhood household remain intact for now. It also occurred to me that it was in my interest to be generous toward her, for the last thing I needed was to have Mrs. S. turn up as a hostile prosecution witness.

She served us tea and coffee in the dining room on very starched linen doilies Sally and I had bought in a Connecticut antiques barn during a thunderstorm. Sally and I were happy that rainy day. How'd we let it get away?

Despite my democratic requests that Mrs. Schmidt sit down with us, she refused and flitted about. Undoubtedly it was her way of handling discomfort.

Arnie admired the setup. "Nice place you have here, Malone. Must've been hard to give it up." Given the circumstances, not the most politic observation for my divorce lawyer to make in front of the staff.

I picked up a sticky bun, dipped it in my coffee, and asked Mrs. Schmidt, "What did you want to talk about?"

She cleared her throat several times, as if to speak, but instead left the room to refill the creamer.

All this postponement was making me very hungry. I started a second bun. Mrs. Schmidt returned with the creamer and set it back down in front of Arnie, who was also busily stuffing himself. "Mrs. Schmidt, it's better if you just get it off your chest, whatever it is," I exhorted her.

"What my sister says, too." She rubbed her hands together with imaginary lotion. "I haven't been able to sleep well since the missus . . ." She broke off. "I should have

told you sooner. Then maybe you wouldn't be with so
many problems."

I tried my best to relieve her guilt. "It's okay, Mrs.
Schmidt, I'm sure you did what was right." *Just tell
us, please, before I eat another two thousand calories of
cholesterol.*

"The Wednesday of that week," she began.

Arnie, ever the lawyer, interrupted. "What week?" he
asked, unable to let her tell her story her way.

She gulped. "The week the missus passed. They'd had
such a terrible fight. I was so afraid, I'd never seen him
like that. Not even when he was a little boy. He was
yelling and throwing things." She reached into the sideboard and brought out pieces of fractured crystal. "Look,
he broke the candleholder." A wedding present from my
great-aunt. No loss. We'd both hated it.

"What was the fight about?" I asked.

"I didn't want to listen, Doctor, I'm not that kind of
person," she assured me, "but it was so loud, I couldn't
help it."

This was going to be like pulling teeth. "We understand, Mrs. Schmidt," I reassured her.

"If he were my son I would have washed his mouth
out."

"What did he say, Mrs. Schmidt?" Arnie asked, unable
to handle the slow pace.

Mrs. Schmidt started to cry. "He called her a cold bitch.
Over and over and over. And then he said, 'My mother's
like a whore. You did that.' The missus said to him, 'No,
that's not true. Where'd you get that idea?' 'A little birdie
at school.' Then he quieted down and started making bird
sounds and I thought the fight was over. And I went back
to my dusting. But then he started up again, screaming
again at the missus." Mrs. Schmidt dabbed at her eyes

with a hankie and then focused her dry vision someplace faraway.

"What did he say then?" Arnie prompted her.

She never looked at either of us, but answered, " 'None of your f-dash-dash-dash-ing business, you phoney bitch.' I couldn't help it but I came in here because I could hear the missus crying and I thought maybe Jess would stop if I was there."

"Did he?" I asked.

"No. He didn't care."

"What happened next?" I asked.

"The missus was trying to hug Jess. She said she could explain. But he wouldn't listen, he pushed her away, and she knocked herself, here, against the table, and later I had to give her some massage on the back."

"Do you remember anything else Jess said?" I asked Mrs. Schmidt.

"Yaa. Something like, 'Why didn't you tell me? Everyone else knew.' And he started using bad words again. 'The law and crime is f-dash bull-dash for other people. Not you. You get on television and give interviews and say you're for this and against that and all that other stuff you say you fight. You're worse than all those people. You're a phoney. A piece of s-dash.' "

"I'm not sure I get why you're telling us all this now, Mrs. Schmidt," Arnie said.

"I didn't want to cause trouble for the boy. He's a good boy, really. I don't know why he was so upset," she answered.

"I think what Mr. Glimcher means, Mrs. Schmidt, is what's so urgent today?" I asked.

"I sit in the courtroom yesterday, yes. I understand everyone thinks you killed Mrs. Malone. I don't believe it, I know you," she cried.

"And you were afraid Jess did?" I asked.

"I don't know, I don't know."

"Mrs. Schmidt," I put my arm on her shoulder, "Jess was away. He couldn't have done this."

"He's a smart boy. Somehow it's possible," she confided.

"None of us knows what happened here. Did anyone else have keys to the house?"

"No," she said softly.

"It's no time to keep secrets. Mrs. Malone is dead. Are you sure no one else had keys?"

"I'm sure. No one."

"Did you ever see any clothes or anything in Mrs. Malone's bedroom that didn't belong there?" Arnie asked.

"No, I don't think so."

"Is there anything else you wanted to tell us, Mrs. Schmidt?" Arnie asked. "Because we're gonna be late for our meeting."

"No. I'm so confused, Dr. Malone. I don't know what to do," she said. And then Mrs. Schmidt finally sat down on one of the side chairs, looking very much older and more fragile than she had when we'd first arrived.

"You've helped us a lot, Mrs. Schmidt. You really have. Don't worry. Everything's gonna turn out all right. Have faith."

"I pray every night for you, Doctor."

"Thank you, Mrs. Schmidt, I appreciate your support." And I did. I'd learned long ago, when you're having trouble, never decline help of any kind from any source, especially the Divine.

# CHAPTER 31

UP until the last block, where we became part of a traffic jam on Madison, Arnie and I rode in silence to the D.A.'s club, the Knickerbocker. Finally I said, "Mrs. Schmidt's a nice lady. She wants to help. But there's no way Jess could be involved. I don't buy it."

"Me either. He's a good kid."

"Yeah," I agreed, relieved.

"He doesn't even look physically strong enough to have done this."

"He isn't," I said. "I just wish we could find the way to tie this to Jennings and Garcia. They're the mules. With them we have another scenario for the jury."

"That's the prosecutor's burden."

"I know the mantra, okay? But if we're right about Gramb's involvement, the burden's going to be ours."

"Hey listen, Gramb's a prick, but maybe he's gonna give us something. Let's keep our peckers dry."

The Knickerbocker Club is a stately pseudo–colonial style building planted firmly on the corner of Sixty-second and Fifth, with a high redbrick wall that encloses a garden and runs along Fifth, preventing passersby from seeing inside, an architectural indicator of the disdain the members have for plain folks.

"I'm probably the first Jew that's ever gotten this far," Arnie whispered to me.

"No, Henry Kissinger's a member," I told him. Badger, one of the chosen, had invited me once and pointed out Henry the K.

"He doesn't count," Arnie said.

"Why not? He's Jewish, he's even a refugee from the Nazis."

"He's a meta-Jew. World class. He's left us behind," Arnie said. Not being Jewish, I'm not really aware of their social stratifications, so I let the subject drop.

The butler or door attendant or whatever you call someone wearing a long waistcoat informed us that Mr. Gramb would be down shortly and in the meantime would we be so kind as to wait in the sitting room, which we did dutifully, admiring the framed portraits of past members hanging from the high-ceiling moulding in regular intervals. After my last and only visit here, Sally had been so impressed it'd taken several days before she stopped quizzing me about the club furnishings and table settings.

"Maybe someday you'll be admitted," she'd remarked, forever betraying her not-so-well-disguised (from me anyway) desires for a social climb or, at the least, step upward. Once on a whim I'd even called, really on Sally's behalf, to ask about membership and somehow I wound up talking to the club secretary, a middle-aged woman, and inquiring as to whether or not they admitted women. She'd responded, unsisterly, in frosty British, "I'm sorry but I cannot give out that information." I did learn, however, on my prior visit, that there was a ladies' dining room where members could bring their female guests, so the place wasn't entirely colonial.

When Gramb appeared and escorted us to our meeting site, I found myself thinking about whether he'd ever taken his deputy district attorney, my wife, to his club and thereby fulfilled her secret fantasies. If the right moment occurred in our conversation, maybe I'd ask him.

We climbed the circular staircase (good exercise for the socially challenged) to the second floor "Governor's Room," an elegant private dining room with only one round table, set for five.

I don't know about Arnie, but I didn't recognize either of our other two luncheon companions.

"Gentlemen," Gramb said to Arnie and me. "Let me first introduce you to Barbara Ames, Commissioner, Investigation Department, and Milt Wagner, the mayor's general counsel." I recognized Barbara Ames's name—she'd headed the Ames Commission investigating the police.

"The drinks are on the sideboard. Help yourself. If you want anything else, we can ring for it." Want, not need, Gramb's social status summarized.

Dressed in his best striped rep tie and Brooks Brothers gray suit, Gramb, whatever else I might say or think about him, was in his element, a perfect host for an imperfect lunch, a political animal with excellent manners. Perhaps because he'd cuckolded me, or was it as a result of the power he could wield as prosecutor? I suspected that no matter how well he imitated Emily Post everyone who knew him had discovered the nastier, more abusive underskin. The others had already made their selections, so Arnie and I chose ours, for me a ginger ale on the rocks, for Arnie, scotch. I roused the carbonic acid bubbles with the swizzle stick, hoping to mask my nervousness with nonchalance.

"Dr. Malone, I want to thank you and Mr. Glimcher for coming here on such short notice." *Oh yes, it was so stressful. I had to cancel five appointments in order to squeeze this one in.* "We hope this get-together will be an open, aboveboard, free exchange of ideas as to how best to resolve our mutual problems." *We are making progress already—our problems have now become mutual.* "We have come prepared to discuss some of the concerns you raised with Mr. Snyder last Friday night." I wondered which untraceable, unsubstantiatable explanation of a joint federal-state-city-top-secret blah blah blah would be evoked to justify why this bureaucratic trinity had nothing better to do with their time than to try to convince me to spend some of mine in jail on a reduced plea.

Everyone, including me, seemed uncomfortable. Commissioner Ames, younger than her résumé would have led you to believe, her youthfulness enhanced by a short Katie Couric haircut, doodled on the linen tablecloth with her swizzle stick, while Wagner—thin-faced, ruddy, his neck skin folds dotted with shaving nicks—who came to nervousness naturally, played with his hair.

"We've taken the liberty," Gramb said, "of ordering you both the poached roulade of chicken. If you want the seared tuna, we can switch."

"It's fine," Arnie said. "Too much fat in tuna." I didn't think so, but this wasn't the time and place for nutrition education.

"Barbara, why don't you begin," Gramb emceed.

Ms. Ames cleared her throat. "Dr. Malone, I'm here to give you my personal assurance that no conspiracy of any kind is in play against you." I picked up a bread stick and melodramatically snapped it in half. "Specifically, we have made a complete check of our procedures with respect to evidence handling in this matter and we've found nothing amiss." Big deal. By then Jennings and Garcia had covered their tracks. As had the Grambs and Mal Snyder.

"Pardon me, Ms. Ames," Arnie started. "But I'm sure you remember last year when the state police claimed the same thing until they found out they had a rogue investigator who was tampering with evidence. How do we know the Department doesn't have the same problem? I'll answer the question: we don't, and, giving you the benefit of the doubt, you don't."

I piped up. "My wife, a deputy district attorney for five years, would regularly complain about evidence screwed up while in police custody. You can't tell me this doesn't happen."

"Dr. Malone, if what you say is the truth, why didn't Sally ever write me a memo or initiate some action in this regard?" Gramb asked.

"That's a good question, Mr. Gramb. Very incisive. But, you know what, it's better directed at yourself. You're the one with the vulnerability." *Doubly so. You're the one who was fucking my wife. And if worse comes to worst, I'm going to use that vulnerability to get a mistrial.*

"You're delusional, Malone," Gramb said, but then he took a very long sip of his drink.

Milt Wagner, the mayor's man, added, "Let's get back to basics, gentlemen." Translation: we're not going to talk about the personal stuff and hope the Achilles' heel repairs itself. "There are some sensitive issues the City . . ." (*here comes the bullshit, hold your nose*) "is grappling with. Some internal investigations have to be protected. At this time, for a variety of reasons, we cannot make certain moves against those two detectives, for example."

"So you still want me to take the fall for something I didn't do in order to protect some hush-hush stuff, is that the scoop?" I asked the mayor's man.

"Doctor," Milt Wagner lingered on the "r," "we'd be the first to help you out. But the two situations are not really connected. Be that as it may, we've taken you at your word and we've tried, as Barbara indicated. There's no way around the DNA evidence. It's your blood at the crime scene. It's your wife's blood at your house, on your clothes. There's no EDTA present. Not even as a normal contaminant. No one spiked the evidence. What can we do about that?" Maybe, I thought, you could ask Donald Gramb or Victoria Gramb. "It's not something we can negotiate. We didn't manufacture the evidence and we can't make it go away."

Barbara Ames added, "Jennings and Garcia haven't been near the police lab. We honestly don't think they're smart enough to have tampered with the blood evidence." Exactly what Figlio had said and what we all believed. Yet why am I so sure they've snookered us?

"Sometimes stupid people can surprise you," I said, which stopped the conversation cold, as everyone paused to privately consider to whom the comment applied.

I looked away and saw a double-decker tourist bus run a red light. Through the floor-to-ceiling French windows, the newly resplendent greenery of Central Park made the silence more suffocating.

Arnie broke the spell with a question to Milt Wagner. "Would you consider an independent review of the police lab?" Wagner looked at the D.A. and then the commissioner, and when no one said anything or raised any eyebrows or scowled he said, "We can consider it. Give us a few days to talk to the people involved."

Arnie's intercession freed me, for the moment, from the dead-end hopelessness. I'd ask Figlio for sure, maybe Steve Kim or an FBI guy I know. Figlio might be reluctant—he wasn't exactly on the most-favored list. "We'll need a guarantee that the investigators we use won't be hassled in any way, now or in the future," I added.

"If we agree to this, you have our word," Milt Wagner assured me.

Good. Don't quit while you're ahead. "One other thing. We'll need to look more closely at my wife's and the Department's files on a lot of matters." A frown passed over Gramb's face. Maybe he knew I was looking to pin his ass against the wall. *You screw my wife, that's the price you pay.* He couldn't have known that I wanted to look at the file on Dr. Feldman's murder and see if hubby was pursuing the case vigorously or was somehow covering for Victoria.

"Under statute, I don't think we can allow that," Gramb declared.

"Maybe it can be done on a 'Don't ask, don't tell' basis," Arnie suggested.

Wagner put his arm on Gramb's to quiet him. "We'll think about it and get back to you."

"Okay, I guess that covers everything," Arnie said. "We might as well concentrate on the food."

"If you all don't mind," I said, "I'm not that hungry. I really need to get some personal stuff done."

"Thanks for coming, Doctor," Wagner said. "If you have any other ideas please feel free to raise them. We'll do the best we can. We're not out to screw you."

I window-shopped homeward. Things were looking up. I must have spooked the biggies. What else could explain the sudden conciliatory atmosphere? Or was it the opposite and actually worse? What if they really weren't hiding anything? What if my legal situation was unrelated to any games they'd played? What if the chain of custody remained unbroken and became a noose around my neck and the DNA stuck tenaciously and couldn't, for the life of me, be washed off?

# CHAPTER 32

SELF-FULFILLING prophecies, by definition, have a way of coming true. At least that's what I told myself as I repeated my mantra: I'm not guilty, I didn't kill Sally, I'm innocent. Thank you for having believed me, ladies and gentlemen.

We're coming up on noon, twenty-four hours since our meeting with the biggies, and we've heard nothing. I tell myself there are a lot of people involved, bureaucratic stuff takes time, but the delay isn't helping my mood. I can't shake the feeling that things are headed to a final, negative result. Arnie and Figlio have each independently picked up on my gloom and call me every four hours. Don't worry guys, I'm not the type to do anything rash, or messy.

I'm also edgy because Diane's away again in Switzerland for another deposition, but her absence has given me the chance to spend some quality time in the kitchen and with Jess. Together we're beginning to make peace. I've told him how scary all this is, how alone I feel, and how I understand how horrible these events must be for him. At one point during dinner last night, he told me he's proud of me—I'm down, but I'm still trying to go forward. I'll always be his dad no matter what, he said.

We've even started talking about Sally and remembering the things we'd done together as a family. The wonderful birthday parties she'd planned, how she'd taught him to ride a bicycle (I was studying for the bar at the time), the computer course they'd taken together at the 92nd Street Y.

This morning at breakfast Jess asked, "Dad, if you go to jail, what's going to happen to me? Where am I going to live?" I told him that we didn't need to worry about that yet, because I didn't have a better answer. But I've been thinking about his question all morning. With my mom in a nursing home, my brother Roger in Seattle was the obvious choice, but we haven't been that close. Figlio? A bit undisciplined. Arnie? Maybe his friend Jasper?

Diane's noon call braked these depressing choices.

"What're you doing for lunch?" she asked.

"Not much."

"Why not join me?"

"Okay. I'll beam myself across the Atlantic." I wasn't being clever, Diane was a Trekkieholic.

"No, I'll beam myself. Bye."

A half hour later, Diane was walking through the front door.

"Nothing supernatural. Just the red-eye from Zurich. This is for you," Diane said, and tossed three stacks of rubber-banded mail on the table from an office pit stop. "Lydia sends her love. She's been assigned to Rob Clark, but misses you."

"Remind me to send her something from prison for National Secretary's Week."

"So the office buzz is right about you. In your pajamas all day. Gloom and doomy."

"Wouldn't you be, in my place? Except for Jess and me doing better these past few days, nothing's progressing."

"Well, that's no small thing."

"And what good will it do either Jess or me if I'm in jail for life?"

"You're not there yet," Diane pointed out.

"The trial's adjourned until Friday, with everyone hoping I'll cop a plea."

"Even Arnie?"

"No, not him."

"Your police buddy?"

"No, not Figlio."

"Who then?"

"Just everybody."

"You're just feeling sorry for yourself. It's understandable. Try to let up on yourself," Diane advised. "For what it's worth, I believe you."

"Why? You're turned on by jailhouse relationships?"

"No, I have a thing for cardiologists."

"I'm retired. Soon to be defrocked."

Diane slipped her hand under my shirt and started stroking my back.

"What are you doing?" I said.

"Defrocking you."

"Diane, I'm not in the mood. I don't have it in me. Really."

"Next you'll say you have a headache."

"I do."

"Oh, I know what to do for that," she said, and continued her ministrations southward, in ever-widening arcs, until she finally arrived at my genitals in a glancing accidental way, fingers out for a skin walk on a sunny afternoon. She played with the ridge along the underside of my penis, it felt like tickling and made me squirm away, but her hand chased after me and wouldn't give up. Slowly, the tension and stiffness of my body was easing, or, some might argue, was in the process of being transferred. I began to welcome the offering and live in the moment: I reached under her blouse and found a breast, and between thumb and forefinger rolled a nipple back and forth, at first idly, but soon with more commitment, until it swelled and hardened. Simultaneously, I moved my other hand over the curved topography of her very firm ass, which had not yet fallen and of which she was justifiably proud. The forces of arousal pulled us closer and we flattened ourselves against each other in a kind of erotic isometric exercise with deep kisses. When we finally disengaged for air, Diane pulled down my pants, waltzed us toward the bed, pushed me down and slid off the oral zone and headed below, leaving a licking trail of wetness all the way. She seemed unfazed by my semihard penis; if anything it appeared to intensify her sucking, a determined response to a challenge that must've served her well in law school. Her focused effort produced the required stiffening. Though the sensation was undeniably exquisite, I pushed her away. "Stop, please. It's wonderful, but it's too alienating. At least, now. Okay?"

Diane was not at all taken aback. Without a word she got up on her haunches, positioned herself astride, and greedily stuffed my now fully erect member into her wet warmth. Together we started going up and down, somewhat raggedly, but within a few cycles we were synchronous, rhythmic, and soon both breathing faster, so much so Diane's nostrils flared. The bed began to squeak as I lifted her whole body into the air with each thrust and, finally, before I blew a fuse or did some other system harm, we both came and she fell down upon me spent and sweaty.

After sex I usually fall asleep. Perhaps because it was the middle of the day, I didn't this time, leaving me with lots of aroused energy, just what you need to tackle old mail. Lydia had carefully separated the wheat from the chaff. The first-class pile was fortunately not too thick. I opened the letters first. Nothing that couldn't wait. Some I'd probably never answer.

At the bottom of the pile was a large Express Mail package that had arrived and been opened sometime after my partners had begun their lockout. Three weeks ago. An involuntary shiver went down my spine and I was reluctant to look at the contents when I saw that the sender was Dr. Abraham Feldman. What possible good could I do him or his organization now? They were both dead in the water. I tossed the envelope on the floor without reading it and finished the rest of the pile.

"Anything interesting?" Diane asked.

"Nothing that can't wait ninety-nine years to life."

"What was the thick one?"

"Oh. Something from Dr. Feldman."

"What was in it?" Diane asked.

"I didn't read it. What's the point, he's dead."

"What are you talking about?" she gasped.

"I'm sorry. I assumed you knew. Somebody murdered him Friday night. The investigating officers told me it looked like a hit. Figlio fished him out of the water."

"Is it connected to you?" she asked.

"Why do you ask? I think so, I can feel it is, the D.A.'s involved somehow, but we don't know how. But Figs is down there trying to poke around."

"And you can't be bothered to look at his package," she said. "What if it has something to do with his murder?" she asked.

"Not very likely," I said. "It came three weeks ago. Abe visited me at the ICU and he never mentioned anything. Probably had to do with the TRO hearing."

"Why don't you just read it and stop feeling sorry for yourself?"

I could continue being stubborn and prickly, and before long I could imagine myself turning pissy and unfriendly and probably ruining the afternoon for both of us. Why go down that well-trodden, neurotic route?

"Okay. Lay it on the bed."

Dr. Feldman or someone on his staff had assembled testimonials from various muck-a-mucks over the years, reprints of professional articles he'd written, quite a few it seems, and a collection of promotional brochures and pamphlets describing the Center and its services. Nothing relevant to his murder, that's for sure, but I restrained myself from telling Diane "I told you so," as she was intently reading the materials.

"Did they have beautiful nurses there?" Diane wanted to know.

"Didn't see any. Why?"

"You never said he ran a sperm bank. Don't you need young nubiles around to help you make the little guys come out?" She giggled.

"They probably had *Playboy* back issues or one of those electric cattle prods," I said.

"Oh, gross."

"Did you know he also stored eggs?"

"Maybe you should make a sperm deposit just in case I can't get a personal pickup," Diane suggested.

"That's not funny."

"Oh, so you're the only one allowed to make morbid comments?"

"Right now I am. You know Dr. Feldman's one of the pioneers of in vitro fertilization and a lot of the other infertility techniques. Even though he won the Lasker Award, which is one step below or before the Nobel, the university wanted him shut down."

"Why?" Diane asked.

"All those family-value types were threatening to withhold contributions unless—"

"I wasn't kidding about the sperm donation, Malone," Diane interjected.

"You must be joking, so I won't bother to feel flat-tered," I said.

"I'm not. I meant it."

"Your timing's not too good," I said.

"Never was. But my clock's ticking."

"So's mine," I reminded her.

"I'll be twenty-nine next birthday."

"You're a kid. You've got lots of time. My prospects aren't looking too good." Pretty soon, in fact, I might be down for the count.

Diane ignored my last comment and continued to leaf through the brochures, occasionally stopping to read a pamphlet more carefully. She was a quick learner; no wonder she'd made law review. One thing they could say about me, or put on my headstone, I suddenly thought, *he was intimate with very smart women lawyers.*

"What's autologous blood banking?" Diane asked me.

"You bank your own blood for future use. Sally's old company pushed it and I gave one time. Most people usu-ally donate right before they have an elective surgery. Cuts down on the risk of infection or transfusion reactions. Bad for business for us poor malpractice lawyers."

"It says you can safely store blood for up to ten years. How come with AIDS it hasn't taken off more?" she asked.

"Well, I don't really know. Dr. Feldman told me that the Red Cross was behind his problems with the university."

"Because they don't want competition."

"Exactly. That's what Abe said. But I didn't buy the logic, and I thought maybe he was a little nutty."

"No, he's right. Blood products are big business. A bil-lion dollars a year. The International Red Cross is a collat-eral defendant in the Swiss action we're pursuing. They're a very tough operation, trust me. You must have been damned good on your feet to get the injunction."

"I got lucky."

Diane started reading the Center's Annual Report. "Boy, Malone, the Center has a lot of major corporate clients. IBM, General Electric, Health and Hospitals Union, Williamson Communications, Viacom. Where'd they store it all?"

It hit me like a shot in the face. "What'd you say?"

"Where'd they store it?" Diane repeated.

"No, about their clients," I clarified. "Who were they?"

I'd heard what she'd said the first time, but I listened again silently, as she reread the list. I needed a few seconds to gather my thoughts. "So?" she said.

Instead of answering I jumped up and hugged Diane so hard she couldn't breathe. "What's going on?" she cried.

"Don't you see. It is my blood. It is my blood. It is my DNA. Goddamn, it is," I shouted.

Diane pushed me away. "If it is, then why are you so happy? I don't understand what you're talking about. You're scaring me, Michael," and she started to sob.

I stroked the back of her hair, nuzzling into her. "It's going to be all right. Trust me. You want something to drink? Iced tea? Beer? Orange juice? Champagne?"

"Nothing," she answered.

"Sally worked for Williamson Communications before she took over the Sex Crimes Unit at the D.A.'s," I said.

"Okay, so?" Diane said.

"Williamson's a big believer in corporate health care benefits. It was one of the reasons I told Sally she shouldn't switch to the D.A.'s, but who listens to me, right? The company had this program . . ." I stopped to wet my lips— I'd been speaking so rapidly my mouth was drying out under the verbal assault. "For five dollars a month deducted from your paycheck you and your spouse could bank up to two units of blood. And we did. Twelve years ago. I never paid attention to where it went, but it must have somehow ended up at the Center for Human Biology. That's where they got my blood and Sally's."

"It wouldn't still be there twelve years later," she said.

"It must have been. Somebody knew it was there and that's how they framed me."

"Do you think Dr. Feldman was involved and that's why he was murdered?" Diane asked. "Maybe that's why he hired you, to throw you off."

"No. Abe was a sweetie. He'd only been director there three years. He wouldn't have been involved with blood record-keeping from twelve years ago."

"How'd Dr. Feldman happen to hire you on behalf of the Center?" Diane asked.

"I represented him years ago. He was an old client."

"Maybe that caught the killer by surprise. Maybe the killer didn't want you and Dr. Feldman to get too chummy," Diane postulated.

"Because we might stumble onto something," I added.

"Exactly."

"You know, I don't mean to sound insensitive. I mean, I care about Dr. Feldman, but right now it doesn't matter what was going on. What does count is the fact that my blood and Sally's were stored at the Center. And if that was the case, and someone could have taken it, then we've got reasonable doubt in spades," I asserted.

"We still have to find out who," Diane declared.

"That's not what Arnie will tell you."

"And why," Diane said.

"We will. *Finally*, I've got something. More than I've had in awhile."

"Now you also have seen firsthand the benefits of daytime sex."

"You'll have to stay home from work a lot more," I said.

"Well, you've had a lot of practice. You could certainly teach me."

"I certainly can," I said, and gave her the deepest kiss of the afternoon.

# CHAPTER 33

"GOOD afternoon. Do you have an appointment?" the receptionist asked.

"Yes, with Dr. Carlino," I announced.

"Who should I say is calling?"

"Ms. Forster and Dr. Malone."

"I'll let Dr. Carlino know you're here."

In a few minutes a short young woman in a long lab coat came out and escorted us to Dr. Feldman's, now Dr. Janet Carlino's, office.

The diplomas, the art, and most of the books that had been Dr. Feldman's were already crated. Only the celebrity photographs remained, though now they were hung on the wall, clustered together, a makeshift memorial.

"I'm very pleased to meet you, Dr. Malone. I'm so sorry it had to be under these circumstances. I can't believe he's not with us anymore." Janet Carlino looked away and wiped her eyes. "Dr. Feldman was so glad that you were able to handle our appeal. As always, his judgment was vindicated."

"Thanks," I said and wondered why the rush to clean out his office.

"Since your call we've begun the process of tracking down your specimens. It might take awhile. They're from the precomputerized days and we need to sort through quite a few handwritten records on index cards. It is possible, as I cautioned you, that a twelve-year-old specimen was on the cusp and might have been discarded on its tenth anniversary. But we wouldn't do that without first notifying the blood customer."

"I never was notified."

"It probably went to your wife. She was the employee of record."

"She never mentioned it, not that it would have seemed important."

"The only documentary evidence that the specimen was taken and banked is the index card and the notification, is that correct?" Diane asked.

"Basically," Dr. Carlino agreed.

"Are the blood specimens stored here or elsewhere?" Diane asked.

"We have several facilities that actually handle the cold storage. We keep some here on the sixth floor. But from what I understand the older samples are mostly maintained in Storm King Mountain upstate. Until we find the locator information on the index cards I can't really answer your question intelligently."

"Are you required to maintain a custody chain?" Diane asked.

"Yes, in a way," Dr. Carlino answered.

Diane arched her back, a litigator ready to pounce. I'd never actually worked with her professionally, but I did know that Badger and buddies considered her a rising star. Not surprising given that most of our international liability insurer clients insisted that Diane represent them at Swiss banking depositions.

"In what way, Doctor?" she asked.

Before Dr. Carlino could elaborate, she was interrupted by the staccato ring of the intercom. "Yes. Okay. Thanks. Keep looking," she said to the caller.

"Dr. Malone. I hope this doesn't cause too much of a

delay, but all the records from eighty-five and eighty-six were shredded last year, so it's going to take awhile to find the actual specimens, if in fact we still have them."

My heart sank. My nervous system couldn't take much more. "Which means there's no proof you ever had our bloods," I said.

"The bloods might still be stored."

"How do you identify them?" Diane asked. "By name or number?"

"Both. They're banked in numerical sequence."

"And like the Swiss accounts," Diane volunteered, "you keep the list of matching names elsewhere, right?"

"Exactly. Without the list or the locator index card, it will take forever. And there's one other added difficulty."

"What's that?" I asked, dreading the answer.

"Our chief lab technician resigned last week and he's the one who knew the system best."

"Why'd he resign?" Diane wanted to know.

"Oh, it's terrible. His wife drowned. But if we need him, I'm sure he'll help. I don't want to bother him unless we have no choice."

"Yes, I understand." I might not have a choice and if that's the situation, you can count on my bothering him.

Dr. Carlino looked pensive, then her face brightened. "There is one other possibility."

"What's that?" I asked hopefully.

"I don't know all the audit protocols Dr. Feldman set up, but if I'm not mistaken we also send a duplicate notification to the medical department of the employer of record, in this case Williamson Communications. Let me call them."

Williamson was in the midst of a merger with NBC, itself a subsidiary of G.E., and despite the directions we'd received from the security desk, it took us several elevator rides before we found the current location of the Medical Department.

What goes around, comes around—I'd helped a Williamson family member years ago and today John Williamson returned the favor. As a result of his personal interest in the request, the Medical Director, Dr. Gloria Vladic, and her team had quickly located the notifications.

"I can give you yours, Dr. Malone. Please sign this release. But I'd better hold on to Mrs. Malone's. We don't have the right to release any of her medical information without her signed consent."

"She won't be able to give it to you," I said, pausing melodramatically. "She's just recently passed away."

"Oh, I'm so sorry," she said. "I didn't know." *No reason you should,* I thought. "Why don't you just sign for both of you," she decided, which I did, whereupon Dr. Vladic handed Sally's card to me without any further red tape or caution. Too often, physicians wear their hearts on their sleeves, eventually propelling themselves into otherwise preventable difficulties. If Dr. Vladic had been my client I would have urged her to talk to in-house legal first. Given my circumstances, such advice wouldn't have been a smart move.

From the pay phone in the Williamson lobby we called Arnie, who put us on hold for what seemed like hours while he arranged everything with the mayor's man. After the meeting was approved and set up, I had, for some unfathomable reason, an uncontrollable urge for Oreo cookies but had to settle instead for a Kit Kat bar from the lobby newsstand.

"Diane, you don't really have to go," I said. "Arnie arranged it and even he doesn't want to."

Diane laughed. "Like a lot of men, he's a bit of a sissy. No, I'd like to. It's the one place my dad never took me."

"Okay. Don't say I didn't warn you."

The Office of the Medical Examiner of the City of New York is a small building abutting the NYU Medical Center. Its outer sheathing of blue-glazed tiles gives the false impression of interior good cheer.

"We're here to see Dr. Kim," I told the security guard at the front desk, who directed us to the rear elevator without asking us if we had an appointment or checking our identification or in any fashion protecting the security of the premises. I suppose, by the time you've arrived at this office, any harm that could have been done has already come to pass.

The stainless-steel elevator cab reeked of formaldehyde, and the odor intensified in the subbasement hallway. To my surprise I didn't pass out. One stress dominating another.

BB-9 was a large room of pale-green–painted cinder block and exposed fluorescent fixtures that cast an unnecessarily harsh light on an already uncongenial venue and made Steve Kim's face, especially when he smiled and puffed out his cheeks, look the color of stale piecrust.

Kim appeared to be as meticulous as ever—his uniform of green surgeon's shirt and white pants was unstained, and not a strand of his shiny, still jet-black hair, precisely slicked back, was out of place. Only the pinpoint shaving nick on his right earlobe betrayed his personal hygiene efforts. He'd always been neat even in the worst of places. The messiness of medical life had never splattered on him in Physio Lab or OB either.

"Steve. How're you doing?" I said too enthusiastically, undoubtedly to mask my discomfort. "This is my associate, Diane Forster." Kim unpeeled his right glove and shook Diane's hand. "I'm sorry we've come about this."

"Occupational hazard," he said. "Are you a lawyer, Ms. Forster?"

"Actually, yes," she answered.

"Great," he said, and brushed some talc dust off the back of his hand. "The mayor's office said to give you my complete cooperation. So what can I do for you?" With his head he did a three-sixty pan of the room. "I don't have a whole lot of time. We're real busy today." He glanced at Diane. "Would you prefer to talk in my office?"

"Not necessary on my account," Diane answered.

Naked bodies lay on each of the four stainless-steel examining tables, while a gathering of gurneys filled the far end of the room with more customers.

The swinging doors flew open as an aide pushed another gurney into the room. "Doc, we got another floater. Where do you want me to take 'er?"

"Recent or frozen?" Kim called out.

"Frozen."

"Put her over there to thaw. In a few hours, see if you can get some prints. Maybe we'll get lucky and get a match."

"This is definitely the time of year for drownings," I said.

"How'd you know?" Kim wondered.

"Friend of mine keeps me posted."

"Still hanging out with weirdos."

"Don't you match by DNA?" I asked.

"No. You can't," he declared.

"How can that be? They're doing it in my case. Without DNA you and I could be renewing our friendship someplace else and I wouldn't be in such deep shit."

"It's totally different. In your case they're comparing blood evidence against a sample of your blood, and they're saying they match. Here, we have a corpse, and the problem is we don't know who it is. It's easy enough to harvest the DNA, but unless we had everyone's DNA profile in the computer, in terms of identifying this body, we've got no one to match against. But the computer has millions of fingerprints and dental records. That's what works best down here. Can I get you guys anything?"

"No thanks, we're fine," I answered quickly. This place's a natural appetite suppressant. "So, Steve, you don't really do much with DNA, is that what you're saying?"

"No, I didn't say that. We use DNA forensically all the time. But not to identify a John Doe from scratch. If we've got a rape victim, we collect the semen from the vagina and see if it matches the suspect's DNA, for example. Do you understand the difference, Malone?"

I nodded, feeling a little let down, afraid Kim wouldn't really be able to help. "What do you know about long-term autologous blood banking?"

"Not much, but I gather it's pretty simple. They deep-freeze your donated blood with a preservative, making it usable for many years. I'm blocking on the name of the cryoprotectant. I've got the AABB tech manual in my office. I've gotta look it up or it'll drive me crazy."

"Still enjoying the autopsy business? Not too cut and dry?" I make lame jokes, especially when I'm anxious.

"Never is."

Steve's office, more a cell block than a place to relax or do creative work, was a windowless ten by ten at the far end of the room. On the wall were some pathology blowups, too disgusting to inquire about, and a photo-portrait of the mayor. Jars filled with body-part specimens functioned as bookends on the shelves above his child-sized desk. Except for Steve's framed pathology board certificate, there was nothing personal—no family pictures, no postcards from faraway places, no newspapers or other escapist literature. Maybe their total absence made it easier for Kim to do this kind of work.

"Here it is," he announced, "page one hundred thirty-one:

> Glycerol, the cryoprotectant, must be added slowly, so as not to disturb the sodium-potassium ATPase pumps, and with vigorous shaking, thereby enabling the glycerol to permeate the red-cell lipophilic membrane. The unit of less than six-days-old packed red cells is rapidly frozen and stored at a temperature below minus sixty-five degrees Centigrade. The technique was first developed in 1978 by Dr. Abraham Feldman.

"Wow. Weird. I just did his post last week," Kim declared.

"It's even weirder than that," I said. "He was my last client. Don't worry, everybody, I've got a witness and an alibi."

Kim wrinkled his high forehead. "Wait. I'm confused."

"No need to be. Listen, Steve. Dr. Feldman's Center banked frozen units of my blood and Sally's twelve years ago, I think, and we need your help to prove this, that someone sprinkled the crime scene and framed me with that same blood."

"You can show that the blood units are missing?" Kim asked.

"No, they're still searching for them. They were banked in the years before computerized records," Diane replied.

"You'd better look harder," Kim suggested.

"Why?" I asked.

"I'm no expert on this, but glycerol's a natural constituent of red blood cells. Big deal if we find it in the blood evidence. I don't see how that helps you."

"Won't you find more of it?" Diane asked.

"I don't know. Depends on the kind of test."

"Shit," was all I could say.

"The one thing I've learned down here, Malone, is that life's not simple, and neither is death."

"An old Korean proverb?" I asked.

"No, I just made it up."

"A natural-born philosopher."

"Mike, I'll retest the blood evidence. I'll keep you posted. . . . Sorry. No pun intended."

# CHAPTER 34

"VERY romantic. I like the swaying motion," Arnie said.

"Suits my purposes."

"Who's Annabelle?" Arnie asked.

"A fantasy. Want another beer?"

"You got anything beside Red Dog?"

"Root beer," Figlio answered.

"How 'bout ice water?"

"You got it." He turned to me. "How're you doin'?"

"I'm fine." At least with respect to beer level. "So now that you've heard the latest, what do you think we should do?" I asked them.

"From where I'm sittin'," Arnie answered, "nuthin'. We got reasonable doubt up the wazoo. That's all we ever needed. Why press our luck?"

"And what if the Center can't find the specimens and what if my buddy Kim can't show the blood evidence came from the frozen blood?"

"That's a lotta what-if's, kid," Arnie said.

"Here's one more," Figlio offered. "What if the people who did this aren't finished and come after Malone or the kid?"

Figlio was right. He'd raised the issue that had been there from the beginning and against which my family still had no defense.

"You don't think it could still be Jennings and Garcia?"

Arnie asked us. "Except," answering his own question with another, "how would they even have known your blood was there?"

"They couldn't even say 'autologous.' They'd have to have had inside help," Figlio declared. "Now Gramb's another story. He's snaky enough to be behind this whole thing."

"Why would he have Sally killed?" I asked.

"Maybe he had no choice. Someone could have been pressuring him. He might have owed someone something. He certainly knows a lot of bad guys," Figlio said.

"So do you, but you don't go around snuffing people," I pointed out.

"You know, Malone, you make a lot of assumptions based on no information—it's one of the ways you get into a lot of trouble," Figlio retorted.

Although I'm not normally superstitious it occurred to me, as I entered the Medical Examiner's the next morning for the second visit in two days, that coming here again, rather than telephoning, was pressing my luck with the gods of the universe.

When I arrived in the subbasement Kim was talking on the telephone and motioned for me to have a seat.

"Asphyxiation. She was already dead when they shot her. I'm positive. You're welcome."

"Great way to start the day," I said.

"You get used to it. So we ran the tests." His tone wasn't what I'd call upbeat, but I tried to put a lid on my worries. "First problem—there doesn't seem to be any kind of chemical test for glycerol. It's a physical test."

"So what?" I said, my arrogant, irrationally confident self flourishing anew.

"Physical tests are harder to quantify. Anyway, we did

an HPLC. High pressure liquid chromatography. It's kind of a horse race among chemicals."

"But you found a difference? Didn't you?"

"Yes, but no D.A. or jury is going to be convinced that you've been framed on the basis of this result."

I could feel the panic washing over me. "But—"

"Mike, it's just my opinion." People had always listened to Kim's opinions because he had that rare combination—clear-eyed thinking and sensitivity.

"Is there any other test we can do?" I asked.

"DNA concentration."

"Which means?"

"DNA is only in cell nuclei. Red cells have no nucleus. The DNA is in the white cells."

"And?"

"When you unfreeze the blood, you have to first do a special kind of washing to eliminate the glycerol. If the person who framed you did the washing properly they'd end up washing away a lot of the white cells, too."

"Which means you won't find much DNA in the thawed blood?" I stated.

"Bingo."

"And that's quantifiable. So we could compare the levels of DNA in the blood evidence against the tube blood the police lab drew from my arm and the lab sample should have a higher concentration of DNA. Right?"

Kim smiled. "How come a lawyer knows so much about biomedicine?"

"You weren't the only smart guy in med school."

"Mike, that's not enough, I'm afraid."

"What's not enough?"

"All that I've said applies to using the banked blood for a self-transfusion. If the person who's framing you doesn't care about the red cells being okay and just lets the sample thaw, and doesn't bother to do the washing, there won't be any less DNA, because the white cells will still be there."

"You did this test already, didn't you?"

"Yeah."

"And?"

"Nothing definitive. It'd be better if you could bring us the frozen bloods. Maybe they have a contaminant or something we can run with. Can't anybody at the Center find them?"

I sighed. "They're looking. But there's a problem. Only Dr. Feldman and the chief lab technician really seem to have known the record-keeping system. And the lab guy resigned, and no one wants to bother him because his wife drowned."

"What was her name?" Kim asked. "I might have done the post."

"I don't know. How many adult female drownings have you had recently?"

"You'd be surprised. For a while it looked like we were on our way to a record year, but then we had to reassign two to last year," Kim said, sounding a little disappointed.

"How can that happen?"

"They were John and Jane Does. No ID, no nothing. We had them credited toward this year when they should have been last year all the time. Sometimes, until a family member or a friend shows up, we're in the dark. The Jane Does are the worst because of the maiden name–married name changes. We finally found the husband for one of those two transfers—a real geeky guy with a ponytail who'd reported her missing at Christmas."

Two neurons, somewhere deep in my brain, made a connection. "What was the husband's name?"

"It was a strange one."

"Compared to Kim, what isn't?" I said.

"Very funny. What the hell was it? I've always been lousy at remembering names."

"Just don't try too hard. Relax."

"Cut it out, Mike, I'm from the land of tae kwon do."

"Could it have been Joralemon?" I asked, choosing the name of a street in Brooklyn Heights. Kim shook his head. "How about Joraster?"

"What kind of names are these, Mike? I'm not an idiot."

"How about Jasper?" I asked.

Kim's pie-shaped face flattened into a broad smile. "How'd you know?"

"Geeky guy with a ponytail and a strange name—Jasper Reynolds."

Kim's smile faded fast. "Reynolds wasn't the wife's last name. She was Mary something else. We had so much trouble with her because she'd been married several times. She was a week away from Potter's Field, instead of Poughkeepsie with her family. It's on the tip of my tongue. Mary Williams. No. Mary Willow." His face brightened. "Willabrand. Mary Willabrand was her name."

"Oh my God," I moaned, and clutched the right side of my abdomen, in the middle of the lower quadrant, where I felt the pain the most sharply.

"Are you all right? Sit down. I'll call someone."

"Don't. I've got to go," I shouted.

"Don't play doctor on yourself, Mike."

"I'm okay. Just give me a second. Just give me a second to think," I grunted.

The Greeks were right. There's no way you can escape your fate.

I stood up to leave. "Where're you going?" Steve asked. "You don't look well. Let me get someone to check you out."

"I have to go. I have to find Jess. Before it's too late."

"What's too late?"

"I have to go," I said, and pushed past Steve.

"Mike, you're scaring me," he yelled from behind.

I ran down the hallway, Kim in pursuit. He caught up and pinned me against the cold tiled wall. I'd forgotten he was a second-degree black belt in great shape.

"Let me go, Steve. Let me go," I screamed. "You have to let me go." Tears were running down my cheeks. "Mary Willabrand was Jess's birth mother."

# CHAPTER 35

I must have looked like a raving lunatic when I arrived, breathless, at the reception area of Jess's school. How I got there so quickly from the Medical Examiner's, I have no idea. All I remember is the fearful look in the eyes of Mrs. Hadley, who must have thought she was my next victim. I regret having frightened her, but it was unavoidable.

"Where's my son? Do you know where Jess is?" I demanded.

"Please sit down, Doctor, I'll ring the upper school principal's office. She'll know his schedule." Mrs. Hadley dialed upstairs.

"He's not here, goddamn it," I shouted. "He went to a chess tournament somewhere."

"Someone will be here shortly. Please sit down. There's coffee on the table, Doctor." *No thank you, I'm already on overdrive, can't you see that?*

How had I let Jasper Reynolds get so close to our family? If only Sally and I had paid more attention to what Jess was doing. You know how teenagers are, they have to push you away. That's what we'd said. At least, I had. I don't know about Sally. Of course, right there is part of the problem. With the separation, neither one of us knew what the other was doing or saying, unless our lawyers mentioned it, which only happened if they thought the point would gain their client a negotiating advantage, and in this kind of climate, Jess got lost in the middle.

"Dr. Malone, I'm Becky Lester, Mrs. Phelan's assistant. You're trying to find Jess?"

"Yes. He went to a chess tournament with the team somewhere."

"It's at Scarsdale High, I believe."

"Is Jasper Reynolds there?"

"No. Mr. Nolan accompanied the team. Mr. Reynolds is attending a family funeral in Poughkeepsie."

"Oh that's great," I said, relieved, exultant almost. "Thank you. Thank you very much." I'm sure my callousness shocked her, but I didn't have the energy to explain what I'd said.

# CHAPTER 36

WITH the assistance of the state police, Figlio flew to Poughkeepsie, served the warrant, and made the arrest.

By 4 P.M. Jasper Reynolds had been booked and transferred up to the nineteenth, which is where I caught up with Arnie, for further questioning.

"Gramb's bein' a real prince. Nice of him to invite us to watch the interrogation," Arnie said.

"Even with a two-way mirror it's not quite kosher, since I'm still indicted and on trial."

"So what if he's got a guilty conscience from shtuppin' your wife, we won't look a gift horse in the mouth. All I can say, kid, is ain't it a pisser how that chain of custody turned out to be a friggin' red herring."

Detectives Levine and Johnson, lead investigators for Sally's murder, and Ianucci and Scavone, heading up the Feldman investigation, and Figlio were all there.

"Mr. Reynolds, you're not helping yourself," Detective Levine said. "We're trying to determine certain facts. The sooner we do, the sooner we can all resume our regular business," Detective Levine told him.

"Abusing people *is* your regular business."

She ignored the comment. "Mr. Reynolds, you worked for the Center for Biology?"

He suddenly laughed. "So, you're a headhunter. Excuse

me. People say companies are downsizing when the truth is, before our very own eyes, they're recruiting everywhere."

Johnson walked over and crouched next to Reynolds, pushing his blue backpack aside. "Listen up, sir. Detective Levine has been very patient, but you're starting to get on our nerves. Just answer her questions, okay?" From behind he twirled Jasper's ponytail and gave it one quick yank.

Jasper screamed, "Cut this shit out, you fucker. I'll file a complaint against you, you scumbag," but his protest was soon over. I must say Jasper's profanity surprised me.

"Are you ready to continue, Mr. Reynolds?" Detective Levine asked in the sweetest, most feminine voice, as if Jasper had just returned from a bathroom break. "As I was saying, Mr. Reynolds, you worked at the Center for Biology and you were a lab tech for how long there?"

"I started in eighty."

"And at that time the Center was involved in long-term blood banking?" she asked.

"Yes, so?"

"And you had responsibilities in this area?"

"Not much," he declared.

"What did you do exactly?" she asked.

"ABO and Rh typing. You know what that is?" Jasper challenged her.

Ianucci leaned over, getting in Jasper's face. "We ask the questions, pal, not you."

"Blood-typing's all you did?" she asked.

"No. Of course not. I got promoted to chief lab technician and then I had responsibility for making sure we were following federal guidelines."

"You got promoted?" Scavone interjected.

"You want my old job?"

Detective Levine ignored the exchange. "So you were in a position to monitor all the blood that the Center stored?"

"Yes."

"And you knew that Mrs. Malone and Dr. Malone stored their blood with the Center?"

"We had lots of clients. There's no way I could have known of them or kept track of their blood units," he declared.

"If someone tampered with any of the blood, you were the person who would find that out and do something, right?"

"It never happened and you've got no proof it did," he said, cockily.

"How can you be so sure?" Levine asked. She stopped to take a sip of water without offering any to Jasper. "Look, Jasper, you didn't like Mrs. Malone, did you? You blamed her for Mary's suicidal depression, right?"

"No, I didn't. I never met the lady. She's just a name to me."

"So Mary never talked about the way Mrs. Malone had robbed her of her son, taken Jess away, is that what you're saying? If it'd happened to me, I would have hated Mrs. Malone. It's very understandable. Believe me, I understand. I worked with Mrs. Malone and she could be very demanding—she thought everything belonged to her. I know what Mary must have felt. I lost a baby once. You never forget, never get over it," Levine confided.

"She missed him. Sure. But she also knew Jess had a good life."

"So Mary kept track of Jess?"

"Yeah. He was her son. Is there anything wrong with that?" Jasper snarled.

"No, not at all," Detective Levine answered, almost

tenderly. "Let me ask you this, Jasper, when Mary disappeared at Christmas you feared the worst, didn't you? And when she didn't turn up after the new year, you knew she never would, right?"

Jasper said nothing.

"So that's when you decided to find a way to worm yourself into the Malone family," Ianucci declared.

"I didn't worm myself into anything," Jasper shouted.

Detective Levine leaned forward. "If there'd been no part-time position available at the school you would've done anything, maybe even volunteered at the school, just so you could get close to Jess. Nothing was going to stop you. You were going to make the Malones pay for Mary's pain and for yours. Isn't that how it happened, Jasper?"

Arnie nudged me. "He's the one, kid, who must have gotten Jess all worked up against Sally."

*No shit, Sherlock.*

Figlio pulled up a chair and sat down facing Jasper. "Did you see what Mary looked like after we fished her out of the river?"

Jasper glared. "Look," he said, addressing Ellen Levine, "I know what all of you are trying to do. But you're wasting your time. I didn't have any connection with what happened to Mrs. Malone. I'm not gonna lose it and confess to anything, because I didn't do anything and you've got no evidence that says I did, so unless you've got more than spit, you can't hold me."

It seemed to me, a trained litigator, though hardly objective, that Jasper was right.

"What if we tell you that the tests we ran show that the blood found at the murder scene and at Dr. Malone's apartment came from the banked frozen blood, not from the victim or Dr. Malone. What would you say?"

"What test did you use?" Jasper asked Detective Levine.

"DNA," Levine answered.

"In that case, I'd say you got jack and you don't know your ass from your elbow," he said.

"Arnie, I can't watch this anymore. He's gonna be released as soon as any decent, even halfway decent, lawyer gets here. I've got to go home and see how Jess is doing."

"Wait a second, kid, I'm comin' too or I'll miss the six forty-five," Arnie said.

"Hey," Jasper added, "unless you come up with something better, the doctor's still your prime suspect. Duhhh."

The way the interview was going, he might be right on all counts.

"Trust me, kid, we're gainin'," Arnie declared.

On the way out we met Detective Levine, who'd excused herself from the interview room. "I'm sorry about your kid," Arnie said to her. "Must have been tough."

"Not really," she said. "I made it up. Never ever been pregnant."

"What a shame," Arnie remarked.

Jess was home watching the Classic Sports Channel retelecast of the Ali-Frazier fight.

"Quite a fight, huh."

"You saw it?" Jess asked.

"Only on TV. So how're you doing?"

"Not too good. I lost all my matches. Three. Mr. Nolan was useless. I wish Jasper had been there—we couldda used his help, but he had to go to a funeral or somethin'."

"Yes, I know. I've just seen him."

"You have? Where?"

"Jess, I have something to tell you." *Someday I hope you'll forgive me.* "Something about Jasper."

"He's okay?"

"Not really," I answered softly. "He's in jail."

"Why? Why's he in jail?"

"A felony."

"What felony?"

"Suspicion of murder."

"Murder?" he cried. "Murder who? You're going to help him. Right?" he implored.

I swallowed hard and sighed noticeably. This wasn't the time to conceal and dissemble. "No, I'm the one who alerted the police. He murdered Mom."

With his left hand Jess crushed the soda can he was holding. "How can you say that? You're really out there. Jasper didn't even know Mom. Why would he kill her?" he screamed.

"I don't have a simple answer, Jess. But he did."

Jess tucked his knees into his chest and covered his ears with couch pillows. "Shut up. Shut the fuck up. I don't care what you say anyway—it's just going to be bullshit. That's all I ever hear. First Mom, now you, too."

"You have to listen, Jess. This isn't easy for me either. You don't know everything. . . ."

"Yeah, that's true. Because of you."

"We did what we thought was best."

"You fucked up, that's what you did."

I lowered my voice. "You're right," I said gently. "We made a mistake. We fucked up. Jess, I understand how you must feel. In your place, I'd be angry. Really pissed off. But you need to understand how afraid Mom was of losing you. She loved you so much, more than anything."

"I was just another purchase for the house," he said softly.

"That's not true, Jess. It's really not. I know you know that. And I know Jasper poisoned you against Mom, but one day you'll forgive her, forgive both of us. Nothing gave anyone the right to take Mom's life away. And you deserved to have your mother."

"She wasn't my mother. She was my *surrogate* mother." He paused. "I want to meet my real mother."

"You can't."

He uncurled himself and jumped to his feet. "Why not? You're jealous of her, too? Well, fuck you, I'm going to find her. And don't try to stop me."

"I would never do that."

"Where does she live?" Jess asked.

"You can't see her, Jess, because she died. I'm sorry you had to find out like this. I only learned about it myself today. That's why I told the police about Jasper."

Jess stared at me with the hollow look one associates with people who've seen or lived through unspeakable horrors. His face was about to crumble. I tried to put my arm on his shoulder, but he pushed me away. "Jasper was married to your biological mother. She was very unhappy and Jasper blamed her unhappiness on your mom and me, and when his wife died it must have set him off."

Jess picked up the TV remote from the end table beside the couch and pointed it at me, as if its beams were laser, not infrared. He made one last try to put his world back together. "You've got good evidence, counselor?"

"The police accept it."

"Yeah, right, the same bozos who were sure you did it. What makes them so smart now?"

"Jasper worked in a blood bank where Mom and I stored our bloods."

"Big deal. That doesn't prove anything."

"So Jasper was able to take our blood, sprinkle it over the crime scene, sprinkle it here, and make it appear like I killed Mom." I had to look away. "Unless you really believe I'm capable of murder and did kill Mom, there's no other way her blood could have landed on my clothes and no other explanation for why the police found mine at our house. Unfortunately for you, one of the people you most care about did this to Mom."

"What was my mother's name?" Jess asked.

"Mary Willabrand."

"Did she die naturally or are you saying Jasper murdered her, too?"

"She wasn't murdered."

"She was sick?" he asked.

"Sort of."

"What did she die from?" he asked, his voice breaking.

I wanted to shield him. "It doesn't really matter, does it?"

"It does to me," he answered.

"She drowned herself in the Hudson."

Jess nudged his right bare foot under the crushed soda can. "Why'd you guys even have to have a kid, anyway? It's not as if you have any time for one." Before I could say anything, he kicked the can in the direction of my face. I ducked. It made a crescent-shaped mark on the wall behind me. "Why didn't you just leave things alone?" he yelled as he fled to the bedroom.

At some basic level, he was, of course, right. We could have adopted. Or we could have been a childless couple. We were paying, all of us, for going against nature.


In the morning, I watched Jess eating his corn flakes, his face buried in the bowl. I wished there were some heartfelt words that I could summon that would somehow bring him immediate unconditional comfort, but that, of course, was just wishful thinking.

"Dad," Jess broke the silence, "last January, when Jasper started at school, by mistake we took each other's backpacks home. They're the same kind and color. That's how he had the keys to your apartment and Sutton Place. That's how he planted the blood."

Sally, the prosecutor, would have been proud. Something extra, not on the DNA, had been handed down.

# CHAPTER 37

IN all the years I'd known Steve Kim, during med school and since, we'd never eaten Korean food together, though in fact it was Figlio who'd suggested it.

Monsoon Gardens wouldn't have been the name I'd have recommended to the proprietors, especially since the place was very cheerful and bright, and without wind or rain. Unlike Chinese restaurants there were no dishes named after inconsequential generals, and therefore I recognized nothing on the menu and deferred to Steve (when in Rome), who selected Korean barbecue specialities—bulgoki and kalbi—which the chef prepared at our table.

"They got any good ballplayers over in Korea?" Figlio asked Steve. "You know, like Japan has. The Mets need some lefty pitching."

"Yeah, lots."

"Only problem is they're all named Kim," I said.

Steve let the gratuitous comment pass. "How's your son doing?" he asked between bites.

"Who knows. He's very pissed at me."

"You know how kids are. He'll get over it," Figlio said.

"If you like very hot, try the brown sauce," Steve recommended. "I remember you gave your parents a hard time."

I dipped some meat in the sauce and tasted the combination. "I suppose so," I said. And then I started coughing. Never try to talk with spicy food in your mouth.

"Are you okay, Malone? I don't wanna do a Heimlich." I waved Figlio off.

"Drink some tea," Steve suggested.

I coughed more and was somehow able to swallow the piece of meat. Except for breaking out in a cold sweat, nothing serious happened. "I'm okay. It went down."

"You sure? You look terrible, Mike," Steve said.

"Not as bad, I hope, as some of the people you meet at work."

"No, not that bad. But you are all flushed," he said.

"Maybe it's the TB acting up."

"TB? How'd you get that?" he asked.

"From a pro bono."

"You're on meds?"

"Yeah, INH. Once a day. I'm almost finished."

Steve poked at his food. "It's a long course of prophylaxis, isn't it?"

The wheels had started turning in my head, too. "Almost a year. Which means it's in my blood now . . ."

"But wasn't twelve years ago," Steve said, finishing my thought.

"Congratulations, Malone, all the doc's gotta do is test your blood evidence for this stuff and then you'll be officially off the hook," Figlio decreed.

"Doesn't get us any closer to putting Jasper on it," I said. "And if we don't come up with something he's going to get away with two murders."

"You're sure he's also responsible for Dr. Feldman's?" Steve asked me. "That could have been a random."

"No way. Friday night, at Jess's school, I told Jasper about Dr. Feldman visiting me in the ICU. Jasper must have been afraid that if the two of us kept talking, one of us, Dr. Feldman or I, would eventually stumble on the Williamson autologous blood bank program."

"How'd he figure you wouldn't to begin with?" Steve asked.

Figlio scratched his nose. "He just took a chance, would be my guess. If worse came to worst and Malone wasn't stuck being the prime suspect, there would still be nothing pointing to him. Either way he must have thought he could get away with it." Figlio turned to Steve. "It's hard to believe, doc, you guys found nothing to connect Jasper to Sally."

"Maybe Steve did and didn't know it," I declared. "Remember, Steve, you told me that DNA is useless for IDing somebody and it's only good when you have someone to match against. Nobody had any reason to suspect Jasper. Damn, damn, damn. Now it's too late."

"No it's not," Figlio announced. "We could exhume her, right, Kim? Look for some DNA under Sally's fingernail or wherever that matches Jasper's." Steve nodded. "Malone, how long does it take to get a court order to exhume someone?"

"Forever," I answered. "It's too late—she was cremated."

"Oh shit," Figlio whispered under his breath.

"Hey guys, wake up and smell the end of the twentieth century," Steve declared.

"What's that supposed to mean?" I asked.

"We've got DNA Southern blots on every organic matter we found on the body. All we need are some fresh samples—hair, blood, or buccal scrapings from Jasper—and we can run them against the unknown DNA's we already blotted."

"I'm gonna pretend I followed that and say it sounds simple," Figlio said.

*Nothing ever is, not lately,* I said to myself.

# EPILOGUE

THE Southern blots matched and Jasper was charged with two counts of first-degree murder. Unable to post the eight hundred thousand dollars bail, he resides, as we speak, on Rikers, behind the DNA eight ball. Speaking of Rikers, the Lopez family received three point eight million dollars from the City of New York and moved back to the Dominican Republic, while Jennings and Garcia were nabbed in the aforementioned joint federal-state RICO investigation, dismissed from the Force, and now spend their days throwing darts at their wallpaper, awaiting further criminal and disciplinary actions.

For many reasons, I resigned my partnership at Badger Weissberg and opened my own firm, taking with me several of the junior associates and control of the silicone settlement, which means I don't need to work too hard for many years to come, and as a result have plenty of time to spend with Jess and Diane, who, by the way, is seriously considering my offer to move in with us.

Figlio, promoted to chief of the harbor patrol, and Arnie, to whom Jess is teaching the intricacies of chess, visit us regularly.

As for Jess and me, we're trying to come to terms with each other. Last Sunday we scattered Sally's ashes in the meadow behind the Connecticut house. And on Labor Day I'm planning to drive Jess to Poughkeepsie to visit his mother's grave.

DON'T MISS THE MOST AUTHENTIC
THRILLER OF THE DECADE!

# REMOTE CONTROL
## by Andy McNab

A former member of the Special Air Service crack elite
force, Andy McNab has seen action on five continents.
In January 1991, he commanded the eight-man SAS
squad that went behind Iraqi lines to destroy Saddam's
scuds. McNab eventually became the British army's
most highly decorated serving soldier and remains
closely involved with intelligence communities on
both sides of the Atlantic.

Now, in his explosive fiction debut, he has drawn on
his seventeen years of active service to create a thriller
of high-stakes intrigue and relentless action. With
chillingly authentic operational detail never before
seen in thrillers, REMOTE CONTROL is a novel so
real and suspenseful it sets a new standard for the
genre.

*From the* New York Times *bestselling author*
*of* THE GENESIS CODE *comes a compelling*
*new novel . . .*

# THE FIRST
# HORSEMAN
## by John Case

In the Norwegian Sea, an icebreaker forces its way
through the heavily frozen waters, carrying the members of a scientific expedition to the graves of long-
dead miners. When they arrive, they find the graves
dug up and the bodies gone.

Elsewhere, everyone in a remote village
mysteriously dies.

The First Horseman is one of The Four Horsemen of
the Apocalypse. The First Horseman is plague.

# DEATH ROUNDS

## by Peter Clement

The bacteria was supposed to be treatable. Until a nurse dies from it. Horrifically. Traced to University Hospital, the infection is raging out of control. Dr. Earl Garnet tries to remain calm. But as more people fall gravely ill—including Garnet's own wife—he uncovers a shocking connection between the crimes.

*No one captures the complex workings of an urban hospital like former ER physician Dr. Peter Clement. His new medical thriller ranges from the realm of microbiology to raw, human rage—in a plot so chillingly authentic it could be happening right now. . . .*

Published by Fawcett Books.
Available wherever books are sold.